Charles Stanford

Joseph Alleine

His Companions and Times

Charles Stanford

Joseph Alleine
His Companions and Times

ISBN/EAN: 9783741186547

Manufactured in Europe, USA, Canada, Australia, Japa

Cover: Foto ©Andreas Hilbeck / pixelio.de

Manufactured and distributed by brebook publishing software
(www.brebook.com)

Charles Stanford

Joseph Alleine

Joseph Alleine:

HIS COMPANIONS & TIMES;

A Memorial of

"Black Bartholomew," 1662.

By Charles Stanford.

"O, sit anima mea cum Puritanis Anglicanis!"—Erasmus.

London:

JACKSON, WALFORD, AND HODDER,

ST. PAUL'S CHURCHYARD.

Printed by G. Unwin,
at the Gresham Steam Press,
Bucklersbury, London.

Author's Preface.

THE following work is an attempt to bring into notice some of our early Nonconformist worthies, the story of whose life-long sufferings for truth and duty is now almost unknown. It professes to be a book of "OBSCURE MARTYRS." True it is, that the chief hero, *Joseph Alleine*, was well known in his own times, but even then he was obscure in comparison with many in the constellation of eminent men around him.

With prophet - like solemnity, *Richard*

Baxter says:—" Let posterity know, that though this servant of *Christ* was exalted above very many of his brethren, yet it is not that such men are wonders in this age that his life is singled out to be recorded." The " Life," in the introduction to which these words occur, was first published in 1672. It includes a narrative, twenty-five pages long, written by his widow; several essays, like prose elegies, contributed by his friends; and also forty of his letters. Only a few facts are related, and although the volumes spread the fame of his worth, it still left much of his life in obscurity.

In our own day, " *Joseph Alleine*" is little more than a name;—a name that stands on the title-page of an old book, called, " AN ALARM TO THE UNCONVERTED ;"—a dead name, without substance, personality, or history. Still less is known of his companions, for, generally speaking, their very names have faded out of remembrance.

It has been said by some of my friends, that the life of some great Nonconformist leader would have been a more attractive subject than that which has here been selected. But we are already well acquainted with *Baxter, Owen, Howe, John Bunyan*, and men who in the same day had similar influence. Accounts of them have been so often and so ably recorded, that little more remains to be told. My preference has been decided in favour of *Alleine* and his companions, because I venture to think that most of the information now offered respecting them is important; and that also, to most of my readers, it will be new. Important, I am sure it is. To know the heroic age of Nonconformity correctly and completely, we must not only know the men who were then influential from commanding genius and station, but we should know something of the average ministers and the provincial congregations. You are invited to live with one of those ministers; to study his principles, and the various influences which tended to fix and try them; to look on some of those external things to which his mind owed its formation and its *in*formation; to be introduced to some of the men and women whom he met in his daily walks and country labours; and to follow him, in thought, both to prison and to death. As you thus accompany him, you are invited to watch, all the way along, the development of the events which led to the Act of Uniformity, and then to observe that Act in its operation.

This is my plan; and although it has been very imperfectly realised, I hope some good will be effected by the attempt to carry it out. I address more especially the younger members of our congregations, and if they are led to examine afresh the reasons of Nonconformity, to search into some of its historical connexions, and above all to emulate the holy lives of its earlier confessors, my principal object will be gained. At the present time, having nearly reached the second centenary of the year when the peculiar sufferings of our ancestors began, and when their good confession was made, it becomes us all to renew our attention to the truths for which they suffered, and also to renew our praise to Him, who, through the growing ascendancy of those truths, has permitted us to see the day of liberty which they desired to see but saw not. "They that are delivered from the noise of archers in the places of drawing water, there shall they rehearse the righteous acts of the Lord, even the righteous acts towards the inhabitants of his villages in Israel."

My cordial acknowledgments are due to the various friends who have kindly answered my inquiries and contributed to my materials; but chiefly to my friend *James Waylen, Esq.,* of *Etchilhampton,* near *Devizes,* who first suggested the idea of undertaking the work, and who has ever been ready to help me with the results of his extensive reading and minute antiquarian research. For courteous permission to see books and papers, in *Dr. Williams's* library most especially, also in the library of the *Guildhall,* in that of the *London Medical Society,* in that of the *Society of Friends* at *Devonshire House,* in that of *Sion College,* and in that of the *Baptist College, Bristol,* the Trustees and Librarians will be pleased to accept my best thanks.

Charles Stanford.

Camberwell, October, 1861.

Chapter I.

Joseph Alleine's Father.

" Was I not borne of olde worthie linage ? "

SIR THOMAS MORE.

N the course of searching for lost facts in the life of Joseph Alleine, a few particulars have come to light in relation to his father, worthy Mr. Tobie Alleine, of Devizes. Slight and disconnected as they are, it would be a pity to let them vanish into darkness again; they are therefore now for the first time presented, and all the more readily, because a notice of them will involve some historic statements which may prepare us to estimate the facts given in the following chapters.

Some old writers on heraldry seem to think that the father of all the Alleines in England, or, at least, of all whose families have been longest established in the counties where they live, was Alan, lord of Buckenhall, in the reign of the first Edward;

stopped under the glimmer of the trees in the market-place to chat with him about the good old times.

Many allusions to him occur in the ancient municipal documents. In 1636, and subsequently, he stands as sponsor for the due appearance and equipment of a musketeer in the town train-bands. At a later period, mention is made of £300 (about £1000 in present value), which he lends the borough authorities to relieve the straits occasioned by the wars. For many years his name is written first in the list of *majores* or "capital burgesses" of the common-council;—these, and similar notices, seem to certify that he was a man of public spirit, that he held a respected but unpretending station in society, and that as to his circumstances, he had neither poverty nor riches.*

He does not appear in the gentry lists of Wilts for the year 1623, though his family had always been thus reported before.† The omission in his instance was only remarkable because, trades-man as he was, he might have been supposed to have some claim to the honours of gentle birth ; and so eager were the heralds to obtain twenty-five

---

* My best thanks are due to Alexander Meek, Esq., town-clerk of Devizes, for permitting Mr. Waylen and myself to examine the borough records for these and other accounts.

† It will be seen by a comparison of the documents in the British Museum, that, although the book for 1623 does contain a pedigree of the Wiltshire Alleines, it is simply copied, without additions, from that of 1565.

shillings, the annual tax for being " a gentleman," that they often returned a tradesman under this title, even if he had no such claim. In such a case the victim was compelled either to pay the amount, or to make a declaration like this: " A. B. hath this day appeared before me, Clarencieux king-at-arms, *and taketh oath that he is no gentleman.*" This declaration, so trying for human nature to make, was actually made by a smart young yeoman of Alleine's acquaintance, and we can readily imagine the burst of broad Wiltshire sympathy that greeted his next appearance amongst his brethren at Devizes. We shall be forgiven for recording these small instances of honour withheld where honour was due, and obtruded where it was not, as affording a curious glimpse of the times in which even the honours of chivalry, from the highest to the lowest, were bought and sold to pay the debts of an exhausted Exchequer and profligate Court.*

We must now hasten to set down facts of greater interest.

> " Kind hearts are more than coronets,
> And simple faith than Norman blood."

His was a higher rank than any that Camden could attest by reference to a brass on the cathedral pavement, or to a richly blazoned family tree. We

---

* Speech of Sir Francis Seymour, M.P. for Marlborough, complaining of the abuse of the heralds in the course of the Wiltshire Visitation.—Journal of House of Commons, 1624.

may style him " a good knight of Jesus Christ." *
One who knew him well, asserts that he was " an
understanding, affectionate, prudent, and signally
humble and experienced Christian."† Various
witnesses give evidence that he was a Puritan, and
that like his son he gloried in the name.

The distinctive principle of a true Puritan was
reverence for the strict letter of Holy Scripture, as
God's direct message to each individual man, and
as forming our final and absolute authority in religion.
Of course, as the immediate and most conspicuous
expression of his creed, the Puritan was a Protestant.
What has been called the severe Scripturism of
Puritanism stood in steadfast protest against the
principle which reaches its culminating intensity in
the church of Rome—the principle of combining
with Scripture the traditional exposition of its
announcements as preserved in the decisions of
Christian antiquity. What has been called the
intense personality of Puritanism stood in equally
steadfast protest against that theory of a church
which also reached its highest development under
the Papacy—the theory which regards the church as
a mother, endowed with changeless attributes, preserving a mysterious life through all ages, untouched
by the actual conduct and opinions of the individuals
who, in their aggregate, are personified under her

---

* Old English translation of 2 Tim. ii. 3.   † Richard Alleine, M.A.

name, and wielding a power so great that salvation itself should be spoken of as if wrought, not alone by one redeeming Person, but also by this redeeming Personification. In consistency with these religious doctrines, and as their vital result, the Puritans were also the foremost advocates of political liberty.

We are chiefly acquainted with them through their ministers, and we therefore look upon Mr. Alleine with peculiar interest as a fair type of another class, which has had few biographers, although it exercised an influence almost equally important, in its rule over the religious changes of the times—the class of average Puritan laymen. Living in an age when the Court and Court-prelates were attempting to put down doctrinal preaching, and to give a stronger papistical tincture to the rubric of the church, he differed in opinion from these fashionable ecclesiastics, as to the two great questions, " What is the Gospel? " and " How should the Gospel be administered ?" When, in 1662, directions were issued to the effect " that no preacher under a bishop or a dean should presume to preach in any popular auditory on the deep points of predestination, election, or reprobation ; or of the universality, efficacy, resistibility or irresistibility of Divine grace," * he was one

---

Directions from the King to the Archbishop, to be communicated to all the clergy in his province. Windsor, August 10, 1632.

who said, " Is our minister forbidden by law to
preach the efficacy of divine grace ?   Then, man
makes that the forbidden fruit which God makes
the tree of life !"   When the bishops began to
apologize for images in churches, for confession to
a priest, for sacerdotal absolution, for bowing at
the altar, for the doctrine of transubstantiation,
which they declared was a school nicety, and for
the theory that the Lord's Supper should be
regarded not only as a sacrament, but as a sacrifice,—he, like many another Puritan layman, made
no secret of his indignation.

Perhaps if you saw some of the thoughts on
this subject expressed in Mr. Tobie Alleine's
memoranda, and could have overheard the strong
words spoken by him in the company of his friends,
your first impression might be that he magnified the
evil importance of the ceremonies Laud was aiming
to revive, and allowed them to inspire him with
too deep a fear of returning Popery.   But if you
could look through the mist of more than two
centuries, and see, as he did, the actual men and
women of that day, with all their living opinions
and emotions—if you could know with a power of
eager realization how ignorant they were, how
ready to follow the religion of those who made the
laws, and how very little the recent and short
ascendency of Protestantism had as yet served to
disperse the darkness induced by the ancient and

long ascendency of Romanism — you would qualify your first opinion. He saw the people sunk in superstition. Most of the countrymen with whom he transacted business came from districts infested with witches; in their journey over the downs they had been in peril from fairies; and in those dreary solitudes more than one had at times seen unearthly sights, or heard bursts of mysterious music. Night and morning, in going out and coming in, in bringing the sheep from the fold or the wool to the market, it was common for them to appeal to the tutelar saints of their respective parish churches. " Good Saint Catherine, stay my oxen!" would a farmer cry, when in chase of his straying cattle. The drover prayed to Saint Anthony. As the pack-horses came sliding and stumbling with obstreperous jingle down the chalk hill-side, the men in charge would invoke the aid of Saint Loy. Not only did they appeal to dead saints, but to graven images. In 1631, Mr. Sherfield, a gentleman with whom Alleine was acquainted, having long observed " many people" pause and bow before a window in his parish church at Salisbury, asked them why they did so. " Because the Lord our God is there," was the reply. On looking more closely into the glass, " all diamonded with quaint device," he found that it contained seven representations of God the Father, in the form of a little old man with a blue and red coat, with a pouch at his side.* This was the diocese which had so long been illumined with the presidency of men like Jewell and Davenant; and if here so much ignorance prevailed, how great would be the darkness elsewhere !

If, by the due consideration of facts like these, we could acquire power to stand in the place and see with the eyes of a man like Mr. Alleine, we should discover a spiritual meaning and dignity in many of the opinions held by him and his brother Puritans, which may now seem like the mere crotchets of morbid scrupulosity. " The surplice was the recognized symbol of the priestly character, and might have a tendency to recal the doctrine of a merely human intercessor standing between God and man. The cross in baptism, and the consecrated font, might, they said, easily bring back with them the exorcisms accompanying the rite of baptism in Roman Catholic churches. The observance of saint's days might suggest the adoration held to be due to those saints. Kneeling at the communion had its tacit reference to the conversion of the consecrated wafer. To retain these ceremonies, it was agreed, even were they innocent in themselves, was extremely dangerous in the English church, which had so recently emerged from Romanism.†

---

* Rushworth's Collections, vol. ii., p. 153.
† J. L. Sanford's Studies of the Great Rebellion, p. 67.

While the superstitions to which allusion has been made, showed how sensitive the poorer people were to the enchantments of Popery, other facts served to keep Mr. Alleine in mind of its persecuting vengeance. In his boyhood, old men sat in the sun who could remember the dying faces of martyrs, and who had told him thrilling things in the story of their own fathers, who had "played the man in the fire" at Salisbury; and now, the crushing tyranny of the church in her courts, her frowns on free thought, and the fervour with which, in the language of the scourge, the pillory and the branding iron, she asserted the religiousness of vestments, of attitudes, of signs, and of a particular quarter in the sky, naturally suggested the fear that scenes like those of the Marian persecution might open again. Perhaps it is not surprising that the church as thus represented should have alarmed rather. than attracted such a man; certainly this is not so wonderful as the fact that all this time, only a few miles off, a bard of such celestial inspiration as George Herbert, should have thus been singing in her praise :—

> " I joy, dear mother, when I view
>   Thy perfect lineaments and hue
>   Both sweet and bright :
>   Beauty in thee takes up her place,
>   And dates her letters from thy face,
>   When she doth write."

It was long thought by most persons, and is still thought by many, that the period of ecclesiastical history which came just before the great Puritan revolution, was a kind of golden age—the age out of whose life we must fetch our highest types of priestly excellence, and our fairest ideal pictures of a Christian people. And, indeed, this must be true, if we are to accept as true the wonders told of the desolation wrought by the later Puritanism. All the learning and eloquence, sanctity and grace which that Puritanism swept away, must have flourished then or never; for, however black and stormy Puritan barbarities were, their first stroke could not have crossed over the age in which they existed, to light on a distant century. The truth is, that most of that ignorance of the people which we have been describing, arose from the incompetency of their spiritual guides,* and especially from the want of a " preaching ministry." Within the memory of man, the sovereign had said, " It is good for the world to have few preachers—three or four may suffice for a county, and the reading of the homilies is enough." For

---

* This is contrary to the commonly received doctrine. See, for instance, some curious remarks in the Introduction to Stephens's Notes, legal and historical, on the Book of Common Prayer.— Ecclesiastical History Society.   The writer says :—" The episcopal clergy of that day were equally eminent for their learning and exemplary character as those of the present day."

a few years, at the beginning of the century, there had been a revival in this and other agencies of public instruction and refinement, but now there was a mournful decline. The calm-judging Selden, speaking of the clergy, says, " they were ignorant and indolent, and had nothing to support their credit but beard, title, and habit."* Milton, in " Lycidas," utters a similar complaint.† Richard Baxter, writing of Shropshire in the days of his boyhood—that is, about 1620, and ten years after—says, " There was little preaching of any kind, and that little was rather calculated to injure than to benefit. In High Ercall, there were four readers in the course of six years; all of them ignorant, and two of them immoral men. At Eaton Constantine, there was a reader of eighty years of age, Sir William Rogers, who never preached; yet he had two livings, twenty miles apart from each other. His sight failing, he repeated the prayers without the book; but to read the lessons, he employed a common labourer one year, a tailor another, and at last his own son, the best stage-player and gamester in all the county, got orders, and supplied one of his places. Within a few miles round were nearly a dozen ministers of the same description: poor, ignorant readers, and most

---

* History of Tithes, preface, p. i., 1618.
† 1637.

of them of dissolute lives."*   George Withers also
remarks respecting such unprofitable servants,—

> " In their poverty they will not stick
> For catechising, visiting the sick,
> With such-like duteous works of piety
> As do belong to their society ;
> But if they once but reach a vicarage,
> Or be inducted to some parsonage,
> Men must content themselves, and think it well
> If once a month they hear the sermon bell." †

Such was the rule, and it is of the rule we now are
speaking, not of a few brilliant exceptions.   Every
step was taken by the higher priests to discourage
preaching, and every proof was given by the lower
ones of readiness to acquiesce.

The Puritans endeavoured to find a remedy for
this evil by supporting *lecturers* — clergymen,
who, having obtained the necessary licence, were
supported by special subscriptions, or by funds
obtained through the purchase of lay-impropriations,
and then employed merely as *preachers*.   Mer-
chants and tradesmen who lived in London were
accustomed to consult and subscribe for the settlement or occasional service of lecturers in the towns
and villages of their native county, where there
appeared to be a deficiency in the ordinary clerical

---

* Orme's Life of Baxter, vol. ii., p. 3.   Fuller, *sub anno* 1630.
Rushworth, vol. i., part 2, p. 150.

† Britaine's Remembrancer, 1628.

means.* In other cases, such lecturers were maintained by the zeal of resident friends. They had no local charge, and their sole vocation was preaching. The pulpit of St. John's was then provided for by the town authorities, the minister was under their patronage, and was almost entirely supported by free contributions.† It is curious to see, from their old records, the vigorous use they made of their rights in inviting lecturers. In the course of the twenty years immediately preceding the Protectorate, very many were the lecturers engaged by the corporation to preach at ordinary and extraordinary times, and we may trace much of this work to the quiet energy of Mr. Tobie Alleine.‡

One of his friends, who was always a cordial helper in work like this, was the worshipful Master John Kent, the aged town-clerk,§ and also member of parliament for the borough, for which service, during the time occupied, he received, according to ancient usage, the sum of two shillings a day.

---

* Account of Clerical Customs in 1630, additional MSS., 4460, f. 80. Social History of the Southern Counties, by George Roberts, Chapter on Lecturers.

† So stated in a petition from Devizes to Parliament against a proposal for settling on Mr. Henry Johnson, minister, the sum of £100 per annum, out of the lands and stock of the borough.—State Papers, 1660.

‡ Devizes chamberlain's books, and other memoranda.

§ Mr. Justice Kent's Ledger Book is in the Lansdown MSS., 231

You may see his effigy—solemn with ruff and robe, and hands clasped as in prayer—in the chancel of St. John's Church.   According to the Latin epitaph there, he was " a man of fervent piety towards God, who so obtained the calm of an untroubled conscience, that he might be said to have anticipated the bliss of heaven."*   These worthies often exchanged formal compliments and quaint courtesies, and held many a grave conference about Church and State.   Like other keen watchers of events, they hardly knew whether they could see in these events the beginnings of a new day for Romanism, or the dismal dawn of civil war.   It was only certain that some disastrous crisis was at hand.

A ray of sober merriment sometimes shot through their gloomiest conversation.   One day, Nathaniel Stephens, a young Oxford student, said to have been related to Mr. Kent, came in with a story which he thus drily told :—

"A clergyman entering the church," (perhaps his father's church at the neighbouring village of Stanton Bernard,) " went up to the chancel to bow to the altar.   It so happened that there was no altar there, but the communion table stood against the east wall, and a boy sat upon it.   The boy, seeing

---

* He died in 1630.   The epitaph was probably written by his grandson, Dr. Philip Stephens, president of Hart Hall, Oxford, and who was ejected for Nonconformity in 1662.

the priest coming towards him, slipt down and stood before the table. At length the priest made a low bow, and the poor boy thinking it was to him the respect was paid, bowed as low to him again ; and the bows were repeated three times on each side ; the boy being surprised at the priest's wonderful civilitie."

Many years after this, when, according to George Fox, the relater of this anecdote had become " one of Baal's priests, and preached in Drayton Steeplehouse," he used to finish the tale with a few solemn words of application, sounding very much like the echo of what might have been said about it by the elders to whom he related it first. " In this case," he would say, " the boy knew well enough who it was he bowed to, but whether or not it was so as to the priest, it is questionable ; for the God whom Christians worship is no more in the east than in the west—no more in the chancel than in the church— nor any more there than in the house or in the field; unless when His people are there ' worshipping him in spirit and in truth.' Before the coming of Christ it was the duty of the Jews in the western parts to worship towards the east, because Jerusalem and the Temple stood that way. (1 Kings viii. 48 ; Dan. vi. 10.) This might be the reason why some Christians in the primitive times took up the fashion of praying towards the east. They Judaized in that as well as in some other things. But now

Mount Zion is no more holy than Mount Gerizim, or the mountains in Wales." *

The matters which suggested talk like this, and which seemed in one way or other to become the theme of every conversation between thinking men, grew in practical importance every day. The spirit of the rival parties became terribly earnest. At last the sword flashed out, and the land rang with war. When the Cavalier, fired with loyalty for the *person* of the King, set up his standard, "invoking every eye for its glance and every tongue for its prayer;" and the Puritan, fired with equal loyalty for principles which he thought involved in the *office* of the King, set up another standard of defiance, greater interests were at stake than those of politics. Events showed that those seers were right who had predicted that the only alternative for the country would be a fight for freedom, or a return to Popery and arbitrary power. Say, if you please, that the Puritans dwelt upon the evils of Popery with an emphasis that was injurious and out of place, and that no grounds existed for their apprehensions of its return. The Pope himself formed no such low estimate of their political sagacity ; and we may remark in passing, as an evidence of the light in which he regarded the war, that a Bull of his was intercepted and sent up to Parliament,

---

* Nonconformist's Memorial.

promising canonization to those Catholics who fell on the side of the King—a mark-worthy fact which has not found its way into any of our histories.*

In the storm of war, Mr. Alleine, like thousands of his countrymen, suffered greatly in trade and estate. The Chamberlain's accounts for 1647 record the discharge of Tobias Alleine, Gent., "from the bond to pay a rent to the corporation for taking ' the tolls of the beams and scales,' on the ground that, owing to the late unnatural wars, the markets were unfrequented, rendering him unable, in consequence, to make up his rent out of the profits."† From this time we gradually lose sight of him, and by 1650 his name entirely disappears from the burgess lists. He had not yet, however, retired into absolute obscurity ; for in the Bodleian Library, bound up with a volume of pamphlets, we find a list of Wiltshire Triers of ministers, which contains his name. The list itself is undated, but if the Triers reported there are those appointed by Cromwell's commission, the date of the appointment must have been about :654 ; showing that he had not by that time ceased to be a man having authority. In this capacity he was associated with thirteen ministers, and sundry country gentlemen, among whom were Sir Edward Hungerford, Sir Edward Baynton,

---

* Commons' Journals, vol. iii., pp. 257, 264.
† Burgus de Devizes, tempore Will. Thurnam, Maioris.

John Ffreme, a Devizes Baptist, and Serjeant
Robert Nicholas, who then represented the town in
Parliament.*

This is the last instance in which he appears in
any public service, for altered circumstances prevented him from filling his former station.   First,
from the wars, then from the penal enactments
against Nonconformists, he sunk into deeper and
yet deeper poverty.   Troubles came crowding on
him, throng upon throng, and in his old age he
often had no home of his own.   In 1666 he was
imprisoned for conscience sake, with his son Joseph;
and a letter is extant, dated from Ilchester Gaol, in
the postscript of which he sends his "tender remembrance" to the beloved people of Taunton,
and says, "I desire you to hold fast what you have
received and heard, and that you be holy, harmless,
exemplary, and without offence in the midst of a
crooked and perverse generation."

In June, 1667, "he died," it is said, "suddenly
but sweetly."   On the morning of his death he rose
about four.   About ten or eleven he came down
out of his closet and called for something to eat,
which being prepared he gave thanks, but could not
eat anything.   His wife, perceiving a sudden change
in him, persuaded him to go to bed; he answered,

---

* The date of the papers collectively is given outside the pamphlet
as 1658.

" No, but I will die in my chair; and I am not afraid to die." He sat down, and only said, " My life is hid with Christ in God;" and then he closed his eyes with his own hand, and died immediately.* "Shut thine eyes a little, old man, and immediately thou shalt see the light of God !†" So it was said to Ananias the martyr, as he knelt to lay his white head upon the block; and so it might have been said to Mr. Tobie Alleine.

---

* Rev. R. Alleine.

† "Paulisper O senex, oculos claude; nam statim lumen Dei videbis."—Sozomen, lib. ii., cap. 11.

Chapter II.

Strange Schools and Schoolmasters.

"The courser's neighing he could ken,
And measured tread of marching men—
The banners tall, of crimson sheen,
Above the copse appear ;
And glistening through the hawthorn green,
Shine helm, and shield, and spear."

SIR WALTER SCOTT.

JOSEPH ALLEINE was born at Devizes, early in the year 1634.* The date of his birthday is lost, but his baptism, according to the register of St. John's Church, was on the 8th of April. He was the fourth child in the family, and after him were several others, including some whose names are not recorded.†

---

* Late in the year 1633, if we reckon by the old style, which supposed the year to begin on the 25th of March, and end on the 24th of March following.

† The following are the names of Mr. Alleine's children, with the dates of their baptism as given in the register :—Edward, 13th

Our immediate aim will be to trace the earliest processes of his education, and to show their earliest effects. Hugh Miller used to complain that with most persons the word " schools " only called to mind the idea of certain buildings devoted to scholastic purposes, and that the word " schoolmasters " only suggested the idea of certain men in desks, teaching in those buildings. He thought this was too narrow a meaning for such words, and that its adoption led to too narrow a view of education. Regarding the matured life of a man in the light of a result; in his opinion, every scene, every event, and every friendship of childhood contributing to that result, should be remembered in the list of our " schools and schoolmasters." This, therefore, was the title he selected for the charming story of his own life. There, the first school that he recognizes is that of *parentage ;* the next is that of *surrounding local circumstances.* In studying the agencies that educed the character of Joseph Alleine, we may with advantage adopt these thoughts and in this order. The nature, in his case, of the first-named class of educating forces, may be inferred from what has already been

---

December, 1618 ; Tobie, 15th January, 1620–1 ; Elizabeth, 21st February, 1626–7 ; Joseph, 8th April, 1634 ; Lettice, 22nd September, 1635 ; Israel, 13th March, 1637–8 ; Mary, 1st June, 1640. After that, there is a long *hiatus* in the book.

said of his father.   The nature of the second now
remains to be described.

It should be remembered that the conflict
between Charles and his Parliament had, by the
time of which this chapter treats, been transferred
from the House of Commons to the battle-field.
In no place, according to its measure, were the
consequences more severely felt than at Devizes.
Instead of opening in a dream of pleasant wonders,
Joseph Alleine's childhood was spent in the midst
of these alarms.

His father's house, with its white gables, striped
and flowered with dark wood-work, occupied the
site of that which now stands next the market-
house.   Right before it, only just across the broad
way, half screened on one side by a ring of elm
trees that stood round a broken cross, rose the
great grey walls of the castle ;—its keep roofless,
and its outworks shattered into picturesque decay ;
but its general aspect still sufficiently royal to show
why the monk, Matthew Paris, had called it " the
most magnificent castle in Christendom."   Even in
its partial ruin it was deemed an important fortress.
Twice, at least, did the boy witness its siege and
the consequent change of its masters, before he was
twelve years old.

To the last, one of the most vividly lighted
scenes in his memory was that siege by Sir William
Waller, the object of which was to recover the

town from the Royalists, into whose power it had recently fallen. The issue of this experiment was the famous battle of Roundway.

From the back of the house might be seen over the roofs, the high, bare Wiltshire plains, where they drop abruptly by a long line of undulating slopes, into a rich valley of trees and pasturage. Roundway is the name given to one of these slopes, just above Devizes. The town is at the highest part of the valley, and from the point where the castle stood, the ground sinks away down into a landscape, in which, to use the language of a local poet, we may descry,

> "Towns, villages, light smoke,
> And scarce-seen windmill sails, and devious woods,
> Chequering 'mid sunshine the grass-level land,
> That stretches from the sight."*

Looking up, early in the morning of the 10th of July, 1643, the child might have seen, through the thin rain that was falling, Sir William Waller's army of 5,500 men in slow motion over the edge of the down. He and the little ones of the family were hurried within doors. Presently, the guns from the battery and the answering peals from the castle shook the roof-tree, and flashed through the chinks of his father's barred and shuttered windows. Soon, he heard eager voices in the

---

* Rev. W. Lisle Bowles.

street, telling the news that the besiegers had
captured large supplies of artillery that were on
their way to the town, and that now the garrison
would only be able to hold out for a few hours.
Shortly after that, he was at work with his mother
and sisters, in hot haste cutting down all the bed-
ropes and collecting all the cordage they could find,
to be boiled and beaten into match for the
musketeers.

Match was furnished by this expedient, suddenly
and conjointly adopted by all the good wives of the
town.   Lead was torn from the church roofs to be
cast into bullets.   Powder was unexpectedly contributed by a townsman who had for some time
been storing it in a pit.   Thus, supplies were found,
and the defence of the place was prolonged for
four days.   Meanwhile, so early as Monday night,
the Marquis of Hartford had stolen away from the
castle, to obtain reinforcements from Oxford; but
Waller, trusting that Essex would intercept them,
felt no anxiety.   On Thursday, however, at about
four o'clock in the afternoon, the reinforcements
came.   A formidable body of horsemen came
thundering over the sward, and attacked Waller
on Roundway, just as he was about by one last
stroke of desperate strength to take the town.
Without staying to relate the intricate history of
the engagement, it will be sufficient to say that the
army of the Parliament was put to flight, and the

result of the day was seen in the fall of Bath, the fall of Bristol, and the restoration for a time of the King's ascendency in the west. The Royalists called it the battle of " Run-away ;" Waller entered it in his journal as a " fatherly chastisement."*

Take another scene from Joseph's childhood :— On Sunday morning, the 18th of September, 1645, he found that a battery of ten guns had been constructed in the night, just before his father's house, and pointed towards the castle gates. Standing on the green margin of the footway, only a few paces from the porch, was a soldier, whose rough, grand look of concentrated authority shot a thrill through the young beholder, and compelled the whisper, " Who is he ?" It was Oliver Cromwell, who, as Lieutenant-General for the Parliament, brought a final summons to the Governor to deliver up the place. There was an answer of defiance. Clouds of arrows whizzed through the air.† For two days and two nights, incessant

---

* Waller's Recollections. The history of this battle is given in Waylen's History of Devizes.

† In 1643, the Earl of Essex had issued a commission desiring all well-affected persons in and about the city of London to " bring in bows and arrows, not doubting but that success will attend the use of that honourable and ancient weapon, heretofore found of good use in this kingdom " Gwynn, in his Autobiography, speaking of this last siege of Devizes, says—" Standing by Sir Jacob Astley a bearded arrow struck into the ground between his legs. He plucked it out with both hands, and said, ' You rogues, you missed your

were the pealings of musketry and the explosions of shells. On the third day the garrison surrendered—Governor Sir Charles Lloyd and his men were permitted to ride away to Worcester;* and at last, high over the old keep, the blue banner of the Parliament was seen flowing in the wind.†

In May, 1646, orders came from the House of Commons for the total demolition of the fortress. Slowly and gradually these orders were carried into effect by the regiments quartered in the town, until almost the last vestige of a wall was gone, and even the white bones and rusty chains in the dungeons were open to the sky. For several years it was a daily excitement to see the warriors at work, now with sturdy swing, handling pickaxe or lever, now pausing to hold a debate on theology, to settle a case of conscience, or to raise the stave of a psalm; and after work was over, often going, it is said, to "a little room in the little house of good dame Ffreme," there to hold those meetings for prayer and exhortation, which formed the first stage in the history of the Baptist Church at Devizes.‡ John Bunyan was at this time a sol-

---

aim.'" Sir Walter Scott remarks on this passage, that it is "perhaps the last mention of the use of the bow and arrow in England in actual battle."

* Sprigg's Anglia Rediviva, part iii., chap. 1.

† So described by Sir John Prestwitch.

‡ MS. Diary of Thomas Webb, a man who prayed that Daniel Defoe might enjoy "the blessings of the upper and nether springs."

dier, doubtless often engaged in similar work and
in similar society, traces of which perhaps we find
in such conversations as those between Mr. Great-
heart and his companions, and in such verse as
that in which they celebrate the fall of Doubting
Castle.

Joseph had yet other strange schools and schoolmasters, of which some account should be given.
When you step down into the twilight of the old
still church at Devizes, you say, "Here, at least, we
may forget the world, and let the mind drink in
holy tranquillity." But it was not so then.
Houses of prayer were often vortices of strife, for
the prelates who a few years before had been " sow-
ing to the wind," were now " reaping the whirlwind ;" and the whirlwind was often wildest there.
The people, having in youth had an ecclesiastical
drill rather than a Christian education, were not all
prepared to use aright their new-found liberty of
conscience. Just rung up in alarm out of their
awful sleep of ignorance, they were all in excitement, and their uneducated enthusiasm found out-
force in many a rude extravagance. To borrow
the wise and eloquent words of the Bishop of
Oxford, though not spoken by him in defence of
the views advocated here, we may truly say that
"it is part of the curse of unrighteous tyranny,
that it not only oppresses its victims during its
supremacy, but that, even in its removal, it still

blights them by the licence which is engendered by its dissolution."*

We may find illustration of this truth in some of the disturbances of which the churches were sometimes the scene, about the time of which we are speaking. The custom has been to point to such disturbances, and call them the effects of Puritanism, although they were in reality only the natural effects of the causes we have described, made more intense by the licence of a civil war. The actors in them were not the Puritans, as such, but soldiers or rioters, and the immediate sufferers from them were often the Puritan ministers.†

One day, late in 1647, when Joseph with his father and all the family were at church, the Presbyterian minister, worthy Master Shepherd, being in the performance of his duties, one Captain Pretty did, with "much admirable incivilitie," command the good man to leave the pulpit, charging him with "a disorderlie walk." The pulpit was vacated in a swift and lively manner, and the congregation "had no lecture that day." This incident seems to

---

* Addresses to Candidates for Ordination, by Samuel, Lord Bishop of Oxford, 1860, p. 218.

† To be informed as to the true authors of the war, let all young Nonconformists consult the actual documents of that day, as given in such works as Forster's "Debates on the Grand Remonstrance," and "Arrest of the Five Members;" Verney's "Notes of the Long Parliament," Camden Society; and Sanford's "Studies of the Great Rebellion."

have furnished Sir Walter Scott with a suggestion for the scene in "Woodstock," where Master Nehemiah Holdenough suffers similar "incivilitie" from the hands of Joseph Tomkins the weaver; who forthwith takes the clergyman's place, and delivers a long exhortation.*

It was no uncommon thing to find a soldier in possession of the pulpit, and the boy Alleine often heard a military preacher. You may still see old manuscript notes of such sermons taken down by hearers. There are notes of one preached in St. John's by Major Barton, about the beginning of the year 1649. It is founded on Numbers xii. 1, 2, 3; and has evident reference to the revolt of the Levellers. Nothing could be more unlike the work of an enthusiast. The constructive skill it displays would have done credit to one of the deposed bishops. It has division within division, in all ninety-seven—subtle, intricate, confounding, pedantic, preposterous. Each has a numerical distinction. The thoughts are dry as petrifactions, and it is difficult to conceive that once they were, as they must have been, full of passionate life.†

---

* One proof that Sir Walter knew of this circumstance, and had it in mind when he wrote this romance, exists in the fact that at this time (1636) *Sir Henry Lee* was one of the capital burgesses of Devizes.—Chamberlain's Accounts.

† "Good Old Simeon Ash wrote to Colonel Barton, when Monk came in, to engage him for the King."—Baxter MS. In the *Public*

" Sir," said " a gentleman all in scarlet," to a
minister, as he was one day stepping out of the
pulpit, " you speak against the preaching of soldiers ; but I assure you, if they have not leave to
preach, they will not fight ; and if they fight not,
you must all fly the land and begone. * * *
These men who are preachers, both of troopers
and commanders, are the men whom God hath
blessed within these few months to rout the enemy
twice in the field, and to take many garrisons of
castles and towns.—I thought good to let you
understand as much, and this is all I have to
say." *

According to Edwards, the author of the " Gangrœna," the violent and insulting interruption of
the Presbyterian ministers by soldiers, in the
time of public service, was an ordinary event.† If
so, the charge must be restricted to those who were
known as the Levellers,—rebels on theory against
all authority, and whose revolt against Cromwell has
just been the subject of a passing allusion. But it
was common even for those of their number who
belonged to that large and superior class whose
praise is in all the histories, to aspire after preach-

Intelligencer for February, 1660, we find the name of Lieutenant-
Colonel Barton associated with that of General Monk. This must
have been the same person.

   * Gangrœna, book i., p. 111.

   † Book i., pp. 106—108.

ing or disputing in the churches. Baxter records
an instance of such a discussion carried on in
Agmondesham Church, between himself and "Pitch-
ford's cornet," one taking the reading-desk, and the
other the gallery.* The Ironsides seemed to claim
an occasional use of their gifts in the pulpit as one
of their rights, and part of their pay.

Such are fair instances of the things which helped
to form Alleine's education. Almost every person
he knew, led a life of anxiety and adventure, everywhere and every day. Thomas Fuller had truly
said, " Janus's Temple was not shut in any parish,
and there was no rest on the earth." The people
of Devizes in particular, had a thousand experiences
to remind them of some lines in a book that was
then lying on many a window-seat :—

> " Ah ! sweet Content, where is thy mild abode ?
>   Is it with shepherds and light-hearted swains,
> Which sing upon the downes and pipe abroad,
>   Leading their flockes, and calling unto plains ?
>
> " Ah ! sweet Content, where dost thou safely reste ?
>   In heaven, with angels, who the praises sing
> Of Him that made and rolls at His beheste
>   The minds and parts of ev'ry living thing ?
>
> " Ah ! sweet Content, where doth thine harbour hold ?
>   Is it in churches with religious men,   .
> Which praise their God with prayers manifold,
>   And in their studies meditate it then ?
>
> " Whether thou dost in heaven or earth appeare,
> Be where thou wilt, thou wilt not harbour here." †

---

* Orme's Life of Baxter, vol. ii., p. 74.   † Barnaby Barnes, 1590.

Many faded letters and diaries bear witness to the fact that thoughts like these, suggested by the troubles of the times, were often employed by the Divine Regenerator to bring about that grand change, which all must feel who " see the kingdom of heaven." " Content is not here," it was said, " where can we find it?" Like the dove of the deluge, that flew to the ark because nowhere else could it fold its weary wing to rest, many were taught by trouble to seek rest in Christ. Young as he was, there is reason to believe that Joseph Alleine was thus taught. It was just at the time of the second siege, when he was about eleven years old only, that he dated the dawn of his new life. At that time his many contrivances for being alone were first observed, and persons coming accidentally where he was at such seasons, found that he was alone for prayer, so absorbed in his simple devotions as not to be aware of their presence. He grew up so much under the influence of great and solemn feelings, that the state of his mind was sometimes an overstrained one. From his gravity, induced partly by this, and partly by his love of study, his companions used to call him " the lad that will not play." It would dishonour the benignant Redeemer to plead for a religion that by its own inherent law

> " Checks a child with terror,
> Stops its play, and chills its song."

But in this case we only see the natural working of
the forms in which religion was first suggested to
his mind, and of the outward forces that first led
him to feel its value. These early events seemed
to cast a shadow all along his future life. Seeing
from boyhood little peculiar to earth besides " the
windy storm and tempest " of sin and consternation,
he was almost led to think that he had absolutely
nothing to do in this world but to hasten through
it to a better, and by means of invitation or
alarm to persuade, if possible, everyone else to
become a companion of his panic flight. Under the
power of God's Spirit, the same circumstances also
tended to educe habits of self-denial, of endurance,
and of hardy, fearless courage in the advocacy or
practice of his faith. It would be wrong, however,
to think that his was only a gloomy religion. Old
tracts say that " even in his childhood he showed a
singular sweetness of disposition," and that " the
whole course of his youth was one even-spun thread
of godly conversation, which was rendered the more
amiable by his sweet and pleasant deportment
towards all he conversed with." *

His eldest brother, Mr. Edward Alleine, was a
clergyman ; but in 1645, when he was only in his

---

* A Brief Relation of his (Joseph Alleine's) early Setting Forth in
the Christian Race, &c. Written by an Eye-witness thereof.—
Also, account of Alleine in Clarke's Lives.

27th year, he died, to the deep grief of many friends, as we learn from more than one paper, in which he is described as " a young minister of rare promise." This, as we have seen, was the year of Joseph's " setting forth in the Christian race." He implored his father that he might be educated to " succeed his brother in the work of the ministry." Glad consent was given, and he was immediately sent to school. It is supposed that the school selected was that at Poulshot, under the care of his father's friend, Mr. William Spinage, fellow of Exeter College, Oxford. There he had praise for unusual diligence, and in four years, broken by long intervals of visiting at home, caused by the confusion of passing events, he obtained such a degree of mastery over the Greek and Latin languages as to be fit, in the judgment of his tutor, for university studies.*

After this he remained for a little time in his father's house at Devizes, reading logic " with a worthy minister of the place." Unusual maturity now displayed itself both in mental and religious life. Jeremy Taylor decides that " some are of age at 15; some at 20; and some never." Joseph Alleine was of age at 15, and his father, whose heart had been almost broken by the loss of his first-born, as he now looked upon the son who was rising to take the place of the departed one, and as

* Anthony Wood.

he proudly augured from what he was, what he would be, would say, " This same shall comfort us concerning our work and toil of our hands. The blessing of thy father shall be upon the head of Joseph, and on the crown of the head of him who was separate from his brethren."

Chapter III.

Life in the Puritan University.

" Youth, with pale cheek and slender frame,
And dreams of greatness in thine eye,
Goest thou to build an early name,
Or early in the task to die?"

BRYANT.

E remained at Devizes more than a year after Mr. Spinage had pronounced him ripe for the university, but there was good reason for the delay. To all appearance that year had been, for the interests of learning, the most dismal and hopeless in all the annals of Oxford. In 1646, after a long siege, it had surrendered to the Parliament forces, but was left in a state so desolate, that men said in their excitement it looked " like Jerusalem in ruins." Broken trees and trampled gardens were seen on every hand. Sculptured stones and pictured windows lay shattered in the grass. Nettles and brambles were growing round the walls of the schools. The rich wood-work in the quadrangle of Christ-church College had been torn down for fuel. The halls had been turned into granaries, the colleges into barracks, the butteries into shops for the sale of food for the garrison; all the treasuries were exhausted; all the plate was gone;* and books had disappeared for the purchase of fire-arms. So long had Mars usurped the place of Minerva, and students been accustomed to exchange cap for helmet, that the scholastic air of the place had almost vanished. Lectures and exercises had fallen into disuse, except in St. Mary's Church, where a scanty remnant of undergraduates used to assemble. Few persons connected with the university remained besides heads of houses and professors.

Even when the soldiers had surrendered, the academics still refused to acknowledge the authority of the commissioners sent down by Parliament to carry out the measures which had been concerted for the reformation of the university. " They held out," says Dr. Walker, " a siege of more than a year and a half; the convocation-house proved a citadel, and each college a fort not easy to be

---

* Plate presented to his Majesty by the colleges, January 20th, 1642, 1610 lb, 1 oz. 10 d.—Collectanea Curiosa, vol. ii., p. 227. This was the first instalment.

reduced."* At length, in July, 1648, this "siege" of mere authority being unavailing, the Parliament expelled by military force those who refused to take "the solemn league and covenant," as they afterwards did those who refused to sign "an engagement to be true to the Government without king or lords." All honour be to the memory of these stout Carolist doctors, with their romantic devotion to the King, their high chivalry, and their noble stand for conscience. We acknowledge and deplore the wrongs they suffered. Yet, if we admit the university to be a national institution, it will be difficult to show why the actual Government of the day, assuming it to be the organ of the national opinion, and the grand executive of the national will, should not have demanded its submission to governmental authority ; and further, if we admit the university to be by right a part of the religious establishment of the State, it is difficult to see why it was not as consistent for the State, when Presbyterian, to enforce its own symbol, as it was, when Episcopalian, to enforce the thirty-nine articles.

While these affairs were in agitation, and Oxford seemed to be but the camp of all chaotic and refractory elements, it was not likely to attract new students, and Alleine, like many others, waited.

---

* Sufferings of the Clergy, pp. 122, 123, 128. Wood's Annals.

Something like order being at last restored, in the
month of April, 1649, he set out for the scene of
his studies.   Amongst the Wiltshire youths riding
with him some part of the way, might have been
seen, we may suppose, "that miracle of a youth,"
Christopher Wren, afterwards the architect of St.
Paul's Cathedral, and Lancelot Addison, now
known only by a fame reflected from that of his
son, the great essayist.   On his arrival, he was
placed at Lincoln College, then under the presidency of Dr. Paul Hood.   He thus began his
curriculum in *the Puritan University*.   We must
give some illustrations of what is meant by that
phrase, and it will best be done by a few historical
scenes and pictures.

Stand by Joseph Alleine, and look at the first
scene.   He had been here but a few weeks, when
he had an opportunity of witnessing the sober
splendours of a Puritan gala-day.   This was occasioned by the ceremony of creating Oliver Cromwell doctor of civil laws.   Late on Thursday,
the 17th of May, the general rode in from Burford,
where he had just quelled the mutiny of the
Levellers, and the university put forth all her
pomp and all her hospitality to greet him.   He,
Fairfax, and a staff of officers, were entertained that
night at All Souls' College, "hitherto," as Prag-
maticus pensively remarks, "a neat nursery of
civility and learning."   In the morning, the heads

of houses waited on him in their ceremonial robes, and Mr. Rous of All Souls' delivered a congratulatory speech. In reply, Cromwell said that " he and his companions were well aware that no commonwealth could flourish without learning; that, whatever the world said to the contrary, they meant to encourage it, and that so far from subtracting any of their means, they meant to add more." Next day, "having been entertained," says Anthony Wood, "with good fare and bad speeches" at Magdalen College, followed by a hearty game of bowls on the green, the visitors went to the schools. There the degree of doctor of laws was conferred on Cromwell and Fairfax, and that of master of arts on their principal officers. The two chiefs, arrayed in doctorial scarlet, were then led in procession. Some of the usual formalities were omitted from the routine. For instance, it was customary for the beadles to march first, bearing the doctors' square caps swung from the tips of their silver staves, but these costly symbols of office had not yet been delivered up by the Royalists ;* and, as to cap and hood, they having

---

* " Procuratores sine clavibus,
    Querentibus ostendas ;
    Bedellos novos sine stavibus,
    Res protinus ridendas."—Allibond on Oxford Univ., 1648.
The staves were kept back until 1651. R. S. to Sheldon;
Ayscough MS.

formed part of the vestments worn by Romish priests, were of course rejected as "mere conjuring garments," and "relics of the Amorites." On the arrival of the procession at the upper end of the convocation-house, all the members standing bare-headed, Zanchy, the Baptist proctor, made a complimentary speech, "such as 'twas," adds our friend Anthony, and presented the new doctors to the vice-chancellor, who addressed them in a similar strain. Ralph Button, the university orator, then delivered a Latin oration, in which he styled Cromwell and Fairfax "the two martial twins," in allusion to Romulus and Remus. Dead and dull as these and other details may look, when we only see them in the old, brown pamphlets of the British Museum, they may help the imaginative student of the past to call into his presence something of the eager animation, light, and colour of the very scene itself, as its changes shifted before the eyes of Alleine and his companions.*

It is fair to suppose that he was looking from the gallery on that high day in February, 1650, when Cromwell's letter was read announcing his acceptance of the chancellorship. "You shall not want my prayers," so ran the document, "that that seed and stock of piety (so marvellously springing up among you) may be useful to that

---

* Mercuries; also Wood's Annals, by Gutch, vol. ii., part ii., p. 621.

great and glorious kingdom of our Lord Jesus Christ, of the approach of which, so plentiful an effusion of the Spirit on these hopeful plants, is one of the best presages. And, in all other things, I shall, by the divine assistance, improve my poor abilities and interests, in manifesting myself to the university and yourselves, your most cordial friend." ·" Which, being read in convocation," remarks Mr. Wood, " the members thereof made the house resound with their cheerful acclamations." *

These acclamations were not echoed by the Royalists. On the contrary, to use the chancellor's own words, they opened a brisk " battery of paper shot " upon him. Rough and unlettered as they chose to call him, they had no objection to address the hero of Naseby as " Dr. Cromwell," and they frequently did so, in an ecstacy of satirical glee; but this last appointment was thought an outrage too profane to be treated with levity, and at the very thought of it the graver sort amongst them almost gave up the ghost. Pity that so much good emotion should have been wasted, for succeeding events amply justified the election, and Oliver, in becoming chancellor, became " the practical saviour of the old university."†

Alleine often saw the dean of Christ Church, Dr. John Owen, not then looking as he does

---

* Fasti, p. 136.   † Guizot.

in those later portraits by which he now is
known—

> " ———— the frail remains
> Of sickness, care, and studious pains ;"

but in the prime of his vigour ;—his dark eyes full
of keen fire ; his raven-black hair thrown back by
the action of his quick, authoritative step ; his
frame still showing the spring and spirit, owing to
which, only a few years before, " no man was more
ready to pull a wherry on the Isis, or wrestle a
fall, or heave a stone on the college meadows, or
join a jolly crew of wild lads to go up on a moon-
light eve into the belfry of Magdalene, and set the
rich bells a clanging till the spire rocked, wakening
the night, and startling the old monastic quiet of
the streets with the joyous outbreak and tintin-
abulatory exuberance of a double Bob Major."*
His manliness, his courtly presence, his strong
will, his rare administrative ability, and, above all,
his sanctified genius and learning, now attracted the
attention of Cromwell, who, as Thurloe remarks,
" sought not places for men, but men for places."
This tact led him to nominate the doctor to be
vice-chancellor, that is, to be chancellor's deputy,
to act in his absence as the virtual judge and ruler
of all academical affairs. Accordingly, on the 26th

---

* Dublin University Essays, No. IV. ; Life and Times of John
Owen, D.D., by the Rev. Richard S. Brooke, M.A.

of September, 1651, he was chosen to that honour by the unanimous suffrage of the senate. He soon effected great reforms. During the five years of his vice-chancellorship, " professor's salaries, lost for many years, were recovered and paid, the rights and privileges of the university were defended against all the efforts of its enemies, the treasury was tenfold increased, new exercises were introduced and established, old ones duly performed."* The once-deserted courts were crowded again, and even in the first few months of his office, four hundred more students were enrolled than in one of the golden years of King James.† The coarse amusements and the shameful vice which had made Oxford so notorious in the reign of that great monarch, and which, if possible, had become worse during the military occupation of the place,‡ were

---

* Oratio ad Richardum Crom.

† In 1622, the total number of students of all degrees was 2,850 ; in 1651, 3,247. " The Foundation of the University of Oxford," 4to., 1651, supposed to have been written by Dr. Langbaine, keeper of the archives.

‡ Sir Henry Blount, Knight, who was at Oxford in Charles I.'s time, " inveighed much against sending youths to the university, where they only learned to be debauched."—Aubrey's Lives.

"That which was most burdensome to me . . . was the debauchery of the university. For the most eminent scholars of the town . . . did work upon me by such endearments as took the name of civilities (yet day and night could witness our madness) ; and, I must confess, the whole time of my life besides I did never so much transport me with drinking as that short time I lived at Oxford, and that with some of the gravest bachelors of divinity there."—

put down by Owen with resolute severity. Yet he
meant only to be intolerant of wickedness. Opinions
and preferences of good men, however adverse
to his own, he treated with respect. The Royalist
visitor to a chapel would see no traces of injury
done to its Gothic effigies or floral mouldings,
but those received in the siege; he would find
few differences in its arrangements, except that
the altar would be " turned table-wise ;" and the
solemn organ still " tossed its music from side to
side ;" at least we know that the organ was still
used in the chapel of the college under the prin-
cipalship of the famous Independent, Dr. Thomas
Goodwin, as well as in some others.* Caps and
hoods were an abomination to Owen's puritanic
tastes, and he said so ; but they were worn without
hindrance by those who liked them. Owing to
the narrow policy of Government, still more
owing to the folly of the bishops, the Episcopalian
service was now proscribed, but every day a few
Episcopalians met to enjoy their forbidden Prayer-
book in a house just opposite his own. They
knew that he might have dispersed them had he

Arthur Young, Gentleman Commoner of Trinity College, Oxford,
in 1631, " Peck's Desiderata Curiosa." lib. xii., p. 470.
  " What few students remained were much debauched, and were
much addicted to swearing, drinking, and profanity."—Wood's
Annals of the University.
  * Evelyn's Diary, 1654.

so minded; but, in the interchange of courtesies
between him and them, as they casually met on
the green outside, he never made inquiry as to
the object of their assembly.*   Congregationalist
as he was, he appointed qualified men to responsible
posts, notwithstanding their presbyterianism or their
prelacy; "for," said he, "I wish that the people
of the Lord, notwithstanding their differences,
may live peaceably one with another, *enjoying
rule and promotion, as they are fitted for employment.*"†

While the doctor was giving all his soul to
the work of raising the university from its fall,
his few recreative hours were spent in penning
some of those folios by which he now is mainly
known.   "Ponderous tomes," says one, "each

---

* It is grievous to think that we cannot say as much for his tolerant
spirit towards the Quakers.   In 1654, two harmless women were, in
their belief, "moved by the Spirit" to speak in a "steeple-house, after
the priest had done," in refutation of what he had said.   They had
also rebuked the students, who in turn treated them roughly, thrusting
them into "the pool called Giles's, and causing one of them to fall
into an open grave."   When the poor women were brought before the
magistrates, the mayor was willing to discharge them. but Owen
insisted on their punishment.   A full account of this was published in
a pamphlet, entitled, "A true Testimony of the Zeal of the Oxford
Professors and University Men, in persecuting the Servants of the
living God."—Lond. 1654.   Owen had a strong prejudice against the
Friends, as appears from his *Exercitationes apologeticæ adversus
hujus temporis Fanaticos.*   Oxon, 1658.

† Sermon before Parliament, 17th September, 1656.

one of which might have been fairly boasted of as the life-work of a man of earnest thought and labour, but which were by him thrown off almost sportively. We gaze upon them with a sort of breathless wonder; wonder increased by the recollection that they were the results of his brief leisure,—and the wonder reaches as far as humanity can entertain it, when we find the man of so many sacred offices, of so many high achievements, and with so many calls upon his time, not only equal to all, but actually going up to Parliament and taking his seat as representative of the university of Oxford."* Such was Owen, and like him were the Puritan scholars round him; miracles of memory and acquisition; men, caring little indeed for the graces of literature, and possessing no admiration of the exquisite; with no ear for the music of language, and no eye for the magic of beauty, but whose minds were filled to overflow with the riches of all old learning, and whose powers were trained to grapple athletically with all great questions in the religious and ecclesiastical controversies of their times.

Oxford was now the refuge of science as well as of learning. In November, 1651, just before Owen's installation, and apparently with reference to it, we find the Hon. Robert Boyle thus

---

* Gentleman's Magazine, January, 1851.

E

writing to a friend:—" As for our intellectual
concerns, I do with some confidence expect a revolution, whereby divinity will be exalted, and
real philosophy flourish beyond men's hopes."*
Shortly after the date of this letter, which was
written from Twickenham, we find Boyle has taken
up his residence at Oxford, mainly, we suppose,
for the cultivation of " real philosophy." It was
the only place in England," remarks his biographer,
" where, at that time, he could have lived with
satisfaction to himself."† Then and there it was
that he and the most distinguished men of science
living held those enthusiastic meetings for experiments which issued in the formation of the Royal
Society. For the convenience of inspecting drugs,
these meetings were first held in an apothecary's
house, at the lodgings of Dr. William Petty, the
ancestor of the present Marquis of Lansdowne.‡

Alleine's course at Oxford was coincident with
the life and labours there of these notabilities.
It requires a capacious faith to believe with Dr.
Walker that " they reduced the university to a
mere Munster ; and that if the Goths and Vandals,
or even the Turks, had overrun the nation, they
could not have done more to introduce disloyalty,

---

* November, 1651.   Ayscough MS., 4162.
† Life of Boyle, by Birch, 1744, p. 110.
‡ Aubrey's Life of Seth Ward.

barbarism, and ignorance." The very utterers of statements like these, when off their guard, refute themselves. Lord Clarendon, their leader, says of Oxford under Owen, " It yielded a harvest of extraordinary good and sound knowledge, in all parts of learning ; and many who were wickedly introduced, applied themselves to the study of learning and the practice of virtue."* Our student needed no sympathy. He had rare advantages, which he used with rare industry, and a Wiltshire place becoming vacant in Corpus Christi College, on the 3rd of November, 1651, he was chosen scholar of that house, " elected in accordance with the old statute ;"† " his merit," says a fellow-student, " being the only mandamus that brought him in."

It was a great satisfaction to him to be introduced to the friendship of Dr. Edward Staunton, the president. Two very different biographical accounts of this gentleman have been left us ; one written in a spirit of deep veneration, the other in that of strong antipathy and disrespect.‡ He had the reputation of being an austere precisian. Well known as a scholar, he was still more famous as " a saint." It was said that " he prayed like an

---

* History of Rebellion, vol. iii , p. 57.   † MS. at Corpus Christi.

‡ Life and Death of Dr. Edward Staunton, 1673, by Mayo. Appendix to the Life, &c., 1672 ; supposed to be by William Fulman.

angel." Men called him "the living Concordance."
His generosity kept him poor, and he ever sought
to relieve the spiritual as well as the temporal wants
of his needy neighbours, giving away "godly books
and catechisms" by hundreds. With him, the un-
seen world was all in all, and life without, important only for its bearings on the life within.
"Joseph Alleine," writes an old memorialist, "soon
became a great comfort to this holy man ; and it
did always revive him to hear of his after-eminence
in the church of God."*

Before the entrance of any student into this college, the doctor had an interview with him in order
to discover, if he could, the "signs of grace." In
the *Spectator*, No. 494, a story is related of such a
conversation. A young Oxford matriculatist is
conducted into a chamber all hung with black, and
lighted by the glimmer of a solitary lamp. At
last, the head of the college makes his appearance,
puts a few mysterious interrogatories, and sums up
all by the question, "Are you prepared for
death ?" which question being misunderstood by
the youth, "frighted him out of his wits," so that,
upon making his escape, he could never be brought
to examination again. This sketch, it has been
thought, was intended to ridicule Dr. Thomas
Goodwin ; but to the scared imagination of many a

---

* Clarke's Lives, 1683, p. 174.

" Roger Wildrake," it would have served equally well for a picture of Dr. Staunton in his audience-chamber.

Besides ordinary anxieties for the piety of the students, was that arising from the fact that Corpus Christi was regarded as pre-eminently the college for ministers. " It was the founder's will, expressed in one of the statutes, that all the fellows and scholars who were of the foundation should, about a year or two after they were masters of arts, be ordained to the holy ministry, one only excepted, who, *ad arbitrium*, should be deputed to the study and practice of physics."* The doctor was conscientiously in earnest, therefore, that this will should be realized, as far as was consistent with the altered condition of university life. Everything was done by him with a view to this object, not only by " putting into force all such statutes as tended to the advancement of learning and religion," but by catechetical exercises, meetings in his own house for prayer and religious conference, and divinity lectures for initiating the senior students into the work of the ministry. Owing to the working of this theory in the doctor's hands, of all colleges in Oxford this would have been generally deemed the most solemn and sombre. It was like a Puritan monastery. Within its awful walls, no

---

* Wood.

language was to be spoken but Greek or Latin;
very strict were its rules, and even in the dining
hour, all were accustomed to listen in silence while
one of the brotherhood read from the Scriptures,
or else joined with the doctor in spiritual discourse.
" Truly," remarks the learned Henry Jessey, in
1660, " I think there was scarce such a place in
the world as Corpus Christi, where such a multitude held forth the power of godliness, and purity
of God's worship.   Even an Eden it was, but now
a barren wilderness."*

This was true in the main, yet it is to be feared
that the " hopeful plants" here and in other colleges were not all so good as they seemed to be;
and we learn from the accounts of the early Friends,
who in some instances suffered violent ill-treatment
from the gownsmen, that the bad were very bad.
Indeed, how could it be otherwise?   Many a wild
lord, who afterwards frolicked in the Court of
Charles the Second,—many scapegraces, who afterwards gave occasion for the blind poet to call them
" sons of Belial, flown with insolence and wine,"—
were now at college; and although perhaps they
could utter the evangelical pass-words demurely as
their companions, it would have been strange had
they not found at intervals some way of indulging

---

* Jessey's Loud Calls, describing "the Lord's strange hand at
Oxford," 1660.

in their favourite revelry, unknown to the mag-
nates of the place.   We need not stain this page by
narrating the doings of alumni like these, especially as such outbreaks were rare and exceptional.
But there were others, who, while never running
to the same vicious excess, sometimes went too
far in the same direction.   As human nature,
though clad in an antique costume, was much the
same then as now, of course we know that some
young Puritans, who had been tutored into miracu-
lous gravity by discipline like that at Corpus
Christi, would, the moment restraint was over,
break out into all kinds of riotous fun.   Small
blame to them, only we grieve to say that even
when no malice was intended, this merriment was
often at the expense of the poor Quakers.   Here
is a company gathered round John Ward, who is
telling them that " a Quaker has just been in to
Sir Harry Vane, to persuade him that he is the
Lord's anointed, and powred a botle of rancid oyle
upon his head, which did make Sir Harry shake
his eares !" Another has something to tell about " a
Quaker debtor, who has just replied to his creditor,
' 'Tis revealed to mee that I ow thee nothing.' "
At last they all go to a " silent meeting," and one
of them, with a lively recollection of Dr. Staunton's
last discourse, preaches to the outraged but uncom-
plaining audience on the subject of " Tobit and
his dog," enlarging on the doctrine with needless

prolixity, sprinkling the sentences with scraps of
most audacious Latin, and quotations from apocryphal fathers, then branching off into interminable
" Vses and points, after the manner of the priests."
At another time, a visitor comes to Oxford, professing to be a Greek patriarch, " by name Jere-
mias," and that he wants from the university
authorities "a model of the last Reformation." He
has " old, long, black raiment, a broad white beard,
and a hat whose brim is of an eastern diameter."
Some of the Royalists repair to him for his blessing ; Harmar addresses a formal Greek harangue
to him ; even Owen resorts to him ; becomes on a
sudden exquisitely and haughtily polite ; all is
found out to be a trick, and to escape the storm of
indignation, the mischievous originator of it is
obliged to abscond.*

Joseph Alleine took no share in these freaks of
Puritan juvenility ; nor even in recreations less
questionable.   He felt no gloom in Corpus Christi.
It was to him, as it had been to Hooker before
him, even as "a garden of piety, of peace, and of
a sweet conversation."   The genius of the place
suited him. - He knew no change in his life, and
asked for none, but what was now and then made
by a "solemn fast," or a new invention of self-

---

* Wood's Annals ; Peck's Desiderata Curiosa ; MS. Common-
place Book of John Ward, 17 vols. ; Tracts of the Friends, in the
Library of Devonshire House.

denial. With all this, it is said, such was the friendliness and liveliness of his spirit, and such the charm of his address, that were it not for his many other excellencies, " he might have been described as *Totus ex comitate*, made up of courtesy." Yet he had such a panic sense of the value of time, and the importance of study, that nothing could induce him to relax his labours.

> " Who studies ancient laws and rites,
>   Tongues, arts, and arms, and history,
> Must toil like Selden days and nights,
> And in the endless labour die." *

This was his student-creed, and he tried to practise it. " He could toil terribly." One of his companions assures us that it was common for him to work from four o'clock in the morning, and often until one the next ; and that it was as usual for him to give away his commons at least once, as it was for others to take theirs twice a day. Like many in those days, he was tempted to look upon that man as the holiest Christian and the worthiest student who was simply least indulgent to the body, scorning it, addressing it in abusive language, and keeping it under, as a mere inconvenience, or a mere dead weight to the soul. He ought to have remembered the sentiment of his favourite Plutarch, " Should the body sue the mind before a court of

* R. Bentley.

judicature for damages, it would often be found
that the mind had been a ruinous tenant to its land-
lord ;" and he might have drawn the inference, that
in such a case the mind would have a formidable
fine to pay.   Wood says he became "a meer
scholar."   This, had it been true, would have been
sufficient penalty, but it was untrue.   His judgment was as remarkable as was his scholarship.
"All who knew him," writes his friend, "knew
him to be as smart a disputant and as excellent a
philosopher as he was a good linguist.   When he
performed any academical exercises, either in the
hall or in the schools, he seldom or never came off
without the applause, or at least the approval, of
all but the envious."

On July 6th, 1653, he took the degree of
bachelor of arts, and an interesting proof of the
estimation in which he was held is afforded by the
fact that he was almost immediately compelled,
young as he was, to become a tutor of his college.
Some impression may also be taken of what he was
himself, from the eminence which some of his pupils
afterwards attained. Dr. Kippis asserts that "several
became very eminent Nonconformists," but the only
one of them known by his present biographer to
have joined the ranks of Nonconformity was
Robert Dod, M.A., who, according to Calamy,
"greatly profited" under his tuition, both in
"serious religion, and in useful, humane learning."

He was ordained by Bishop Juxon immediately after the Restoration, and was rector of Inworth, in Essex, until 1662. All the others who can be traced with distinct certainty were destined to be stars of the church of England. The names of some of them here follow :—

John Rosewell, D.D., sometime fellow of Corpus Christi, afterwards head-master at Eton, and canon of Windsor.—Christopher Coward, D.D., also fellow of his college ; an intimate friend of Sir Kenelm Digby, and Bishop Ken ; he became rector of Dicheat, in Somerset, and prebendary of Wells.—Nicholas Horseman, B.D., author of several learned works.—John Peachell, D.D., admitted master of Magdalen College in 1679.—Another of his pupils was Sir Coplestone Bampfield ; but he does not appear to have reflected the highest credit on his college training.*

In the year 1654, on the occasion of the peace which Cromwell concluded with the Dutch, there was no small stir in the university.

> Straight other studies are laid by,
> And all apply to poetry :
> Some write in Hebrew, some in Greek,
> And some, more wise, in Arabic,

---

* Authority for what is said above will be found in the following works :—Wood's Life of Dr. Nicholas Grey; the Kennett MSS., British Museum ; Kennett's Register ; Bliss's Life of Wood ; Fasti Oxonienses ; and a pamphlet of Andrew Marvell, who says, " Sir Coplestone Bampfield is much addicted to tippling."

> 'T' avoid the critic, and th' expense
> Of difficulter wit, and sense.
>
>   *   *   *   *
>
> The doctors lead, the students follow :
> Some call him Mars, and some Apollo ;
> Some Jupiter, and give him th' odds,
> On even terms, with all the gods :
> Then Cæsar he's nicknam'd as duly as
> He that in Rome was christen'd Julius ;
> And was address'd to by a crow,
> As pertinently long ago."*

After a fashion which Butler ridiculed in this rattling fire of conundrums, the doctors and students of Oxford did honour to the Lord Protector, presenting him in various languages with a garland of poetical addresses of gratitude and compliment, many of which were printed in a volume entitled *Oxoniensium* ΕΛΑΙΟΦΟΡΙΑ. Alleine contributed a Latin ode, but after a long search it has not yet appeared. Certainly it is not in the printed book ; perhaps not inserted there because wanting in the fervour which became the occasion. We know from his own confession that he was unable to join in the highest praise that was given to " Cromwell, chief of men."

Twelve months before he left Oxford, he became chaplain to the college ; preferring this office to a fellowship, which in a little time would have been his own of course and by right.

The companion, whose words have been cited

---

* Butler's Miscellanies.

before, attributes this preference to his delight in
the exercises of devotion. Much of his time in the
early morning was thus spent, and after walking or
discoursing with a friend, he would usually propose
to close the interview with prayer. Most likely,
the most definite motive to this decision for the
clerical engagement was the spirit which was already
visible as the ruling law of his life—"ardent love
to the souls of men," inspiring an impatience to be
occupied in direct ministerial work. He began to
take every opportunity of preaching in the village
churches, and where he thought men were most
forgotten. "He paid frequent visits to persons
who were mean and low, his main design being,
together with relieving their wants, helping their
souls on the way to heaven." The prisoners in
the county gaol attracted much of his sympathy.
Partly as the cause, partly as the effect of great
neglect, prisons were then scenes of such repulsive
wretchedness, and sometimes of such deadly infection,
that to pay them a visit of charity was often a
dangerous venture to the benevolent enthusiast.
Some of the citizens had lately died of gaol fever.
In 1577, when the Oxford prisoners were brought
out of their cells for trial, the chief baron, the
sheriff, and four hundred persons who were present
in the court, all died of infection within forty-eight
hours; and we have no statistics to prove, or reason
to think, that any great sanitary reforms of the

prison had taken place since that " black assize."＊
Who ever thought of the prisoners ? Alleine was
the first friend they were ever known to have had.
It was his custom to preach to them once a fortnight, and during the week of his visit to give them
large allowance of bread.

In October, 1654, he appears to have had certain
offers of high preferment, but of what nature is now
a secret. In the following words, written to a
personage of whom more will be said presently, he
makes reference to the overture, and at the same
time reveals an interesting glimpse of his inner
life : --

" My dear Heart,—My heart is now a little at rest to
write to thee. I have been these three days much disturbed, and set out of frame. Strong solicitations I have
had from several hands to accept very honourable preferment in several kinds, some friends making a journey on
purpose to propound it ; but I have not found the invitations (though I confess very honourable, and such as are
or will be suddenly embraced by men of far greater worth
and eminency) to suit with the inclinations of my own
heart, as I was confident they would not with thine. I
have sent away my friends satisfied with the reasons of
my refusal, and am now ready with joy to say with David,
" Soul, return unto thy rest." But, alas ! that such things
should disturb me ! I would live above this lower region,
that no passages of providence whatsoever might put me

---

* Baker records the fact in his Chronicle, p. 353. Lord Bacon
ascribes it to the infection brought into the court by the prisoners.

out of frame, nor disquiet my soul, and unsettle me from my desired rest. I would have my heart fixed upon God, so as no occurrences might disturb my tranquillity, but I might be still in the same quiet and even frame. Well, though I am apt to be unsettled, and quickly set off the hinges, yet methinks I am like a bird out of the nest, I am never quiet till I am in my old way of communion with God, like the needle in the compass that is restless till it be turned towards the pole. I can say through grace with the church, ' With my soul have I desired thee in the night, and with my spirit within me have I sought thee early ;' my heart is early and late with God, and 'tis the business and delight of my life to seek Him. But, alas ! how long shall I be seeking ? How long shall I spend my days in wishing and desiring, when my glorified brethren spend theirs in rejoicing and enjoying ? As the poor imprisoned captive sighs under the burdensome clog of his irons, and can only peer through the grate, and think of, and long for, the sweetness of that liberty which he sees others enjoy : such, methinks, is my condition ; I can only look through the grate of this prison, my flesh ; I see Abraham, and Isaac, and Jacob sitting down in the kingdom of God ; but, alas ! I myself must stand without, longing, striving, fighting, running, praying, waiting, for what they do now inherit."

Evidently, he was open to no invitations but such as would lead him into a sphere of laborious ministry. Tempting offers of this kind were presenting themselves to some of his acquaintance. For example, Mr. Robert South, of Christ Church, had lately been recommended as assistant minister to the reverend Mr. Richard Baxter, of Kidder-minster.   There had been some correspondence on the subject, but it had now ceased.   Perhaps, that "trier of Satan's subtleties" recoiled from the suggested alliance, on the ground of some supposed incongruity between himself and the sharp young graduate.   South was a flatterer of Cromwell, Baxter was not ; the one was a little too frivolous, the other a little too grave ; the one was too politic, the other too crotchety ;—at any rate, the union was never consummated.   How Alleine would have rejoiced at the prospect of such a co-pastorate ! He was destined to a life of service very similar to it, for in 1655 a letter came to him from Mr. George Newton, expressing his desire for his assistance at the church of St. Mary Magdalen, at Taunton. This occasioned his leaving Oxford without taking his master's degree, so eager was he to fulfil the grand vocation of his life ; but before the final step, he resolved to ride down to Taunton and survey the land.

Chapter IV.

A Visit to Taunton and its Old Pastor, in the Spring of 1655.

" *How should the hearts of saints within them bound,*
When they behold the messengers that sound
The gladsome tidings ;—yea, their very feet
Are beautiful because their words are sweet.
Thrice happy land! which in this pleasant spring
Can hear these turtles in their hedges sing.
Oh, prize such mercies !"

JOHN FLAVEL.

N the spring of 1655, he paid a visit to Taunton, to see the old pastor there, and to pass through the usual course of a probationer.

Just then, perhaps, there was no town in England that had a wider fame, or whose affairs were watched by politicians with a keener scrutiny. Its population, if not actually, was relatively very large.* It had long been influential on account of its woollen

---

* In 1689, 20,000 persons.

manufactures, although the war with Spain, breaking out this very year, had just for the crisis almost
destroyed its trade.*   It was distinguished for its
free, intelligent, unconquerable public spirit.   Notwithstanding some impediments just at first,
through all the vicissitudes of the great war, it had
been faithful to the cause of liberty.   Twice had
it been closely besieged by Goring, and twice
defended with heroic steadfastness by Robert
Blake.   When food had risen to twenty times its
market value, when many of the inhabitants had
died of starvation, when half the streets had been
burnt down by a storm of mortars and rockets, the
defenders still held their ground, and Blake
announced to the besiegers his grim resolve not
to surrender " until he had eaten his boots."   The
rage of the Royalists at this prolonged resistance
knew no bounds, and " in the pages of Clarendon,
their loud wail and gnashings of teeth are still
audible."†   At last, in July, 1645, the besiegers
were obliged to withdraw.   Just ten years had
now elapsed since that event, but there was no
change in the spirit of the people.   To the end of
the century, Taunton could be regarded by none
without interest, although there was a great dif-

---

* Fuller's Worthies, 1655, pp. 15, 19. Twenty years later it
had quite recovered, and we hear of " the great trade and riches of
Taunton."—Yarranton, 1677.

† Hepworth Dixon's Life of Blake.

ference between the kinds of interest felt in it by
different men.* One party called it "the metro-
polis of faction in the West," and the other thought
that of all places in that quarter, " this deserved
most praise." William Lilly, the astrologer, had
said that "whatever happened materially in England,
whether for good or ill," would most likely " show
itself for the most part in the West." According
to his own report, he was moved to deliver this
sage but safe prediction by the appearances of
Saturn " being in Gemini, and in the ayery tripli-
city;" but we must be allowed to think that he
also had an eye on Taunton.†

The Taunton man of those days was tempted to
be proud. He gloried in his local interests and
histories. He thought there was no town like his
town, and no church like " Mary Magdalen," up
whose stately tower he and his companions had
often mounted in the war, to watch the manœuvres
of the enemy amongst the gardens, or under the
elms that arched the deep green lanes in the vale
below. Standing near the town wall, he thought

---

* North ; A. Wood ; Bishop Sprat. An " Informer," writing to
Sir Leoline Jenkins, says, " was this wicked town brought down to
obedience, all the West of England would then be very regular."—
State Paper Office.

† A Peculiar Prognostication, astrologically predicted, according
to Art. By William Lillie, Student in Astrologie. Published for
generall satisfaction. Jan. 6, 1649.

few sights on earth pleasanter than the view across
that vale, and he was right; not on account of its
" solemn glooms, or sudden glories," not because
it ever rises into grandeur or breaks into wildness,
but because it wears a look so peaceful, so cheerful,
so homely.   Trees all aglow with apple blossoms,
hedges white with may ; meadows, orchards, che-
quered squares of cultivation, stretch away in rich
level variety, mile after mile, till all the gay colours,
and all the innumerable tiny traceries of the scene,
softly distinct in the sunshine, melt into the waves
of the blue dreamy hills in the distance.   So it
was when Alleine saw it first, and so it is now.
The Puritans who were with him—peace be to their
memory!—might have pretended not to see this
broad illuminated beauty; they might have thought
of it in the light of a temptation, they might have
felt half afraid that it betrayed a carnal affection to
admire it ; yet they did admire it, and their delight
would sometimes burst forth in Bible language.
A certain hill, about half a mile from the town,
they used to call Mount Nebo, in allusion to the
prospect it commanded ; and the vale itself, they
said, was " even as a land flowing with milk and
honey."*

But the true glory of Taunton was its Puritanism, and the great light of its Puritanism

---

* Savage's History of Taunton, p. 7.

was Mr. George Newton, the pastor. He was master of arts of Exeter College, Oxford. He had received episcopal ordination at the hands of Laud, when that prelate was bishop of Bath and Wells. After that, he was for a short period minister of Hill Bishop, near Taunton, a perpetual curacy, then in the gift of Sir George Farewel; and in 1631, became vicar of Taunton Magdalen, by the presentation of Sir William Portman and Mr. Robert Hill. He soon became a noted "gospeller." Though naturally timid, "strength was made perfect in weakness," and he was not timid in the assertion of his principles. According to Fuller, Somersetshire was the earliest field of the Sabbatarian controversy, and it appears that Mr. Newton was one of the earliest champions in the field, if not the very first, taking the side of the Sabbath against the profane decrees of the King. When, in 1633, the "Book of Sports" came out by order of council, and was commanded to be read in all the churches, he read it, but said immediately to his congregation, " These are the commandments of men." He then read the 20th chapter of the book of Exodus, saying, " These are the commandments of God; but whereas in this case the laws of God and the laws of man are at variance, choose ye which ye will obey." Thus, regarding it as an iniquitous law, he contrived at once to defeat its object, to evade its penalty, and to set an example of protesting decision to the ministers in all the country round.*

The year 1636 was the date of a remarkable episode in the annals of his eventful pastorate. This arose out of the emigration of some enterprising members of his flock, to establish an evangelical colony in America. Burning with zeal to spread God's truth abroad, unable to bear the yoke of ceremonies imposed upon them by the prelatical faction at home, and unwilling any longer to pay exhausting fines for nonconformity, they resolved to strike out this noble course of independence. The fact, since the time of its occurrence, has scarcely been heard of here until lately, and has not been published in England until now. After grave conference, many tears, and many a meeting for prayer, the pilgrims at length set sail, with the blessing of their pastor on their cause. We are unable to report their numbers, and most of their names have dropped out of human memory; but amongst them we find Rossiter, Blake, Deane, Strong, Attwood, Reed, Hall, and Thomas Farewell,—names still represented in Taunton, and showing that we have still amongst us the families from which the emigrants sprung. It was the distinction of this enterprise that it was led by a lady.

---

* Fuller's Church History, _sub anno_, 1633.   Calamy's continuation.   Savage's History of Taunton.

Dux fœmina fa&i. Governor Winthrop calls her "an ancient mayde, one Mistress Poole," and informs us that "she endured much hardship in the undertaking." "An ardent love for religion," writes another annalist, "and an enthusiastic desire of planting another church in the American wilderness, impelled this pious Puritan lady to encounter all the dangers and hardships of forming a settlement among the Indians."* No actual documentary evidence exists to show that she first roused her friends at Taunton Magdalen to think of "that great secret, America;"† or that her fortune mainly helped them to meet the expenses of the voyage,—from her generous and resolute spirit, even this is likely; but we have positive proof that she became their leader after their disembarkation at New Plymouth. It was sometime in the year 1637, that, starting from Dorchester, she led them, and others who joined them there, on their pilgrimage in search of a home. The country was scattered over, though not always crowded, with "oak, fir, beech, walnut-trees, and exceeding great chestnut-trees."‡ Sometimes cutting their path through the netted vines that hung from tree to tree, sometimes plunging up to the neck through

---

* Historical Memoirs of New Plymouth, by Hon F. Baylies, vol. ii., p. 2.

† Sir Thomas Brown.

‡ Journey of Winslow and Hopkins in 1621.

the tall weeds and grasses, now stooping to peer
about a spot that was black with the cinders of an
old camp-fire, and printed with the footmarks of
unknown forerunners; now fording a stream, now
toiling over grey blocks of projecting stone, but
generally winding along between the stems of the
forest with comparative ease; ever catching sight,
through the leaves, of scudding rabbits, and of
antlers wafting silently away into the distance ;—
on the travellers went, until they reached a clear
space by the borders of the river Titicut.   Here
Mistress Poole purchased lands of " the salvages,"
and the adventurers established their encampment.
The spot was about twenty-six miles from Plymouth, and about thirty-six from Boston.   It
was a still, wild place.   Millions of ancient trees
rustled between them and the world, and the scenery
seemed to look much as it might have done before
the creation of man; but to them it was all holy
ground.   A poet says, although with something of
a poet's license —

> " Yes, call it holy ground,
>   The spot where first they trod ;
> They left unstained, what there they found,—
>   Freedom to worship God."

To this place they agreed to give the name of
TAUNTON.*   A street of cabins soon sprang up,

---

* It was not generally known by this name, but retained its
Indian name, Cohannet, until its incorporation in 1639.

but there can be little doubt that their unpretending temple, built of logs and twisted roots, was completed first, for their first idea was worship. Regarding themselves not as a band of worldly emigrants, but as a church led to this place by the "pillar of cloud," that they might declare the wonders of the Lord amongst the heathen, one of their first collective acts was to choose a pastor, and the choice fell upon William Hooke, a kinsman of Oliver Cromwell,* and "a learned, holy, and humble man."† Fresh parties joined them. Grist mills and saw mills, farms and factories, brick fields and iron works gradually gave life to the river-side. Here, the first forge ever known in America was set up ; and here, let it be recorded with due solemnity, was manufactured the first American shovel.‡ Great as was their industrial energy, their spiritual energy was greater, and its results were still more decisive. The Sabbath was observed with austerity, stringent rules were passed for social decorum, and frequent use was found for the whipping post, sometimes called, irreverently, the Puritan Maypole. Moreover—for the truth must be told—they did, they certainly did perse-

---

* So Mr. Emery asserts in his interesting work on the Taunton Ministry, but Hooke is not mentioned as one of Cromwell's relations by Noble in his memoirs of the Protector's family.

† Cotton Mather.

‡ At Raynham, a spot included in the original purchase.

cute Baptists and Quakers. When, in 1651, certain Baptists and Quakers at Boston were whipped or banished from the colony, the people of Taunton gave their voice against them.* The Tauntonians came to America for " freedom to worship God." They advocated liberty of conscience, suffered for it, fought for it, would have died for it ; but when they extended the privilege to others, it was with the cautious definition afterwards given by Mr. Knickerbocker, " Liberty of conscience is liberty to think what you please, *provided you think right.*" We are amazed at the intolerance of these fathers, we are grieved by it, but the reverence due to them because they were in many things before their age, must not be withheld, because in a few things they were only on a level with it. " In the court of posterity," remarks Sir James Stephens, " it is a settled point of law, that in mitigation, if not in bar of any penal sentence, the defendant may plead that the generation to which he belonged did not regard as culpable the conduct imputed to him as criminal by men of a later age." Let us give them the benefit of this consideration, and then turn with

---

* Letter from Obadiah Holmes, of New England, to the well-beloved brethren John Spilsbury and William Kiffin, in London, 1652. He narrates the persecution of himself and brethren ; says that four petitions were sent to the Plymouth Court, urging "some speedy course to suppress the Baptists," and informs us that one of these petitions came from " the church at Tanton, as they call themselves."—Mass. Hist. Coll., vol. ii., fourth series.

relief to the story of their nobler deeds. Their sternly earnest spirit made them indefatigable catechists and missionaries; and we are told that in connexion with such labour, many of the Indians were converted to God. Whether engaged in work or worship, the old country was as dear as ever, and they had their fasts or thanksgiving days according to the nature of the news that reached them of our national sorrows or joys. Sermons preached on such occasions found their way across the waters, were printed here, and may still be met with on old book-stalls.*

Meanwhile, a correspondence was maintained with them by their former friends, and during the course of their early difficulties, it appears that public collections on behalf of their mission were made in the church of Taunton Magdalen. Some passages are to be found in Mr. Newton's sermons that were evidently delivered on such occasions. Here is one of his appeals :—

" Now, I beseech you, my beloved, cast an eye

---

* New England's Teares for Old England's Feares. Preached on July 23, 1640, being a day of Publike Humiliation, &c. By William Hooke, minister of God's word, &c. Sent over to a member of the honourable House of Commons, who desires it may be for publike good. London, 1641.

New England's Sence of Old England and Jreland's Sorrows." By William Hooke, minister of God's word at Taunton in New England. London, 1645.

upon them" (the people of American Taunton).
"Travel thither in your thoughts and meditations; there shall you see some servants of Jesus
Christ, once our fellow-labourers, spending themselves, undergoing difficulties without number or
measure to convert souls and gather Christians
among blind heathen;—there shall you see the
Gospel blossoming, the church enlarging her tent,
and striking forth the curtains of her habitation,—
' the doves flocking to the windows.' What shall
we do now, beloved, and how shall we behave
ourselves in this dispensation? Shall we, as many
have done heretofore, condemn the instruments, as
if they went beyond themselves in this business?
Shall we mock at these beginnings of the building
of the temple? Shall we despise the day of small
things? Shall we, like Gallio, care for none of
these matters? Truly, the least we can do is to
comply with Jesus Christ in this design of His, for
which He sends His ministers into the world, and
to promote this glorious work to the utmost of
our power. It is in the hands of those, for whom,
as you have heard, it is too heavy. As the men of
Macedonia, they seem to call over to us for help.
O, let not such a work miscarry, or fail of being
driven on, for want of any help that we can yield
it. Truly, my brethren, if we can help it in no
other way, we can help it by our prayers and our
purses. We can help it by our prayers. Let us

remember that we have a little sister in America, and that now is the day of speaking for her, for now her case is in agitation ; and therefore now let us be in earnest with the Lord ; let us pray, and pray hard, let us not be cold and dead in such a suit as this. We can help by our purses and estate, and this is especially what we have in hand at this time. We, methinks, that share not the difficulties and dangers that others of our brethren undergo amongst the Indians, should be content to share a little of the costs ; and therefore I beseech you, my beloved, enlarge your bounty more than ordinary, in such a choice and extraordinary work as this.

"' Go, preach my Gospel to every creature,' saith Christ. Churches are to be planted all over the world. This is the meaning of that famous pro- clamation of our King himself, ' From the rising of the sun even to the going down of the same my name shall be great among the Gentiles ; and in every place incense shall be offered unto my name, and a pure offering ; for my name shall be great among the heathen, saith the Lord of Hosts.' —Mal. i. 11. ' So a great multitude, which no man can number, of all nations, and kindreds, and tribes, and people, and tongues, stood before the throne, and before the Lamb, clothed with white robes, and palms in their hands.'—Apoc. vii. 9. And then shall that triumphant voice declare,

' The kingdoms of this world are become the kingdoms of our God and of His Christ; and He shall
reign for ever and ever.'—Apoc. xi. 15.　　Help
this choice work by your purses and prayers ! "*

A missionary sermon more than two hundred
years old will be regarded by some persons as a
curiosity.　It is strange when turning over leaves
on which, perhaps, the light of the nineteenth
century never shone before, in a book which may
have been forgotten for many generations, to find
sentences that flame with such evangelic intelligence and liberality as these.　You go back in
thought to the day of the Commonwealth ; you
enter a church ; you see the minister stand, quaintly
garmented, with hour-glass at his side ; you hear
him preach a wonderfully complicated sermon ; he
quotes " Plutarch, his witty sarcasm," and also
what " Tully " or " Austin saith."　Perhaps he
tells you that something which he is saying is " as
Bernard phraseth it ;" or, " as the Greek philosopher
hath well observed ;" or, " as Rabbi David Gantz
hath summed up."　Then he has a word or two

---

* These passages occur in a folio with this title, " An Exposition with Notes unfolded and applied on John xvii.　By
George Newton, minister of the Gospel.　Dedicated to the Honourable Colonel John Gorges, governour of the city of Londonderry
and the castle of Cullmore in Ireland, my duly honoured and dearly
beloved brother."　Though not published until 1660, he says these
discourses were preached when he had no assistant.

strongly flavoured with personality for the squires
in the chancel, reproving them for wasteful expen-
diture in " hawks and hounds ;"* after that, with
startling unexpectedness, very striking by force of
contrast with all the old-fashioned things in the
connexion, he preaches about foreign missions just
as your minister might have done last Sunday.

But we are now chiefly thinking of New
Taunton. If the preacher had been gifted for the
moment with the vision of a seer, and had been
able to look down the long perspective of its future
course, he would have been almost ready to say,
"Lord, now lettest thou thy servant depart in
peace." Since the day when he thus pleaded on its
behalf, it has gone from stage to stage of development. For a long time this was not known here.
"Out of sight, out of mind." After the first
generation, correspondence dropped, and the story
of " the little sister in America" was forgotten
until the year 1856, when the successors of the
original emigrant church sent a message of inquiry
and love to the successors of the ancestral church
in England. With this came cheering information.† They have been honoured from the commencement with a long line of eminent ministers,

---

* These and similar references are to be found in Mr. Newton's
various sermons.

† Appendix I.

many of whom still live in their writings, and whose biographies, ably narrated by the pastor who now succeeds them, will long edify thousands.* Taunton has become the parent of seven other towns, all within the limits of the original settlement. Not only is the Christian community first formed, still existing, but with it forty others, all in the same cluster of towns. Comparing the old lists in the parochial register here with the lists of those who have signed the various church covenants there, we find that the children of George Newton's hearers are treading in the steps of their fathers, and are inheriting a legacy of good results from the ministry of their father's pastor. The hardy virtues of Puritan Somersetshire, that struck root in the far wilderness so long since, are living still, " sending out their branches to the sea, and their boughs to the river ;" and the seeds cast by an English lady on the waters of the Atlantic are " seen after many days," flowering with the thousand glories of spiritual life and usefulness.

We must return to the main line of the story. In the year 1642, Taunton being besieged by the Royalist forces, Mr. Newton was obliged to make his escape from the place. When the town was recovered for the Parliament, it was still too closely

---

* The Ministry of Taunton. By Samuel Hopkins Emery. 2 vols. Boston, 1853.

invested to admit of the fugitive pastor's easy return. During the siege, therefore, he exercised his ministry in the abbey of St. Albans. We find him in his old pulpit again in 1646, at the anniversary of the town's deliverance, taking for his text, " Surely the wrath of man shall praise thee : the remainder thereof thou shalt restrain."* In 1654, he was placed by ordinance on the commission for inquiry into " scandalous, ignorant, and inefficient ministers,"† a thankless post, and the recollection of it by Mr. Wood, when writing the short notice of his life, gave new pungency to that writer's acid sentences.

Great as Mr. Newton's provincial influence undoubtedly was, it would be wrong to speak of him as an eminent man in comparison with the eminent men of his day. He was no type of " great greatness," but only of an average Puritan minister. " *Pastor vigilantissimus, doctrina et*

---

* Man's Wrath and God's Praise. A Sermon on Psalm lxxvi. 10. By George Newton. London, 1646. Many sermons were preached on this occasion by various other ministers. In one preached before Parliament the preacher said,—

" O give thanks to the Lord, for He is gracious, and His mercy endureth for ever ;

Who remembered us at Naseby, for His mercy endureth for ever ;

Who remembered us in Pembrokeshire, for His mercy endureth for ever ;

Who remembered us at TAUNTON, for His mercy endureth for ever."—Walker's Sufferings of the Clergy, p. 18.

† Wood's Fasti.

G

pietate insignis," says one of his friends. "Very much the gentleman," remarks another ; a peacemaker, "keeping out of the town those divisions that did so much mischief in other places," adds a third. He was a sound scholar, a faithful preacher, and, in his day, not without name as a theological writer. Both in preaching and writing his style was prolix, negligent, and leisurely as fireside chat, though sometimes breaking out into minute originalities of fancy, and into words that rang with a quaint alliterative tinkle. Now and then he might be too elaborate in his attempts to win the verdict of the clothworkers for a new rendering of some Hebrew text, and would too readily assume their perfect familiarity with things that could only be drawn from obscure and remote springs of learning. Yet they profited much by his preaching and more by his life, for it was a life of holiness and love. Bright, benign face ; head comforted with a velvet cap ; brown locks touched with silver, soon to be changed into a glory of snowy whiteness, flowing down to his broad bands and prim Geneva gown ; the Bible in his hand ;—his very appearance a sermon.* Such was George Newton, when he and Alleine had their first conversation.

---

* Thus represented in a coloured drawing preserved in the Wilson Collection of Prints. This collection includes 1145 portraits and other engravings illustrative of Nonconformist biography.

The elder minister was most urgent in renewing his request for the assistance of the younger. " I soon observed him," said he, " to be a young man of singular accomplishments, natural and acquired. His intellectuals solid, his affections lively, his learning much beyond the ordinary size, and, above all, his holiness eminent. He had a good head and a better heart." Not yet more than twenty-one, it appeared to be a premature honour to be nominated as the associate of this old divine. We must remember that it was not as a pastor, but only as an assistant that he was thought of. To him the offer had the aspect not only of a new sphere for Christian services, but of a new stage in his education,— it would gradually fit him for those higher functions of his calling, for which there can be no training but that which is acquired in the school of experience. But a call from the congregation, as well as from Mr. Newton, was required. During the few Sundays that preceded this formal election, he preached a series of discourses on the obedience of subjects to the supreme magistrate, founding them on the sentence, " Let every soul be subject to the higher powers." This was a strange topic at such a time, and to take it was a delicate experiment in such a place. We have in this fact an unexpected precedent for political sermons ! His motive seems to have been a wish to be quite transparent in his dealings with the people, that they might know at first, the particulars in which his sentiments differed from their own. He was a Royalist. In his interpretation of the text in question, he brought out principles that clashed with the views of many a sturdy republican there. Some were offended. For the most part, however, they liked him all the better for his outspoken spirit. Whatever his political theories might be, there could be no doubt that he was a true man, and a true preacher of the Gospel, and this they valued above all things, so they asked him to be their teacher. In the course of time, as we shall see, most of them adopted his politics. There was a parting visit to the vicarage, when, the two friends having sat and talked together, and then prayed together, the student rode back to his college chamber to pray alone.

Chapter V.

Alleine's Settlement.

"Being now, therefore, settled in that sweet and civil country, ... the uncouth solitariness of my life, and the extreme incommodity of that single housekeeping, drew my thoughts to condescend to the necessity of a married estate; which God no less strangely provided for me; for walking from church, . . . with a grave and reverend minister, I saw a comely and modest gentlewoman standing at the door of the house . . . . and enquiring of that worthy friend whether he knew her. 'Yes,' quoth he, 'I know her well.' . . . . . When I further demanded of him an account of that answer, he told me that she was the daughter of a gentleman whom he much respected . . . . advising me not to neglect opportunity . . . . not concealing the just praises of the modesty, piety, good disposition, and other virtues that were lodged in that seemly presence. I listened to the motion as sent from God; and at last, upon due prosecution, happily prevailed."

BISHOP HALL'S ACCOUNT OF HIMSELF;
Scripsi, May 29, 1647.

E have been detained too long in the company of Mr. George Newton; for there is another personage, of greater importance to this history, to whom we ought to have sought introduction earlier. This is Mistress Theodosia, the daughter of "that reverend man," Mr. Richard Alleine, kinsman of Joseph, and parson of Batcombe, in Somerset. He and this gentlewoman were on excellent terms. In August, 1654, they had met at the rectory—they had become friends—then, there was the old story of friendship blooming into love. Do not expect a romantic tale. Besides the fragment of an epistle, already given in the account of his life at Oxford, the only memorial of this time is a letter written by him on the subject of the Taunton invitation. For its style as a love-letter, it might have been composed by John Knox; but there is every reason to believe that it interested its first reader, and, for its spirit of beautiful godliness and manliness, it ought to have a charm for every one :—

" My dear Heart,—By this time I hope thou hast received mine by Martin, and also an answer touching their resolution at Taunton. My thoughts have been much upon that business of late, so small as the outward encouragements in point of maintenance are, and methinks I find my heart much inclining that way. I will tell thee the principles upon which I go.

" First, I lay this for a foundation, that a man's life consisteth not in the abundance of the things that he possesseth. It was accounted a wise prayer that Agur put up, of old, that he might only be fed with food convenient for him. And certain it is, that where men have least of the world, they esteem it least, and live more by faith and in dependence upon God, casting their care and burden upon Him. O, the sweet breathings of David's soul! the strong actings of his faith and love, that we find come from him, when his condition was low and mean in the world. How closely doth he cling, how fully doth he rely upon God! The Holy Ghost seems to make it a privilege to be brought to a necessity of living by faith, as, I think, I have formerly hinted thee, out of Deut. xi. 10, 11; where Canaan is preferred before Ægypt, in regard of its dependence upon God for the former and latter rain, which in Ægypt they could live without, and have supplies from the river. And certainly could we that are unexperienced, but feel the thorns of those cares and troubles that there are in gathering and keeping much, and the danger when riches increase of setting our hearts upon them, we should prize the happiness of a middle condition much before it. Doubtless, godliness with contentment is great gain. 'Seekest thou great things for thyself?' saith the prophet to Baruch; 'seek them not.' Certainly a good conscience is a continual feast, and enough for a happy life: no man that warreth intangleth himself with the affairs of this life, that he may please Him who hath chosen him to be a souldier. We should be but little encumbered with the things of this world, and withal free from a world of entanglements, which in a great place committed wholly to our charge, would be upon our consciences as no small burden.

" Secondly, I take this for an undoubted truth, that a dram of grace is better than a talent of wealth; and therefore such a place where our consciences would be free, and we had little to do in the world to take off our hearts and thoughts from the things of eternity, and had

the advantage of abundance of means, and the daily opportunities of warming our hearts with the blessed society
and conference of heavenly Christians, and no temptations to carry us away, nor discouragements in our walking with God, and the due performance of our duty; is
(if we pass a true and spiritual judgment, as the Holy
Ghost in Scripture would,) without comparison before
another place, void of those spiritual helps and advantages.
Let us think with ourselves, what though our purses, our
estates, may thrive better in a place of a large maintenance? yet where are our graces, our souls, like to
thrive any way answerable to what they are in this?
We should have but little in this world; but what
is this, if it be made up to us, as it will surely be, in
communion with God and His people? If we thrive
in faith and love, humility and heavenly-mindedness,
as, above all places I know, we are likely to do there,
what matter is it though we do not raise ourselves
in the world? The thing itself may well be accounted
but mean; but let us look upon it with a spiritual
eye, and then we shall pass another judgment of it.
Who would leave so much grace, and so much comfort
in communion with Christ and His saints, as we may gain
there, for the probabilities of living with a little more
gentility and handsomeness in the world? 'Tis a strange
thing to see how Christians generally do judge so carnally
of things, looking to the things that are seen and temporal,
and not the things that will stick by us to eternity.
What is it worth a year? Is the maintenance certain and
sure? What charges are there like to be? These are
the questions we commonly ask first, when we speak of
settling. But, though those things are duly to be considered too, yet what good am I like to do? what good

am I like to get ?—(both which questions I think might
be as comfortably answered concerning this, as any place
in England)—these should be the main interrogatories,
and the chief things we should judge of a place to settle
in. What if we have but a little in the world? Why
then we must keep but a short table, and shall make but a
little noise in the world, and must give the meaner
entertainments to our friends. Will not this be abundantly made up, if we have more outward and inward
peace, as we may well count we shall have? One dram
of saving grace will weigh down all this. Let others hug
themselves in their corn, and wine, and oil, in their fat
livings, and their large tables, and their great resort, if we
have more of the light of God's countenance, more grace,
more comfort, who would change with them? Surely,
if Paul were to choose a place, he would not look so
much what 'twas a year, but would wish us to take that
where we might be most likely to save our own and
others' souls.

 " Thirdly, That the best and surest way to have any
outward mercy, is to be content to want it. When men's
desires are over-eager after the world, they must have thus
much a year, and a house well furnished, and wife, and
children, thus and thus qualified, or else they will not be
content ; God doth usually, if not constantly, break their
wills by denying them, as one would cross a froward
child of his stubborn humour ; or else puts a sting into
them, that a man had been as good he had been without them, as a man would give a thing to a froppish
child, but it may be with a knock on his fingers, and a
frown to boot. The best way to get riches, is out of
doubt to set them lowest in one's desires. Solomon
found it so. Alas, he did not ask riches, but wisdom and

ability, to discharge his great trust; but God was so
pleased with his prayer, that he threw in them into the
bargain. If we seek the kingdom of God, and His
righteousness in the first place, and leave other things to
Him, God will not stand with us for these outwards;
though we never ask them, we shall have them as over
measure; God will throw them in as the vantage. And
to this suits the experience of our dear Honoratius;
indeed (saith he, speaking of God), Honoratius finds
that his only hiding-place and refuge, and a place of
succour, from the storms that fall upon him, and hath had
such helps at a dead lift there, that he is engaged for ever
to trust there. For when he had been lowest and in the
greatest straits, he hath gone and made his moan heaven-
ward, with free submission to the rightful Disposer of all
things, and he hath been so liberally supplied, as makes
him very confident the best way to obtain any mercy, or
supply, is to be content to be without it : and he is persuaded nothing sets God's mercies further off, than want
of free submission to want them. Certainly God will
never be behind-hand with us. Let our care be to build
His house, and let Him alone to build ours.

" Fourthly, That none ever was, or ever shall be, a
loser by Jesus Christ. Many have lost much for Him,
but never did, never shall any lose by Him. Take this
for a certainty, whatsoever probabilities of outward comforts we leave, whatsoever outward advantages we balk,
that we may glorify Him in our services, and enjoy Him
in His ordinances more than others where we could, we
shall receive an hundredfold in this life. 'Tis a sad thing
to see how little Christ is trusted or believed in the world:
men will trust Him no farther than they can see Him,
and will leave no work for faith. Hath He not a

thousand ways, both outward and inward, to make up a little outward disadvantage to us ? What doth our faith serve for ? Have any ventured themselves upon Him in His way, but He made good every word of the promise to them ? Let us therefore exercise our faith, and stay ourselves upon the promise, and see if ever we are ashamed of our hope.

" Fifthly, That what is wanting in the means, God will make up in the blessing. This I take for a certain truth, while a man commits himself and his affairs to God, and is in a way that God put him into : now if a man have but a little income, if he have a great blessing, that's enough to make it up. We must not account mercies by the bulk. What if another have a pound to my ounce, if mine be gold for his silver, I will never change with him. As 'tis not bread that keeps men alive, but the word of blessing that proceedeth out of the mouth of God ; so 'tis not the largeness of the means, but the blessing of the Lord that maketh rich. Oh ! if men did but believe this, they would not grasp so much of the world as they do. Well, let others take their course, and we will take ours, to wait upon God by faith and prayer, and rest in His promise ; and I am confident that is the way to be provided for. Let others toil to enlarge their income (but alas, they will find they go not the right way to work), we will bless God to enlarge our blessing, and I doubt not but we shall prove the gainers.

" Sixthly, That every condition hath its snares, crosses, and troubles, and therefore we may not expect to be without them, wherever we be; only that condition is most eligible that hath fewest and least. I cannot object any-thing against the proposal of Taunton, but the meanness of the maintenance; but if our income be but short, we can, I hope, be content to live answerably. We must fare the meaner, that will be all the inconvenience that I know, and truly I hope we are not of the nature of that animal, that hath his heart in his belly. I know how Daniel thrived by his water and pulse, and think a mean diet is as wholesome to the body, yea, and far less hurtful than a full and liberal is ; and persuade myself it would be no such hard matter for us contentedly to deny our flesh in this respect. But let us consider how little and utterly inconsiderable this inconvenience is, in comparison of those we must reckon upon meeting with, if God cast us into another place ; and whether this be not a great deal less than the trouble we shall have for want of comfortable and Christian society, for want of the frequent and quickening means we shall here have, in wrangling and contending with the covetous, or else losing our dues, in the railings and scandalous and malicious reports, that are we see raised upon the best, by the wicked in most places, in their contentions about their right to the sacraments, in our entanglement in the cares and troubles of this life, &c., all which we should be here exempted from. Upon these and the like considerations, I find my heart very much inclined to accept of their offer at Taunton. I beseech thee to weigh, and thoroughly consider the matter, and tell me impartially thy thoughts, and which way thy spirit inclines, for I have always resolved the place I settled in should be thy choice, and to thy content. The least intimation of thy will to the contrary, shall overbalance all my thoughts of settling there, for I should account it the greatest unhappiness if I should thus settle, and thou shouldst afterwards be discontented at the straitness of our condition. But I need not have writ this, hadst not thou fully signified thy mind already

to me, I had never gone so far as I have. Well, the
Lord whose we are, and whom we serve, do with us as
it shallseem good unto Him. We are always as mindful
as is possible of thee here, both together and apart. Captain Luke desired me to entreat thee to meet him one two
hours in a day, for the commemoration of mercies upon
the twenty-third day of every month. Send word to me
of their resolution at Taunton, in two letters, lest possibly
one of them should miscarry, though never a one did yet.
I dare not think of settling under £60* at Taunton, and
surely it cannot be less. I have written as well as I
could on a sudden my mind to thee. I have been so
large in delivering my judgment, that I must thrust up my
affections into a corner. Well, though they have but a
corner in my letter, I am sure they have room enough in
my heart; but I must conclude. The Lord keep thee,
my dear, and cherish thee for ever in His bosom. Farewell, mine own soul,

"I am ever thine own heart,

"Jos. ALLEINE."

"*Oxon, May* 2⁷, 1655."

---

* Although he only anticipated this, he actually received £80,
which, it appears, was raised by *voluntary contributions.*—(Life,
p. 99.) This, though small when measured by the scale of alms-
giving which he thought it right to maintain in a parish where there
were so many poor, will appear to have been in reality no very mean
stipend when the different value of money in those days is taken into
account.

Dr. Hook remarks on it thus :—" When the Dissenters had aided
in the rebellion, he, as a zealous Puritan, was provided for out of the
confiscated property of the church."

Ecclesiastical Biography : containing the Lives of Ancient Fathers
and Modern Divines, interspersed with notices of Heretics and
Schismatics.

Theodosia consented to these views. In a few weeks Mr. Alleine is seen in Taunton streets again, and shortly after that we hear of his ordination.

In the early days of Presbyterian ascendency, young ministers, who had been nominated by patrons or elected by parishes, presented themselves for ordination or induction before a committee of ministers, formed under the sanction of the Westminster Assembly. After a time, it was voted to be inconvenient for the gate of the ministry to be in the charge of Presbyterians only, because they would allow Presbyterians only to enter it. It was Cromwell's principle that all able and godly preachers, of what " tolerable opinion soever they were," provided they were not openly opposed to the reigning Government, or the accepted orthodoxy of the day, should be on equal terms in the State. In order to this, by an ordinance dated March 20, 1653, the powers of the old clerical committee were transferred to " the Triers," a new examining board, approved by the council or the parliament, and consisting of divines and laymen of various religious persuasions.* This commission held its sessions in London, but sub-commissioners were employed to act for it in distant places.†

---

* Scobel, p. 279.

† " That a certain number of ministers and others be appointed to sit in every county, to examine, judge, and approve all such per-

The Triers have been burlesqued as endeavouring

> " To find, in lines of beard and face,
> The physiognomy of grace ;
> And by the sound of twang and nose,
> If all be sound within disclose."

They certainly owed their office to arbitrary power, and sometimes exercised its functions in a narrow spirit. Amongst them were some who thought " grace " in a minister atoned for the comparative absence of " gifts ;" and others, of whom complaint might have been made in the words of John Howe,—" It is not enough that a man should say to them, *Sib*boleth ; but he must say *Shib*boleth, or they will slay him for an Ephraimite." Yet, when you study the list of eminent men who were on the commission — " the acknowledged flower of English Puritanism "*—you would feel unable to believe that they would elect incompetent

---

sons as shall be called to preach the Gospel."—Order of the House, April 5, 1653. Whitelock, p 528. This order with reference to the appointment of Triers "*in every county,*" never appears to have been fully carried out ; for John Goodwin, whose Arminian principles brought him into trouble from the London Commissioners, calls them " hyper-archepiscopal, and super-metropolitan," and complains of them for holding their sittings exclusively in London. Βασανισται, or the Tryers (or Tormentors) Tried and Cast, 1657, p. 25. There must have been some ground for the charge, although it was overstated.

* Carlyle's Cromwell, vol. iii., p. 323.

deputies to serve in the remoter counties. There
is ample evidence to show that in the main the
Triers performed their task with thoroughness and
with tenderness, rejecting no applicants who were
good and competent ministers of religion, whether
Presbyterian, Independent, Prelatist, or Baptist,
—unless, indeed, though good and competent in
other respects, their avowed opinions were dangerous
to the ruling powers.

Through this " strait passage" Mr. Alleine had
to pass when down in Somersetshire in the month of
August. Among the local Triers were Thomas
Lye, M.A., of Wadham College, then minister of
Chard ; William Thomas, M.A., rector of Ubleigh,
the friend of Bishop Bull ;* and Edward Bennett,
M.A., of New Inn Hall, then minister of South
Petherton. When we find a detailed account of
the ordeal, we may expect to see connected with it
the name of Henry Jessey, M.A., the well-known
Baptist minister, who was then rector of St. George's,
Southwark ; for just at this time he was on a
visit to the Baptist churches in the neighbourhood.
He was one of the most famous members of the
Supreme Court of Triers ; and it would have been
strange if the deputies, whom he had helped to
appoint, knowing him to be near, had not invited
him to take part on the occasion,—an occasion in

* Nelson's Life of Dr. George Bull, p. 15.

which he would feel peculiar interest from his knowledge of Mr. Alleine, gained by visits to Corpus Christi. But this is conjecture ; we only know that Alleine passed through the trial without obstacle, and was, at the close, presented with parchments, to certify that he was confirmed in his appointment by authority of council.

He was a Presbyterian, and therefore had yet to be ordained by the presbytery. From Philip Henry's account of the first stages in his own ministerial course, we learn that it was usual for this to take place *after* receiving the license of the State from the Triers.* The process opened with a new series of examinations. When the candidate appeared before the neighbouring presbyters, inquiry was made as to " his experience of the work of grace in his heart." Verses in the Hebrew and Greek Scriptures were given him to read and construe. He was examined in logic, natural philosophy, and systematic divinity. To test his skill in exposition, his opinion was asked on some obscure text in Scripture. A case of conscience was stated for him to solve. He was questioned in church history. He was requested to prepare in Latin a thesis on some given subject, to be read at the next meeting ; and, lastly, certificates

---

* Philip Henry's Life. Appendix. He was ordained in 1657, two years later than Alleine.

H

of good character were required from the university,
and also from well-known ministers.   After all
this, the actual ordination service was appointed
to take place a month later.   A written announce-
ment of the approaching solemnity, accompanied
with a notice to the following effect, was read on
the next Sunday from the pulpit, and afterwards
nailed on the church-door :—

"If any man can produce any just exceptions
against the doctrine or life of Mr. Joseph Alleine,
or any sufficient reason why he may not be ordained, let him certify the same to the clerk of the
presbytery, and it shall be heard and considered."

No objection arising, Mr. Alleine was set
apart to the ministry on the day specified, at a
public association meeting held at Taunton ;* the
nature and order of the service being the same
as adopted by modern Dissenters.   Such were the
forms through which, in the days of Cromwell,
a young Levite had to pass before he entered upon
the exercise of his calling.

One object in life was now gained ; but he had
yet another in view.   Thoughtful people, with
much concern, saw him every fortnight set out
for a ride of twenty-five miles, on some mysterious
errand, into the country.   It was an exciting fact,
especially (if we may descend to a thing so trivial),

---

* Mr. Alleine's account.

when the state of the roads was considered. So
primitive were they that, according to one authority,
" it would not have cost more to make them
navigable, than fit for carriages ;"* and, according
to another, after a hard frost, the unhappy traveller
had " to lead his horse with one hand, and with
the other to use a strong staff for breaking the
ice, nine miles out of ten."† The autumn rains
were beginning to fall, the rural journeys were not
beginning to slacken. What would become of the
minister, and why, oh why, did he perform this
penance ? Mr. Newton was in the secret, as
perhaps you are; had some talk with him on the
subject of the expedition, and then advised him
to get married. Knowing that through his lavish
generosity he was not yet able to furnish a house,
he drew a touching picture of his own widowed and
lonely life,‡ and urged that he and Theodosia
should have their home at the vicarage. His
eloquence prevailed. They were married on the
4th of October, 1655, " contrary to our purpose,"
remarks Theodosia, "we resolving to have remained
much longer single." They became his guests,

---

* Such was the complaint, even when civilization had marched
the stage of a century beyond this time.—Speech of Thomas
Prowse, Esq., in the House of Commons, when Taunton applied
for a Turnpike Act, in 1752.

† Locke's MS. Savage's edition of Toulmin's History of Taunton,
566 ; Roberts's Life of Monmouth, vol. ii., p. 295.

‡ Mr. Newton's second wife died December 31st, 1645.

and he " entertained them courteously for the space
of two years."

To their honour and to his own infamy, Mr.
Wood seems to have darted all the venom of his
nature into the account he has left of this lady
as well as of her husband.   Before he died he seems
to have relented somewhat ; for, in a manuscript
of his, preserved in the Ashmole Museum, he
says :—" Theodosia Alleine was accounted among
her partie, a religious woman, and a good neighbour."   This praise was well deserved ; for she was
her husband's true helper and solace in all his life
of manifold sacrifice and benefaction, in all his
labours and imprisonments, in all his last long
agonies, and much of our knowledge of his personal
history we owe to her pen.

Amongst the letters of congratulation Alleine
received on his marriage, was one from an old
college friend, who said that he had some thoughts
of copying his example, but wished to be wary,
and would therefore take the freedom of asking
him to describe the *inconveniences* of a married life.
He replied,—" Thou wouldst know the inconveniences of a wife, and I will tell thee.   First
of all, whereas thou risest constantly at four in
the morning, or before, she will keep thee till
about six ; secondly, whereas thou usest to study
fourteen hours in the day, she will bring thee to
eight or nine ; thirdly, whereas thou art wont to

forbear one meal at least in the day for thy studies, she will bring thee to thy meat. If these are not mischiefs enough to affright thee, I know not what thou art."

"At the end of two years," writes his wife, "hoping to be more useful in our station, we took a house, and I, having always been bred to work, undertook to teach a school, and had many tablers* and scholars, our family being seldom less than twenty, and many times thirty; my school usually fifty or sixty of the town and other places."† And the Lord was pleased to bless us exceedingly in our endeavours; so that many were converted in a few years that were before strangers to God. All our scholars called him father; and indeed he had far more care of them than most of their natural parents, and was most tenderly affectionate to them, but especially to their souls."

This happy period of his life was still further brightened by a few special friendships. One or two of his friends we will name now on our way to the description of certain events in which perhaps they may have to take a part. His most intimate companion was Mr. John Norman,

---

* Boarders.

† "The daughters of gentlemen of good ranke far and near."— Letter written by "a Conformable minister," his familiar acquaintance.

minister of St. Mary's, Bridgewater. He was a strong thinker, a delicate casuist, and became well known through the country for the piety and scholarship that shone in his life and writings.* He had been acquainted with Alleine at Oxford, although he was there much his senior, and took his master's degree when the other had not long matriculated. They were like brothers, and right glad were they to be neighbours. Mrs. Alleine always called him " My brother Norman," because, it is said, her sister had been his first wife. His present wife was daughter of Humphrey Blake, and niece to the great admiral.

Another of his friends, although in a more distant and reverential way, was the Lady Farewell, of Hill Bishops, who was granddaughter to the Duke of Somerset, Lord Protector in the time of Edward the Sixth. She was frequently seen at Taunton Church. Warm was the welcome that he was wont to receive at her home,—

" The house, quaint-gabled, hid in rooky trees;"

and many were the opportunities there enjoyed of refined and graceful intercourse, " sanctified by the word of God and by prayer." After the

---

* Christ's Commission Officer, 8vo., 1658. Warning to God's Watchmen, 8vo., 1659. Cases of Conscience, 8vo., p. 400. Family Governors exhorted to Family Godliness. Christ Confessed, 1665.

death of this lady, in 1660, Mr. Newton thus magnified her excellences, in a letter addressed to her son; he had just been speaking of her husband, Sir George, who had died twelve years before her.

" *They were lovely and pleasant in their lives, and in death* (I rest assured) *they are not divided.*

" Indeed they were awhile divided, as she was left a solitary turtle in a vale of tears ; where she *lived, not in pleasure,* but in a strict performance (not of the easiest only, but) of the *hardest* and *severest private duties,* and in diligent attendance on the *publique ordinances,* in her own and in the neighbour congregations ; under which, while some were *hardened,* she *melted,* and closely dropt many a silent, secret tear (I speake it upon good assurance), which, though she covered, God observed and received into His bottle.

" How glad she was on all occasions *to go up to the house of the Lord,* to which she went in a religious equipage, attended with her train. She said not *ite,* but *eamus ;* not ' Go ye,' but ' Let us go.' In every holy duty she was first, being resolved, with Joshua : ' *I and my house will serve the Lord.*' Not ' my house, and not I ;' not ' I, and not my house ;' not ' my house and then I ;' but ' I, I first, and then my house ; I and my house ; I, with my house, will serve the Lord.'

" Among many other graces which I have not room to mention, her *humility* was orient. Herein she was an *example,* I may say, *tantum non, beyond example.* Though she had many things to stand upon—birth, title, education, &c.—so that she might have said, with reference to others of her quality, ' *Whereinsoever they are bold, I am bold also;*' yet she seemed not to know it. She had exactly learned *Bernard's* golden rule, which he illustrates with a similie : ' *As he that goes in at a little low door, it matters not how much he stoops, but if he beare himself one inch too high, he is in danger.*' So she regarded not how low she stoopt, nor how far she condescended, *in doing any office,* or in *bearing any burthen,* wherein *she might fulfil the law of love.*

"To say the truth, her whole demeanour was so incomparably sweetened with this amiable grace, that it was strangely taking and obliging, with all that had the happiness and honour to converse with her. And for her *habit ;* she was clothed with humility—that was her richest ornament. She did not (as *Tertullian* speaks of some) *wear grounds and groves and manors on her backe.* She look't not after the adorning of the outward man, either with garish or with gorgeous rayment; but after the *adorning of the inward man,* with holynesse and grace, *which is of great price in the sight of God;* whose *pure eyes* ladies and gentlewomen should rather strive to please, than the *wanton eyes* of men.

"She was a lady of a choice temper, and had a singular command upon her passions, *transcendantly* beyond the ordinary measure of her sex. She had the *government of her own spirit,* and the *possession of her soul* in patience, while others use their soul in passion. No *injuries of men* transported her into those wilde extravagancies and excesses, which some are carried out into, upon very slight occasions. And when the *hand of God* was on her in any way, she humbled herself. *Humble* she was in the most flourishing and prosperous state, but then especially she *humbled herself.* She was not only *humiliata*, but *humilis* too. She stoopt and kisst the rod, was *dumb* and *said nothing;* not a word either to *justifie herself*, or to *charge God foolishly.* In her last sicknesse, she reflected in her thoughts, and her discourses, on the long time of health she had enjoyed, that she might take occasion thence, both to *bring down* and to *lift up* her own heart. To bring it down to meekness and *submission*, to lift it up to *thankfulnesse.* To rayse it and to enlarge it (as she did) in the high prayses of the God of her mercy.

" As her meekness and *humility*, so her *charity* abounded. *To her power, yea, and beyond her power* sometimes, *she was willing of herself.* For the poor *she devised liberal things, considered them*, observed and studied their condition, and drew out (not her purse only but) *her* very *soul* to the needy. She *made her friends of the unrighteous mammon*, which she dispensed to the *righteous, especially to the household of faith.*

" I wander in so wide a field that I forget the narrow limits of a short epistle. I shall perhaps be twitted with the gate of *Mindus*, and be told that it is wider than the city. As Tygranis said in derision of the Roman forces under Lucullus—' This is too little for an army, and too much for an embass ;'—this is too little for a life, and too much for an epistle.' . . . .

" Let me take up with that allusion of the bishop of *Winchester*, Dr. *White*, who preach't Queen Marye's Funeral Sermon; wherein, comparing her with her unparalleled successor, Queen *Elizabeth*, he gave the latter a few cold faint praises. ' But yet,' said he, ' (according to my text), *I commend the dead rather than the living, and it will always be true*, Mary *hath chosen the better part.*' Sir, I may confidently say the same of this our

eminently gracious Lady *Mary*, and with far greater
truth than he, as he applyed it : the better part she chose,
and the better part she hath, yea, more than the better
part.   *She is dissolved, and is with Christ, which is best of
all.*   And, though the latter days in which she liv'd were
rough and boysterous, she dyed *in peace*, and *in a time of
peace.*   For, in a lucid interval, when all was husht, she
stole away into the *place of silence.*   She was not gather'd
by a *wanton hand*, nor blown down by a *furious wind*
while she was green, but being fully ripe, she dropt
away.   Fragrant and sweet she is, now she is but
newly fallen ; but she will be sweeter yet, when she is
mellowed.

" Sir, you are happy beyond many others of your rank,
that you had two such worthy patternes.   I beseech you
eye them well, and follow them as closely and exactly as
you can.   So live, and so walk, according to the faith
and holynesse which you have seen exemplified in your
excellent parents, that you may meet them in the great
day of account, *with joy, and not with grief.*   That you
may stand on the same hand of Jesus Christ at the time
of separation, and sit on the same throne to *judge the
world*, with them and others of the saints, and not to be
judged by them.   O, what a sad thing would it be
if, while your parents, both of them, are *sitting on the
bench*, you should be standing at the bar !   And if you
should be judged and condemned by them, though but
(as some expound that place of the Apostle Paul) by their
example.   Let this consideration quicken you to *walke
as they walked*, and to be a follower of them as they were
of Christ ; that keeping on the way wherein they went,
you may at length attain to the place where they are.
And when you also come to dye, you may *sleep with your*

fathers, and be gathered to your fathers ; your body to the same earth, and your soul to the same heaven." *

* From the epistle dedicatory to a sermon entitled " Magna Charta : or, the Christian's Charter Epitomized, in a Sermon preached at the Funerall of the Right Worshipfull the Lady Mary Farewell, at Hill-Bishops, near Taunton, by Geo. Newton, minister of the Gospel there.

> D. FareweLL obIIt MarIa saLVtIs In anno
> Hos annos posItos VIXIt et Ipsa VaLe."

This sermon is now so rare, that I have not been able to meet with a copy, and the above extracts are from a MS. lent by the Rev. William Arthur Jones, who is, by marriage, one of the representatives of the old Farewell family. To this gentleman, also, I am under obligations for other instances of kind assistance in research.

Chapter VI.

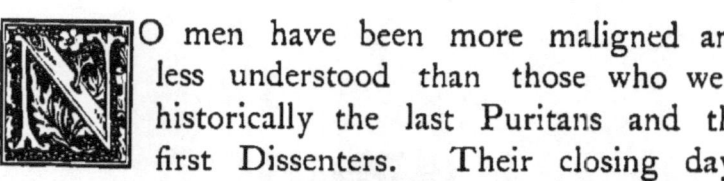

𝔚𝔬𝔯𝔡𝔰 𝔞𝔫𝔡 𝔚𝔞𝔶𝔰 𝔬𝔣 𝔱𝔥𝔢 𝔏𝔞𝔰𝔱 𝔓𝔲𝔯𝔦𝔱𝔞𝔫𝔰.

" Although they were not understood,
Yet from their spirit and their blood
Did flow a fair and fertile flood
Of thoughts and deeds both great and good."

THOMAS JORDAN. 1645.

NO men have been more maligned and less understood than those who were historically the last Puritans and the first Dissenters.   Their closing days were so vexed with the necessities of conflict, flight, and melancholy change, that they had little time or inclination to write about themselves.   The popular knowledge of their principles has often been drawn from the writings of men whose estimate of them was only as the estimate of Raphael by a blind critic, or of Newton by his dog Diamond.   Victorious enemies were their first historians,—and " when the man, and not the lion was thus the painter," it was easy to foretel with what party all the virtues, and all the nobilities would be found. It becomes our duty to look into our old family cabinets and libraries, and from the moth-eaten letters and tracts of our fathers to find out what manner of men they really were, how they used to spend a day, whether they did the eccentric things imputed to them, and if so, why. From such sources let us seek to know what were the opinions and manners that prevailed at Taunton when Alleine was there, and while Puritanism was putting forth some of its later forms. At that period there was scarcely a town in England where those forms were more broadly reflected.

You have before been reminded, that the radical principle of Puritanism was " reverence for the strict letter of the Scripture, as God's direct message to each individual man, and as forming our sole, final and absolute authority in religion." We may object to some applications that were made of this doctrine. We may think that the Bible is intended to rule us chiefly by its evangelical revelations, which, operating in the heart by the power of the Holy Spirit, become the regulating forces of the life, adjusting themselves, few and simple as they are, to the ever-changing conditions of the outward state; but many devout scripturists betrayed a tendency to regard the legislation of the Bible as proceeding on the system of a precise rule for a precise question, something like

that of the Mussulman code, with its 75,000 special precepts.   They were unquestionably right in
the respect they paid to the plainly stated laws and
precedents of Scripture ; but in attempting to find
laws and precedents to govern every minute and
particular action, they were often mistaken in
thinking they had found what they sought, and
were often in needless bondage.   Still, with all
their faults, " the Bible, and the Bible alone, was
the religion " of the Puritans ; and their very faults
grew out of this principle misunderstood, or misapplied.   Now, look at some of its every-day
workings, as it was understood by the people of
Taunton.

They, and those of like faith elsewhere, *never
called their ministers, in distinction from other
Christians,   " priests,"   or   " clergymen."*   " A
priest," said one, whom they held in high esteem,
" importeth a sacrifice."*   In their opinion, the
only sacrifices accepted under the Gospel are
the sacrifices offered by all believers ; so, amongst
the followers of Christ, the people are the priests.
—1 Peter ii. 5.   " Clergyman," was also a term
which, if used by them at all, would, by the same
Scripture rule, have had the same wide meaning.
" Poor men !" said one of their writers, speaking of
the Episcopalian ministers in reference to the mem-

---

* Latimer.

bers of their communion, "are you the clergy, and
not *they?* Read 1 Peter v. 3 : 'Not as lords
over God's clergy,' (κλήρων). Are they the laity,
and not *you?* Read Romans ix. 25 : 'I will call
them my laity,' (λαόν μου)."* Out of such inter-
pretations of texts relating to the priesthood
sprang that dislike of priestly vestments, which
sometimes startles us by its extravagance. Mitre,
crosier, cap, hood, surplice, were all denounced as
"instruments of a foolish shepherd," only because
they were the symbols of a priestly caste.†

They had no fixed forms of prayer, because it was
said the Scriptures have prescribed none ; and we
have already seen that in their view there was no
other prescribing authority in existence. When
two collects were printed and recommended to be
read in churches, one on "the horrid decollation of
King Charles the First," and the other on the
Restoration, Alleine had resolved to read them, but
owing to the strong opposition that was excited,
felt it prudent to desist.

They observed no saints' days, because the Scriptures appointed none ; but many were their days
of special religious solemnity, because this was
the custom of inspired men, and what they did as
well as what they said from the afflatus of inspiration, was viewed as having the authority of law.

---

* Preface to Henry Jessey's Life, 1672.　　† Vavasor Powel.

For example, they observed many fasts, including the monthly fast appointed by Parliament during the unsettled state of the nation; and many festivals, such as the day of rejoicing to commemorate the happy close of their siege.   On such occasions, the people met early in their own houses to pray,* and then crowded to the church.   Days of private thanksgiving or fasting were also kept; and on one of these days, George Trosse, a gentleman commoner of Pembroke College, who was often at Taunton, is said to have spent eleven hours upon his knees.†

They observed no rites and ceremonies, but such as were appointed by the plain decrees of the New Testament.   As might be expected, the ministry of ceremonies was displaced by the ministry of the Word.   This led to the sin of long sermons, of which the critics of Puritanism complain so loudly. Yet it should be admitted that this was not exclusively a Puritan habit, but a fashion of the times, of which all Protestant sects were guilty. Alleine sometimes preached for two hours, but Isaac Barrow has kept his patients three hours and a-half.   The young people were sometimes warned against regarding the sermon as a " meer passtime."

There was no organ allowed at St. Mary's

---

* Oliver Heywood, MS.   † Hallet's Funeral Sermon for Trosse.

Church. The reason for this may be given in the language of a Puritan doctor : —" There is not one word of institution in the New Testament for instrumental musique in the worship of God ; and because the holy God rejects all that He doth not command in His worship, He now, therefore, in effect, says to us, ' I will not hear the melody of thine organs.'"* Vocal music they cultivated, ⊀ because they had distinct New Testament authority for it, and the fame of the psalmody in Taunton Church rang far and wide.

They had no religious reverence for the mere building in which worship was offered. A person entering the church while Mr. Alleine was preaching, would see every man there keeping his steeple-hat on. The old "Mercuries" mention it. Many devout people were scandalised by it. When Colonel Turner, a gallant Cavalier, was hanged for burglary, he told the crowd gathered round the gallows that his mind derived great consolation from the thought that *he* " had always taken his hat off when he went into a church ;" but to whatever extremity the Puritan might be brought, he had no such consolation in reserve. "Some holy Nonconformists I have known," says Mr. Baxter, " that would rarely mention God but with their hats put off, or bowing down

---

* Cotton Mather.

I

their heads, and it hath often affected me more than a sermon."* Yet the sight of these holy men at church would have alarmed the religious sensibilities of Colonel Turner, for they would certainly have worn their hats while listening to the minister; though, when he commenced prayer, they would have uncovered. How was it? In those days, let it be understood, wearing the hat in-doors was an ordinary habit, and the lords on whom Mr. Pepys bowed attendance never thought it implied discourtesy to do so even at the dinner table; but actually taking it off with reference to anything religious was thought to imply worship,— taking it off at church, merely because it was a church, was thought to imply worship to the mere building. These precisians only meant to show their reverence for the Scriptures, and to utter their protest against the notion of specially consecrated ground, because they believed the Scriptures had declared it to be abolished.† Right or wrong,

---

* Baxter against Schism, Part II., p. 8, 1684. An Enquiry on a Question relating to Divine Worship; by Samuel Stoddon, 1682. "Though I am against superstitions, I am against putting on your hats in prayer." Mr. Jenkin's Farewell Sermons, 4to., 1662. In the second volume of Farewell Sermons, 8vo., 1663, there is an engraving showing a minister addressing a hatted congregation.

† John iv. 21. The Nonconformists also said that Christians had a church in the house, as well as in the public building; that acts of worship belonged to the one place as to the other; that the places, therefore, had equal sacredness.—Rom. xvi. 5; Philemon.

they only acted in this respect like the first reformers of the church of England, whose true successors and living representatives they were. In a rare old book by Archbishop Parker, there is a wood-cut representing that prelate preaching to a congregation of men all sitting with their hats on.*

They looked with no favour on any kind of symbolical beauty of form or colour in the structure or adornment of the churches. In Mr. Newton's time, the glories of the stained windows, in which the monks had taken so much pride, were nearly all destroyed ; and those windows, to use the language of the times, " were *beautified* with white and bright glasse." † Such Gothic destructiveness arose out of a misapplied scripturism. One motive to it was the sense the iconoclasts attached to such instructions as are contained in the Epistle to the Hebrews, which, as they understood them, taught that the religion of Solomon's Temple, with its types, emblems, and rich material splendours, was now fulfilled in the facts of the Gospel, and superseded by a system of spiritual worship, which such symbols would only hinder and becloud. Another

---

* De Antiquitate Britanniæ Ecclesiæ et Priviligiis Ecclesiæ Cantuariensis cum Archiepiscopis Eiusdem, 70, an. dom. 1572, folio   Only twenty-one copies are known.

† Expression used by Samuel Hinde to set forth how John Bruen, of Bruen Stapleford, Esquire, reformed the Popish window of his family chapel. Life of Bruen. 1641.

motive, still more strongly felt, was their intense hatred of all things that might lead to Romanism. They looked on such things just as the primitive Christians looked on the relics of classic art, without a thought of the genius they might display, but only of the superstition they might foster, and therefore gave them over to ruin or neglect. Here, again, they did but follow the steps of the first Anglican reformers. Few amongst them would or could have carried these principles further than was taught in the homily " Against peril of Idolatry, and superfluous decking of Churches." " My little children, saith St. John, deeply considering the matter, keep yourselves from images, or idols. He saith not now, keep yourselves from idolatry, as it were from the service and worshipping of them, but from the very shape and likeness of them . . . . think you, the persons who place images or idolls in churches and temples, take good heed to St. John's counsel?" Thus, in many passages, wrote the homilist, Bishop Jewell. It was natural, under the circumstances, that such principles should by many be adopted without intelligence, and carried out without discrimination. This, therefore, led through the next century to the destruction in churches, not only of religious images, but of many a noble work of art besides, in glass, wood, and stone. Let us, however, be fair to the Puritans. Many of the disfigurements of churches that are assigned to the period of the Commonwealth, belong in reality to the period of the Reformation ;* many others were wrought for which no religious party is accountable, but which were the reckless deeds of rioters, in the time of civil war ; and in all cases where works of art not Romanistic in their design were shattered, it was in direct violation of the very ordinance for the removal of Popish badges, in which it was specified, " This ordinance shall not extend to any image, picture, or coat of arms, in glass, stone, or otherwise, in any church, chapel, or churchyard, set up by or engraven for a monument of, any king, prince, nobleman, or other dead person, which has not commonly been reputed or taken for a saint."†

It must not be denied that serious evils were developed under the reign of the Puritans. There was much intolerance, and at the same time there was much division in the church. Both sprang from a harsh and mistaken application of their primary doctrine—that the laws of religion, and all that belongs to it, must be taken from the written Word alone. Spending their strength in attention to the letter of the Scripture, they were apt to overlook the spirit of

---

* Archæological Journal, vol. ii., p. 244. Godwin on Ely Cathedral.   Catalogue   of   Bishops,   1601.   Weaver's   Monumental Antiq., p. 18.

† Husband's Collections, p. 307.

the Scripture; giving all possible emphasis to its truth, they were in danger of slighting its charity — yet both are equally divine. The first result was intolerance. "We have undoubtedly found in the Bible," thought they, "certain great truths, and a certain scheme of church order; then for a man to question those truths, or to deviate from this order, is not so much a sin against us, as a sin against God." "Polupiety, is Impiety."* The next result was division. All history shows that whatever among an intelligent people demands religious uniformity, does, in the same degree, raise the spirit of discord. Amongst the Puritans, not only was this spirit of discord sometimes rampant as the effect of such intolerance, but as the effect of the reception and consequent perversion by intolerant minds of another article of the Puritan creed, namely, that the Bible being God's message to every individual man, every man has a right to judge of its meaning for himself. The article itself is gloriously true and important, but it is easy to see that its operation in the hands of intolerant men, exasperated by the intolerance of others, would lead to much division, not only in faith, but in feeling. One consequence was, that during the Commonwealth a wonderful number of new sects shot into consequence, some of them having strange

---

* Edwards.

and wonderful names, to which, perhaps, the Royalist, Dr. Beaumont, has a sly allusion in his catalogue of heresies, filling twenty-nine lines with words like these :—

> " Tertullianists, Arabics, Symmachists,
>   Homousiasts, Elxites, Origenians,
>   Valesians, Agrippinians, Catharists,
>   Hydroparastates, Patripassians,
>   Apostolics, Angelics, Chiliasts,
>   Somosatenian Paulianists." *

We think that the cure for religious division is not renouncing the Biblical doctrine of the Puritans, but keeping it in the spirit of Christ. Many did thus keep it, as we shall presently see ; many more were more generous in practice than in theory ; but the true nature of Christian liberty had yet to be learned.

Sometimes this intolerance took the form of church discipline. " Wondrous narrow " were the laws of the churches, and very harsh was the occasional dealing with offenders, thereby provoking harsh recrimination. A few years after his settle-

---

* Ephraim Pagitt, in his Heresiography, describes between forty and fifty sects. Another writer, evidently a more moderate man, wrote a pamphlet with the following title, " A Discovery of Twenty-nine Sects here in London, all of which, *except the first*, are most divellish and damnable."—Guildhall Library.

Edwards gives a list of 180 flagrant heresies ; Baxter has also left a doleful catalogue ; Ford, Vicars, and Featley have given equally wonderful reports ; but the witnesses do not agree, and all make very foolish distinctions.

ment, Mr. Alleine was much disturbed by an instance of this kind, in which some of his relatives were affected.   Cousin Tobie Alleine, with his wife, Mistress Marie, were both Presbyterians at Exeter.   Mr. Lewis Stuckley, a gentleman of ancient and knightly family, and one of the preachers in the choir of the cathedral, was an Independent. They went to " behold his Gospel order ;" and in the course of time joined his church.   Gradually they saw many things which they disapproved, be-came irregular in attendance, and at last went back with all repentance to their old pastor, Mr. Mark Downes.   They were therefore excommunicated by the Independents ; and Mrs. Marie, a lady of uncertain temper and much velocity of speech, was "delivered over unto Satan."   Then came forth a pamphlet, bearing the tremendous title, " Truths Manifest ; or a Full and Faithfull Narrative of all passages relating to the Excommunication of Mrs. Marie Alleine, lately delivered over unto Satan by Mr. Lewis Stuckley and his Church at Exon ; with a Brief Answer to Mr. Stuckley's Sermon." 8vo., 1658.   This was followed by " Diotrephes, detected, corrected, and rejected ; and Archippus admonished by a soft Answer to an angry Sermon and Book." After that appeared "Truths Manifest Revived."*
A testimony to Mr. Tobie's " good name and

---

* These pamphlets are in the Bodleian Library.

reputation " was published, and signed by the
sheriff, the mayor, and twenty-five aldermen and
burgesses; but although he and his wife were
treated in a way most inquisitorial and severe, his
conduct in the affair does not appear to have been
without blame, and his spirit through the controversy is certainly not to his credit. These matters
may seem to some to be trivial as the politics of a
rookery, but they are given here as specimens of
the unseemly confusion that might occasionally
occur under the dynasty of the Puritans, and from
a wish to be perfectly fair in sketching their manners, both bad and good.

It is now time to turn from the churches, that
we may direct our thoughts to the social life of the
first Nonconformists. You will there find that,
of many grotesque things imputed to them, some
were the pure inventions of festive malice, and
that others lose their look of absurdity when truly
understood. You expect to see the immortal
oddities of Hudibras start up before you ; you
expect to meet half-gloomy, half-comic wonders, at
every step of your inquiry ; at the very beginning
you expect, at least, to find that George Newton's
people have outlandish names, such as *Kill-sin*
Pimple, or *Weep-not* Billings, for all the historians
from Hume to Macaulay have told you that
this was the fashion. They all appear to have been
mistaken. It may be allowed that names remotely

like these, because formed out of a religious dialect,
were occasionally given by the settlers in Mas-
sachusetts to their children, and that a very few
might also have been given to children in England ;
it must be asserted, however, that where they were
in use, they were always imposed in infancy, and
never selected by the parties themselves.   Please
to remember, that if such names were worn by the
men and women of the Protectorate, they had been
conferred upon them at the font in the reign of the
British Solomon.   We have ample evidence that
the habit was occasional then, but it really seems to
have declined by the time of which we are writing.
If existent anywhere, it surely might have been
expected in the place where those charged with
adopting it had their stronghold ; but not one such
name is to be found in the copious Taunton
register of that date, and not one in all the numerous parochial registers of the same era which the
present writer has examined.*

Imagine yourself leaving Taunton Church on
some thanksgiving-day, and walking with a grave
burgher to his home.   Take notes of what you
see.   His life there, just as much as in public

---

* Confirmation of these statements will be found in Camden's
Remains, p. 42, 1629; Harris's Cromwell, p. 342; and Lower
on English Surnames.   This writer gives instances of such names
from a Sussex jury list, which he assigns to about the year 1610, and
from the parochial register of Warbleton, 1617.

worship, is ruled by Scripture texts. Texts are woven into all his conversation, for the language of the Bible is with him the language of common life ; he applies it to everything, and uses it most, not as you might suppose, when most artificial, but when most in earnest. Looking round, you see *texts* painted on the doors and over the fire-places, stamped on kettles and skillets, wrought in garments, and even carved on the wooden cradle in the corner where the child lies asleep. A Nonconformist, who was young in Oliver's time, after praising his father for great care in the religious instruction of his children, adds, " Let those Scriptures upon the chimney-stone in the parlour be witness."* There were thirteen texts there. In a few cases, as might have been expected, satirists wrote merrily about this Puritan use of texts, especially on their appearance in the ladies' embroideries. A personage in one of the comedies is represented as saying—

> " Nay, Sir, she is a Puritan at her needle too :
> She works religious petticoats ; for flowers,
> She'll make church-histories ; besides,
> My sleeves have such holy embroideries,
> And are so learned, that I fear in time
> All my apparel will be quoted by some pure instructor."†

In one of Beaumont and Fletcher's plays we read

---

* Life of John Machin, p. 19.   † Jasper Mayne's City Match.

of " a neat historical shirt. *"   From such passages
it appears that the custom was of earlier origin
than the period of the Commonwealth, although
it was then in the height of its observance.

You are not to infer from all this, that your
burgher friend leads a life of holy dulness or
illiteracy on account of his biblical notions.   Why
should he ?   He enjoys a *recreative* hour as freely
as any other man, thinking it lawful, however, not
so much because it is natural, as because he can
show you chapter and verse for it.   " Recreation,"
he will say, " is an exercise joined with the fear
of God, conversant with things indifferent, for the
preservation of bodily strength and the confirmation
of the mind in holiness.   To this end hath the
Word of God permitted shooting (2 Sam. i. 18);
musical consort (Neh. vii. 67); putting forth
riddles (Judges xiv. 12); hunting of wild beasts

---

* Beaumont and Fletcher's Custom of the Court. The statements
given above are supported by the traditions and relics of three or
four Nonconformist families known to the author, in the west of
England.   One venerable member of his former congregation, a
gentleman who lived to the age of ninety-four, used to tell of a
ramble he had when a boy over the old house of a Nonconformist
baronet, which was printed over in this way; and he remembered
how his youthful mind was impressed by an inscription in the
dormitory anciently used by the handmaidens of the family, and
which was intended to strike the eye the first thing in the morning,—" Arise, ye vvomen y^t are at ease."   It is a wonder that
the witty enemies of the Nonconformists have not made more of
these things.

(Cant. ii. 15) ; searching out, or the contemplation of, the works of God (1 Kings iv. 33)."*

You find him almost *insensible to the beautiful or awful in art;* but not so much from religious scruples, as from strong religious excitement, and the effect of distracting war. In time of war, the best man thinks more of the forces that ensure protection than of the graces that decorate repose. He is more likely to be occupied in barring his gate, than in training the rose that clusters over it.†

On the same account you will find him *indifferent to written poetry.* You are not likely to see a new poem in his house. We are told, it is true, that in the houses of a certain western town—

> " Poems were pasted up on every hall
> As thick and thin as cobwebs on the wall:—
>
> Here you might view Haman in all his pride,
> And, like a rogue, hanged and then dittified.
> Each kitchen, parlour, chamber, were all drest here
> With Samson, Joseph, Daniel, or Queen Hester." ‡

But this was a local accident,—these were the effusions of an inspired parish clerk ; and Nathaniel Miers, " the clarke that did the christenings"§ in Mr. Newton's absence, was not inspired. If, in any of the houses at Taunton in the time of the Commonwealth, you saw amongst the broad sheets on the wall, one that was covered over with

---

* Master Perkins.   † Wilmott.
‡ Batt upon Batt : a Poem. 1680.   § Register of Mary Magdalen.

what at the distance of a few yards looked like poetry, a nearer approach would show you that it certainly had not been selected for its poetical merit. We owe most of our written poetry to the remembrance in peace of past excitement; but the crisis of excitement is not itself the season when poetry is most likely to be written or read. The lives of the Puritans were often instinct with the very soul of poetry; only, " instead of singing it like birds, they acted it like men."* Poetical authorship was next to impossible amidst their trials; yet, even in this respect, they were not deficient in comparison with their opponents. They had, at least, George Wither, John Milton, and " the glorious dreamer," John Bunyan.

After the noon-day meal, *your host confesses to you his delight in goodly music,* and quotes in support of his views, the saying of one of his ministers: "Of all beastes, saith Ælian, there is none that delighteth not in harmony, save only the asse; strange would it be for men to love it not." Singing begins, and, perhaps, to the accompaniment of the lute: but, although playing on the lute is mentioned by Alleine with approval, it was a question with some of his neighbours whether they ought to conform so far to the habits of the ungodly. At a meeting which the members of the Baptist church

---

* Kingsley on Plays and Puritans.

at Taunton held with the members of sister churches at the Bridgewater Association in 1655, the question was proposed, " Whether a believing man or woman, being head of a family in this day of the Gospell, may keep in his or her house an instrument or instruments of musique, playing on them, or admitting others to play thereon ?" The answer was, " It is the duty of the saints to abstain from all appearance of evil, and not to make provision for the flesh to fulfill the lusts thereof, to redeem the time, and to do all to the glory of God ; and though we cannot consider the uses of such instruments to be unlawful, yet we desire the saints to be very cautious lest they transgress the aforesaid rules in the use of it, and do that which may not be of good report, and so give offence to their tender brethren."* Keeping the " aforesaid rules " in mind, your friend will venture to use the lute, and invite you to join in a song, not, however, one of the songs of this world. (When you have time, if you have courage, look into one of the Roxburgh or Luttrell Collections of Songs of the Seventeenth Century, preserved in the British Museum, and you will soon see the reason.) Since all the living literature of music was too tainted for the pure to use, he gives out a canticle from a little black volume, called " The Booke of Psalmes ; close and

---

* Baptist Church Book, Lyme Regis.

proper to the Hebrew; smooth and pleasant for
the Metre; plain and easy to the Tunes. By
W. B., 1654." Out of this book, Alleine and his
family were accustomed to sing after dinner, though
sometimes he would substitute the *Te Deum*, which
he much rejoiced in ; and it was said, when he pronounced the sentence, " The noble army of martyrs
praise thee," it was always with "a certain exaltation."

You will find your companion *severe in his
notions as to simplicity in dress.* When a Somersetshire lad came home one day, in a coat broidered
with broad gold lace, his mother in great alarm cut
it all away, and he himself afterwards remembered
his " vaine apparel " with great anguish, saying,
" My buttons, gold, and the silk on my sleeves
lay on my conscience, a burden weighty as a
world."* Some of the elders of the people, while
they held grave opinions about adornment in
" gold, pearls, and costly array," expressed those
opinions to the weaker brethren with edifying
moderation, desiring that " they should be proceeded against with all sweetness, and tenderness,
and long-suffering, it being not so clearly and
generally understood as other things that are more
contrary to the light of nature."† After all, the

---

* Life of Trosse.

† Papers of Western Association of Baptist Churches in 1655.—
Baptist College Library, Bristol.

standard of dress adopted by the Puritan would more closely approximate to modern laws of taste and propriety than would that of the Cavalier, with his silks, feathers, laces, and gaudy streamers of ribbon.

Your friend exacts from his family the most strict respect to the injunction, "*be not conformed to this world.*"* But knowing what was meant by "the world," in the life of any one of the Stuarts, you are not surprised. If those gallants the "bright exhalations' of knighthood"— so often placed by Sir Walter Scott in enchanting contrast to the rude and gloomy Puritans—were walking the earth now, you would not call them gentlemen, nor wish to see them at your table. Of course we are speaking not of exceptions on either side, but of the average Puritan and the average Cavalier.

In the evening, you leave the burgher's house to take a view of life among the poorer classes. You hear the music of family praise floating through many a stone-shafted lattice as you pass along the streets. It used to be so even in London,†

---

* We must hope that extreme measures to secure family order were not often resorted to; but in one of Mr. Newton's books there is a publisher's list, which announces an interesting new work with the following title: "The Husband's Authority Unveiled; wherein is moderately discussed whether or no it be lawful for a good man to beat his bad wife."

† "Time was when one could not have come through the streets of London, even on a week-day, but we might hear the praises of God, in singing of psalms."—Mr. Case, 1663.

K

but more especially in the better instructed provincial towns.* At last, you enter the cottage of a labourer. Pasted upon the wall are various folio sheets, with such titles as these :—" Old Mr. Dod's Sayings ;"—" Another Posie out of Mr. Dod's Garden ;"—" Plain Directions for the more profitable hearing of the Word," by Joseph Caryl ;— " Memorables concerning our life before God, by one desirous of Poor Folks' Salvation;"—"Sayings, &c., which may be pasted on a Man's Chamber-door for a Memoriall." In the place meant to be most public and honourable, there is a sheet, broad as a leaf of the *Times* (you are not to forget the nineteenth century), bearing the title, " Mr. Joseph Alleine's Directions for covenanting with God : also, Rules for a Christian's Daily Self-examination."† A few godly books lie on a shelf near the window.

If you have been much in Puritan company, you must have learned that, although no large Society was at that time in existence for the diffusion of religious knowledge amongst the poor, sheets and books for this purpose were often distributed privately, or by concert of two or three

---

* Baxter says of Kidderminster, "You might hear a hundred families singing psalms and repeating sermons as you passed through the streets." And this, he elsewhere tells us, was not an uncommon thing in other towns.

† British Museum. The Rev. John Wesley afterwards issued an abridged publication of these " Directions," giving them high praise.

persons, to the extent of hundreds of thousands. When, for instance, Alleine's treatise on conversion came out, a Nonconformist minister proposed that an edition should be printed for gratuitous circulation, and immediately paid down £50 towards the cost. Others joined him, and the result was, that an impression of 20,000 was dispersed without sale, and another impression was, by the same method, sold under rate.* In these ways, together with the system of catechising, on which so much stress was placed in those days, the poorer people were remarkable for their religious intelligence. The poor man, into whose cottage your spirit is now glancing, is ready to open a dialogue with you like one of those reported in the " Pilgrim's Progress."

If you wish to see what Puritan life was like in " the high places," go with Mr. Alleine and his brother Norman to spend an evening with Admiral Blake at his country-house at Knowle, two miles from Bridgewater. Suppose it to be during the period of his brief visit to England in 1656. Suppose his friend Colonel Hutchinson to be staying there. There would be a simple meal,—the Bible would be brought in,—there would be prayer,— there would be conversation such as Christians

---

* Life and Funerall Sermon of the Reverend Mr. Thomas Brand, M.A., by Dr. Samuel Annerly, 1692.

love, and which they can only have when in "their
own company;"—there would probably be discourse,
in logical forms, on some of the mysteries of Christian truth,—of course there would be reasonings
over some " case of conscience ;"—Mr. Newton
would be apt to get prosy in discussing the opinions
of Fragosa, Tolet, Sayrus, and Roderiques ;—then
there would be a flow of graceful and varied talk,
not only on politics, but on books, pictures, gar-
dening, or the last scientific experiments of the
Oxford Society,—and the great sailor, who had so
often made the Dutch tremble at his sublime
audacity, " would affect a droll concern to prove
before the ministers, by the aptness and abundance
of his Latin quotations, that in becoming an
admiral, he had not forfeited his claim to be considered a good classic."*   You could not find
better types of the winning yet stately Christian
gentleman, than amongst the Puritans.

They had amongst them men of narrow and
negative opinions ; men of vehement, disputatious
independence ; men who had no love for the lovely
in the works of God or man, and who were accustomed to think that in the exercises of religion the
eye and the ear were only in the way ; men who
seldom relaxed the stern strain of the faculties
which the exigencies of their day demanded, and who

---

* Hepworth Dixon's Life of Blake, p. 267.

therefore made Christianity look forbidding. They were often joined by men who though with, were not of them, and who only misrepresented them to the world; who put religiosity in place of religion, and displayed a false Puritanism, " as like and as unlike the true, as hemlock is to parsley ;" men to whom plain, downright Lewis Stuckley said, when referring to the signs over the tradesmen's doors, " You have glorious signs, but ill customs ; an angel for a sign here, a lamb for a sign there, but within devils and cheats."* Still, the true principles of Puritanism were favourable to strength and refinement of character, to domestic purity and love, and to all kinds of commercial prosperity. While they were ascendant, " there was scarcely an instance of bankruptcy heard of in a year."† " Many places," remarks Baxter, when writing of Alleine, " were so seasoned by the great abilities and holy lives of their pastors, the great market-towns have become as religious as the selected members which some think only fit for churches." " In those years, between forty and sixty," Philip Henry testifies, "though on civil accounts ' the foundations were out of course,' yet, in the matters of God's worship, things went well ; there was freedom and reformation, and a face of godliness was upon the nation, though there were some that made a mask of it.

---

* Gospel Looking-Glasse.   † Neale's History, vol. iii., p. 46.

.   .   .   .   This, we know very well, let men say
what they will of those times."*

A clear conception, it is hoped, may now be
formed of the people among whom Allcine laboured,
whom he used to call "loving and most endeared
Christians," and whose excellencies so won his
heart, that in his long last illness he used to say,
"If I should die fifty miles away, let me be
buried at Taunton."

---

* Life of Philip Henry, by Sir J. B. Williams, p. 89.

Chapter VII.

Alleine in the Sabbath of his Life.

" A Father's tenderness, a Shepherd's care,
A Leader's courage, which the cross can bear,
A Ruler's awe, a Watchman's wakeful eye,
A Pilot's skill, the helm in storms to ply,
A Fisher's patience, and a Labourer's toil,
A Guide's dexterity to disembroil,
An Intercessor's unction from above,
A Teacher's knowledge, and a Saviour's love."

BISHOP KEN.

RABBI JOSE BAR JEHUDAH once gave this decision :—" He that learneth of young men, is like a man that eateth unripe grapes, or that drinketh wine out of the wine-press; but he that learneth of the ancient, is like a man that eateth ripe grapes, and drinketh wine that is old." Such, at first, was the spirit of the comparisons drawn between the old and the young minister, by many a little group of critics that stood about in the churchyard after service ; but gradually such murmurs were hushed, and awe-struck crowds walked home in silence.

"This young Timothy was, at his first entrance on his ministry, despised for his youth, by those who after with shame confessed their errour, and deplored their rashness, resolving after for his sake no more to judge according to appearance, but to honour for their work, and intrinsick worth, those whom age hath not made venerable."*

His composition was slovenly. He never studied the art of casting thought into form ; never uttered language that was stately, periodic, or delicately musical ; and never, unless by mere chance, used words lit up with secondary or imaginative meanings ; yet we should always remember, when reading sermons preached by him and his brethren to Puritan congregations, that many things in the matter which are to us truisms, were to them startling truths ; and that much of the style which may seem to us tiresome and common, was not felt to be so then. Long familiar use of such language in the pulpit has worn away the freshness and sharpness of its figurative stamp, but it was then vivid and poetical, not because the speaker cared to make it so, but because he was so full of life that he could not help it. He would have disdained to care about it. "The King's business requireth haste," was his constant feeling, and he could not stay to study the structure of sentences

---

* Mr. Newton.

while dying men were waiting for the word of
life. Had the young preacher at St. Mary's been
advised to think more of verbal refinement, he would
probably have replied in language like that of John
Owen, " Know that you have to do with a person,
who, provided his words do but express the sentiments of his mind, entertains a fixed and absolute
disregard for all elegance and ornaments of speech."
His addresses had far higher elements of excellence.
They all breathed a winning tenderness, and all
revealed an amazing power of rapid, homely, shat-
tering appeal. The thoughts were all impetuous
with a rush of fresh and glowing life; and though
there was the prophet's rough mantle, there was
also his chariot of fire. Every meaning was clear,
every stroke told, every gesture seemed to speak,—
*vividus vultus, vividi oculi, vividæ manus, denique
omnia vivida.* One of his hearers tells us that
" he never preached without a long expostulation
with the impenitent, vehemently urging them to
come to some good resolve before he and they
parted, and to make their choice for life or death, expressing his great unwillingness to leave the subject,
till he could have some assurance that he had not
fought against sin ' as one that beateth the air ;' and
that much of his power arose from the point and
seasonableness of his words, spoken as they were
with an intimate knowledge of the individual cases
of those who formed his auditory." There was

piercing directness—the shafts of living Scripture flew straight to their intended mark, and each swift sentence had an aim clear as had the arrow found on the ancient battle-field, bearing the motto "For Philip's eye."

The bows of eloquence, it has been said, are buried with the archers, and the life of rhetoric perishes with the rhetorician; it darkens with his eye, stiffens with his hand, freezes with his tongue. No full idea of what Alleine was in this respect can be gathered from his writings; we are nearly dependent for information on the testimonies of those who heard him, and to cite these would be almost endless, but we may cite a few.

"Few ages have produced more eminent preachers than Mr. Joseph Alleine," says Oliver Heywood. Baxter speaks of his "lively seriousness," and of his "great ministerial skilfulness in the public explication and application of the Scriptures—so melting, so convincing, so powerful." "He had a powerful and charming rhetoric," adds Mr. Mayo, when telling of his reputation at Oxford. Pearse, an Episcopal clergyman, who heard him preach, commends him as "eminently learned and excellent." Mr. Newton thus speaks :—"His ministerial studies were more than usually easie to him, being of a quick conceit, a ready, strong, and faithful memory, a free expression (which was rather nervous and substantial, than soft and deli-

cate), and, which was best of all, a holy heart that
boiled and bubbled up with good matter. This
furnished him, on all occasions, not with warm
affections only, but with holy notions too. For
his heart was an epistle, written not with ink,
but with the Spirit of the living God. In the
course of his ministry, he was a good man, and in
his heart a good treasure ; whence he was wont
continually to bring forth good things, both in
publick and private.

" He was apt to preach and pray, most ready on
all occasions to spend himself in such work : when
my sudden distemper seized upon me, putting him
at any time (as many times it did) upon very short
and suddain preparations, he never refused ; no,
not so much as fluctuated in the undertaking ; but
being called, he confidently cast himself upon the
Lord, and trusted perfectly to His assistance,
who had never failed him ; and so he readily and
freely went about his work without distraction.

" He began upon a very considerable stock of
learning, and gifts ministerial and personal, much
beyond the proportion of his years ; and grew
exceedingly in his abilities and graces in a little
time ; so that his profiting appeared to all men.
He waxed very rich in heavenly treasure, by the
blessing of God on a diligent hand, so that he was
behind in no good gift. He found that precious
promise sensibly made good, ' To him that hath

(for use and good employment) shall be given, and
he shall have abundance.' He had no talent for
the napkin, but all for traffique, which he laid out
so freely for his Master's use, that in a little time
they multiplied so fast, that the napkin could not
hold them. I heard a worthy minister say of him
once (not without much admiration), 'Whence hath
this man these things?' He understood whence he
had them well enough, and so did I,—even from
above, whence every good and perfect gift proceedeth. God blessed him in all spiritual blessings
in heavenly things, and he returned all to Heaven
again; he served God with all his might and all
his strength; he was abundant in the work of the
Lord; he did not go, but run the wayes of His
commandments; he made haste and lingered not;
' he did run, and was not weary; he did walk, and
was not faint.' He pressed hard towards the mark,
till he attained it; his race was short and swift, and
his end glorious.

" He was infinitely and insatiably greedy of the
conversion of souls, wherein he had no small
success in the time of his ministry; and to this
end he poured out his very heart in prayer and in
preaching; he imparted not the Gospel only, but
his own soul. His supplications, and his exhortations, many times were so affectionate, so full of
holy zeal, life, and vigor, that they quite overcame
his hearers; he melted over them, so that he

thawed and mollified, and sometimes dissolved the hardest hearts. But while he melted thus, he wasted, and at last consumed himself."

Another contemporary writes as follows :—

" His judgment was as the pot of manna, wherein were found and conserved all wholesome, soul-feeding doctrines. His memory was as the tables of the covenant, and as the sacred records kept in the ark, God's law being his meditation day and night. So tenacious it was, that it needed not and wholly refused those helps by which it is usually kept. What had once engaged his love was, without delay or difficulty, possessed of his memory."

* * * * * *

" His phansie was as Aaron's rod budding, ever producing fresh blossoms of refined, divine wit. His affections were strong and fervent, never enkindled but with a coal from the altar. He had a great acquaintance with the chief sects of the philosophers, especially of the academics and stoicks, of his insight into whom he made singular use, by gathering their choicest flowers to adorn Christianity withal ; and scarcely did he preach a sermon wherein he did not select some excellent passage or other out of them, whereby to illustrate and fortify his discourse. His prolation or manner of speech was free, sublime, and weighty. It will be hard to tell what man ever spake with more holy eloquence, gravity, authority, meekness, compassion, and efficacy to souls."

Such are a few of the expressions written about him, years after his death, by a minister of the church of England who knew him well.

The theme of his preaching was always " Jesus Christ and Him crucified ;" and we are informed that his views of the central peculiarities of the Christian system were the same as those held by Dr. Davenant, bishop of Salisbury, and Mr. Baxter.   The sentiments of the former may be inferred from his threatened suspension by King James, in 1630, for asserting in a sermon the doctrine contained in the seventeenth article of his Church ; *—the sentiments of the latter are not so easy to define; but his declared approval of the Assembly's Confession and the Synod of Dort's Conclusions, with some slight exceptions, seem decisive on the point that he was essentially a Calvinist ;† although it was certainly the aim of his life to adjust the balance between the two great doctrinal systems, and to bring their respective adherents to closer communion.

Alleine's theological doctrines have not been given to us in any form of scientific unity, but we may suspect that the critics who asserted their likeness to those of Baxter, had special reference to his constant call to the unconverted, and to the fact that he dealt with every man as a free and respon-

---

* Fuller, Book XI., p. 138.   † Orme's Life of Baxter, ii., 76, 77.

sible agent, open to receive the invitations of the
Gospel. Although even the most rigid followers
of the Genevese reformer preached the " glad
tidings " to the unconverted, they often did so in
strains made so cold and mysterious by subtleties
of qualification, and led the people round to the
waters of life through such a tangled brake of
logical refinements, that their invitations seemed
scarcely to be given in good faith ; and they sometimes even seemed afraid, lest, through their own
mismanagement, some of the wrong persons might
get saved after all.   But Alleine, on the other
hand, feeling no embarrassment and no reserve,
and shackled by no theoretic misgivings—with
shouting voice, flashing eye, and a soul on fire
with love, proclaimed a completed and gratuitous
salvation to all who were willing to accept it. The
Spirit of God gave his message great effect, and
multitudes, through all the days of heaven, will
remember Taunton Magdalene as the place where
they first beheld that great sight—" the Lamb of
God who taketh away the sin of the world !"

But this great evangelist was not great merely,
or even chiefly, in the pulpit.   Other agency was
needful to touch the many thousands for whom
there was no room within church walls.   It was an
age of wondrous evangelic activity, but the uncertain tenure of government discouraged the erection
of new churches, and in that populous town there

was only one small church besides his own. The Baptist conventicle was the only worshipping assembly of any other kind. The various opinions now represented by Dissenters—separation from the State, of course, excepted—had then place and voice within the ecclesiastical buildings belonging to the nation ; comparatively, only a few objected to the State control of religion.*   Nearly everything had to be done, therefore, by the unassisted action of the parish ministers.

By these circumstances he was stimulated to almost incredible labours as a catechist. Several hours were spent on each of the seven days of the week in work of this kind, and in the following way : —On the Sunday morning he preached from his own pulpit, and when Mr. Newton, owing to infirmity, was disabled from taking his turn in the evening, he would then preach the same sermon again, after-wards calling forth several youths to give an account of its leading thoughts from memory.   In either case he constantly catechised in the after-noon, before a great congregation, the youth of each sex, the children of the magistrates and of other gentry with the rest.   The Assembly's Cate-

---

* Perhaps this may help to illustrate the statement made by the Rev. Dr. Cottle—that, in the time of the Rev. Joseph Alleine (one of the former clergymen), "there were no Dissenting places of worship in the parish."—Some Account of the Church of St. Mary Magdalen, p. 73.

chism was the basis of the exercise, but along with it were questions in writing which he had given out in the previous week.

On Thursday afternoon he also catechised in the church, street by street, whole families, except the married or more aged, in order. In the remaining five afternoons, from one or two o'clock until seven in the evening, he would adopt the same method more privately. Mrs. Theodosia Alleine says, "In this work, his course was to draw a catalogue of the names of the families in each street, and so to send a day or two before he intended to visit them. Those that sent slight excuses, or did obstinately refuse his message, he would speak some few affectionate words to them, or if he saw cause, denounce the threatenings of God against them that despise His ministers, and so departed ; and after would send letters to them so full of love as did overcome their hearts, and they did many of them afterwards receive him into their houses. Herein was his compassion shown to all sorts, both poor and rich."

Another witness adds, " When he came, and the members of the family were called together, he would first be instructing the younger sort in the principles of religion by asking several questions in the Catechism. Then he would be pressing the practice of them upon their consciences, with the most cogent arguments and considerations, minding them of the great

L

priviledges they did enjoy, the many Gospel-sermons
that they did or might hear, the many talents they
were entrusted withal, and the great account that they
had to give to the God of heaven. Telling them
how sad it would be with them another day, if after
all this they should come short of salvation. Those
that were serious and religious, he would labour to
help forward in holiness, by answering their doubts,
resolving their cases, encouraging them under their
difficulties. And before he did go from any family,
he would deal with the heads of that family, and such
others as were grown to years of discretion, singly
and apart; that so he might (as much as possibly
he could) come to know the condition of each particular person in his flock, and address himself in
his discourse as might be suitable to every of them.
If he did perceive that they did live in the neglect
of family duties, he would exhort and press them
to set up the worship of God in their families, and
directing them how to set about it, and to take
time for secret duties too. Such as were masters of
families, he would earnestly desire, as they did tender
the honour of Christ and the welfare of their children
and servants' souls, to let them have some time every
day for such private duties, and to encourage them
in the performance of them ; neither would he leave
them before he had a promise of them so to do."*

* Account of his catechising, by Mr. John Glanvil, M.A.,
minister of St. James's, Taunton.

After this, every Saturday morning, he catechised the free-school of the place,* "excellently
explaining the answers in the Assembly's Catechism,
discovering a mine of knowledge in them and in
himself."†

While thus careful that all should understand
those doctrines which he himself received, without a
doubt, as the clear dictates of Heaven, he was
equally in earnest that these should be translated
into a resolutely holy and active life. Some
called him a legalist, because, with young and old,
high and low, he was severely practical, both as a
preacher of righteousness and a fearless reprover of
sin. When any person had been detected or
suspected of promise-breaking, deceitful trading, or
of not being diligent in his calling, he would be
sure to hear of it from his minister, whatever the
event might be. "The failings of professors
touched him to the very quick, and brought him
low; drew prayers, tears, and lamentations, both by
word and letter, from him."‡ Life, he told the
people, was not to be spent in saintly reverie, and
"Religion was not a thing that knew only how to
kneel, but not to walk, or work."

---

* The free-school was founded in 1522, by Fox, bishop of
Winchester. Dr. Toulmin, when speaking of a gentleman who
was head master in 1730, says it was the largest provincial school
at that time known in England.

† Portraiture of a Compleat Gospel Minister. ‡ Newton.

" Beyond his labours in that great congregation wherein he was fixed," observes his father-in-law, " the care of many other congregations was daily upon him.   He went forth frequently into several places about the country, among the poor ignorant people that lived in dark corners, and had none to take care of them, and both preached to them himself and stirred up many of his brethren, whose forward minds readily joined with him."

At that time the ministers in the west of England—Episcopal, Presbyterian, and Independent—had formed themselves into an Association for their mutual assistance in the ministry.   This was parted into seven divisions, which met quarterly, and into many sub-divisions which met once in six weeks. In their quarterly meetings, the moderator opened the engagement with a Latin prayer ; then there was a thesis on some question in divinity, and a disputation, in which the ministers present opposed the respondent ; after that would be words of inquiry and advice in relation to the local interests of religion.   All the various divisions had a yearly united meeting at Exeter.*   Mr. Alleine's influ-

---

* Calamy's Account, vol. ii., p. 227.   The writer would here say, that there is every evidence short of the most distinct assertion that the Ministers' Association, of which Alleine was a conspicuous member, was that of which Calamy has given an account as above. He thinks it clear enough to be assumed as certain.   Palmer says that amongst the many episcopal ministers who belonged to it

ence with the ministers thus convened was great. On one occasion, after a debate on the best methods of promoting family instruction in their respective charges, he was appointed to prepare a paper on the subject, which was afterwards printed. On another occasion he advised his brethren to set apart the two hours immediately before eight o'clock every Monday morning for special prayer secretly, or in concert with selected friends, on behalf of the church and the nation. This rule, originating with him, and supported by the sanction of the western ministers, was observed for many years by Nonconformists far and wide,—it was observed in London, and the practice extended even to Wales.*

It may be wondered how so young a man could have wielded so much power. There were several reasons for it. One source of his power was his own character, which drew expressions of respect from the most reluctant lips. " The tongues of all did pay tribute to his good name, which was

---

were—Drs. Hutchinson, Gandy, Fulwood, Ashton ; Messrs. Ackland and Banks.—Nonconformist Mem., vol. ii., p. 391. Voluntary associations of Episcopal, Presbyterian, and Independent ministers were also formed in other places. For an account of one in Shropshire, see P. Henry's Life, 1698, p. 60. For a reference to one in Lancashire, see Life of Heywood, by Joseph Hunter, F.S.A., p. 109.

* Among other references to this, see P. Henry's Life, p. 151.

a thing so entire and sacred that scarce a Rab-shakeh or a Shimei could find a passage to invade it." "He was both a first table-man and a second table-man—that is, his religion had constant respect both to God and man; and much as he loved hours of divine communion, he was not so much in the mount with God as not also to come down to his neighbour, whom he did accost as Moses, with both tables in his hand, on which his life and doctrine did constantly and excellently comment."

Another source of his power was his own assurance of his divine calling as a minister. Evidently, if a thing so extravagant could visit the imagination, as that in the changes of life the magistracy should ever say to him, "Be silent; it is against the law for you to speak—you are not a minister;" the effect would be much the same as in olden time it would have been, if the civil government had told Elijah that he was not a prophet. This belief in his commission made every thing he did bold and impressive. Confidence begets confidence. All felt its effect. He was young, but every moment he seemed to hear a voice from heaven say, "These things do, and speak with all authority. Let no man despise thee;" —and no man did.

Another secret of his power was the charm of his presence. "He was tall and erect, with a counte-nance sprightly and serene, yet with such an inde-

scribable gravity and look of command, resulting
from a mind ever in awe before God, that his very
look struck an awe on all with whom he conversed,
and composed them to a true decorum. So that
as reverend Mr. Bolton, when walking the streets,
was so much clothed with majesty that the notice
of his coming in these words—'Here comes Mr.
Bolton!'—would, as it were, charm people into
order when vain or doing amiss; so this most grave
divine, wheresoever he came, was as a walking
spirit, by his presence conjuring them into a grave
deportment, his countenance ever pointing out his
awful soul. What the image of Sennacherib did
speak, much more did this lively image of the most
high God speak: 'He who looketh to me, let him
be religious.'"*

Another spell that he had was his known generosity. His aged father, and divers of his brethren
with their large families, being fallen into decay,
he gave pensions to some, portions to others,
education to the rest. He gave much alms daily.
When trade was low, he would give beyond his ability
to assist godly tradesmen to recover their standing.
Pease and flitches of bacon would he buy for distribution twice in the year in the severe weather.
Several children did he keep at school at his own

---

* Abridged from " An entire and exact Delineation of this holy
Person."

cost, bought many books and catechisms, had many
thousands of prayers printed and circulated ; gave
largely to the assistance of poor ministers, and took
many journeys to the gentry in the country on
their behalf; partly by his own gifts, and partly by
exciting the liberality of others, established lecture-
ships in the dark villages.   Every remarkable
mercy was acknowledged by a " thankoffering" in
the shape of a special donation to the poor.   There
seems to have been some alchemy required to conjure all these golden results out of a minister's
income; but it should be remembered that his
resources were at this time greatly augmented by
his wife's school.   All that we would say is, that
he appears to have been generous to the last limit
of possibility.*

In this life of almost seraphic ministry, that
seemed to ask no recreation and to know no pause,
he yet found time for scholastic labours scarcely
less remarkable.   At the oak lectern in his library
he studied the Fathers, became acquainted with
much of the learning contained in more than one
living language, and through his peculiar skill in
" the three languages which Christ sanctified at the
Cross,"† unlocked many a treasure of ancient

---

* Accounts by Mr Newton, Mr. R. Alleine, Mrs. Theodosia,
and others.

† Ludovicus Vivos.

thought. Some results of these explorings were given in a work on the harmony between revelation and nature, as shown by a comparison between the doctrines of Scripture and those of ancient philosophers. The work was in Latin, and was entitled " Theologia Philosophica. 1. De cognitione Dei. 2. De Existentia Dei. 3. De Nominibus et Substantia Dei. 4. De Attributis Dei in Genere, et Speciatim de ejus unitate. 5. De Perfectione Divina. 6. De Decretis Divinis. 7. De Providentia Divina. 8. De Cultu Divino de Precibus." " In all which," remarks his friend Richard Baxter, " he delivereth, in a very good Latin style, the Christian doctrine ; and then, by way of annotations, addeth the testimony of the philosophers . . . . such a promptuary for any one who hath not leisure to peruse, or to gather for such particular uses the philosophers themselves, that I know not where you can find the like. For every sheet or two of his doctrine on the subject, you have eight, ten, twelve, or more sheets of collected attestations."

Only one volume of this work received the author's final touches, and was licensed for the press ; and the following is its title-page :—" Theologiæ Philosophicæ, sive Philosophiæ Theologicæ specimen : In quo Æterni Dei Providentia solius Naturæ lumine comprobatur, validissimis rationum momentis demonstratur, quoad Partes, Species,

Objecta, et explicatur; contra omnes denique adversariorum Objectiones firmatur; ex Aristotele, Platone, Chalcidio, Sallustio, Firmico, Empirico, Jamblico, Antonino, Epicteto, Proclo, Simplicio, Cicerone, Seneca, Macrobio, Porphyrio, Xenophonte, Galeno, Plutarcho, Plotino, Tyrio, Apuleio, Alcinoo, aliisque Philosophis, Oratoribus et Poetis, tum Græcis tum Latinis, ad Atheorum convictionem, et Orthodoxorum confirmationem; Elucubratione J. A., anno dom. 1661."

These manuscripts were never printed, and are now lost; but speaking of the evidences they gave of the writer's profound capacity, and wide classical reading, Baxter says, " All these in a man so young, as unless in one Giovanni Pico Della Miranola, one Keckermann, one Pemble, in a country, are rarely to be found."*

Yet he was not a mere man of books. His acquaintance with some of the patriarchs of the Royal Society, who were then busily collecting the facts which other ages were more fully to interpret and classify, kindled in his mind an interest in

---

* It is believed that this manuscript was in the possession of the Rev. Dr Toulmin, and shared the fate of the doctor's papers. The Rev. Arthur Jones, of Taunton, writes : " All Dr. Toulmin's MSS. were lost in the wreck of the vessel in which they were being conveyed to America, to Judge Harry Toulmin, the son of the doctor. The house of the same Judge Toulmin was afterwards burnt down by accident, and his library destroyed."

science. One of his friends notices "his considerable skill in anatomy, acquired by frequent dissections ; this," he continues, " led him to compose, with Galen, hymns to the Creator, whose infinite wisdom, displayed in wonders herein disclosed, he was often heard to admire."

Minds, like fields, need a rotation of crops to keep them from becoming wastes of exhausted soil. Collateral studies increase the working power of a minister, and tend to give freshness, variety, and striking life to his teachings. It was so here ; but there were persons in the congregation who thought differently. They looked with disfavour on their minister's short excursions into the regions of science, poetry, and classical reading, for they dimly feared that such pursuits robbed them of something, and that the time thus occupied was so much time taken from duty. Unhappily, wiseacres like these are still to be seen here and there in the land of the living. Let us hope that the day is at hand when we shall only know them as fossil memorials of an extinct species, shelved amongst our historical curiosities.

Another of his habits claims our special notice, for we may discover in it the foundation of his life's efficiency. "At the time of his health," writes his wife, "he did rise constantly at or before four of the clock ; and would be much troubled if he heard smiths or other craftsmen at work at their trades, before he

was at communion with God : saying to me often,
' How this noise shames me ! Doth not my Master
deserve more than theirs ?' *   From four till eight
he spent in prayer, holy contemplation, and singing
of psalms, in which he much delighted, and did
daily practice alone, as well as in his family."
Sometimes he would suspend the routine of parochial engagements, and devote whole days to these
secret exercises, in order to which, he would contrive to be alone in some void house, or else in some
sequestered spot in the open valley. Here there
would be much prayer, much meditation on God
and heaven. Baxter's " Saints' Everlasting Rest"
was a common " companion of his solitude ;" and
such was the vehement heavenliness of his spirit
that his favourite employment was praise. We
could scarcely find a more eminent example of
thankfulness under all the vicissitudes of a troubled
career. It was the peculiar grace and light of his
life. Nearly all the scattered notices of him found
in the letters of his survivors contain allusions to it.
" The greater part of his public devotions con-
sisted of thanksgiving." He was never so much
in his element in preaching as when extolling the
marvellous love of God in Christ ; neither did
he forget to sound forth the praise of His

---

* An expression perhaps suggested by the saying imputed to
Demosthenes.

perfections in His works, as witnessed in the fields
and woods, and he has been often heard to
say, " Man is the tongue of the whole creation,
appointed as the creature's interpreter, to speak
forth and make articulate the praises which they
but silently intimate." * " He did delight in his
devotions to converse with the fowls of the air, and
the beasts of the field, with streams and plants did
he delight to talk, and all these did utter in his
attentive ear the praise and knowledge of his
Creator ; afterwards, in his unsettled sojournings
from place to place, he did often (to use his own
words) look back with sweetness and great content
on the places of his former pleasant retirements,
setting, as it were, a mark on those which had
marvellously pleased him in his solitudes, by ad-
ministering to his contemplative delight." †

He had a poet's enjoyment of nature, but only
along with a Puritan's love of the Bible. Every scene
was looked upon in the light of the sacred page ;
and he indulged in no imaginations but such as
were vividly biblical. While alive to all the num-
berless changes of morning music and beauty, he
felt yet more alive to the higher realities of which
they reminded him. When on his way home from
early prayer in the woods, he stood still in the
rapture of peace to watch the orchard trees crowned

* Life, p. 131.   † Ibid.

with the foam of blossoms, he would all the while
be saying to himself, "As the apple tree among
the trees of the wood, so is my beloved among the
sons." Stopping, light-hearted, at other times, with
the glee of a child to listen to the lark, to peer
into a bird's nest in the hedge, to shake the rain
out of a rose, or to notice the gossamer as it lay
laced across the sparkling grass; he would only be
consciously thinking of the "Rose of Sharon," the
"Dew of Israel," the "Sun of Righteousness," or of
the promises, the thought of which Christ has
connected with the sight of the "fowls of the air,"
the "grass of the field," or the array of the lilies
in more than Solomon's glory. We know that
there are other springs of pure pleasure in God's
works, and other lessons to be read there, besides
those found by Alleine; but if we all found as
much as he did, our hearts would be larger and
happier than they are. It is not altogether owing
to a truer philosophy that we fail to find in creation
remembrancers of texts and types of things divine.
If, indeed, we believe that creation and redemption
are both wrought by one Mediator, and are parts
of one great system, it is not inconceivable that the
first work should be constructed in subservient
reference to the highest and last,—that it should
be filled with Christian emblems and cyphers, waiting to be interpreted by each prepared spirit, under
the guidance of the "more sure word of prophecy;"

and that although nature is not commissioned
to preach the Gospel to the lost, it should be full
of evangelical meaning to the saved. Let us take
heed that we are not ruled by a principle more
narrow and realistic than that at which we smile.

These were days of rare happiness. He was
happy in his hours of holy thought; happy in the
calm society of books; happy in his labours.
Could you have seen him, after his hours of solitude,
enjoy the hour of cheerful converse and peaceful
devotion with his family, and then, " rejoicing like
a strong man to run his race," go forth to the work
of the day, you would have thought that the time
of his ministry at Taunton Magdalene was the
Sabbath of his life.

Chapter VIII.

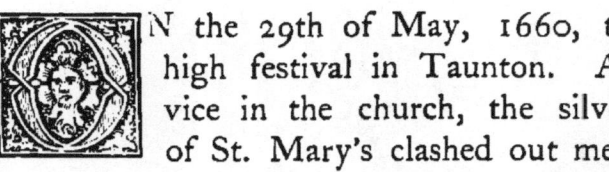

The Act of Uniformity.

" O sacred Peace ! whither art thou fled ?
What region hides thy drooping head ?
Fled from the Church, fled from the State,
Fled from the poor, fled from the great !

Peace for the wicked ne'er was known ;
But peace is now from Zion flown,
Driven to the deserts and the woods,
And there pursued by dragon-floods !"

UNKNOWN WRITER OF THE SEVENTEENTH CENTURY.

N the 29th of May, 1660, there was high festival in Taunton. After service in the church, the silvery bells of St. Mary's clashed out merrily, the guns of the castle boomed, the streets were alive with clamorous crowds, banners and oak boughs waved everywhere, joy was on every face and in every voice, for the King had come " to enjoy his own again." This is only mentioned as a sample

of the delight that burst forth through the length
and breadth of merry England soon as the event
became known. It was not known everywhere at
once ; news travelled slowly in those days ; and
there were towns in which the bells were not set
ringing until a fortnight after the proper date,—
the surprising discovery having then been suddenly
made.

By degrees, unfolding from this event, grew a
train of consequences so important to our history
that this chapter must be separately devoted to
their recital ; therefore, parting company with
Alleine for a few moments, and reserving for the
present all matters relating exclusively to Taunton,
we must now look at the " Act of Uniformity,"
tracing it from some of its springs to some of its
outfalls.

Generally speaking, the Puritans were attached
to the monarchy. Its overthrow had been occasioned, not by them, but by the late misguided
King ; and when, after that, confusion followed confusion, and there was no way out of the maze until
Oliver Cromwell rose to the supreme executive, the
new rule was accepted by them, not as the best in
itself, but as the best the case would allow. On
the death of that great magistrate, most were
willing, and many were eager, that Government
should return to its former course, and wear its
ancient symbols ;—there seemed, indeed, to be no

M

alternative but this or anarchy. There seemed also
to be now no fear that its re-establishment would
bring any danger to their dearly-bought liberties ;
for, surely, the King had been taught to respect
these by his father's fate, and by his own adversity.
Some, indeed, boded evil from the fact that his
companions in adversity had been his father's evil
counsellors,—some of the very men whose advice
had urged on that illegal exercise of prerogative
which had led inevitably to the revolution,—

> " Of a tall stature and a sable hue,
>   Much like the son of Kish, that lofty Jew,
>   Ten years of need he suffered in exile,
>   And kept his father's asses all the while." *

The ministers were more hopeful, perhaps because they were more loyal—it was to their influence, very largely, that King Charles owed the
happy turn in his fortunes ; † and it was the candid
saying of a church dignitary after the restoration,
that " if the Nonconformist ministers could not
drink the King's health, they helped to pray him
to his throne." ‡   He had lately still further won
their hearts, good souls! by putting on signs of
piety.   He had sent over from Breda a proclamation " against debauchery and profaneness."   When
several of their number attended as a deputation

---

* Andrew Marvell.
† Baxter's Life, p. 216.
‡ Conformist's Plea for the Nonconformists, p. 37.

from the Lords and Commons to invite him back
to England, it was their happiness one morning,
while waiting at his command in an antechamber,
to overhear him at his prayers, in which " he
thanked God that he was a covenanted king ; and
hoped that the Lord would give him a humble,
meek, forgiving spirit, that he might have forbearance to his offending subjects, as he expected
forbearance from Heaven."* Upon which, old
Mr. Case, one of their number, lifted up his hands
to heaven, and blessed God.† He had also sent
a declaration granting a general pardon to all his
loving subjects who should lay hold of it within
forty days, except such as should be excepted by
Parliament. " We do also declare," said he, " a
liberty to tender consciences, and that no man
shall be disquieted or called in question for differences of opinion in matters of religion which do
not disturb the peace of the kingdom."‡ With
regard to the structural arrangements of the church
the Presbyterians were willing to make large con-
cessions; and they expected to be comprehended
with others in a church-scheme after the model
suggested by Archbishop Usher, in which the main
points of difference between them and the Episco-

---

* Crosby's History of Baptists, vol. i., p. 357.
† Palmer, vol. ii., p. 43.
‡ Lord Somers' Collections, 4to., 1795, p. 349.

palians should be left open.   " In things essential,
unity ; in things indifferent, liberty ; in all things
charity."   In these expectations they were sustained
by the result of the conferences which they had
invited with Dr. Morley and the chief clergy.
But these gentlemen meantime were receiving their
secret instructions from Chancellor Hyde, who thus
wrote to them from Breda :—" The King very
well approves that Dr. Morley and some of his
brethren should enter into conferences with the
Presbyterian party, in order to reduce them to such a
temper as is consistent with the good of the church ;
and it may be no ill expedient to assure them
of present good preferments ; but, in my opinion,
you should rather endeavour to win over those,
who, being recovered, will both have reputation and
desire to merit from the church, than be over-
solicitous to comply with the pride and passion of
those who propose extravagant things."*

On the occasion of his triumphal entry into
London, his majesty was pleased still further to
dulcify the Presbyterians, by receiving from their
aged spokesman, Mr. Arthur Jackson, a richly-
embossed Bible,—declaring, as he did so, " that he
intended to make that blessed book the rule of his
conduct ; assuring the ministers, at the same time,
that he attributed his restoration, under God, to

---

* Life of Dr. Barwick, p. 525.

their prayers and endeavours."* He also admitted ten of their number into the list of his Court chaplains, and, "for once a martyr to the public good, submitted himself to the penalty of hearing four of their sermons. That with which Baxter greeted him, could not have been recited by the most rapid voice in less than two hours. It is a solemn contrast of the sensual and the spiritual life, without one courtly phrase to relieve his censure of the vices of the great."†

The opening of the new reign was a morning full of promise, but after a few hours, threatening clouds began to gather. First, an Act was passed for restoring the sequestered clergy to their livings. All ought to allow that it was only a righteous thing to restore the worthy men who had been ejected simply on account of their conscientious objection to Cromwell's government; but it must be borne in mind, that great numbers of the sequestered were utterly unworthy of the clerical station, and had been displaced from it simply on account of infamous incompetency or vice. As Christian legislators, the framers of the Act felt that there were some who could not be reinstated with propriety. Even royal charity must have its limits,—a line must be drawn somewhere. Many

---

* Conformist's Fourth Plea, 4to., 1683, p. 69.
† Sir James Stephen.

of the old clergy were still objects of popular
derision for their illiteracy, or for their tavern-
haunting propensities, but these were not unpardon-
able sins.   Others, however, of the unhappy men
had so degenerated since their ejection, that they
had actually professed republican politics ; and,
such is human nature when left to itself, there were
others who had gone so far as to become Baptists !
These two extreme offences were not to be forgiven ; but besides these two things, nothing
" scandalous " was recognized as a bar to restoration.   It was therefore enacted, that " Every
sequestered minister who has not justified the late
King's murder, or declared against infant baptism,
shall be restored to his living before the 25th of
December next ensuing, and the present incumbent shall peaceably quit it, and be accountable for
dilapidations, and all arrears of fifths not paid."
By this Act, " some hundreds of Nonconformist
ministers were dispossessed of their livings in the
first year of the King's reign," " but in every instance
where the old incumbent was dead, the living was
confirmed to the actual possessor."*

The clouds grew darker.   Soon as the clergy
were in their old places again, they loudly lauded
the King's Act of Oblivion; but sometimes in a way

---

* Neale ; Toulmin's edition, vol. iii., p. 40.   See also Henry
Jessey's " Loud Call," p. 2.

not the best adapted to advance its avowed object.
Sunday after Sunday, before the King, before the
judges, on great occasions as well as in the regular
course of their ministry, did they minutely enume-
rate the things that were to be forgotten, and
lengthily expatiate on the enormities that were to
be forgiven. Take, as one instance out of many,
an Assize Sermon, preached by Dr. Creede on
September 6, 1660 :—

"I am resolved, in imitation of the King's unparalleled Act of grace and perpetual oblivion, not
to meddle with any persons or parties concerned in
that Act. . . . . The instruments of all our
miseries could never have been able to have done
anything against us, unless God had not only given
them in charge, but assisted them to do it. We
blame their pride, and covetousness, and ambition,
and we do not amiss. But our spoils and plunder
were the wages God bestowed upon them for their
service ; and they were God's hirelings when they
knew it not, and only designed to serve their lusts
and obey their own ambition. Even heathen
Cyrus was God's anointed, though he was ignorant
of Him. . . . . This should help us to
bury our animosities on all sides. Consider we,
that they have been God's instruments, His fire
and hammer to break us for the furnace, and melt
us from our dross and tin. The Devil, God's
excutioner, and wicked men his substitutes" (such

as Newton and Alleine), " are all but in a chain.
. . . . Though God put you into the melting-
pot, yet it was not your just crimes, but your
steadfastness and constancy in your adherence to
the King and the laws, and the primitive doctrine
and discipline of the church, threw you out of your
places and callings."*

These exhortations to forgetfulness were not
successful ; indeed, they seemed rather to exasperate
party remembrances than otherwise. The Puritans
were betrayed, but they ought not to have been
surprised. They never had been, and they never
could be, really popular,—their religion was altogether unfitted to be the instrument of the State.
It was not in human nature for the clergy to regard
them with anything but a retaliative spirit, after
enduring so much provocation at their hands.
When, therefore, they had assisted to place the
King upon the throne, they were no more wanted,
and were to be treated henceforth only as a defeated
faction.

---

* Judah's Purging in the Melting-Pot : a Sermon preached in the
Cathedral at Sarum, before the Rev. Sir Robert Foster, and Sir
Thomas Tyrell, Knights, Judges for the Western Circuit, at the
Wiltshire Assizes, Sept. 6, 1660. By W. Creede, D.D., Arch-
deacon of Wilts, and Canon-Resident of Sarum. Dedicated to the
above Knights and the Justices of Peace in the County of Wilts.
Dr. Creede was a man of great influence. See the Kennett Collec-
tion, Lansdowne MSS., 986.

The sky was lowering every moment. In 1661, an Act was passed for "The better regulating of Corporations," the effect of which was to expel all the Nonconformists from the various branches of the magistracy; and before the close of the following year, not a municipal officer was left who was not entirely devoted to "church and king." * John Bunyan was watching all this, and in the "Holy War" we are told how Diabolus remodelled the captured town of Mansoul, turning out Mr. Conscience the recorder, and bringing in a new set of aldermen and burgesses.

As a consequence of this measure, and through the appointment of justices who asserted the principle that "the old laws returned with the King," the ministers were treated as men who held an illegal and therefore undefended office. They were insulted in the streets, they could not even worship God in their own dwellings without liability to interruption by persons blowing horns, or flinging stones at their windows; and there was little chance of redress. Their public ministry was open to still greater disturbance, and although the discipline of the church was understood by those in highest authority to be in suspension, they were continually hearing of old friends being sequestered from their livings,

---

* Neale, vol. iii., p 4.

and cited into ecclesiastical courts for not using the surplice in the ceremonies. In March, 1662, the grand jury at Exeter found bills of indictment against more than forty eminent ministers, for not reading common prayer. The diaries of ministers who were not deprived, abound at this time in entries like these :—

"Strong reports I should not be suffered to preach to-day; but I did; and no disturbance. Blessed be God, who hath my enemies in a chain !"

"In despite of my enemies, the Lord hath granted the liberty of one Sabbath more. To Him be praise."

"Common Prayer-book tendered again. Lord, they devise wicked devices against me ; but in thee do I put my trust. Father, forgive them !"

"They took the cushion from me, but the pulpit was left. Blessed be God !"

"Day of preparation for the sacrament. . . . . The good Lord pardon ! Full of fears lest we should be hindered ; for our adversaries bite the lip at us."

"Through the good hand of God upon us, we have this day enjoyed one sweet Sabbath more. They did us all the hinderance they could ; but, notwithstanding, we proceeded."*

---

* Passages from Philip Henry's Diary in 1661 and 1662.

All through the two years immediately following the renewal of monarchy in England, the Independents and Baptists, especially those who had not been included in the ecclesiastical framework of the State, only petitioned for toleration ; but the Presbyterians, who were already thus included, and who still desired to be so, were occupied in unceasing conferences with the men in power, hoping to gain their consent to a system so modified as to admit of their own continued comprehension within its pale. After many fair but evasive speeches, the King appointed a meeting between them and the diocesan clergy to consider the possibility of such a comprehension. They met at the Savoy, on the 25th of March, 1661, and after a discussion drawn through four months, episcopal tactics brought this clerical tourney to a feeble if not a ludicrous close—"a conclusion in which nothing was concluded."

Before the Savoy conference was over, the two houses of convocation assembled. On the 20th of November, by the authority of the King, and also, it was pretended, by the request of the Presbyterians, they commenced the revision of the Prayer-book and the forms of ordination, in order to fix the standard of uniform worship. Clarendon was the secret ruler of the proceedings, but the chief agents here, as at the Savoy, were Bishops Sheldon and Morley ; and Burnet says that, in reality, everything was directed by them.* These men were vehement representatives of the party that aimed to place the crown above the laws, and the church above the crown. It is also notorious that Sheldon was a man of profligate character, and a rival of rakes like Sedley in eccentricities of degrading vice.† It was therefore easy to foresee the result of this council, and after the labours of a month, the result came forth.

A list had been given them of the liturgical changes which the Presbyterians desired ; but although, according to Tenison, afterwards archbishop of Canterbury, about six hundred small alterations or additions were made,—according to Burnet, " care was taken that nothing should be altered as it had been moved by the Presbyterians, for it was resolved to gratify them in nothing."‡ It was known that no Presbyterian minister could confess the nullity of his previous ministrations, or allow that his ministry could have two beginnings ; § therefore, contrary to the decision of Archbishop

---

* Burnet's History of his Own Times, vol. i., p. 184.

† Diary of Mr. Pepys ; Bohn's Edition, vol. iv., 29th July, 1667.

‡ Burnet, vol. i., p. 183.

§ " Pray, Sir," said the bishop of Exeter to John Howe, " what hurt is there in being twice ordained ?" " Hurt, my lord," rejoined he ; " it hurts my understanding ; the thought is shocking ; it is an absurdity, since nothing can have two beginnings. I am sure I am a minister of Christ, and am ready to debate that matter with you, if your lordship pleases, but I cannot begin again to be a minister."

Grindal and the first English churchmen,—contrary to the statute and practice which, at the close of the sixteenth century, allowed scores if not hundreds of clergymen to officiate in the English church who had not been ordained episcopally, they now denied the validity of the orders of all who had been ordained during the last twenty years, and required every man who had been thus ordained to make the same virtual denial, by submitting to episcopal ordination on pain of being deprived of his benefice. It was known that the Puritans disliked the saints' days,—" In 1604 and 1662 the legendary storehouses of Rome were ransacked . . . . . and the feelings of the Puritan party were wantonly outraged by the insertion of the names of fifty or sixty of the mythical or semi-historical heroes of monkish legend . . . . and the names of a few Popes were considerately included in the list." It was known that they objected to the apocryphal lessons,—the bishops therefore added another, containing the story of " Bel and the Dragon." It was known that they objected to the sacerdotal and sacramental theories of the Prayer-book,—consequently, " all the matters about which they scrupled were now made prominent, and a coherence and systematic consistency were for the first time given to those sacerdotal and sacramental theories which had previously existed in the Prayer-book only in an embryotic condition ; and certain dogmas, which, by

the moderation of the reformers, had been couched
in vague and general terms, were now expressed in
ample and emphatic phraseology."*   It was known
that the aim of the Presbyterian section of the
Puritans was to make the church of England com-
prehend all who hold essentially the common faith
of Christians.   The aim of the bishops was to
make this comprehension impossible,—at least it
was resolved to exclude every Puritan.   " It is to
be called a *comprehensive* church," said the bishop
of Ely, when preaching before the King; " though
I think it might better be called a *drag-net*—a
Trojan horse with a comprehensive belly."   To
prevent such a profanation, he and his brethren
studied to incorporate into the Prayer-book things
new and old, to which the Puritans most strongly
objected; and next, they demanded not merely the
promise of conformity to all these in practice, but,
what is a very different thing, the profession of
conformity in principle—conformity the most full,
distinct, and particular—" unfeigned assent and
consent to all and everything contained and prescribed in and by the Book of Common Prayer."
The present organic forms of the church of
England, therefore, owe their very existence to a
protest against the doctrine of comprehension.
When the earl of Manchester told the King that

---

* The Liturgy and the Dissenters, by the Rev. Isaac Taylor, M.A.

the proposed terms of conformity were so hard that
he feared many who were now ministers would not
be able to comply ; " I am afraid they will," said
Sheldon ; " but now we know their minds, we will
make them all knaves if they conform."

This work of re-constructing the Prayer-book
having been effected, it was sent to the King and
his council, and from thence transmitted with the
seal of his majesty's approval to the houses of legis-
lature that it might pass into law.

Meanwhile, the course of proceedings was felt to
be impeded by the royal promise from Breda that
" no man should be disquieted or called into question for differences in religious matters not disturb-
ing the peace of the kingdom." To remedy this
inconvenience, reports were circulated of a general
insurrection on the part of the Nonconformists.
By forged letters and secret agency they were charged
with plots laid in thirty-six different counties.
Undoubtedly, a spirit of passionate opposition to
Government was simmering in many parts of
England, and documents in the State Paper Office
show that there was a readiness on the part of a
few to fight for liberty again. But this was confined to members of the disbanded army, and to
separatists who repudiated the connexion of the
church with the State. The charge, as brought
against the Presbyterians, was a transparent fiction ;
but, fiction as it was, it suited the temper of the

times, stung the mob to fury, and furnished a pretext for the intended Act. *

At length, by a majority of six votes, the Commons passed the Bill for " the uniformity of public prayer, and administration of sacraments, and other rites and ceremonies," &c., &c., in the church of England. After much discussion, the Lords concurred ;—on May the 19th it received the royal assent, and was ordered, by strange fatality or daring defiance, to take effect from the feast of St. Bartholomew, August 24, 1662. One of the provisions of this Act was, " that before St. Bartholomew's day, every parson, vicar, or other minister whatsoever, should, on pain of deprival, declare openly and publicly his unfeigned assent and consent to everything contained in the Book of Common Prayer, to renounce the solemn league and covenant, to acknowledge that the oath taken to maintain it involved no moral obligation, and, further, to declare that it was unlawful, under any pretence, to take up arms against the King." † Those who were not clergymen, but only teachers,

---

* Ample information respecting these sham plots may be found in the writings of Baxter, Oliver Heywood, Calamy, Rapin, John Locke, and also in Captain Yarrington's narrative, exposing the forgery, published in 1681. This last book I have not seen, but great stress is laid upon it by Calamy in the first volume of his Account, and also in his Letter to Archdeacon Echard, 1718, p. 20.

† The clause about the covenant was only in force until 1682. The clause about taking up arms against the King was suspended in 1688.

were, in case of non-compliance with the Act, to be visited with heavy penalties. It was further ordered that a copy of the revised service-book should be printed and sent to every minister recognized by law, before the day appointed for giving it effect; but the issue from the press was so late, that not one in ten had an opportunity of seeing it. At the hour of decision, therefore, the large majority declared their "unfeigned assent and consent to all and everything" in a book which they had not seen.* About three thousand refused to subscribe; and when the terms of subscription were fully known, about two thousand of these took their final station in the ranks of Nonconformity.† Thus the cloud burst, and the long-threatened rush of desolation came at last.

The history of the two thousand men, who in this way "nobly acted what they nobly thought," was henceforth one of peril and solemn sorrow. Their loss of worldly means, their constant liability to persecution, and the consequent necessity of studying every method of concealment consistent

---

* "Not one in forty could have seen it."—Locke's Works, vol. x., pp. 203, 204.

† Baxter puts the number of the ejected and deprived as from 1,800 to 2,000 —Life, p. 384. Calamy gives it as 2,400, including fellows of colleges not in orders. A catalogue in Dr. Williams's library gives 2,257 names. A manuscript by Oliver Heywood gives 2,500.

with their convictions of duty, made all this in-
evitable.

Some died broken-hearted; some left the country;
some became physicians; others, famous once, became private tutors, and were heard of in the world
no more.*   Many, with their families, had to
exchange a life of refinement and competency for
a life on the verge of starvation, gentlemen and
scholars as they were.   Many had to adopt the
calling of farm-servants or artisans.   Let one
instance be accepted as a specimen.   The lady of
a country squire was dangerously ill.   The clergyman was sent for, but returned word that " he was
going out with the hounds, and would come when
the hunt was over."   " Sir," said one of the
servants to the afflicted husband, " our shepherd,
if you will send for him, can pray very well; we
have often heard him pray in the field."   The
shepherd was immediately summoned to the side
of the sufferer, and prayed with such astonishing
pertinency and fervour, that when he rose from
his knees, the gentleman said to him, " I conjure
you to inform me who and what you. are, and what
were your views and situation in life before you
came into my service ?"   Upon which he told him
" that he was one of the ministers ejected from
the church, and that having nothing of his own

---

* Ἢ τέθνηκεν ἢ διδάσκει γράμματα.

left, he was content for a livelihood to submit to
the honest and peaceful employment of keeping
sheep."* The good man was an Oxford master
of arts; in better days he had been noted as a
Hebraist, and had been much revered by his
brethren for his varied excellencies of mind and life.
Several of his beautiful letters written in those days
may be seen in Dr. Williams's library, and one of
them seems to show that we owe to his suggestion
Baxter's valuable autobiography.

Some of these confessors were too old to support themselves by such new modes of labour.
The writer of these pages has before him a manuscript written by one of them in the winter after
his ejection.† He was then in his seventy-ninth
year, and had been for fifty years the honoured
minister of his parish, but now he was a wanderer,
without means of subsistence. He had been
spoken of as " one of the most eminent preachers
of any age;" but just before writing this letter,
one of the magistrates had plucked his grey beard,
and insulted him with epithets too foul to be

---

* Peter Ince, of Brazenose College. This well-known story was
communicated to Mr. Palmer by Mr. Josiah Thompson, who had
often heard it related by Mr. Bates, an aged minister at Warminster.
—Dr Rippon's Register, vol. iv., p. 338. The name of the country
gentleman is there given as Grove; but this must have been a mistake,
as Mr. Grove was a celebrated Wiltshire gentleman, mentioned in the
Baxter MSS. as Mr. Ince's friend in the days of his prosperity.

† Elkanah Wales, A.M , Trinity College, Cambridge.

repeated.   It was no longer safe for him to remain in the district where he was known, and the rest of his days had to be spent amongst strangers ; yet his spirit was fresh and joyous as ever, and he could still write of himself and his wife as follows :—
" We are in tollerable case for bodily health, save that this sharp, piercing weather doth pinch us and make us shrink ; but I hope after a little time it will grow warmer, and the air will become more calm and favourable to old, colde, thinne boddys."

Most of these pastors felt that no human authority could free them from their ordination vows.   Through the years of persecution occasioned by the Act of Uniformity, and the successive penal enactments made to enforce it, they still assembled their scattered flocks for prayer.   Such meetings would be convened by the Bristol pastors in some secluded spot under the open sky, far away from the city, the congregation sometimes drenched with the rain, sometimes standing in the deep December snow.*   The Puritans at Andover met in a dell four miles from the town, or in a private residence which they would enter when their neighbours were asleep, and then, having fastened the door and window-shutters, and even extinguished the candle-light, lest its flicker might be discovered through a crevice by some spy without,—they con-

---

* Broadmead Records.

tinued in prayer until the ray of dawn, slanting
down the chimney, warned them away.*   Flavel's
congregation met at midnight in the hall of Hud-
scot Manor-house; other congregations met at the
same hour in woods.   All were in peril, but that
of their leaders was of course the greatest.   Habited
like a husbandman, with a fork on his shoulder
and a Bible in his pocket, the venerable Richard
Chantyre used to set out in the twilight to his
distant conventicle, thus contriving to evade the
informers for years.†   Other ministers adopted
similar disguise; but, after every expedient for
secrecy and escape, there were few of these brave
men who had not to suffer from hunger or the
chain.

This Act still stands unchanged.   To change it
in any essential respect would be to shake the very
foundations of Anglican episcopacy, for it is the
political rock on which the church is built.   No
wonder, therefore, that the Act itself should still
have its defenders; but we may well be surprised to
find, as we do, that many good men still defend the
very way in which it was first carried into effect.
One of its modern apologists, having spoken of it as

---

* Pearsall's Rise of Congregationalism at Andover, p. 94.
† Nonconformist's Memorial, vol. iii., p. 244. Many facts like
those just cited may be found in the above-mentioned works, and
many more in the various records of old Nonconformist churches,
as also in family papers and traditions.

"absolutely necessary," adds, "on the passing of this Act *only* 2,000 ministers who had appropriated to themselves the livings of the church, refused to conform. These 2,000 are much to be respected for having acted on conscientious motives; they followed the example which had been set them in the time of the rebellion by 7,000 clergy of the church of England. The excuse for the Government after the restoration is,. that their conduct to the Nonconformists was lenient compared with that of the Presbyterians and Independents, when in power, towards the members of the church."* This language of a distinguished living clergyman is not meant to be unfair. It does but describe the transaction as it is set forth in all the books from which men educated within the charmed circle of State orthodoxy, gain their knowledge of it. But even if, for the sake of argument, we admit the justice of his views, first, as to the province of the magistrate in matters of religion, and then, as to the duty of the State to establish episcopacy alone; it strikes us as strange that such an accomplished historian should have fallen into the mistakes as to fact which disfigure this statement. We are obliged to think there is a mistake as to the fact of *numbers.* Every reader should know that Walker, whose work on the sufferings of the clergy is the ultimate

---

* Hook's Ecclesiastical Biography. Art. Alleine.

authority for nearly every assertion like this, has
been convicted of often reckoning each clerical
dignity and place as a separate clerical individual,
—that, for instance, if one clergyman possessed
four dignities, these would be reckoned as four
distinct sufferers—that the like is observable in the
case of pluralists—and that by this ingenious method
the chronicler has conjured up an army nearly
8,000 strong.* Calamy says that we can only
reckon about 1,700 whose sequestration was certain and undoubted; and the facts and calculations
given by him and others of equally high credit, in
support of such an estimate, should at least qualify
our willingness to take on trust the statements of
the romantic Dr. Walker. It is a mistake to speak
of all the sequestered clergy as *sufferers for conscience in reference to religion.* Only a few were
displaced for refusing the covenant, the one simply
religious test; the large majority suffered on fair,
evidence for vice, insufficiency, or resistance to
Government. Martyrs indeed they were; but if
we may believe a royalist looker-on, "Martyrs for
Venus and Bacchus, more than for God and
loyalty." Mr. Baxter says, that in all the counties

---

* This is demonstrated in the following tracts :—Remarks on Dr.
Walker's late Preface to his Attempt, &c., by John Withers, 1717.
Vindication of Dissenters from the Charge of Rebellion, 1719.
Calamy's Church and Dissenters Compared, 1719. Reply of Withers
to Agate; Appendix. All are in the British Museum Library.

with which he was acquainted, " six to one, at least, if not more, were by the oaths of witnesses proved insufficient, or scandalous, or both."* Fuller, the church-historian, declares " that many of their offences were so foul, it is a shame to report them."† The facts published by authority of Parliament all testify to the same thing.‡ It is a mistake to assume that the Nonconformist secession was one of *numerical insignificance.* " *Only* two thousand ministers were ejected." But these two thousand ministers were thrust out of the church only because conscience made them un-

---

* Life and Times of Baxter, p. 74.

† Church History, Cent. XVII., Book xi., pp. 31—34.

‡ The First Century of Scandalous and Malignant Priests, &c. Printed by order of the Committee of the House of Commons, by John White, chairman, 1643. "The introduction of Bills for the eviction of scandalous and inefficient ministers is pretty generally supposed to have been a contrivance of the Long Parliament for mere sectarian purposes. But this is an entire mistake. Laws of this kind, and bearing similar names, had been upon the statute-book ever since the first session of King James's first Parliament. In the Commons' Journals you may find records of such laws on the 22nd of June, 1604; in the sessions of 1605—1606, 1609—1610, 1620, 1627. The Long Parliament did but put into faithful execution Bills which the Court and the prelates had before systematically gagged."—Mr. James Waylen. The commissioners in the time of Cromwell were, no doubt, often guilty of executing such measures with great severity. But we should hear both sides, and if you read the tracts written to complain of this by some of the sequestered clergy, such as Mr. Bushnell, Mr. Gatford, Mr. Sadler, and Dr. Pordage, you should in fairness also read the answers to them. Most of them may be found in the British Museum.

willing to conform. If conscience had allowed
them to be willing, they might have remained in it,
however tyrannical the conditions offered them were.
It was left with their own conscience to accept or
refuse those conditions, for none were excluded, as
in the contrasted case, on account of moral or
intellectual unfitness for their office. Their number,
then, it must be asserted, was not small in comparison with that of the clergy who had been previously sequestered under corresponding circumstances. It was not small in comparison with that
of any similar secession in former days. Even one
of their antagonists has said, "It may be observed
of the clergy of olde that in Henry the Eighth's
time, they were first for the Pope's supremacy, and
then for that of the King ; with King Edward the
Sixth, they were all Protestants ; with Queen Mary,
Papists again ; with Queen Elizabeth, they faced
about, and of 9,000, only 400 stood firm."* We
are inclined to think that this secession of 2,000
clergymen, made voluntarily, and simply for the
sake of principle, is a fact without parallel, and is
the glory of Puritan history alone ; it certainly
seems unfair to insinuate that it was comparatively
an insignificant thing. There is also an obvious
mistake as to the question of *comparative leniency*.
The ejected Episcopalians were allowed a fifth part

---

* Clerico Classicum, by John Price, 1648, p. 18.

of their livings, on retirement ;—the ejected Presbyterians had no such allowance. So far from this,
the terms of conformity were imposed before Michaelmas, when the payment of the year's tithes would be
due ; they were therefore deprived of their last year's
income, and in many instances reduced to absolute
want.* Still further, to borrow the language of a
clergyman of that day, whose views on this subject
differ essentially from those of his brother divine
just quoted, " The plunderings and ravages of the
church ministers were owing, many of them at
least, to the rudeness of the soldiers and the chances
of war ; they were plundered, not because they
were Conformists, but because they were Cavaliers.
. . . . Who can answer for the injustice of actions
in a civil war ? . . . but these ministers were ejected
not only in a time of peace, but in a time of joy to
all the land, and after an Act of Oblivion, when all
pretended to be reconciled and made friends, and
to whose common rejoicing these suffering ministers had contributed by their earnest prayers and
great endeavours."† In honour to the church
of England (we are still speaking as Anglicans),
let us be slow to confess the shameful faith that it

---

* St. Bartholomew's day was pitched upon, that, if they were
thus deprived, they should lose the profits of the whole year, since
the tithes are commonly due at Michaelmas.—Bishop Burnet, vol. i.,
p. 184.

† Conformists' First Plea, pp. 12, 13.

is essential for it to retain as its Magna Charta the
Act which Archdeacon Hare so righteously brands
as " that most disastrous, most tyrannical, and most
schismatical Act of Uniformity ;" but if, indeed,
we must confess it—if, with the dean of Chichester,
we feel compelled to say that it was " absolutely
necessary" to pass that Act—absolutely necessary
to exclude from the church-system sanctioned by
the State a host of men called, by John Locke,
" worthy, learned, pious, and orthodox divines,"—
men who will ever be revered as chief among the
creators of our noblest theological literature,—men
so great and holy, that no true student of their
books and lives can fail to see that in the former,
they alone, among the men of their day, represented
the first teachers of the English reformed church,
and that in the latter, they alone represented its
first martyrs—if we really do think all this was
absolutely necessary in order to establish the church ;
then, soul-struck with shame, let us at least deplore
that the miserable expedient of necessity was not
brought about in a more gradual and considerate
way.   Sentiments like these will be deepened as we
remember the kind of men who remained, when
the Puritans were gone. Take the account given by
.a beneficed clergyman, who wrote the year after the
Act of Uniformity came into force. In his tract
the church of England is personified, and thus
made to speak ; her first complaint is of undue

ordination :—" Of young men, I have a call of
3000. . . . Those pulpits that were filled
with ancient fathers are now desks for young children . . Of debauched men ordained I have 1500."
. . . . Is there any need of authorizing
patterns of impiety? Alas! a man at once a divine
and a beast! Consecrated to God, and devoted to
sin; an abomination in the holy place. . . Of
unlearned men ordained, I am ashamed to see a
roll of 426 tradesmen introduced in four years.
. . . Of factious ministers now ordained 1342,
must a sad race of Dissenters run parallel with the
orthodox succession. Alas, to see men once Presbyterians, then Independents, now Episcopal! Is
a good living their only creed, and a good preferment their only confession of faith?* It was a
miracle that Peter could convert 3000 at one sermon ; it's nothing now, that his Majesty hath converted such multitudes by the glance of his eye!"
The church then complains with indignant eloquence of the habits of the clergy, " Reverend in
function, yet shameful in lives! Ministers, yet
given to wine! In holy orders, yet in riotous disorder! Bound to walk circumspectly, and yet reel!

---

* By "a sad race of Dissenters," the clergyman means all the
ministers who had been ordained to officiate in the Establishment
during the twenty years preceding the Act of Uniformity ; it
appears that 1,342 of these now submitted to be ordained a second
time ; and he regrets that they were not all unconditionally ejected.

Conversation in heaven, yet in alehouses and taverns! Studying eternity, yet trifling away time! In communion of saints, yet in the company of the scorner. I thought," she continues, "the late complaints of scandal were only from malice and hatred. Holy men excused you, but now you refute and contradict them. You must needs justify malice itself." She further says, "Out of 12,000 church livings, 3,000 or more are impropriate, and 4,165 non-resident livings; what a poor remainder is there left for a painful and honest ministry!"*

The argument was not all on the side of the ejected ministers. They suffered cruel wrong, but it might have been shown that much of their suffering only resulted from the working of some of their own principles in other hands. In the opinion of most modern Dissenters, it might have been said to them,—You complain that Government has decided against the interests of true religion, but a representative Government can only represent the average ethical character of the people; and until the people are truly religious, it is only likely to decide against the interests of true religion. Individually, or through their representatives, those who are not "spiritual men," are not judges of spiritual things,† and are of course utterly unquali-

---

* Extracts abridged from a pamphlet called Ichabod; or, Five Groans of the Church. Cambridge, 1663.   † 1 Cor. ii.

fied to legislate for the church as to what doctrine
shall be trusted as true, what worship shall be
observed as scriptural, and what discipline exercised
as wise or holy ; if, therefore, they ever do venture
to legislate in a province so foreign to their own life,
it is only natural that the results should be like
those you now deplore. You complain that the
church is not at liberty to decide for itself in things
relating to itself; but when any church is connected
with a free State, it cannot itself be free. It may
not appoint a minister, nor make a form, nor use a
prayer, without permission. Though a heavenly
thing, it must be ruled by an earthly thing ; that is,
by worldly policy. Like everything else connected
with the State, it is so, that it may be ruled, and it
may not rule the rulers. You complain of your
ejection, but when in your official capacity you
received State endowment, in justice to the nation
you were, in that capacity, placed under State control. From the nature of the case, your power
depended on the life of a ruler, or on the trembling
balance of a parliamentary majority. The State
was your master; every master may dismiss his
servant when the services are no longer required.
Your services were no longer required, therefore it
is not of the fact of your dismissal that you should
complain, but only of its circumstances. You complain that Episcopalians employ the powers of the
State to enforce their ecclesiastical order on you ;

but you once employed those very powers to enforce yours on them. You complain of the demand for uniformity ; but some of you demanded uniformity. You complain of the schismatical spirit that excludes from the communion and ministry of the church, men like Baxter and Howe, on account of their Presbyterianism or Independency ; but some of you were guilty of exactly the same spirit, when you excluded such men as Bishops Hall and Taylor on account of their Episcopacy. Doubtless, the charge against the ministers of having helped the enforcement of uniform worship ought to be greatly qualified. Under Cromwell, ministers of all denominations were allowed to take part in the religious endowments of the nation. For political reasons alone, the forms of Episcopacy were forbidden, but even the Episcopalian clergy shared the common privilege. They were not required to pledge their assent to anything contrary to their own peculiar tenets, they were only required to promise their obedience to the existing Government. Having taken such an engagement, multitudes exercised their ministry, and some even continued to use the Book of Common Prayer.* Thus qualified, the charges now

---

* A clergyman who lived in those times says, "I can reckon up many clergy that had livings in Cromwell's day in the City, and preached without any let. There were Dr Hall, Dr. Ball, Dr. Wilde, Dr. Harding, Dr. Griffyth, Dr Peirson, Dr. Mossome, A. Faring-

expressed might have been brought against some
of the ministers with substantial justice; but after
all attempts to plead for the Act of Uniformity as
an act of imperious necessity, or of wise precaution,
or of measure for measure, we are obliged to regard
it as one of the most wonderful acts of wickedness
ever wrought under pretence of supporting the
cause of that kingdom which is not of this world.

✗

don, and many more, besides abundance in every county."—Conformists' Plea.   These instances might be indefinitely multiplied.
Doctor (afterwards Bishop) Bull used the liturgy at St. Philip's,
Bristol; Sanderson used it in his parish of Boothby Pagnell, and
when informed against, a message was conveyed to him expressing
the reluctance of those in power to abridge his liberty.—Izaak
Walton.

Chapter IX.

Black Bartholomew and the Two Ministers.

" *Must I be driven from my bookes ?*
From house and goods, and dearest friends ?
One of thy sweet and gracious lookes,
For more than this will make amends !
As for my house it was my tent,
While there I waited on thy flock ;
That work is done, that time is spent,
There neither was my home nor stock.
Would I in all my journey have
Still the same inne and furniture ?
Or ease and pleasant dwellings crave,
Forgetting what thy saints endure ?
My Lord hath taught me how to want
A place wherein to put my head ;
While He is mine, I'll be content
To beg or lacke my daily bread.
Heaven is my roofe, earth is my floore,
Thy love can keep me dry and warm,
Christ and thy bounty are my store ;
Thy angels guard me from all harm.

O

As for my friends, they are not lost ;
The severall vessels of thy fleet,
Though parted now, by tempests tost,
Shall safelie in the haven meet."

RICHARD BAXTER, 1662.

HE appearance of "Black Bartholomew" at Taunton was ushered in by many forerunners of evil omen. The day of delirious joy at the King's return was followed by many years of disaster. Most Christian men of various professions had hailed the enthronement of a prince whose title was undoubted, whose rule might reconcile all parties, and whose sacred word, already pledged, might give to their " Gospel day" a security of continuance—the one thing it wanted. His public acts soon woke them from their dream, and their loyalty was turned into gloomy estrangement, created by the King's treachery to the nation, and confirmed by the vindictive spirit of the successful party towards their own town. Before the first year was out, this was shown in an attempt, by means of a forged letter, to involve some of the most influential Nonconformists there in the charge of a desperate plot against the new Government.

Colonel Francis Basset, a Taunton Baptist, was the son of Admiral Sir Francis Basset, of Cornwall; a stanch friend to church and king, and a devoted lover of game-cocks ; who, no doubt, was as highly

exasperated by the degeneracy of his son, as Admiral
Penn was by the unsound principles of William.
It was pretended that the letter in question was
written by this young colonel to a friend ; and the
scheme was contrived with a view to ruin not only
him and his provincial associates, but with them,
certain eminent men of the same religious persuasion
in London. Having referred to the death of the
Princess of Orange, he is made to say—" There
are many that groan to see these times, and the
King's unfaithfulness, and the breaking of his covenant, that they do not fear to do anything for their
liberty. Therefore, pray brother Jesse, and as many
as are at hand of the brethren, not to draw back their
hands from doing the Lord's work ; for it is said by
the Lord that ' One shall frighten a thousand ;'
and, therefore, lay hold on the Lord's promise, for
His word is true, and there are thousands of His
saints who will be ready to lay down their lives to
do the work of the Lord. We desire you to be
careful to get into your hands powder and arms,
as many as you can, between this and Easter.
. . . . I pray let this be shown to my brother
Jesse and brother Kiffin."* The letter was in·

---

* Letter from B. F. (Col Francis Basset) to Nathaniel Crabb, at
his house in Gravel Lane. Taunton, 23rd Dec., 1660. Endorsed
by Nicholas as received, 9th October, 1651 ; and the original
delivered by Captain Will. Dale to the Lord General. It seems
probable that this letter was intended to suggest a suspicion that the

tercepted; Kiffin, Jesse, and Crabb were arrested, and their fate seemed to be hopeless. While the soldiers were guarding them to Serjeants' Inn, the place appointed for their examination, a great concourse of people gathered round the coach, crying out, " Traitors, rogues, hang them all !" When, however, they were brought into the presence of Judge Foster, Kiffin triumphantly proved the document to be a forgery ; first, because it was dated

---

Baptists were parties to Venner's insurrection ; but, according to Jessey, Venner declared that there was not one Baptist in his party, and that if they succeeded, the Baptists should know that infant baptism was an ordinance of Jesus Christ.—Crosby's History. In 1661, Jessey and the leading Baptist ministers signed a memorial to the King respecting Venner's insurrection, in which they say, " We appeal to the all-seeing God, the Judge of all the earth, to vindicate us. . . . . In whose presence we protest that we neither had the least knowledge of the said late treasonable insurrection, nor did any of us, in any kind or degree whatever, directly or indirectly, contrive, promote, assist, abet or approve the same."—Thomas Grantham, Christianismus Primitivus, book iii., chap. 1, p. 9. Besides the paper discussed above, others are preserved at Whitehall with reference to supposed plots among the country Baptists.—Katherine Hurlestone to Secretary Nicholas, 6 February, 1661. Papers by Nicholas on Mr. Ratcliffe. Sir John Finch to Lord Conway, and other documents among the State Papers for 1661. It is just possible that these were not all forgeries. There were then living many persons made mad by oppression, beclouded in their judgment by their training in the school of war, and still further misled by the then too common habit of taking precedents of action from the stories of a repealed economy, and the martial achievements of faith wrought by " Gideon and Barak, Samson and Jephthah, David also, and Samuel and the Prophets ;" and it is not unlikely that some of these persons were ready to draw the sword for liberty.

three days before the Princess died ; next, because
the interval between the time of her death and the
time of their arrest, was too short to allow of a
letter to be sent from London to Taunton with the
tidings from the Court, and then for a letter to come
from Taunton to London in consequence.* Never
was the father of lies convicted of a more artless
oversight, or a more unaccountable lapse of memory.
Perhaps the excuse was, that he never before had
so much bewildering work upon his hands. The
case was clear ; the prisoners were acquitted ; the
Somersetshire people were of course also cleared of
the charge, and went their way exultant, but burning with a stern indignation.

This letter is to be seen in the State Paper
Office, but without any marginal intimation that it
is a detected forgery. Attention has just been
called to it by the new Catalogue of the Series of
Domestic Papers relating to the opening events in
Charles the Second's reign. Most likely some
writers are preparing to use it, and others like it,
as evidence to justify the proceedings of the Carolist
Government against the Nonconformists ; but let
the fact just related be a warning against trust
in such documents as independent materials of
history.

The people of Taunton continued to suffer from

---

* Remarkable Passages in the Life of William Kiffin, pp. 28—32.

the malice of their adversaries.   In the year 1662,
they received stroke upon stroke of outrage.   First
came news of the insults offered to the body of
their own dead hero, Admiral Blake.   It had been
buried in Westminster Abbey, as a distinction due
to one whose name will ever be one of England's
glories.   It had been followed thither by Taunton
men, all filled with venerating love bordering on
worship ; but now, by order of the Council, it was
torn from the grave and flung with many other
bodies into a pit in St. Margaret's churchyard.
They were not afraid of Blake now!   Living or
dead, it was an honour to any man to be disowned
by that base age ; but, at the time, the intended
indignity alone was felt.   Next came the order
for the demolition of their town-walls.   To mark the
King's displeasure at the part the people took in
the wars of the Parliament, those walls to which
they had been accustomed to point with pride, and
which had witnessed that noble defiance of despotic
power, whose wonders, it has been said, " would
give life to a story that should outlive the world," *
were so effectually levelled, that the present inhabitants are unable to trace where they stood.
Next came the law which displaced the members of
their corporation, and along with it came the
rumour of an impending enactment, which soon

---

* Savage's History of Taunton, p. 423.

came in force, depriving them of their municipal
charter. At last came the Act of Uniformity,
which robbed them of their two beloved ministers.

" Before the Act of Uniformity came forth,"
writes Mrs. Alleine, " my husband was very
earnest, day and night, with God, that his way
might be made plain to him, and that he might not
desist from such advantages of saving souls with
any scruple upon his spirit. He seemed so moderate, that both myself and others thought he would
have conformed—he often saying, that he would
not leave his work for small and dubious matters ;
but when he saw those clauses of *assent and consent*,
and *renouncing the covenant*, he was fully satisfied.
But seeing his way so plain for quitting the public
station he was in, and being thoroughly persuaded of this, that the ejection of the ministers
out of their places did not disoblige them from
preaching the Gospel,—he presently took up a firm
resolution to go on with his work in private, when
his ministry in the church had ceased." "Blessings
brighten as they take their flight," and most precious
to him were his few remaining opportunities of
preaching in the great congregation, and carrying
on his work from house to house as a lawful
minister. He worked as one who knew that the
night was coming when, perhaps, he might no
longer work ; and in this spirit he delivered a
course of sermons — his last from the church

pulpit—on the words, " Redeeming the time, because the days are evil."* So evil were the days, and so vexed with interruptions, that the ministers were obliged to anticipate the time of ejection appointed by the State, preaching their farewell sermons on the Sunday before.

The wild love and keen sorrow felt by thousands on that final day never can be told. What Mr. Alleine said has not been reported, but we know that in the evening the old pastor preached from the words of Paul, " I am persuaded, that neither death, nor life, nor angels, nor principalities, nor powers, nor things present, nor things to come, nor height, nor depth, nor any other creature, shall be able to separate us from the love of God, which is in Christ Jesus our Lord."† As in every other farewell sermon preached on that Sunday, and surviving to our own times, there was an utter absence of party spirit, of any attempt to excite pity for the preacher, or anger against his enemies, and the personal allusions were few, simple, manly, and dignified. " It is good," said he, " to part with each other in the consideration of that, from which those that are God's shall never be divided, that is, ' the love of God in Christ Jesus our Lord.' . . . . As to the particular divine providence now ending our ministry among you, whatever happeneth on

---

* Ephesians v. 16.　　　† Romans viii. 38, 39.

this account, let it be your exercise to cry out for
the Holy Spirit of Christ, and He will grant you a
greater support than you may expect from any man
whatever. . . . . The withdrawing of this present
ministry may be to cause you to pray for this Holy
Spirit, day and night; and Christ promiseth that the
Father will give it to them that ask it. . . . . If
I cannot serve God one way, let me not be discouraged, but be more earnest in another. You
may also think it is a time for you to exercise what
you have learned. God is calling you to see if you
have not lost all the advantages He hath allowed
you; ' Ye have been a long time *learning*,' He is
saying to you, ' let me now see what you can now
do or *endure*.' If you have forgot all, Christ hath
made a promise, ' the Spirit shall bring again to
remembrance' when there is occasion for it. Consider, also, Christ is touched with a feeling of the
infirmities of a people in such a condition. Let
none of you be troubled in your heart; you believe
in God, believe also in Christ Jesus. . . . . He
hath promised to give you pastors according to His
own heart, that shall feed His flock with truth and
with understanding. He can find one, or frame
one, that shall fulfil His ministry better than this
weak instrument. He is the great Bishop of our
souls, and is never non-resident, and hath always a
care of His flock. Let not your hearts be troubled,
but let us commend you, yea, each other unto God,

and let Him do what is good in His eyes.   Let us pray."

THE PARTING PRAYER.

" To thee, O Lord Jesus, we commend our-selves : to thee, who judgest rightly, thy poor servant resigneth and committeth this congrega-tion.   The Lord pardon unto me wherein I have been wanting to them : the Lord pardon unto them, wherein they have been wanting in the hearing of thy Word, that we may not part with sin on our hearts.   Unto thee who judgest uprightly, I com-mend them.   The Bishop of souls take care of them ; preserve them from the love of the world ; teach them to wait on thee, and to receive from thee whatever any one, or any family, may stand in need of.

" Provide them a pastor according to thine own will ; only, in the meantime, give us of that anoint-ing which shall lead us out of our own will and wayes, that we may walk in the wayes of the Lord Jesus.   The Lord Jesus say now unto them, ' I am your Shepherd, you shall not want.'   Say to them, as thou didst to thy disciples, ' Let not your hearts be troubled ; you believe in the Father, believe also in me.'   So far as we are able, we put thy name upon them ; we name the name of the Lord Jesus over them.   The Lord Jesus bless them ; teach them to follow holiness, peace, and a heavenly conversation.   The Lord make them use-

ful to each other. The Lord Jesus be a blessing
to them, to me, and to all ours. The God of
peace and consolation fill them with blessings,
according as thou seest every one to stand in need
of. To thee, O Father, we commend them; do
thou receive them, that, under thy counsel, they
may be preserved blameless until the day of Jesus,
when we may all meet, crowned with glory.
Amen."

On the Sunday after the ejection, divine service
was performed in the parish church according to
the restored ceremonial. Crowds came to witness
it, for in the large population of the town and the
near hamlets there were now many who, from
various motives, were eager to show that they had
no sympathy with the Nonconformists. The exciting scene was described in a letter that was sent
the next day to the *Mercurius Publicus*, which is
here reprinted for the first time after an oblivion of
two centuries :—

"'Taunton, Monday, August 25.
" The parish of Taunton in Somersetshire, being destitute of a minister to preach, &c., by the nonconformity
of Mr. Newton,* a very worthy gentleman, Mr. Thomas
James (late of All Soule's Colledge, in Oxford), yesterday being St. Bartholomew's day, supplied his place.
The neighbour gentry purposely were there present, and

---

* Mr. Alleine is not mentioned, because he was only an assistant.

Mr. James being furnisht with the Book of Common Prayer, church vestments, &c., according to the late Act of Parliament, read the whole service for Morning and Evening Prayer, and christened two children accordingly, and (I cannot but acquaint you) the whole town was present, behaving themselves as if their minister had carried away with him all faction and nonconformity. The church was so very ful that severall persons swounded with the heat; and to the honour of this town I cannot but mind you, that 'tis very observable that a people that have been so ill-taught as they have been, should now obey his majesty and the church according to the Act of Parliament without the least hesitation. The mayor and aldermen were all in their formalities, and not a man in all the church had his hat on either at service or sermon, which gave the gentry of that county great satisfaction, who (to do them justice) deserve thanks for their care and vigilancy in setling the church and county according to the laws established." *

Affairs being thus victoriously " setled," the church was closed for many weeks successively ; and although, after that, a public service was held at rare intervals, the parish had no resident minister for the next nine months.

From a station of ancient and well-merited fame Mr. Newton was flung at once into obscurity and contempt. He was insulted by name, along with

---

* This letter also appeared in the " Kingdom's Intelligencer " of the same date.

others, in a lampoon written by the author of
Hudibras, with a view to ridicule the pretensions
of Englishmen to liberty of conscience.* He
might have said, " Now they that are younger |
than me have me in derision, whose fathers I would
have disdained to set with the dogs of my flock."
When scorn and peril first gathered round him,
he seems to have lost heart. For a year or two,
he sought concealment in the houses of various old
friends in London. There let us now leave him,
with the prospect of meeting again before writer
and reader part.

Meanwhile, we have to trace the steps of Mr.
Alleine. On the 21st of August, being the
Thursday after his farewell services in St. Mary's,
he appointed a day of solemn humiliation. What
immediately followed will be best related in the
language of his widow :—" On the solemn day
of humiliation, he preached to as many as would
adventure themselves with him at our own house ;
but, it being then a strange thing to the most professors to suffer, they seemed much affrighted at the
threatenings of adversaries ; so that there was not
such an appearance at such opportunities as my
husband expected. Whereupon he made it his work
to converse much with those he perceived to be

---

* A Proposal humbly offered for the Farming of Liberty of
Conscience, by Samuel Butler. Folio sheet. Guildhall Library.

most timorous, and to satisfie the scruples that were
on many amongst us ; so that the Lord was pleased
in a short time to give him such success that his
own people waxed bold for the Lord, and His
Gospel. And multitudes flocked into the meetings, at whatsoever season they were, either by
day or night ; which was a great encouragement
to my husband, that he went on with much
vigour and affection in his work, both of preaching, and visiting, and catechizing from house to
house.

" He went also frequently into the villages and
places about the towns where the ministers were
gone, as most of them did fly, or at the least
desist for a considerable time after Bartholomew
day. Wherever he went, the Lord was pleased
to give him great success ; many were converted,
and the generality of those were animated to cleave
to the Lord and His ways.

" But by this the justices' rage was much
heightened against him, and he was often threatened
and sought for ; but by the power of God, whose
work he was delighted in, was preserved much
longer out of their hands than he expected. For
he would often say, if it pleased the Lord to grant
him three months' liberty before he went to prison,
he should account himself favoured by Him, and
should with more cheerfulness go, when he had
done some work. At which time we sold off all

our goods,* preparing for a gaol, or banishment, where he was desirous I should attend him, as I was willing to do; it always having been more grievous to me to think of being absent from him than to suffer with him.

" He also resolved, when they would suffer him no longer to stay in England, he would go to China, or some remote part of the world, and publish the Gospel there."

This last statement brings to mind an interesting fact. The first Nonconformists were, in England, the originators of Christian missions to the heathen. When they officiated in our national churches, they were the first who preached and collected money for the work of evangelizing the Indians in America; and when they were cast out of those churches, they still burned with zeal for the same enterprise on a wider scale. " There are many here, I conjecture," wrote Baxter to Eliot, " who would be glad to go anywhere—to the Persians, Tartarians, Indians, or any unbelieving nation—to propagate the Gospel, if they thought they could be serviceable; but the difficulty of their languages is the

---

* Some few articles were reserved; among these was a clock, which the writer has often seen at the house of the Rev. John Bayly, late vicar of Chilthorne, Somerset. This gentleman claimed relationship to Alleine by collateral descent; and the family relic in question had been bequeathed to him, with the charge " that he should never part with it unless he wanted bread."

great discouragement."* It was Baxter "who obtained, through one of his most zealous disciples, the charter which incorporates the *original* Society for the Propagation of the Gospel."†

The idea of missions was treated by the party in power with infinite scorn. It could not be understood by men without souls,—they were only disposed to speculate on the sanity of those who entertained it. Basil Kennett, lord bishop of Peterborough, thus commented on the missionary spirit of Alleine and his companions :—" Even some (the Nonconformists) had a strong impulse, which they termed a call, to go abroad and propagate the Gospel. Thus, Mr. Joseph Alleine, deprived for nonconformity from Taunton St. Mary's, in Somerset, at length receiving a *third* call for the propagation of the Gospel, he would by all means, forsooth, go into China to do it ! But, being dissuaded by the brethren, he fed the flock of God's people in private."‡ Had he gone to China, he would have become the Protestant Xavier.

---

* Baxter MSS.

† Sir James Stephen's Ecclesiastical Biography, vol. i., p. 31. He adds in a note :—" The Society which now bears that name is an institution of later date, founded on the model of that for the establishment of which Baxter laboured, and designed to supersede it ; just as the National School Society followed on the British and Foreign School Society, or King's College, London, on the London University."

‡ Kennett's Register, December, 1662.

For nine months immediately following his ejection he went on with his work, often threatened, yet never actually interrupted. "In these months," continues Mrs. Alleine, "I know that he hath preached fourteen times in eight days, ten often, and six or seven ordinarily, at home and abroad, besides his frequent converse with souls; he then laying aside all other studies which he formerly so much delighted in, because he accounted his time would be short. The Lord, as he often told me, made his ministry far more easy to him by the supplies of His Spirit both in gifts and grace, as was evident both in his doctrine and life, he appearing to be more spiritual and heavenly and affectionate than before. The example of his re-solution made the people grow so bold that they came in great multitudes, at whatever season the meetings were appointed, the same persons coming generally twice a Sabbath, and often in the week."

John Wesley, grandfather of the illustrious founder of Methodism, was his enthusiastic fellow-labourer. He had been ejected from his benefice at Whitchurch, in Dorset; and from the 11th of March this year until the beginning of May, he was preaching almost every day, dividing his time between Mr. Alleine's people at Taunton and Mr. Norman's at Bridgewater, also occasionally minis-tering to congregations of Baptists and Independents at both places.

Mrs. Alleine says :—

" On Saturday, the 26th of May, about six o'clock in the evening, my husband was seized on by an officer of our town, who would rather have been otherwise employed, as he hath often said, but that he was forced to a speedy execution of the warrant by a justice's clerk, who was sent on purpose with it to see it executed, because he feared that none of the town would have done it.

" The warrant was in the name of three justices, to summon him to appear forthwith at one of their houses, which was about two miles from the town; but he desired liberty to stay and sup with his family first, supposing his entertainment there would be such as would require some refreshment. This would not be granted, till one of the chief of the town was bound for his speedy appearance. His supper being prepared, he sat down, eating very heartily, and was very cheerful, but full of holy and gracious expressions, suitable to his and our present state. After supper, having prayed with us, he with the officer, and two or three friends accompanying him, repaired to the justice's house, where they lay to his charge that he had broken the Act of Uniformity by his preaching; which he denied, saying, ' That he had preached neither in any church, nor chappel, nor place of publick worship, since the 24th of August ; and what he did was in his own family, with those others that came there to hear him.' "

" When that would not do, they accused him of being at a riotous assembly, although there was no business met about but preaching and prayer. Then he was much abused with many scorns and scoffs from the justices and their associates, and even the ladies as well as the gentlemen often called him rogue, and told him that he deserved to be hanged, and if he were not, they would be hanged for him, with many such like scurrilous passages,* which my husband receiving with patience, and his serene countenance showing that he did slight the threatenings, made them the more enraged. They then urged him much to accuse himself, but in vain. Having no evidence, therefore, yet did they make his mittimus for to go to the gaol on Monday morning, after they had detained him till twelve at night ; abusing him beyond what I do now distinctly remember, or were fit to express."

"As soon as he returned, it being so late, about two o'clock, he lay down on the bed in his clothes, where he had not slept above two or three hours at the most, but he was up, spending his time in converse with God, till about eight o'clock ; by which hour several of his friends were come to visit him ;

---

* This style of conversation was common amongst the ladies after the Restoration. A curious confirmation of this appears in the Life of Col. Hutchinson, whose wife says, " Scurrilous discourse, *even among men*, he abhorred."—Life, p. 34. Bohn.

but he was so watched, and the officer had such a
charge, that he was not suffered to preach all that
Sabbath, but spent the day in discoursing with the
various companies that came flocking in from the
town and villages to visit him; praying often with
them, as he could be permitted.   He was exceeding cheerful in his spirit, full of admiration of the
mercies of God, and encouraging all that came to
be bold, and venture all for the Gospel and their
souls, notwithstanding what was come upon him
for their sakes.   For, as he told them, he was not
at all moved at it, nor did not in the least repent
of anything he had done, but accounted himself
happy under that promise Christ makes to His,
in the 5th of Matthew, that he should be doubly
and trebly blessed now he was to suffer for His
sake; and was very earnest with his brethren in the
ministry that came to see him, that they would not
in the least desist when he was gone, that there
might not be one sermon the less in Taunton; and
with the people, to attend the ministry with greater
ardency, diligence, and courage than before; assuring them how sweet and comfortable it was to him
to consider what he had done for God in the
months past; and that he was going to prison full
of joy, being confident that all these things would
turn to the furtherance of the Gospel, and the glory
of God.

   " But he not being satisfied to go away, and not

leave some exhortations with his people, appointed them to meet him about one or two o'clock in the night, to which they showed their readiness, though at so unseasonable a time. There was, of young and old, many hundreds; he preached and prayed with them about three hours.

"He prayed for his enemies, as the martyr Stephen did for those that stoned him, ' That God would not lay this sin of theirs to their charge.' The greatest harm that he did wish to any of them was, ' That they might throughly be converted and sanctified, and that their souls might be saved in the day of the Lord Jesus.'

"And so, with his yearnings towards his people, and theirs towards him, they took their farewell of each other—a more affectionate parting could not well be.

"About nine o'clock he, with two or three friends that were willing to accompany him, set out for Ilchester; the streets being lined on both sides with people, and many following him on foot several miles out of the town, with such lamentations that (he told me after) did so affect him, that he could scarce bear them; but the Lord so strengthened him that he passed through them all with great courage and joy, striving both by cheerful looks and words to encourage them.

"He carried his mittimus himself, and had no officer with him. When he came to the gate of the prison, finding the gaoler absent, he took that opportunity of preaching once more before he entered, which was afterwards considered a great aggravation to his former crimes. When the gaoler came, he delivered his mittimus, and was clapped up in the Bridewell chamber, which is over the common gaol. He found there Mr. John Norman, who, for the like cause, had been committed a few days before him."*

Crowded in this one apartment night and day, he, with his companions, spent the next four months. Fifty Quakers were there, seventeen Baptists, and very soon thirteen ministers were brought, all taken like himself, for the high crimes of preaching and prayer. The stifling atmosphere was made more stifling still by the many visitors. The summer sun struck fiercely on the roof all day, and so low was the roof-tree, that at night, when lying on their mattresses, they could touch the glowing tiles. Gasping for life, they had sometimes to break the glass, or rend away one of the tiles for air. Night and day they had but the same scanty accommodation; their beds were their only tables, and all the privacy that they could

---

* Mrs. Alleine's Narrative, thus given, does not appear in full in any single edition of the "Life and Letters." After the first edition, some of the facts were suppressed from prudential motives, and for other reasons, at different times, other facts were added.

contrive, was made by a mat drawn across the room. Night and day their ears were stung by the songs, the curses, and the clanking chains of the felons in the cells below. If they ventured out of their deadly vapour-bath into the prison court, besides these sounds, they were still more afflicted by the sights of loathsome and pestilential wretchedness that crossed their path, for the criminal prisoners were sure to be all there too. When they rushed back to their chamber, and sought peace in united prayer, sad to say, they were disturbed by some of their associates in suffering for conscience sake. Mrs. Alleine says, that " the Quakers would molest them by their cavils in the times of their preaching, praying, and singing, and would come and work in their callings just by them, while they were at their duties."

A few words seem needful both to account for the conduct of these poor men, and to describe the circumstances of their imprisonment at the same time with Mr. Alleine. It is plain that they misrepresented the true principles of Quakerism. The essence of the system seems simply to be, that the reception of Christ into the heart is the grand essential to salvation. Christ, it is said, does at some period or other visit the heart of every man, for He is the true light that lighteth every man that cometh into the world. This inward light may be resisted ; but if received, it will develope itself in a life of righteousness, and the man who thus receives Christ will be justified, not indeed by his own works, but by the works of Christ within him. This life is the truth, even the Scripture itself being regarded as secondary and subordinate to it—the mere declaration, not the fountain, and only known to be Scripture by the central testimony of the Spirit. For this reason, all worship must be offered from the immediate dictate of the Spirit of Christ. Baptism and the Lord's Supper must be taken inwardly, not outwardly, and true religion owns no outward apparatus, no outward law, or outward force. It was natural for such a system to arise at such a crisis in the history of religious thought. Honest George Fox, its founder, was guiltless of taking the idea from Origen, or the Neo-Platonists, although it glimmers in some of their speculations. He had a deep spiritual nature, that felt unsatisfied on the one hand with the teachings of the Puritans, who too often made religion look like mere mechanical obedience to the letter of the Scripture; on the other, with the dogmas of the Laudists, who made it look like a ceremony. Extremes beget extremes, and in re-action from that " bodily exercise which profiteth little," he adopted and proclaimed what seemed to look like the religion only of a disembodied spirit. George Fox was often right in his assertions, but often wrong in his denials ; noble truth was honoured, but there was also the error

which results from truth pushed too far. To speak
with the utmost charity, and to say the very least
that may seem severe, there was danger of slighting
the historic facts of Christianity. There was danger
lest a theory so delicate and so intensely inward
should be misunderstood by followers of coarser
natures than his own. There was danger lest the
religious inquirer should make his last appeal, not
to his Bible, but to himself. It was easy for many
a well-meaning though ignorant man to mistake
the working of his own impulses for the mystic
illapse of the Spirit, and the inward language of
nature for the whispers of grace. A spirit which
he thought was from heaven would often move him
to interrupt the public worship in the steeple-
house ; to insult the ministers in the streets ; to
scream out frantic announcements of coming wrath
upon the land, or to go about in some fantastic
habit for a sign. The doctrine of the inward light
often seemed in its actual workings to be simply
the doctrine that every man may do and ought to do
what seems right in his own eyes, whatever law may
say to the contrary. Of course it attracted many
of the disbanded " Levellers," and many mutinous
and discontented persons, who used the system as a
mere outlet for the spirit of contradiction, or a mere
pretext for insolence to men in authority. As
Quakerism had not as yet formed a distinct Christian community, it had no organic laws by which

it could exclude or disown those who knew nothing of its nature, but who did much evil in its name. These men often suffered as the disturbers of the public peace, and they deserved to suffer. It must also be allowed that even the good men with whom they connected themselves, often did things with a religious meaning, which were punished by the magistrates, not on religious grounds, but as the same things would be punished now—that is, simply as sins against society. Yet it must not be denied that a very large proportion of the sufferings endured by the Quakers was purely for their views of Christian principle ; and that it was inflicted in a spirit of insane hatred to that principle in whatever form it appeared, but more especially when in the form of demur to the church establishment. This hatred was now heightened by alarm at the rapid growth of Quakerism. By the year 1680, it had reached a numerical strength equal to about one person in 130 of the general population ;* at the period of which we are writing it was already immense, and the instances of imprisonment were in proportion. Five thousand Quakers were now in bonds.†

At Ilchester, besides the fifty in ward with Mr.

---

* Rowntree, p. 76.

† Sufferers in prison before the Restoration, 3,179 ; sufferers since the King came in, 5,000.—Address to the King and Both Houses of Parliament, 1661.

Alleine, thirty-one were confined in an old monastic building at the other end of the town. These, one of their pamphlets informs us, "were taken from the highways, from the plough, from their houses, were kicked, beaten, and wonderfully abused ; they were not suffered to have provisions brought them, and the gaoler denied them permission to see their wives and children. Many clothiers were taken away that set many families to work, and some had been driven by horsemen into ditches, some into pools, to the endangering of their lives."*

Chief in this company of sufferers was John Anderdon,† a gentleman of Bridgewater. He was a thoughtful and learned man, one of the earliest professors of the tenets taught by Fox, and both by tongue and pen one of their most animated advocates. Eight of his works, all written in prison, now lie before the present writer. When Alleine came to Ilchester, this gentleman was fettered to a felon with iron chains ; and with five other Quakers, fettered to five other felons, was often dragged along the streets with pitiless cruelty. He lived twenty years in prison, and there at last he died. We must pardon such poor men for

---

* Pamphlet 4,230 in the Library at Devonshire-house ; title— This is to thee, O King, and to thy Council, and all the Officers and Magistrates ; 1660.

† Tanner's Lectures on the History of Friends in Somerset.

their treatment of our own beloved confessor. Life had not been to them a school of chivalry. They had only known controversies where both parties used rough, strong language, asked for no quarter and gave none. They had only seen the worst side even of the best men. After all, many of them were men of heroic piety; and if some of them, in their treatment of the ministers, displayed all the frenzy of zeal without knowledge or charity, we must remember that the Quakers, who had treated Bunyan, " one of Gog's army,"* in a similar way, afterwards did him a kind service when it came within their power, and that most likely they would have done the same for Alleine. He called them " railing Rabshakehs," and they called him " a murthering priest ;" but if they had been free they would have spent much and travelled far to release him from his bonds, still testifying to the last, that he was " a deceiver of the stock of Ishmael and the seed of Cain."

When Mr. Alleine arrived at the prison, his first act had been to preach and pray, and this he called " holding a consecration service." Subsequently, and to the last, he and his companions in turn preached and prayed publicly once, and sometimes twice, every day, the minister generally speaking through the prison-bars to the congrega-

---

* Term applied by Burrowes the Quaker to Bunyan.

tions that flocked from the various villages within a distance of ten miles.*   All the rest of the day he constantly spent in converse with those who thronged to him for counsel and instruction; and in consequence of this, says Mrs. Alleine, he was forced to take much of the night for study and secret converse with God.

The vitiated atmosphere and staring publicity of the prison-life made it peculiarly hard to one who so loved the bright morning air, and had been accustomed to be so much alone with God in the woods and fields.   We are glad to hear that he was soon permitted to curtain off a corner of the room all to himself.   It was large enough to hold his bed ; and as Mrs. Alleine had resolved to share his imprisonment, this little triangular space was not a little luxury.   After a few weeks he was suffered to walk out for a mile or more into the country, morning and evening, though sometimes interdicted by the passion of the keeper.   His friends brought supplies of money and abundance

---

* The imprisoned ministers did the same in many other places. A Stuartine poet complains that the Nonconformist

> " Commits himself to prison to trepan,
> Draw in and spirit all he can ;
> For birds in cages have a call
> To draw the wildest into nets,
> More prevalent and natural
> Than all our artificial pipes and counterfeits."
> Pindaric Ode on a Hypocritical Nonconformist.

of wholesome food.   His health continued good
and his spirit elastic, and "the voice of rejoicing"
was often heard in that "tabernacle of the righteous,"
Ilchester Gaol.

Mrs. Alleine says :—"On the 14th of July,
he was brought to the sessions held at Taunton,
and was there indicted for preaching on May 17th ;
but the evidence against him was so slender that
the grand-jury could not find the bill.   So that
he was not brought to his answer there at all ; and
his friends hoped he should have been dismissed,
it being the constant practice of the Court that if a
prisoner be indicted and no bill found, he is freed
by proclamation.   However, my husband was sent
to prison again at the assizes, and to his friends, who
expected his enlargement, he said, ' Let us bless
God that His will is done.' "

Chapter X.

Trial at Taunton Castle.

" Though wrong in justice-place be set,
Committing great iniquitie ;
Though hypocrites be counted great,
And still maintain idolatrie ;
Though some set more by things of nought
Thàn by the Lord that all hath bought :
    Blame not my lute.

" Blame not my lute, I you desire,
But blame the cause that we thus play ;
For burning heat blame not the fire,
But him that bloweth the coale alway ;
Blame ye the cause, blame ye not us,
That we men's faults have touched thus :
    Blame not my lute."

JOHN HALL'S DITTY ON THE WICKED STATE AND ENORMITIES OF
MOST PEOPLE IN THESE PRESENT MISERABLE DAIES.

IS judge at the Taunton assizes was
Sir Robert Foster,* lord-chief-justice
of England. " After the Restoration,"
remarks Lord Campbell, " it was con-

---

* Western Circuit—Mr. Justice Foster and Mr. Serjeant Archer,
Taunton Castle, August 24 —*Mercurius Publicus,* Thursday, July
9th, 1663.

sidered necessary to sweep away the whole of the judges from Westminster Hall, although they were learned and respectable men. Immense difficulty was found in replacing them. . . . At last, a chief-justice was announced, and his obscurity testified the perplexity into which the Government had been thrown in making a decent choice. He was one of the few survivors of the old school of lawyers which had flourished before the troubles began. He had been called to the degree of serjeant-at-law on the 30th of May, 1636, at a time when Charles the First, with Strafford for his minister, was ruling with absolute sway,—was imposing taxes by his own authority,—was changing the law by proclamation, and hoped never again to be molested by Parliament."* In his obscurity he might have been thought a man of mean but negative character ; but now, to borrow a metaphor which has been applied to another worthy, he had passed the chrysalis state, in which he was only a kind of intermediate grub between sycophant and oppressor, had put off the worm and put on the dragon-fly. It was Judge Foster who brought about the conviction and execution of Sir Harry Vane. He had treated the Quakers with fierce cruelty, and his present object was to exterminate all nonconformity.

---

* Lives of the Chief-Justices, vol. i., p. 493.

The barrister who engaged to take the lead in the defence was Mr. Thomas Bampfield, brother to Sir John Bampfield of Poltimore. He had been a member of many Parliaments, speaker to the House of Commons in Richard Cromwell's time, and for some years recorder to the city of Exeter. The gentlemen of the west appointed him to carry their "Remonstrance" to encourage General Monk in bringing back King Charles.* In religious opinion, like his learned brother,† he was a Baptist. Baxter says of him, " He was a man of most exemplary sincerity and conscientiousness. He never took an oath in his life, till he was a member of the Parliament that brought in the King, and then he was put upon taking the Oath of Supremacy, which I had much ado (he being my much dear and valued friend) to persuade him to, so fearful was he of oaths, or anything that was doubtful, and like to sin."‡ Latterly, this spiritual sensitiveness seems to have been attended by great nervous susceptibility ; therefore, * though a very considerable lawyer, he was wont to give his advice at home, and did not appear at the

---

* Vindication of Dissenters.—John Withers, 1717, p. 60. Also State Papers, 1660.

† Francis Bampfield, M.A., of Wadham College, Oxford. For Christ's sake he suffered many years' imprisonment in various gaols, and in 1683, died in Newgate.—Crosby's History of Baptists.

‡ Reliquiæ Baxteriana, lib. 1., part ii , p. 432.

bar."*   His friendship for Alleine tempted him for
once to break this rule.   Accustomed from birth
and office to an honoured place among the calm
grandees of England, but now scorned, vilified,
suddenly ruined, just discharged from prison for
nonconformity, he certainly had to plead his friend's
cause amidst great disadvantages.†

The account of Mr. Alleine's trial, given in his
own handwriting, is still preserved amongst the
Baxter manuscripts in Dr. Williams's library ; and
such is its minute finish and precision as a report,
that it almost brings us into the presence of the
judge.   We seem to see the venomous glitter of
his eye, and to hear the snap of his quick, short,
sharp, testy sentences.   This document has been
little heard of, and perhaps never read, since old
Richard Baxter brightened his spectacles, and drew
nearer the light, the better to decipher its small
and delicate lines.   It is best, perhaps, to give
it entire, although it touches on some facts which
have been already related.

MR. ALLEINE'S CASE.

Joseph Alleine was taken up May 23, 1663,

---

* Life of Rosewell, p. 63.

† There seems to be a reference to this gentleman's friendship in the
following passage from Alleine's letter to " Pylades." " I find some
jealous passages in thy last lines.   But canst thou think that T. B.
can be put in ballance against my old friend, my own, my covenant
Pylades ?"

by a warrant from M. Clarke and M. Sydenham;
and being then accused of preaching, he was by
them and M. Hawley charged for breaking the
Act for Vniform (worship), (although the said
Joseph never preached in any publique place :) as
alsoe for being at a riotous assembly; although
there were noe threats nor dangerous words, noe
staves nor weapons; noe feare so much as pretended to be strucke into any; noe other unlawful
businesse met about than to pray for the King's
Majesty, themselves, and the peace of the nation,
and to instruct the people (that came in with his
own family) their duty to God and their soveraigne;
and prevent those discontents that might arise
from their being left quite like heathens; the
meetings at which he was, not being where there
was anything done at the church, noe minister
being settled in the towne for three-quarters of a
yeare together, nor any service of God at all in the
publique congregation for very many weeks successively.   After his committment, strenuous
endeavours were used to get evidence of the fact,
and several were menaced to sweare against him.

At the sessions, held July 14, he was endicted for
preaching on May 17, (when there was no worship of
God morning or evening in the publique place, the
said Joseph being well-knowne to be a frequenter of
the church, when there was any minister to officiate
there.)   The grand-jury did not find the bill;

whereupon he expected to be freed, according to
law and justice, but could not obtaine it, though
others on the same businesse, their bills not being
found, were acquitted. Nor could the saide Joseph,
upon his earnest petitioning to the judge and
benche, obtain the favour soe much as once to be
called, or to appeare before the Court to say a
word for himselfe. Yet a justice of peace upon
the benche at the assizes did complaine that he was
a most obstinate man, and that although they sent
for him three or four times, he would not come to
them at the sessions, when he was said to be sent for
to the Court.

At the assizes, when he was againe brought
forth, all possible endeavours were made to get
evidence against him, and because none could be
found in Taunton that could be depended upon,
they sought for it at Bridgewater, where there
were sundrie persons that were suspected to be able
to give evidence against him, sent for by warrants,
but got out of the way, onlie some malicious persons came, and offered to give evidence, but were
rejected, as insufficient in their testimony. Here-
upon, they who had imprisoned Alleine, seeing how
much their credit was at stake to prove somewhat
against him, since he had bin in prison three
months by their meanes, hunted up and downe, and
sent officers for those that were suspected to be
able to give evidence, many of whom got out of

the way, and three men were committed to prison by the judge for refusing to give evidence. Strange, that a man should be three months in prison, and then that men should be to seek for, to give evidence against him !

Proofe being still short, one of the justices that imprisoned Alleine came to a fellow prisoner, and desired him to give evidence against Alleine, which if he would doe, he himself might fare the better in his cause. To another he came, and tolde him that he was a young man, and capable of preferment, and that it lay in his power to doe them a courtesy, by giving evidence against Alleine; and if he would doe it, he should have the favour of the gentlemen of the Court. What sinister endeavours were used with others, afterwards follows as taken from their owne mouthes ; but when all these vigorous attempts would not availe to get more evidence (which lasted from Monday till Wednesday in the afternoone), they resolved to put to it with what little they had. Wednesday night, Alleine was called for.

CLERKE.—Thou art here indicted by the name of Joseph Alleine, for that on the 17th day of May, 1663, thou with twenty others, to the jurours unknowne, did by force of armes, unlawfully, routously, riotously, and seditiously assemble and segregate yourselves together, contrary to the peace of our soveraigne lord the King, and to the great terrour of his subjects, and the evill example of all others.   What saist thou, Joseph Alleine, guilty or not guilty ?

ALLEINE.—My lord, before I plead to this indict-ment, I desire to know upon what account I now stand as a prisoner here, ffor I have bin endicted for this very thing at the ses-sions, and was acquitted by my country, and yet (I know not by what law) returned to prison againe.

JUDGE.—If there were any such indictment, or proceeding, it would appeare.   Where is any such thing to be found ?

> *Note.*—That my lord had, in court, long before this, called for a coppy of Alleine's indictment at the sessions, and upon reading of it was very angry with the clerke, and said it was erroneous *in omnibus*, and fined him, and blamed the justices about Alleine's indictment, who put it off from one to another, and none would owne it ; and moreover was heard to say, as it was thought in Alleine's case, that " iff he were a divell he should have justice."

ALLEINE.—My lord, I endeavoured for a coppy of the indictment and could not obtaine it, but I shall be ready to prove before your lordship by the oathes of the grand-jury, that I was acquitted ; and I beseech your lordship, as you are counsell for the prisoner, to declare whether

a man may be indicted for that of which he
hath bin acquitted.

JUDGE.—If a man be acquitted for a fact committed
yesterday, and commit the same againe to-
morrow, shall he expect any benefit by pleading his being acquitted for the former offence ?

ALLEINE.—My lord, that is not the case; for this
indictment was for the very same day, and
is for the very same thing, for which I was
acquitted at the sessions.

JUDGE.—That does not appeare.

ALLEINE.—My lord, I have offered to prove it by
the oathes of the grand-jury, if you would
accept it; and I beseech your lordship to call
for the records of the session, and there you
shall find the indictment recorded, and the
ignoramus entered.

But this was angrily rejected.

ALLEINE.—I beseech your lordship to enquire of
M. Hunt, who was judge of the sessions,
and he will be able to informe your lordship
that the bill was not found.

But this would not be granted neither, but he
required Alleine to plead presently guilty or
not guilty, or else he would forthwithe pro-
ceede to judgement againste him.

ALLEINE.—If I must plead to such an indictment,
my answer is, that as for preaching and praying, which is the truth of the case, if this be

to be guilty, I am guilty ; but for riotous, routous and seditious assemblies, I abhor them from my heart, and am a loyall subject of his Majesty.

JUDGE.—This is the manner of you and your brethren, you go for to cast dirt upon the Government, as if they were against preaching and praying.   Sir, preaching and praying are good, but under pretence of these you seduce the people, and gather proselytes, and it is against your rogueish meetings that we are.

ALLEINE.—My lord, I am humbly glad to heare your lordship declare that praying and preaching are not crimes.

JUDGE.—Sirrah ! sirrah ! what doe you goe for to catch me !   I said not soe ; but I tell you that it is not against praying and preaching that we are, but against doing it in such a manner, in private conventicles, in a seditious way.   If you will pray, there is the house of prayer for you.

ALLEINE.—My lord, I was expressly indicted for preaching and praying the last session.

JUDGE.—I cannot stand to hear you prate ; plead guilty or not guilty.

ALLEINE.—Not guilty.

CLERKE.—Then prepare for your answer to-morrow morning.

Thursday morning Alleine was sett again

to the fellon's bar, and they proceeded to his
tryall.

ALLEINE.—My lord, I make it my request to your
Honour that I may have liberty to enter my
traverse* to prosecute it the next assizes.

JUDGE.—That you shall, but then you must provide me sureties to prosecute it next assizes,
and get good security, that you will be of the
good behaviour in the meantime.

ALLEINE.—As for securities to prosecute my traverse, I shall be ready to give them ; but for
the good behaviour, I desire your lordship to
excuse me ; for I understand that is not usuall
in this case, and I beseech your lordship not to
turne the water out of the constant course
where it hath ever run.

JUDGE.—I must tell you that you are a fellow of
such evill fame, and I have received such
information of you, as are sufficient grounds
for my requiring the good behaviour.

ALLEINE.—Your lordship hath noe eyes to see,
nor eares to heare, but what is brought here
before you, in the publique judicature ; and if
any will make it here appeare that I have
broke the good behaviour, I shall be ready to
give sureties.

JUDGE.—The grand-jury have found you guilty,

---

* Traverse—to arrest judgment.

and that is sufficient for me to require the good behaviour of you.

ALLEINE.—My lord, that is not sufficient ground, because I have bin already acquitted of that, for which they have prosecuted me; and I beseech your lordship will not require the good behaviour of me for that of which I have bin already acquitted.

JUDGE.—Noe such matter.

ALLEINE.—My lord, I doe here offer your lordship in the face of the Court, and avow it before my countrey, that I am ready to bring the grand-jury now, to prove it upon their oathes, that I was acquitted; which *this* grand-jury might not know.

JUDGE.—Sirrah! will you charge such worthy gentlemen that they did they know not what?

ALLEINE.—My lord, I said not that they knew not my case at all, but that they might not know I had bin already acquitted of that for which they have now prosecuted me.

JUDGE.—I must have the good behaviour of you (*with much passion*).

ALLEINE.—My lord, I have done nothing but what belonged to my duty as a minister.

JUDGE.—When were you made a minister?

ALLEINE.—Eight yeares since.

JUDGE.—By whom?

ALLEINE.—By the Presbytery.

JUDGE.—Who gave them power to ordaine?

ALLEINE.—My lord, they have that power by virtue of their office, as they are ministers of Christ.

JUDGE.—Your ordination is nothing worth; you are noe minister.

ALLEINE.—My lord, I hope you will not assert that which shall overthrow all the ministry of the whole Christian Protestant world, except here in England; for your lordship is not ignorant that they have no other ordination than by the hands of the Presbytery, just as I have. And for my ordination, I shall be ready to maintain it before any whom your lordship may appoint.

JUDGE.—You are no minister of England, of the church of England.

ALLEINE.—I will undertake to show that in the judgement of many, very many bishops and archbishops of the church of England, ordination by the Presbytery is valid.

JUDGE.—I cannot stand here to heare you prate in your self-confidence; you love to heare yourselfe talke. Will you give me security for your good behaviour or not?

ALLEINE.—If you will have securities for my good behaviour, I desire your lordship to explaine what you meane by this good behaviour.

JUDGE.—You fit to be a minister, and not know what belongs to the good behaviour! How can you preach to others and not know what that meanes?

ALLEINE.—My lord, what is vulgarly understood by the good behaviour I know, and in that sense I shall be ready to give securities for it; but if your lordship by this intends to bind me from my duty, and that which belongs to my office as a minister, I cannot yielde to it.

My lord being very angrie, the jaylour pulled M. Al eine away; but he desired, as he was being pulled backe, that if his lordship would not accept of his offers, he might put it upon present issue. But the clerke speakes softly to my lord, in the hearing of a friend, that the evidence was yet very short, and soe his lordship was not ready to heare Alleine. Whereupon he called out a second and a third time that he desired to have it put upon present tryall. Then my lorde spake to the clerke, " Let us then try it presently." So Alleine was put to the barre againe. The first witnesse was John Lake.

J. LAKE.—Once since Christmas, I went to M. Alleine's house to see one that had formerly liv'd with me; and when I came, I heard him preach in his family.

JUDGE.—Were there none but his own family?

J. LAKE. — I know not who were there, but there were many families that did live with him under the same roofe.

ALLEINE. — My lord, I desire that counsell may be heard in my case.

JUDGE. — With all my heart; where are your counsell?

ALLEINE. — I desire they may be called.

JUDGE. — Do you looke that I should call your counsell?

ALLEINE. — No, my lord, I desire the cryer.

CRYER. — I warrant you have Bampfield.

ALLEINE. — Call M. Sidderson and M. Bampfield.

It must be noted that the day before, M. Bampfield, being seen in the Court, Sir Hugh Wyndham, foreman of the grand-jury, spake in M. B.'s hearing to the judge — " We are informed that here is a councellour in the towne, that is come to plead for the ministers, who is an excommunicated person, a Nonconformist, &c., &c. I desire to know of your lordship, whether we shall present him or indict him?" JUDGE — "Which you will, and God's blessing on your hearts."—This was thought to be done to affright M. Bampfield from appearing; and he not coming, in a cause wherein he was expected (upon some weighty reasons), it was said by some that they had frighted away Bampfield; but as soon as he came into the Court, the judge spake to him very angrily, " M. Bampfield, I must tell you, before you plead for another—I must tell you, that you had need answer for your-selfe. You are here presented to me, for being a Nonconformist to the churche of the land, and an abettour of Nonconformists." M. Bampfield answered, " My lord, to that charge I shall answer in due time and place."

ALLEINE.—I desire my first witnesse may be heard againe, before my counsell. He was heard, and afterwards another witnesse was called, by name George Tweagle.

TWEAGLE (*in a hurry*).—Upon the 17th day of May, I went to M. Alleine's house, and there I hearde the singing of a psalme, and that was alle.

JUDGE.—Were there none there but of his own family ?

TWEAGLE (*pulleth at his front hair, in sign of reverence.*)—Yes.

JUDGE.—How many doe you thinke ?

TWEAGLE.—I thinke there might be twentie there.

JUDGE.—Were there not forty there ?

TWEAGLE.—I thinke there were.

JUDGE.—Were not sixty there ?

TWEAGLE (*looketh simple*).—I thinke there were sixty.

JUDGE (*mildly*).—Come, come, old man, speake the truth and shame the divell; never goe

to helpe a lame dogge over a stile; were there
not eighty there?

TWEAGLE (*in like mild manner*).—Sure, I thinke
there might be eighty there.

MASTER BAMPFIELD.—Upon the oath that you
have taken, did you see M. Alleine there?

TWEAGLE (*thundereth out*).—NOE. (*A pause*).

BAMPFIELD (*foolishly*).—Did you *heare* him there?

TWEAGLE.—I cannot sweare I did; but I believe
it was his voice.

BAMPFIELD (*somewhat nervous*). — My lord, it
will come to this point in law, whether it can
be rout, riot, or unlawful assembly, according
to the indictment, there being no appearance
of any fforce, which the law determines to be
necessary to every one of these—ffor a riot, I
conceive—a riot is when three or more do
meet—and by fforce—ffor some unlawful act.
A riot, I conceive—a riot is when they meet
and move towards it—an unlawful act by
fforce.*

---

* What Mr. Bampfield really meant to say may be inferred from
the following opinion with reference to another case. It is copied
from a MS. in his handwriting, and preserved in Vol. V. of the
Baxter MSS. (Treatises) :—" A riot by common law, is when three
or more doe any unlawful act; an unlawful assembly, is when three
or more assemble to commit a riot, and doe not commit a riot. In
both cases I conceive the act done, or to be done, ought to be such
as has force accompanying it ; but I think, beyond doubt, to make it
riot, the unlawful act ought to be actually done, or else 'tis no riot ;

JUDGE (*measuring M. Bampfield with his eye*).—
You conceive and conceive, but all the country
knows that M. Bampfield's conceptions are
none of the wisest. A meeting to do that
which is not allowed by law, is an unlawful
assembly.

BAMPFIELD.—My lord, this is not my single
opinion, but all the bookes that I can meet,
do make a force to be necessary to that which
in law is called an unlawful assembly. My
Lord Cooke, Marrow, and many authours
were now cited, and he repeated the evidence
above-mentioned to the jury, showing them
that here was noe appearance of force, but only
peaceable serving of God in instructing the
family with others, and singing with them, and
soe he should leave it upon their consciences
whether they could find it according to the
indictment, for an unlawful assembly.

Before the jury went out, the judge spake
to them to this effect :—

JUDGE.—You have heard what the witnesses have
sworne ; and though the evidence be not so
full, I desire you to remember, that the grand-

---

and if the act be not done, 'tis but an unlawful assembly and no riot,
which difference between a riot and unlawful assembly is manifest,
and ought not to be confounded."—Legal Opinion (T. B.'s) on Bail.
As in Alleine's case no unlawful force was intended, attempted, or
actually used, there was no rout, riot, or unlawful assembly.

jury have, partly upon the evidence, and partly on their own knowledge, found him guilty, and they are upon their oathes as well as you.

Retirement of Jury.—While the jury were out, it was confidently thought in the Court that Alleine would be found " Not guilty ;" and the sheriffe said to a friend of Alleine's excusingly, " However shorte these witnesses are now, they swore more to the purpose yesterday."

VERDICT.—The jury quickly brought in Alleine GUILTY. Mr. Bampfield asked, " What! guilty according to the evidence of the indiĉtment? They answered *" guilty of the indiĉtment."*

CLERKE.—In the afternoone, Alleine being set to the barre, was asked by the Clerke what he had to say why judgment should not be pronounced? Mr. Alleine said that he desired his counsell might be hearde.

M. BAMPFIELD. — Then M. Bampfield urged the invalidity of the indiĉtment, for that in every good indiĉtment of the kind, three or more of the rioters ought to be named, for want of which this was essentially erroneous. Many more things he urged, but was, with much passion, overcome in all.

CLERKE.—Then the Clerke asked Alleine whether he had anything further to say.

R

ALLEINE.—My lord, I am glad that it hath appeared before my countrey, that whatever I am charged with, I am guilty of nothing but doing my duty; all that did appeare by the evidence being, that I had sung a psalme, and instructed my family (others being there), and both in mine owne house; and if nothing that hath been urged will satisfy, I shall with all cheerfulnesse and thankfulnesse accept whatsoever sentence your lordship shall pronounce upon me, for so good and righteous a cause.

JUDGE.—Inasmuch as you are the bell-wether of a naughtie flocke, and a ringleader of evil men; and this county, and especially this place, are noted for these seditious meetings, by reason whereof the King and the Counsell are in many feares, and new warres like to be hatched, and as you doe, insteade of repenting, aggravate your fault by your obstinate carriage, the judgment of the Court is that you be fined a hundred markes, and lie in jayle till you have paid it, and given security for the good behaviour.

ALLEINE.—Glory be to God, that hath accounted me worthy to suffer for His Gospell!

And soe he drew off the barre.

Note.—The evidence upon which Alleine was found guilty at the assizes, was the very same upon the insufficiency whereof he was not found guilty at the sessions ; J. Lake and G. Tweagle being the only witnesses in both cases. What handsome attempts, in their want of evidence, were used to get it, further appeares by this that is subjoyned.

John Lake saies that he was threatened by J. W. and R. H., that if he would not take an oathe against Mr. Alleine for preaching divers times since Bartholomew day, they would send him to gaole, swearing awfully in their talke.

Tweagle saithe that he was vehemently urged to sweare before the justices, and that they used many arguments with him, both by persuasions and threatenings. Among the reste that noe dammage should come to him, for which they offered to lay downe £5. But if he would not sweare, he should lose Sir William Porteman's* custome, and Mr. H. saide he would rid him out of the lande.

Mr. Norman was next placed at the bar. The following is a specimen of what passed between him and the judge in the course of the trial :—

" Sirrah, do you preach ?"

" Yes, my lord."

" And why so, sirrah ?"

---

* "Sir William Portman ; in hopes to be a lord, much priest-ridden."—Andrew Marvell. List of principal Labourers in the great designs of Popery and Arbitrary Power. Amsterdam, 1677.

" Because I was ordained to preach the Gospel."

" How were you ordained ?"

" In the same manner as Timothy."

" And how was that ?"

" By the laying on of the hands of the presbytery."

The judge said to himself, in a musing way, " Ordained like Timothy ? Timothy ?" He had met with a person of that name somewhere, but now, not being able to recal the particular case referred to, he prudently changed the subject. Still, the question troubled his mind, and shortly after, when a gentleman called at his lodgings on business, Sir Robert kept him waiting two hours in an ante-chamber. On his appearance " he gave for his excuse that he had been searching his books about an odd answer a fellow made him in the West, who told him that he was ordained like Timothy, by the laying on of the hands of the presbytery, which he could make nothing of."

Calamy says, that " although Mr. Norman was a man of a very grave presence and carriage, the judge treated him very roughly." After he had been thus roughly addressing him, and at the same time pouring unmeasured contempt on other Non-conformist ministers, Mr. Norman " with great gravity told him that their learned education in the university, and holy calling in the ministry, not stained with any unworthy action, merited good words from his lordship, and better usage from

the world." This woke up a fresh tempest of
invective. " Sir," answered the prisoner, "*you
must ere long appear before a greater Judge to give
an account of your actions, and for your railing on me,
the servant of that great Judge.*" Perhaps Mr.
Norman saw the shadow of coming death on the
face of the poor old man who glared upon him,
trembling and white with passion—this was only a
natural perception ; but when the judge died suddenly on the circuit, in little more than a month
after,* the country people remembered the speech,
and called it a prophecy.

On his way back to Ilchester Gaol, whither he
was taken in pursuance of a sentence like Alleine's,
the officers insisted upon stopping to rest at the
sheriff's house. Lady Warre, the sheriff's wife,
came to look at the prisoner and to insult him with
cruel taunts. Among other things, she said, " Mr.
Norman, *Where is your God now ?*" " Madam,"
he replied, " have you a Bible in the house?"
" Yes ; we are not so heathenish as to be without
a Bible." A Bible was brought, and turning to
the prophecies of Micah, he read the words—
" Rejoice not against me, O mine enemy ; when I
fall, I shall rise ; when I sit in darkness, the Lord
shall be a light to me. I will bear the indignation

---

* Sir Robert Foster died 4th of October, 1663, and was buried at
Egham in Surrey.

of the Lord, because I have sinned against Him ;
until he plead my cause, and execute judgment for
me : He will bring me forth to the light, and I
shall behold His righteousness. *Then she that is
mine enemy shall see it, and shame shall cover her
which said unto me, Where is the Lord thy God?*
Mine eyes shall behold her ; and now shall she be
trodden down as the mire in the streets."* The
lady retired in silence, and " the dealings of God with
the family not very long after," adds the narrator,
" made this to be remembered." These two inci-
dents will serve to show the half-superstitious reverence in which many of the people regarded the
sufferers. They looked upon them as the people
of Scotland did upon the martyrs of the covenant,
who were often supposed to speak in " something
like prophetic strain." They saw in them the
" spirit and power" of the old seers, of whom they
were daily reading—the same sanctity—the same
intense life—and it would have been no surprise
to find that in some awful moments they were
gifted with the same strange intelligence. This
disposed them to hear as prophecies, words that
were only meant as warnings ; and stories of things
that mysteriously came true, just as they had predicted, long haunted the country-side. It was
partly owing to this, in a few cases at least, that

---

* Micah vii. 8, 9, 10.

witnesses against them were found with so much difficulty. Many were "willing to wound, but afraid to strike." Hundreds of men in Taunton, haters of the Gospel, who might have appeared against Alleine, hung back — some indeed from shame, some from a sense of honour, but some from "fear of a judgment." Sudden calamity, it was said, had often lighted on informers, and it had been known to come in fulfilment of something the persecuted men had spoken.

Chapter XI.

Doings in Ilchester Gaol.

" Though men may keep my outward man
Within their locks and bars,
Yet by the faith of Christ I can
Mount higher than the stars."

JOHN BUNYAN'S PRISON HYMN.

ILCHESTER, says an old chronicler, " is a little town in no wise remarkable, save that it sendeth two burgesses to Parliament." This statement does it injustice. It is remarkable for its historical prison. It is remarkable for having had there, in Protestant times, and simply for proclaiming Protestant truths, without the permission of a Protestant State, some of the best ministers of religion known in any age. It has the honour of having been the scene of more imprisonment for righteousness' sake than most other country towns were, during the same period of time —the time when, in the language of John Bunyan,

" Those who had most of the spirit of prayer were all to be found in gaol; and those who had most zeal for the form of prayer were all to be found at the alehouse." The scandal of this distinction, if there be any, rests with those in whom the responsibility centered, but the glory belongs to Ilchester.

After the assizes, the prisoners were greatly multiplied. Mr. Alleine and his friends were placed in their old chamber, where they suffered all their old grievances. Amidst the clatter and tinkle of tools plied by industrious Quaker fingers " for a sign," and the war of crossing voices at the same time raised against them " for a testimony," they resumed their old engagements. The ministers still continued to preach, generally through the window-grate; but this part of the labour was now lightened, owing to the greater number who could officiate in turn. The names of the preachers cannot now be all ascertained ; but amongst them, besides those already given, were the following :—
Mr. Stephen Coven, late rector of Sanford Peveril, then well known by his book called " The Military Christian.—Mr. Thomas Powell, M.A., late of St. Sidwell's, Exeter, an Independent minister, author of several works still highly valued.—Mr. Humphrey Phillips, M.A., of both universities, and fellow of Magdalen College, Oxford ; he had already been in the prison several months, and, several months after this, he was taken one

snowy day to the prison at Wells, where he was
put into a chamber which he said was " like unto
Noah's ark, full of all sorts of creatures."—Mr.
Henry Parsons, a learned man, who, like South,
had been episcopally ordained by one of the
deprived bishops ; but who, not having South's
flexible principles, could not give unfeigned assent
and consent to all and everything in the new Book
of Common Prayer.   The usual consequences followed.   He was not imprisoned with the others at
the summer assizes ; but one day, some time after,
the door opened and he dropped down among them
—wet, soiled, ghastly, and marked· with blood.
He had been serving Alleine's bereaved people at
Taunton, and had now been brought to the gaol
direct from a numerous congregation to which he
had been preaching.   The officers had pulled him
from his horse at the beginning of the journey,
and by strokes of their riding-whips had driven
him along the rough road on foot.—Mr. Tobias
Willes, one of the Baptist ministers at Bridgewater,
who, writing at the time to the churches at Chard
and Wedmore, thus expressed himself: "For our
profession we are now in bonds, as many of our
fellow-brethren are ; yet notwithstanding do hope
that the Gospel shall no whit suffer loss thereby,
but shall more abundantly break forth in power
and purity, and shall run conquering and to con-
quer.   Oh, brethren, go on, though you are in the

wilderness, look to the cloud of God's presence; we have no cause to discourage you from what we find, for God is very good to us. Here strangers do not intermeddle with our joys; we have liberty in bonds; yea, the greatest liberty is here. Therefore, brethren, do not fear, gird up the loines of your minds, and be sober and hope to the end; trim your lamps, see that each has oil in his vessel, for the night is upon us, and at midnight there was a great cry made, ' Behold the bridegroom cometh !'"* The name of one more minister was on this illustrious roll-call, and he was the Nestor of the company, who on many accounts deserves more particular attention.

This was Mr. John Torner, M.A., late parish minister of North Cricket. In the war he had been chaplain to the regiment of Sir John Fitzjames. So highly was he esteemed by Mr. Edmund Prideaux, attorney-general to the Long Parliament, that at the commencement and close of every session the two friends used to spend a day of prayer together. He was now nearly seventy, but still sound in body and strong in spirit. In religious decision, stern, straightforward, fearless; in natural temper, hopeful and cheerful; in bodily presence, if the picture before our minds be correct—

---

* Letter from Ilchester Gaol in 1663, signed by Tobias Willes and S. Wade.— Baptist Register.

> " A man of glee,
> With hair of glittering grey ;
> As blithe a man as you could see
> On a spring holiday."

Old as he was, he seemed to retain all the fire of
youth, and could lift up his voice like a trumpet.
The roll of that great voice was amazing.   It was
unquestionably a rare gift ; but as Nonconformist
ministers were commanded to be silent, he hardly
knew what to do with it.   At last, his friends
invented a way of turning it to a useful account.
Tradition says that he was wont to hold a service
with his family in one of the cellars of Ford
Abbey.   There he sat in the open door-way—all
the other doors and windows in that part of the
house being left open up to the attic.   The whole
place was soon filled with John Torner's thunder.
If, at the same time, every room happened also
to be filled with quiet people on a visit to Mr.
Prideaux—even if a few villagers happened to be
standing in the dark among the trees outside—how
could he know, or why need he care, for what harm
was he doing ?   A father was teaching his own
children—" that was alle."   Only his children and
grandchildren were in the cellar with him, and was
that an unlawful assembly ?   He afterwards found
that while he had been innocently sitting at the
cellar-door talking to the family within, he had
also been preaching to ten or twelve different con-

gregations—preaching to them all at once, though they all met at different places, and he had not been present at one of them. Truly it was wonderful, but was it wicked ? Romanist saint never wrought a greater miracle, but what law did it break ? Unhappily, the interpreter of the law decided against him ; and John Torner, instead of being canonized, was sent to prison as a warning to all sinners.

Even there, scope was found for his peculiar faculty ; for after preaching his own sermonsd own to the congregation in the street, he would rehearse the sermons of others, and transmit messages from his brethren whose exhausted voices unfitted them to speak for themselves. One day, the veteran was holding forth from the window in his own hearty way, when the gaoler fired at him. Owing to a sudden movement of his head, quite accidentally as it seemed, the shot missed.* " The circumstance of being fired at," remarks a judicious writer, " is apt to produce a momentary confusion in a man's ideas." Not so with John Torner ; he continued his discourse, only giving it a personal application to Harrison Skinner,† the foolish per-

---

* A soldier shot a brace of bullets at Vavasor Powell, when he was preaching from the window of his Montgomery prison, but God preserved him.—Life and Death of Powell, 1672, p. 125.

† Harrison Skinner was appointed in October, 1660.—State Papers.

son who had discharged the pistol, addressing him in language so nervous and racy that he " did make him quake and tremble." Mr. Torner was kept in prison five years, but it is cheering to know that he lived to the age of 94, in great honour and comfort; and that before he died, many persons assured him that they owed all their happiness to his prison sermons.

There must have been something highly exasperating, you are about to say, in sermons that made the gaoler think that he might shoot the preacher, without risk of losing his own place or offending the gentry who had just appointed him. Let us inquire. Torner had no reporter, but we can form some judgment of the kind of preaching in which he took a share, from some surviving specimens of the sermons that were delivered by others in the same course, and of those delivered in like circumstances elsewhere. They were not elegantly finished performances—that you would hardly expect in discourses preached from so rough a rostrum, and so likely to be interrupted in their delivery by exploding gunpowder. But, on the other hand, they were not wild words flung off in the heat of passion. They were only the ordinary addresses of the Puritan pastors to their flocks, laying down the laws of Christian duty in logical inference from Christian doctrine, with all their usual learning, and all their usual hair-splitting casuistry.

When read over now, some of them make us
wonder that they could ever have produced a
popular effect. Depend upon it, these cold, heavy,
spent thunderbolts were electric when they struck.
These extinct sentences were once all flame, and
rushed burning from soul to soul; but their flame
was all from Heaven. There was no party spirit
in them. They breathed no complaints. They
made no allusions to the common trial, except to
suggest comfort, to urge constancy, and to enjoin
obedience to the magistrate in all things within his
province. Their only tendency was to make bad
men good, and good men better.

Here are some extracts from a book by Mr.
Norman, evidently the record of sermons preached
at this time, and most likely from the prison window. They will help you, not only to know
what such exercises were like, but what the people
were like who flocked every day from the villages
all round, and stood in the streets for hours
together to hear them. The subject is, " Confessing Christ."*

He first explains what it is to confess Christ.

---

* The title is, " Christ Confessed : written by a Preacher of the
Gospel, and now a Prisoner." Printed in the year 1665. 4to., pp.
114. The work consists of some rough notes which had long been
circulated in manuscript, were never intended for the press by the
author, but which were at last printed by some stranger. The style
is often very loose and wordy, and some of the quotations now given
have been abridged.

" We are to acknowledge our dependence on Him in *point of light.* He is the only supreme Teacher of the church, and the church is not to admit offices of human invention, nor ordinances of human appointment, nor doctrines of human imagination. There is no truth which Christ hath taught which we may part with, or must not profess, due circumstances attending.—We are to acknowledge our dependence upon Him in point of *life.* He is the only Priest of the church, without colleague or successor ; and we are not to admit any other order of priesthood, or any observances, such as altars and ceremonies, properly belonging to the abrogated priesthood, for to His office pertaineth absolute perfection.—We are to acknowledge our dependency on Him for *law*, that is, for the application of the work which He has wrought out with a view to the regulation of our lives ; and so it is His sole prerogative to be King and Head of His church, to constitute church laws, to substitute church officers, to institute church seals and censures, and to have the sole investiture of the conscience."

" *Our principles must be seen—they must be serviceable.* There is not one talent, but it is to trade with. Faith, hope, love, are all for exercise, and so for the praise and honour of the Giver, though not for ostentation by the user." " True grace is compared to light, and to fire, which are not only communicative of their virtues, but carry a self-evidence. Can you believe Christ in your heart, and not confess Christ with your mouths?"

" His followers are known by their confession, and by having His Father's name written, not occultly in their backs, or in their breasts, or in their hands, but in their *foreheads*." " Gird up the loins of your mind, then. A saint! A Christian! Yet afraid to confess Christ! How unlike it is to the spirits of the saints that breathed in the primitive times and stories! Those offered themselves frequently to the test and tormentors. They loved not their lives to the death, and suffered joyfully the spoiling of their goods. What mean these subterfuges and shifting fetches, this shyness and these straitening fears, which so hold or oppress you? Come, show yourselves to be men, if not saints. Be followers of them who through faith and patience do inherit the promises."

" There is no time wherein we may do anything contrary to what we should at *any* time allow to be our duty concerning Christ." Confession of Christ must be maintained,

" 1. *Though the defection be never so general.* ' Though truth faileth, and he that departeth from evil maketh himself a prey, or is accounted mad,' as in Isaiah's time. Though we should be left alone, as Elijah was; or have the whole world against one, as Athanasius: yet one Elijah,

one Athanasius, must be against all the priests of
Baal, against the whole world of heretical and ungodly men.   Our rule is, 'We must not follow
a multitude to do evil.'   We must not be conformed to this world, we must not run into the
same excess of riot, however strange it be reputed ;
but keep our uprightness and profession in the
middest of a crooked and perverse nation ?"

" 2. *Though the danger be never so great,* we
must hold fast our profession without wavering,
and may not cast away our confidence, whatever it
cost us.   Let the constellation of martyrs excite
you.   Did they boggle at this duty because it
would bring danger?   No dungeon, no den, no
distress, no stones, no straits, no fire, no furnace,
no bonds, no banishment, no bloody tortures could
move them from this duty, when they saw 'a manifest door open' for them thus to administer to
others' good and God's glory. . . . Doubtless, it
was their duty, else they were madmen rather than
martyrs.   If it were their duty to confess Christ in
extremities, how have you got a dispensation ?
Cease from the wisdom of this world.   If it saith,
' Better sin than suffer, better turn than burn,
better dissemble, or deny, than die, better strain a
point in profession than starve in prison,' say,
' This thy way is thy folly, and will surely issue in
damnation.'"

He thus encourages timid confessors :—

" You are secured in your *lives* till you have finished your testimony ; immortal till your witness is delivered and your work is done ; and who can desire to live longer, that liveth for God here, and hopeth to live with God in glory hereafter, when he hath finished his work ? 'Tis said, ' when the two witnesses had finished their testimony, *then* (and not till then) the beast that ascended out of the bottomless pit overcame and killed them.'* They never fell, till their testimony was finished. O, ye believers, the year, month, week, day, hour, of your end or death, and of effecting their design, is under a divine limit. When our Saviour taught in the treasury, and therefore to the very teeth of His adversaries, so that they might have easily taken Him (looking at second causes), and by wicked hands have slain Him, yet, full of enraged malice as they were, ' no man laid hand on Him.' Why ? ' His hour was not yet come.' But when that hour came, forthwith they laid hands on Him and led Him away. ' Fear not them that can kill the body,' for not only have they no more that they can do, but they are under an almighty restraint in this also. Not only the essential and integral parts of confessors, but ' the very hairs of their heads ' are under the lock and key, the care and custody of the Lord Christ ; and when you have finished

---

* Rev. xii. 7.

s 2

your course and filled up your confession, let the
enemy *kill* you, he cannot *hurt* you."

" You are secured as to your *liberty* too, so far
as it will further your testimony.   And can you
reasonably expect or endeavour more ?   So long as
liberty will best serve the ends for which you are
made, or maintained, or converted, you shall be
sure to have it, that is, so long as it will be most
useful for you to serve God by it.   He ensured
Paul as much, and you may by faith warrant your
interest in the same promises, as far as concerns the
profession, and your continued liberty will promote
the same ends."   .   .   .   " Away with your fears,
then, and act faith.   'Tis true, your profession may
cost some of you a prison ; and what is a prison
with God's presence, and for professing Jesus ?   A
prison perfumed, a palace, a paradise, a living
extacie, a lower heaven, a little emblem of the
liberties of eternity, if you will believe the experiences of God's prisoners.   .   .   .   Sirs, if you
are good earnest Christians, you have enough not
only to quicken you, but to quiet you when dis-
tracted and discomposed, to give cheerfulness when
drooping and despondent.   Shake off all discouragements then ; 'Stand fast in the faith, quit
you like men, be strong.' "

" We must buy the truth at any rate, whatever
it may cost us, but may not sell the truth at any
rate, whatever it may yield us."

He thus addresses confessors who may be tempted to equivocate or dissemble, in order to escape the penalties attending decision.

"*We may not, in the confession of Christ, dissemble in matters of faith.* As there was no guile found in the mouth of the Saviour, so neither may there be in the mouth of His saints. . . . Both the doctrine and the grace of faith is characterised by the apostle to be ἀνυπόκριτος (1 Tim. i. 5 ; 2 Tim. i. 5) unfeigned ; or, as the same word is rendered (Rom. xii. 9), without dissimulation. We are called to a plain confession of our faith in Jesus, and may not seek the covers of ambiguous phrases, or clothe the chaste and holy verities of Christ with the meretricious terms of the heathen or the heretic who examines us, then think to make it up by an after salvo of distinctions. If such frauds in matters of faith were passable, what fools were our Marian martyrs, to deal so openly on the points of *merit, satisfaction, real presence,*—who could but know that those terms might receive a construction that comported with the sense of Protestants as well as Papists ; but these holy men of God had better studied the simplicity of the Gospel, than that their confession should be in deceit or guile."

" We may not by equivocal expressions, or compliance with the adversaries' dialect, prevent the trials which are probably not far off. For this doth virtually seek the patronage of their sin to

the protection of yourselves. It doth foully slur
the evangelical perfection, together with your own
profession, however you may pre-apprehend a
possibility of evading by the door of an after-ex-
position and distinction. Nay, this liberty would
make void the scope and spirit of confession.
This were, indeed, to cover the faith, not to confess it. . . . Your business is not to hold fast
a form ' of *safe* words,' but of ' *sound* words ;' and
to speak sound truths in sound terms. We are to
abstain from all appearance of evil in doctrinal
positions, as well as in dues of practice. Though
Judah be cast among idolaters, Judah must call
God ' no more by the word Baali, but Ishi,'
because, although Baali also signified Lord, it was
vulgarly known to be applied to the heathen idol."

" We may not, then, dissemble in words, nor in
any other way, when called to a confession of our
faith in Christ. There is no allowance to Arrius
of the paper in his bosom, nor of the acts of the
Priscillianists, to lie behind the curtain. These are
fleshly artifices that harden the adversaries against
the honesty and sincerity of your profession.
. . . Your works in this case would give your
words the lye. . . . You must avoid not
only the sins, but the signs of idolatry."

" There may be no act carrying an appearance of
idolatrous worship done by us. God chargeth His
people that they shall not herein do like the

idolatrous heathen round about them.* How memorable to this purpose are the instances of Eleazer and Auxentius ! Who, though they might preserve their own lives and liberties by such an appearance of conformity, dared not thus stain their holy profession, or scandalize their brethren, or strengthen the hands of their persecutors,—the one by setting the branch of a vine-tree, loaden with clusters, at the feet of Bacchus, his image ; the other, by using his own provision which was lawful for him to eat, yet make as if he did eat the flesh of the sacrifice commanded by the King.† There may be no allowance of any evil or idolatrous act of worship done for us . . . and so to have fellowship with a work of darkness which we are rather to reprove. The signal zeal of Valentinian I may not pass by in this particular, who, when the priests had besprinkled him with their paganish holy water, as he passed before Julian into the Temple of Fortune, broke off those parts of his garments on which the water fell, and burned with just indignation against the priest himself." " You countenance a sin negatively when you do not, according to your place, discountenance it,—when you do not what in you lies regularly to reprove it."

Confession is urged on the ground of God's

---

* 2 Kings xvii. 15. † 2 Mac. vi. 18.

glory. " Is not this your end, and doth not conscience dictate the present usefulness of this means in order to that end? Let every tongue confess that Jesus is Lord, to the glory of God the Father. Who may dare to be mute when the Lord is to be magnified ?"

It is urged on the ground that the Gospel will be best proclaimed by it. " Must we not all pray that the word of the Lord may have free course and be glorified? Then surely we must, according to our place and calling, do our best and most to promote it. . . . Yea, rather than not profess it, ' you must be partakers of the afflictions of the Gospel according to the power of God, and not be ashamed of the testimony of the Lord, nor of such as are His prisoners.' "

It is urged on the ground of the good done to souls by it, especially under the existing circumstances. " No man should seek his own only, but every one another's welfare. Ye may not hide yourselves in whatsoever concerns your neighbours' estates, but help them even to their straying brutes.* Much less may you hide yourselves in what concerns their souls. Ah, Sirs! who should be silent when souls lie at stake ?"

He thus answers the question, whether it be lawful, and when, for persecuted confessors to flee.

---

* Deut. xxi. 1—6.

" You may take the liberty of flight, if the aforesaid ends will be better furthered by your flight than your stay. In this case, God Himself instructs Elijah to hide himself, first at Cherith, afterwards at Zarepath, for a sanctuary. Paul and Barnabas frequently provide for their own safety by a timely retreat from popular fury. The woman flees into the wilderness, and God prepares her not only place and provision but wings for flight."

" You must tarry, and may not flie without sin, when these ends are best accomplished by your stay. While Paul may best forward the concerns of Christ at Corinth by his continuance there, he will not flinch or flie one foot from thence. Religious Stephen will ride out the storm at Hierusalem, though it rain stones and slaughter, so long as the Gospel may rise and live by his death and downfal. As you are now circumstanced, will these ends be best provided for by your standing your ground? Then do not either face about or flie away. Say rather, with stout and resolute Nehemiah, ' Should such a man as I flie? and who is there, that being as I am, would go into the temple to save his life? I will not go in.' Though our Saviour did prudently decline those politic engines whereby the Pharisees did seek to ensnare and apprehend Him, yet when His hour was come wherein He might best glorifie His Father and give an example of

endurance to His faithfull, He went forth to meet
the officers."

One of the questions discussed is, " To what
degree of explicit confession are we bound in the
times whereupon we now are cast ?"   In answer to
this, he says that though no man can be discharged
by any peril or calamity whatever from the most
open possible profession of Christ, yet sometimes
circumstances dictate that the great ends of confession may be best advanced by greater privacy in
the mode of profession than would be right at
other times;   as Christ Himself, under varying
circumstances, sometimes preached in a small company, sometimes to the great congregation.   The
same causes should influence us in the selection of
the special truth we should most emphatically profess.   " It should always be that which is most
under present question and contradiction."

He further speaks of the spirit that will best
quicken and encourage a good confession.

" Quicken and keep up love.   If you love
Christ, how can you be loath to confess ? Holy love
fetcheth in, fixeth, and fireth the interiour mind and
exteriour members to and for its beloved ?   ' The
love of Christ,' saith Paul, ' constraineth us ($\sigma\upsilon\nu\acute{\epsilon}\chi\epsilon$) ;'
it hath, hems in, and holds in the whole man
together, and there is no getting out from the siege
and co-arctation of this holy love.   Love unites
the strength of the soul within itself and upon its

objeƈt. . . . Love is venturous, vehement, viƈtorious, and will at no hand be flattered or frightened, or beaten from Christ, or any of His concernments. . . . Love makes the cross easie, amiable, admirable, delicious. Did Jacob's service seem but a few daies to him for the love he had for Rachel? O! how easie will be the yoak, how light the burden of confession to hearts once overpowered with divine love to this dear Redeemer!

" Quicken and keep up hope. . . . Sirs! this holy hope will assure and rejoice your hearts, and that in the greatest straits that can come upon you for confessing the name of Jesus. This hath cordial and celestial water in its hand for you, to revive you in every swoon and refresh you in every sadness. O Christians! ' rejoice in hope of the glory of God,' and then ' glory in tribulation also.' No marvel if your hearts are sad when your hopes are sunk. Quicken hope, and look to the end !"

" Quicken and keep up joy. Joy aƈts upon the doore of the soule to let in all encouraging means and motives. Fears shrivel and contraƈt the heart, but joy dilates and widens and enlarges it to do the utmost duties and endure the utmost dangers that may come upon us for confessing Christ's name. . . . The joy of the Lord is our strength. . . . ' I am filled with comfort,' saith Paul, ' I am exceeding joyful in all our tribulation.   Maintain your comforts, then, as you would maintain the interest of Christ, and let your confession be full of ingenuity and freedom.   Count it joy—all joy —when you fall into divers temptations."

He then proceeds to show that these animating affections are imparted by the Spirit of God through prayer.

" Be strong in the Spirit.   The flesh will pull you back, and at best profits you nothing.   The Spirit alone can savingly empower you to a suitable confession.   ' No man can say that Jesus is Lord, but by the Holy Ghost.' . . . Solicit Heaven then that thou mayest ' be strengthened with all might by the Spirit in the inner man.'   In that thy strength is so little, and the service so great, ply Heaven the harder, and fetch down a daily influx of divine help. . . . Run to Him in every difficulty, and repose thyself on Him in every duty. Draw strength from Him that thou mayest declare His sufficiency.   ' Blessed is the man, O Lord, whose strength is in thee.' "

His appeal at the close is a charge to confess Christ " Vnderstandingly, Vndoubtingly, Vndauntedly, Vndividedly, Vnfeignedly, Vniversally, Vnoffensively, Vltimately for God."

We can only spare space for some of his remarks under two of these divisions.   " Confess Christ," he says,—

" *Vndividedly.*" " Gebal, and Ammon, and
Amalek combine in ungodliness, and shall the
godly quarrel with each other about the Gospel ?
Oh, where are the golden taches of the Tabernacle
that should unite the many curtains into one tent
of confessions ? Alass ! for the staffe of beauty
and the staffe of bands, so strangely broken !
When shall Christians stand fast in one spirit, with
one mind, and strive *together* for the faith of the
Gospel, and no more *against* one another in
ungodly factions ? The unity of confession will be
their own glory and His also, whom they confess.
'Tis the badge, 'tis the beauty, 'tis the blessing of
the church. ' My dove is but one,' saith Christ;
' the daughter saw her and blessed her.' Yea,
' there the Lord commandeth the blessing, even
life for evermore.' Confesse Christ

" *Vnoffensively.* ' Give no offence, no, not in
anything,' nor unto any man, that the blessed
Gospel ' be not blamed.' Lord it not herein over
other men, as if their faith were to be limited by
thy faith, much lesse by thy phancie. Be lowly
and meek in your answers to them that ask you,
yea, though they. are adversaries to you. Set aside
whatever matters or modes of expression may
justly harden or provoke them, and study to please
wherein thou mayest profit them. Comport yourselves agreeable to the circumstances you are in :
others may lose the benefit and yourselves the

blessing of your confession by an unbecoming circumstance therein.   Mind what they *now* can bear
who are private men, and whose authority they also
bear who are publique magistrates, that your zeal
for God may be tempered with submission to
governours as it ought, so that they take not just
offence."

While these appeals were sounding from the
prison windows, the King came into the neighbourhood.   On the 29th of August he visited Bath,
where he remained for a little time to drink the
waters and enjoy the gaiety.   Addresses full of
humility, miracles of metaphor, floods of adoring
eloquence were called forth by this amazing act of
royal condescension.   The recorder welcomed his
Majesty in "a pithie and rhetorical speech," in the
course of which he glorified him as "the preserver
of all the felicities of the nation," and said, "The
greater number of our visitants come to receive
health from *Vs;* your Majestie (God be prais'd)
does us this honour without that necessity, and
the very *sight* of you (for not only is your *touch,*
Sir, medicinall) is able to give more health here
than the virtue of all our bathes !"*

In contrast with this, read an address that was sent
shortly before this time from Ilchester Gaol.   It was
from the Quakers.   An epistle from members of

* The Newes, September, 1663.

the Society of Friends to "Comus and his crew!"
Thus they wrote to him whom they called "Our
good friend Charles:"*—

"Forasmuch, O King! as our sufferings are
augmented, and our number in this place so greatly
increased, as that we cannot any longer well hold
our peace, we do in the fear of God, and in true
humility in thy sight, in all lowliness of mind, after
long imprisonment, present thee, in this thy progress and day of prosperity, with our grievous
sufferings for our conscience in things relating to
God; our souls being subject to the Lord that
made heaven and earth: and against thee, O King,
have we not done or imagined evil, but do,
according to the truth and righteousness in our
hearts, desire thy peace and prosperity, and that
mercy may establish thy throne in equity and
justice. And whereas we who are called *Quakers*,†

---

* "We are come to testify our sorrow at the death of our good
friend Charles, and our joy for thy being made our governour."—
Address to James II. Library of Devonshire House.

† George Fox was committed to the Derby House of Correction,
October 30, 1650, by a mittimus signed by Gervase Bennett and
Nathaniel Barton. "Barton was an Independent . . . When
G. Fox bade him tremble at the word of the Lord, he took hold of
this weighty saying in such an airy mind, that from thence he took
occasion to call him and his friends, scornfully, *Quakers*."—Sewell.
From that time they were generally known under this scornful title,
although they declared that their true designation was "The Children of Light." The people persisted in thinking "Quakers"
to be their proper name. One writer seemed to think he had found

because of the fear of God, and to keep our consciences void of offence, cannot take any oath, many of us are by a severe sentence deprived of all the goods we have in this world, and our wives and innocent children thereby exposed to utter ruin, unless the execution thereof be prevented ; and others by fines beyond their abilities adjudged to perpetual imprisonment ; and that for matter of pure conscience only, and not for any design of evil or wrong intended towards thee, O King, nor any of thy subjects, as hath been largely testified by many years' experience through many trials and hardships in bonds, wherein the Lord hath been with us, and preserved us innocent and upright in our hearts toward thee ; and for this we appeal to the witness of God in all men, whether we have not so approved ourselves this day, in the sight of God and man.   And as an addition to our present sufferings the gaoler's cruelty so abounds, that many of us are likely to be exposed to famishment and utter destruction, being thrust together in such great number, and denied such necessary accommodation as is ordinarily given to the worst of men,

---

a kind of prophetic reference to them, as such, in the Bible, for he applied to them a text in 1 Sam. xiv. 15, which he thus translated :— " And there was trembling, or *quaking*, in the host, in the field, and among the people ; the garrisons, and the spoilers, they also trembled, and the earth *quaked*; so it was a very great *quaking*."—Quakerism Unmask'd by Will. Prynne of Swainswick, Esq , 1664.

besides what is daily further threatened. We therefore, as to our outward man, being objects of thy mercy and clemency, it being in thy hands to dispose of us at thy pleasure, do in all due submission make an appeal to thee, as unto one who is able to relieve us; and the Lord open thy heart to consider our innocency and distress, and to acquit us from our grievous sentences, and our imprisonment. And it is the desire of our hearts that in truth and righteousness the God of peace may prosper thee to reign; and what profit will the death of the innocent be to the King?

"From the prisoners called Quakers, in Ilchester, the 4th day of the seventh month, 1663."*

Strange does it seem to us, that between the writers of these noble and pathetic words, and the ministers who were their fellow-sufferers, there did not exist a more perfect sympathy. Strange must it now seem to them, as they review their trials from the world of love, for we know they now "see eye to eye, and with the voice together they do sing."

Let us return to our own company. As the winter came on, the ministers found the cold of the Bridewell chamber as bad to bear as had formerly been its furnace-heat. It had no chimney, and the ragged fractures of roof or window, once so needful, now threatened to be only inlets for the drifting

---

* Besse's Sufferings of the Quakers. Somerset.

T

snow.   After long negotiation with the magistrates, and much difficulty, they obtained permission to be transferred to the ward, a place more convenient in every respect.

The first use Mr. Alleine made of this increased seclusion was to write his " Call to Archippus," an eloquent appeal to the Nonconformist ministers, charging them, though in the face of danger and suffering, " to fulfil their ministry," to rally their scattered congregations,—if free, to preach to them just as ever ; or if in prison, to teach them by pastoral epistles.   The effect was immediate and extensive; and proof might be given that the church owes many valuable instructions, both oral and printed, to the stimulus of these burning lines.

Next, he wrote an " Exposition of the Assembly's Shorter Catechism,* with an affectionate Letter annexed, and Rules for Daily Self-examination." Directly this was printed, he sent a copy to every family under his own ministerial charge, so that the Christian education of the children might not suffer through the withdrawment of their minister.

After this he wrote for his flock a treatise called " A Synopsis of the Covenant."   This was at first circulated separately, and then included in the Third Part of the *Vindiciæ Pietatis* of his father-in-law, Mr. Richard Alleine.   The senior John

* Exposition of Assembly's Catechism, pp. 176.

Ryland calls it "that glorious synopsis, the gem of the book." He also wrote the chapter entitled, "A Soliloquy representing the believer's triumph in God's covenant, and the various conflicts and glorious conquests of faith over unbelief." He had contributed before his imprisonment to the first part of the same work.* If it could tell its own story, it would be found that few books could match it for romantic adventures. Sheldon refused to license it.† It was published without a license. It was then rapidly bought up, and "did much to mend this bad world." Not being licensed, Roger Norton, the king's printer, caused a large part of the impression to be seized and sent to the royal kitchen. On second thoughts, it seemed to him to be a sin that a book at once so holy and so saleable should be consigned to a fate so obscure. He therefore bought back the sheets, says Calamy, "for an old song," bound them, and sold them in his own shop. This was complained of, the honest man had to beg pardon on his knees before the council-table, and the remaining copies were sentenced to be "rubbed over with an inky brush,"

---

* Mr. Alleine's *Vindiciæ Pietatis* appeared successively in three parts, issued in 1660, 1663, and 1665.

† In the Act of 1661, for regulating the press, it was enacted, *inter alia,* that no book of divinity should be printed without the license of the lord archbishop of Canterbury or bishop of London for the time being.

and sent back to the kitchen for lighting fires. The mission of the book was not ended yet. It was re-issued by the author, was read by high and low ; and among other instances of good effected by it which he lived to see, was one in the case of a Yorkshire thief, who, attracted by the glitter of its binding, stole it from a stall at Woodend, took it home, read it, then brought it back to the owner, confessing his crime in stealing it, but thanking God for making it . the means of his conversion.   At the present moment, this book, so eventful in its story, is on its travels in various lands, speaking in various languages, and, we hope, not speaking in vain.

His labours in the ward were not merely those of a writer. " Here," writes his wife, " he and his companions had very great meetings, week-days and Sabbath-days, and many days of humiliation and thanksgiving. The Lord's days many hundreds came." Here, too, he held constant conferences with his people ; here he taught all the children who were sent to him, and invented plans for the elder to teach the younger when he was gone. He also sent out catechisms to be distributed among the poor families of Ilchester and the surrounding villages. The gaol chaplain falling ill, he dared to take his place, and, until prohibited, was much with the felons, preaching to them, talking to them, and, by gifts to relieve their physical misery, trying to win his way to their souls. Unhasting, unresting, month after month, he thus worked on, and sometimes after these varied toils all day, kept on his day-clothes all night, having only time for one or two hours' sleep; for he always rose at four o'clock in the morning, to begin those secret prayers which he felt to be more essential than ever.

Labours like these were not to be tolerated. Merely to punish the "unauthorised ministers" with bonds was a weak leniency, and it really seemed to do more harm than good. Other measures were thought of, as we learn from Mrs. Alleine, who says :—" My husband and brother Norman had many threats from the judges and justices that they should be sent beyond sea, or be carried to some island, where they should be kept close prisoners." " This banishment," she says, " they constantly expected." Do you know what this meant ? In this and the following reign the sugar-trade had remarkable prosperity.* There was a great desire to procure white labourers instead of negro slaves to work in the West India plantations.† To meet this demand, and at the same time to relieve the

---

* In an old folio sheet, 1666 is mentioned as the year of its greatest prosperity.

† Complaint was sometimes made of the deficiency of white convicts.—Rise and Progress of the West India Colonies, 1690, p. 41.

country of serious expense, many convicts were sent over.* This was an old practice, and Cromwell had thus punished, for treason, seventy persons who had taken part in the rising of Penruddock and Grove. But it was now occasionally done in a secret and fraudulent way. Certain magistrates were known to take peculiar interest in the prisoners who were sentenced to transportation, and were suspected of having been anxious to secure the passing of such a sentence, in order that they might receive money for the convicts, and virtually sell them to the planters. For the same purpose, some of these guardians of justice used to induce men liable to death or hopeless imprisonment, to escape the terrors of the law, by engaging to go to the colonies for a given period.† Such culprits were employed in grinding, digging, and working at the furnaces; lived under the lash, were sold from planter to planter, and but few came back to tell the woeful tale.‡ Sound divines like Mr. Alleine and Mr. Norman began to be highly valued by men of that generation, and were considered to be worth at least "from ten to fifteen pounds apiece." This was the estimate formed by Judge Jefferies, twenty years later, of what some prisoners might

---

* Lingard's History, 1849, vol. x., p. 183.
† The magistrates of Bristol, for instance.
‡ Burton's Diary, vol. iv., pp. 254 to 273.

fetch who were taken in the Monmouth rebellion.*
We should be sorry, however, to be unjust to our
friends the Taunton magistrates, for perhaps, after all,
they only contemplated a perfectly open transaction,
according to the forms of law; bringing no pecu-
niary advantage to themselves, and having no aim
but the honour of the church. We know that the
transportation of Nonconformists was now first
publicly talked of, and that it was thought the
system would work admirably. "Our phanatiques
here," wrote the Dover correspondent of *The Newes*,
a 'little later in the year, " begin to be startled
with the fear of transportation, hearing that some
of their fellows are adjudged to be sent away,
which will certainly do much more with them
than their imprisonment, where, as the matter is
generally handled, they have more freedom of
communicating, and at least as much of scrib-
bling as they have abroad."† Along with other
matters of gossip and advertisement, the old news-
papers contain many notices of Nonconformists
being transported to Barbadoes and other places;
but while their fate was talked over by some with
brutal jests, by others with heartless indifference;
while Alleine daily suffered threats from his enemies
of being sent into the same dreadful oblivion,

---

* Letter dated Taunton, September 19, 1685.
† *The Newes*, August 23, 1664.

and fully expected that one day they would keep
their word and do their worst, his spirit was undis-
mayed, and none of these things moved him to
make the slightest change in his course.   " There
is another life after this," said he, in a letter to a
friend ; " I regard myself as *already* in banishment,
and am content . . . .

    " It was the divine argument that Epictetus used
for comfort in banishment : *Ubique, habenda sunt
colloquia cum Deo.* I met lately with a passage out of
one of the Fathers, which I engraved upon my heart.
*Cui Patria solùm placet nimis delicatus est; Cui omnis
Terra Patria, is sortis est ; Cui omnis Terra exilium,
is sanctus est.* That is worthy of a saint, indeed,
to account himself always in the state of banishment, whilst in the state of mortality ; like the
worthies who sojourned even in the land of promise, as in a strange countrey. Such a sojourner I
wish both myself and you ; and may the moveable-
ness of our present state fix our desires upon that
kingdom which shall never be shaken !"

    Our confessors were not transported from the
country,—" the Lord preserving them by His
power, and so ordered it that their imprisonment was
a great furtherance to the Gospel, and brought
much glory to Him."*

---

* Mrs. Alleine.

Chapter XII.

Cardiphonia.

" O sacred Providence, who from end to end
Strongly and sweetly movest! shall I write,
And not of thee, through whom my fingers bend
To hold my quill? Shall they not do thee right?

" Of all the creatures both in sea and land,
Only to man thou hast made known thy ways,
And put the pen alone into his hand,
And made him secretary of thy praise."

GEORGE HERBERT.

HILE he was a prisoner, it was his custom, until interrupted by press of occupations, to send once a week a letter to his people. This was to serve for a sermon ; and when, every Sunday morning, worthy elder Rossiter carried it round to the various meeting-places, and read it to company after company, it often seemed as if no sermon had ever been so eagerly waited for, or so solemnly received. About forty of these letters have been preserved in different books, besides others addressed to the destitute churches at Luppit, Honiton, and other

places.   Matthew Henry has truly said that they
all have " a mighty tincture of peculiar prison
comforts and enlargements."   John Wesley has
pointed out their resemblance to those of the eminent
Rutherford, and though they are not in the same
degree picturesque with many images, and tinged
with the colours of genius, every line is alive with
the same holy love.   We must not, however, try
them by the laws of literary criticism, for they are
only the free impetuous overflowings of his full
heart—a heart charged with enthusiasm for the
glory of his Master, and with a passion of anxiety
for the spiritual welfare of his flock.   If any study
had been spent upon them, it was only to make
them so simple that no poor servant from the mills
or fields might miss the meaning of a single sentence,
or fail to feel its urgency.   A few specimens here
follow.   The first was written a day or two after
his first imprisonment by sentence of the county
magistrates.

PREPARE FOR SUFFERING.

" *To my dearly beloved the Flock of Christ in Taunton, Grace
and Peace.*

     " MOST DEAR CHRISTIANS,—My extream straits of time
will now force me to bind my long loves in a few short
lines ; yet I could not tell how to leave you unsaluted,
nor choose but write to you in a few words, that you
should not be dismayed, either at our present sufferings or
at the evil tidings that by this time I doubt not are come
unto you.   Now, brethren, is the time when the Lord is

like to put you upon the trial ; now is the hour of temptation come. Oh ! be faithful to Christ to the death, and He shall give you a crown of life. Faithful is He that hath called you, and He will not suffer you upon His faithfulness to be tempted above what you are able. Give up yourselves and your all to the Lord, with resolution to follow Him fully, and two things be sure of, and lay up as sure grounds of everlasting consolation :—

" 1. If you seek by prayer and study to know the mind of God, and do resolve to follow it in uprightness, you shall not fail either of direction or pardon ; either God will shew you what His pleasure is, or will certainly forgive you if you miss your way. Brethren, fix upon your souls the deep and lively affecting apprehensions of the most gracious, loving, merciful, sweet, compassionate, tender nature of your heavenly Father, which is so great that you may be sure He will with all readiness and love accept of His poor children when they endeavour to approve themselves in sincerity to Him, and would fain know His mind and do it, if they could but clearly see it, though they should unwillingly mistake.

" 2. That as sure as God is faithful, if He do see that such or such a temptation (with the forethought of which you may be apt to disquiet yourselves, lest you should fall away when thus or thus tried) will be too hard for your graces, He will never suffer it to come upon you. Let not, my dear brethren, let not the present tribulations or those impending move you. This is the way of the kingdom ; persecution is one of your land-marks ; self-denial and taking up the cross is your A B C of religion ; ' you have learnt nothing that have not begun at Christ's cross.' Brethren, the cross of Christ is your crown ; the reproach of Christ is your riches ; the shame of Christ is

your glory; the damage attending strict and holy
diligence, your greatest advantage; sensible you should
be of what is coming, but not discouraged; humbled, but
not dismayed; having your hearts broken, and yet your
spirits unbroken; humble yourselves mightily under the
mighty hand of God; but fear not the face of man; may
you even be low in humility, but high in courage; little
in your own apprehensions of yourselves, but great in holy
fortitude, resolution and holy magnanimity, lying in the
dust before your God, yet triumphing in faith and hope,
in boldness and confidence over all the power of the
enemies. Approve yourselves as good souldiers of Jesus
Christ, with no armour, but that of righteousness; no
weapons, but strong crying and tears; looking for no
victory but that of faith; nor hope to overcome, but by
patience; now for the faith and patience of the saints,
now for the harness of your suffering grace. O gird up
the loyns of your mind, and be sober, and hope to the end.
' Fight not ' but ' the good fight ' of faith; here you must
contend, and that earnestly. Strive not but against sin,
and here you may resist even unto blood; now see that
you chuse life, and embrace affliction rather than sin.
Strive together mightily and frequently by prayer; I know
you do, but I would you should abound more and more.
Share my loves among you, and continue your earnest
prayers for me, and be you assured that I am and shall
be, through grace, a willing, thankful servant of your
souls' concernment.   " JOSEPH ALLEINE."

" *From the common Gaole, May* 28, 1663."*

---

* Printed May 2, in some of the old copies of his letters. In
many of these old copies the dates are inaccurate, and appear to have
been added by the printer, most of the MSS. being undated.

When at the Quarter Sessions, July 14, 1663, it was resolved that he should still be kept in prison, although the grand-jury could not find the bill, he wrote next day the following letter to console his people under their bitter disappointment : —

RIGHT REASONS IN SUFFERING.

" *To the most loving, and best beloved, the Flock of Christ in Taunton, Grace and Peace.*

" MOST LOVING AND DEARLY BELOVED,—I know not what thanks to render to you, nor to God for you, for all the unexpressable love which I have found in you towards me ; and not terminatively to me, but to Christ in me ; for I believe it is for His sake, as I am a messenger and embassador of His to you, that you have loved me and done so much every way for me ; and I think I may say of Taunton, as the Psalmist of Jerusalem, 'If I forget thee, let my right hand forget her cunning; if I do not remember thee, let my tongue cleave to the roof of my mouth.' I would not, my dear brethren, that you should be dejected or discouraged at the late disappointments : for through the goodness of God I am not downcast, but rather more satisfied than before : and this I can truly say, nothing doth sadden me more than to see so much sadness in your faces. As on the contrary nothing doth comfort me so much as to see your chear and courage. Therefore I beseech you, brethren, faint not because of my tribulation, nor of God's delays, but hold up the hands and the feeble knees. And the Lord bolster up your hands, as they did the hands of Moses, that they may not fall down till Israel do prevail. Let us fear lest there be some evil among us, that God being angry with us, doth send this farther tryal upon us. Pray earnestly for me, lest the eye of the most jealous God should discern that in me which should render me unfit for the mercy you desire. And let every one of you search his heart, and search his house, to see if there be not cause there. Let not these disappointments make you to be less in love with prayers, but the more out of love with sin. Let us humble ourselves under the mighty hand of God, and He shall exalt us in due time. And for the enemies of God, you must know also that their foot shall slide in due time. Let the servants of God encourage themselves in their God : for in the things wherein they deal proudly, He is above them : therefore, fret not your-selves because of evil doers ; commit your cause to Him that judgeth righteously. Remember that you are bid, if you see oppression of the poor, and violent perverting of judgment and justice in a province, not to marvel at the matter ; verily, there is a God that judgeth in the earth : and you have the liberty of appeals : rest in the Lord, and wait patiently for him, and fret not yourselves, because of the men that bring wicked devices to pass : take heed that none of you do with Peter begin to sink, now you see the waters rough, and the winds boysterous : these things must not weaken your faith, for they are great arguments for the strengthening of it. What clearer evidence can there be for the future judgment of the ungodly, and coronation of the just in another life, than the most unjust proceedings that are here upon earth : shall not the Judge of all the earth see right to be done ? We see here nothing but confusion and disorder, the wicked receiveth according to the work of the righteous, and the innocent according to the work of the wicked. The godly perish, and the wicked flourish ; these do prosper, and they do suffer. What, can it be ever thus ? No, doubtless, there must be a day when God will judge the world in righteousness, and rectifie the present disorders, and reverse the unrighteous sentences that have been passed against His servants. And this evidence is so clear, that many of the heathen philosophers have from this very argument (I mean the unrighteous usage of the good) concluded that there must certainly be rewards and punishments adjudged by God in another world.

" Neither must these things cool your zeal : now is the time that the love of many doth wax cold : but I bless God it is not so with you : I am sure your love to me is, as true friends should be, like the chimneys, warmest in the winter of adversity ; and I hope your love to God is much more, and I would that you should abound yet more and more. Where else should you bestow your loves ? Love ye the Lord, ye His saints, and cling about Him the faster now ye see the world is striving to separate you from Him. How many are they that go to knock off your fingers ! Methinks I see what tugging there is. The world is plucking, and the devil is plucking : hold fast, I beseech you ; hold fast, that no man take your crown. Let the water that is sprinkled, yea, rather poured upon your love, make it to flame up the more. Are you not betrothed unto Christ ? Oh, remember, remember your marriage covenant : did you not take Him for richer for poorer, for better for worse ? Now prove your love to Christ to have been a true conjugal love, in that you can love Him when most slighted, despised, undervalued, blasphemed, among men. Now acquit yourselves, not to have followed Christ for the loaves ; now confute the accuser of the brethren, who may be ready to suggest of the best of you, as he did of Job, ' Doth he serve the Lord for nought ?' And let

it be seen that you loved Christ and holiness purely for
their own sakes; that you can love Christ when there is
no hope of worldly advantage, or promoting of self-
interest in following Him."

Two days after he was sentenced by Judge
Foster to prolonged imprisonment, he addressed a
message to his people, part of which is now given.

" To those who are in the City of Refuge, and to those who
are only in its Suburbs.

"Most dearly Beloved,—I have been through mercy
many years with you, and should be willingly so many
years a prisoner for you, so I might eminently and effectually further your salvation. I must again, yea, again
and again thank you for your abundant and intire affections to me, which I value as a great mercy, not in order
to myself, if I know my own heart, but in order to your
benefit, that I may thereby be a more likely instrument
to further your good. Surely, much as I do value your
love, yet had I rather be forgotten and forsaken of you
all, so that your eyes and hearts might be hereby fixed on
Christ. Brethren, I have not bespoken your affections for
myself. I am perswaded that I should much rather choose
to be hated of all, so this might be the means to have Christ
honoured, and set up savingly in the hearts of you all.
And indeed there is nothing great but in order to God;
nothing is material as it terminates in us. It matters not
whether we are in riches or poverty, in sickness or health,
in honour or disgrace, so Christ may be by us magnified.
Welcome prison and poverty, welcome scorn and envy,
welcome pains or contempt, if by these God's glory may
be most promoted. What are we for but for God? what

j

doth the creature signifie separated from his God ? Just so
much as the cypher separated from the figure, or the
letter from the syllable, we are nothing, or nothing worth,
but in reference to God and His ends. Better were it
that we had never been, than that we should not be to
Him. Better that we were dead than we should live,
and not to Him. Better that we had no understandings,
than that we should not know Him. What are our
interests unless as they may be subservient to His interest ?
or our esteem or reputation, unless we may hereby
glorifie Him ? Do you love me ? I know you do ; but who
is there that will leave his sins for me ? I mean, at my
requests. With whom shall I prevail to give up himself
in strictness and self-denial to the Lord ? Who will be
intreated by me to set upon neglected duties, or reform
accustomed sins ? O, wherein may you rejoyce me ? In
this, in this, my brethren, in this you shall befriend me,
if you obey the voice of God by me ; if you be prevailed
with to give yourselves up thoroughly to the Lord. Would
you lighten my burden ? would you loosen my bonds ?
would you make glad my heart ? Let me hear of your
owning the ways and servants of the Lord in adversity ;
of your coming in, of your abiding and patient continuing
in the ways of holiness. O that I could but hear that
the prayerless souls and families among you, were now
given to prayer!' That the profane sinners would be
awakened, and be induced by the preaching of these
bonds, which heretofore would not be prevailed with, to
leave their drunkenness, their loose company, their lying
and deceit, and wantonness! I warn you of staying in the
suburbs of the city of refuge. O what pity is it that any
should perish at the gates! that any should escape the
pollutions of the world, and do many things, yea, and

suffer it may be too, and yet should fall short of the glory of God, for want of a thorough work of grace! You halting Christians, that halt between Christ and the world, that are as Ephraim like a cake not turned, professors that have lamps without oil, that cry Lord, Lord, but do not the will of our Father which is in heaven, how long will you stay in common workings and external performances? Even out of my prison I cry after you, and make one tender of mercy more!"

During the few months just following his renewed imprisonment, he had reason to feel much concerned for the stability of his people, who, every day, had more terrible trials of principle and fewer outward supports. At the beginning of September he writes :—" See to it, my dearly beloved, that you stand fast in the holy doctrine which we have preached from the pulpit, preached from the bar, preached from the prison to you; it is a Gospel worth the suffering for." At the close of the month he says :—

" I see so much mercy in this very gaol, that I must be more thankful for this than for my prosperity. Surely the name of the place is, ' The Lord is here :' surely it may be called Peniel. Be strong in the Lord, my brethren, be patient, stablish your hearts, for the coming of the Lord draws nigh. In nothing be terrified by your adversaries. ·Now let those that fear the Lord be often speaking one to another. I hear that Satan is practising to send more of you after me; I desire and pray for your liberty; but if any of you be forced hither for the testimony of the

Gospel, I shall embrace you with both arms. Fare you well, my most dearly beloved; be perfect, and be of good comfort; be of one mind, live in peace, and the God of love and peace shall be with you. My brethren in bonds salute you with much affection, rejoycing to behold your order and the stedfastness of your faith in Christ: share my heart among you, and know that I am the willing servant of your faith and joy."

In the month of October he is told that the courage of some is beginning to waver; he therefore sends this earnest message :—

" Let it not be a strange thing to you, if the Lord do now call you to some difficulty; forsake not the assembling of yourselves together, as the manner of some is. I plainly see the coal of religion will soon go out, unless it have some better helps to cherish it than a carnal ministrie, and lifeless administration. Dear brethren, now is the time for you that fear the Lord, to speak often one to another: manage your duties with what prudence you can, but away with that carnal prudence that will decline duty to avoid danger. Is the communion of saints worth the venturing for? Shut not up your doors against godly meetings. I am told that it is become a hard matter, when a minister is willing to take pains with you, to get place: far be this from you, my brethren. What, shut out the word! Suppose there be somewhat more danger to him that gives the minister entertainment, is there not much more advantage accordingly? Did not Obed-Edom and his house get the blessing by entertaining the ark there? or do you think God hath never a blessing for those that shall with much self-denial entertain His messengers, His saints, His worship? Are you believers, and yet are afraid you shall be losers by Christ? Do you indeed not know that he that runs most hazard for Christ, doth express most love to Christ, and shall receive the greatest reward? Away with that unbelief, that prefers the present safety before the future glory."

In another letter he thus seeks to inspire cheerful bravery :—

"Fear not, little flock; stronger is He that is with you, than he that is against you. What though Satan should raise all his militia against you? Adhere to Christ in a patient doing and suffering His pleasure, and He shall secure you. The Lord will not forsake you, because it hath pleased the Lord to make you His people: God hath entrusted you with His Son: you are His care and His charge. Many will be lifting at you, many will be plucking at you, but fear not, you shall not be moved, none shall pluck you out of Christ's hand, He hath all power.—Matt. xxviii. 8. Can omnipotence secure you? He is all treasures.—Col. ii. 3. Can unsearchable riches suffice you? In a word, He is all fulness.—Col. i. 21. Can *all* content you? Can fulness fill you? If so, you are blessed, and shall be blessed.

"Beloved, we lose unutterably for want of considering, for want of viewing our own privileges and blessedness. O man, is Christ thine, and yet dost thou live at a low rate and comfort? Is thy name written in heaven, and yet dost thou not rejoyce? Shall the children of the kingdom, the candidates of glory, the chosen generation, the royal priesthood, be like other men? O Christians, remember who and whence you are; consider your obligations, put on a better pace ; bestir yourselves, run and wrestle, and be strong for the Lord of Hosts ; (and earnestly, yet peaceably) contend for the faith once delivered to His saints. What, shall we make nothing of all that God hath said and done for us ? O Christians, shall he that hath gotten an inriching office boast of his booty ? or he that hath obtained the king's patent for an earldome, glory in his riches and honour, and shall the grant of heaven signifie little with thee ? Shall Christ's patent for thy sonship and partnership with Himself be like a cypher ? Shall Haman come home from the banquet with a glad heart, and glorying in the greatness of his riches, the multitude of his children, and all the things wherein the king had promoted him above the princes; and shall we turn over our Bibles and read the promises, and find it under God's own hand, that He intends the kingdom for us, that He will be a Father to us, that He gives and grants all His infinite perfections to us, and yet not be moved ? Beloved Christians, live like yourselves ; let the world see that the promises of God and privileges of the Gospel are not empty sounds, or a meer crack. Let the heavenly cheerfulness and the restless diligence, and the holy raisedness of your conversations prove the reality, excellency, and beauty of your religion to the world. Forget not your prisoner."

The secret of spiritual strength is often set forth, and the timid Christian is summoned to be "strong in the Lord." This passage occurs in one of his appeals :—

" We must learn to have no subsistence in ourselves, but only in Christ, and to stand only in Him. Study the excellent lesson of self-annihilation. A true Christian is like a vine that cannot stand of itself, but is wholly supported by the prop it leans upon. It is no small thing to know ourselves to be nothing, of no might, of no worth, of no understanding, nor reality; to look upon ourselves as helpless, worthless, empty shadows. This holy littleness is a great attainment; when we find that all our inventory amounts to nothing but folly, weakness, and beggary; when we set down ourselves for cyphers, our gain for loss, our excellencies for very vanities, then we shall learn to live like believers. A true saint is like a glass without a foot, that set him where you will, is ready to fall every way till you set him to a prop. Let Christ be the only support you lean unto. When you are throughly emptied and nullified, and see all comeliness to be but as a withered flower, dead, dried, and past recovery, then you will be put upon the happy necessity of going out to Christ for all."

Chapter XIII.

Freedom Found and Lost Again.

" Think with mingled joy and fear
On the freedom thou hast found ;
Know, while yet we linger here,
Perils ever hem us round.

" Art thou faithful ? then oppose
Sin and wrong with all thy might ;
Care not how the tempest blows,
Only care to win the fight."

LYRA GERMANICA.

AFTER an imprisonment of twelve months, Mr. Alleine was set free on the 20th of May, 1664.*

Free at last! Out again,—out, in the broad, clear glory of the open country. Away, through great spaces, where, amidst scattered clumps of gorse or fern, the sheep are grazing ; through lanes, where high over-head the crossing

---

* Twelve months, wanting but three days.

arches of young foliage make a wavering green
radiance; through woods where hyacinths are all
about the oak-tree stems in a rich mist of beauty.
"Flowers peep, trees bud, boughs tremble, rivers
run." The freed prisoner is alive to all these things;
no man more than he. Like him who wist not
that it was true which was done by the angel, but
thought he saw a vision, the joy of deliverance will
surely be bewildering—he will need a pause to
think, to look around him, to drink the air of this
May morning, and to feel the ecstacies of escape
from his dismal cage. But no, the time is short;
the church is mourning; and just as Paul would
have done in like circumstances, he hastens "to
work for God more earnestly than ever," for he
says, "Necessity is upon me, and woe is me, if I
preach not the Gospel!" Obeying this law, we
find him preaching to his congregation four times
on the very first Sunday after his release.

Great changes had taken place amongst his
people, and many old faces were missing. This
was natural; for, although actual persecution had
not yet been extensively directed against the so-
called laity, the position of a Nonconformist was at
best, as it ever must be, one of social indignity and
loss. Besides those of his parishioners who had
left him out of thoughtful preference for the religion of the State, many others who had once helped
to swell the great crowd in his church, were now

gone. All who had been Puritans only by accident,—all who had become lax in life, and who were therefore inconvenienced by the laws of Christian fellowship, and the restraints that belong to union with one particular " congregation of faithful men,"—all who were bent on finding the easiest path to promotion of any kind,—all who supremely cared for the great prizes of education,—all who were sensitive to what was thought about them by the majority, " Mr. Byends, Mr. Facing-both-ways, and Mr. Anything ; Mr. Worldly-wiseman, Mr. Legality, and that pretty young man, his son, Mr. Civility,"—all who were afraid of adopting any form of religion that implied the probable absence of honoured social rank, had gradually dropped away. But it was cheering to find that, after all, great numbers flocked round him, and all the more cheering, because it might be fairly presumed that those who now remained were at least disinterested and sincere. So large was the congregation, that it was needful to make permanent arrangements for dividing it into four separate sections on the Sunday, and into many others in the week, that he might preach to each one in succession, and so secure the privilege in turn to all.*

On the 1st of July, 1664, a month after this

---

* Baxter's Introduction to Alleine's Alarm. Mrs. Alleine's Account.

arrangement had been made, the Conventicle Act
came into operation.   Hitherto the law had only
punished the pastors, now its penalties lighted on
the flocks.   It was enacted that if any person above
the age of sixteen attended any meeting under colour
of a religious exercise not allowed by the liturgy or
practice of the Church of England, where five
or more persons were present besides the household, he should for the first offence suffer three
months' imprisonment, or pay a sum not exceeding £5 ; for the second, six months' imprisonment,
or pay £10 ; for the third, to be banished to
certain specified plantations for seven years.
" With refined cruelty it was provided, that the
offender should not be transported to New
England, where he was likely to meet with sym-
pathising friends."*   If he returned to his own
country before the expiration of his term of exile,
he was liable to capital punishment.   A jury was
unnecessary.   A single justice of the peace, and the
oath of an informer were sufficient, and this Act
was to continue in force for three years after the
next session of Parliament.

From this time scenes became common such as
Mr. Pepys thus describes :—" I saw several poor
creatures carried by constables for being at conventicles.   They go like lambs, without any resistance.

---

* Macaulay.

I would to God they would either conform, or
be more wise, and not be catched!"* All the
county gaols, like those in London, were soon
filled with Dissenters, and hundreds of families
were brought to ruin, either by fines or seizures on
property. As usual, the Quakers were the greatest
sufferers, and the pamphlets they issued at this
time, though sometimes apt to provoke a smile by
their quaint wording, furnish accounts of wrongs
done to them, which no true man can read without
starting to his feet in a storm of indignant emotion.† Not a few of the Taunton Dissenters were
carried off from the praying assemblies to prison,
but how many, or for how long a time, is not
known. The only notice of their imprisonment is
this incidental reference to it in a sermon delivered
several months later, when they were again at
liberty :—

" Brethren, it is your privilege that God gave
you hearts to own Him in times of danger, and
blessed be God He was not behind hand with you
in that He owned you in your prison state. Doth
not God speak to you as the apostle, ' Which of you
goeth a warfare at his own charges ?' When

---

* Diary, August 7, 1664.

† In the Library of Devonshire House there is one preserved with
this title :—" A Trumpet Sounded in the Eares of Persecution, with
the lowing of oxen, the bleating of sheep, neighing of horses,
rattling of pots, kettles, skillets, dishes and pans, taken from an Innocent People," &c.

our Saviour sent forth His disciples without scrip or shoes, says He, 'Lacked ye anything?' and they answered, 'Nothing.' May you not say so? If He say, ' Lacked ye anything?' we must reply, ' No, He poured out His kindness upon us.' God did send bread, and not by a raven, but by friends. Whoever wants, God will be sure that His prisoners shall not want. The king took care of Jeremiah, ' Then Zedekiah the king commanded, that they should commit Jeremiah to the court of the prison, and that they should give him daily a piece of bread out of the bakers' street until all the bread in the city was spent.'—Jer. xxxvii. 21. When Jeremiah was in prison, God would be sure that he should not want as long as there was any bread to be had in the city. So God commands concerning His prisoners."*

Try to picture the effect on any modern congregation of such penalties as these, softened as they were by the ministries of Christian pity. " To some Christians," says John Foster, " there is something formidable even in a certain quantity of rain-drops—they have a reverential awe of the weather." If such agencies serve to thin our churches, how many worshippers would be there, if they anticipated as the probable consequence, the payment of a fine, suffering in a prison, or the

---

* Alleine's Remains.

chance of slavery and death beneath the blaze of a tropical day?

Even Mr. Alleine's brave people were so far dispersed by these terrors, that he deemed it sufficient to hold henceforth two Sunday services instead of four; still continuing, however, his various other labours in the week, both at home and in the villages.

His own languid health yet more imperatively required him thus to lessen his usual amount of work. The prison had made him an old and weary man. It had made his life wither as a flower will wither if the fire has once passed over it. His iron power of endurance, his elastic spring of recovery had gone for ever. He could hardly hold on his way, and at last he broke down utterly. At the close of August, having travelled sixteen miles to visit a church which had been deprived of its pastor, he sank into such utter exhaustion after preaching, that he could not be removed for three or four days, and then was with great difficulty borne back to Taunton. For many weeks his strength consumed away so fast, that his friends thought he would soon die. In October he began to revive, but even then his disorder so affected him, that he could not use his arms so as to write letters, or put off and on his clothes.

About the beginning of his illness he received a letter from a clergyman to thank him for the religious good gained in former years from his preaching. In January, he was able to dictate a reply, some sentences of which shall be given here :—

TO A CLERGYMAN WITH TWO PARSONAGES.

" Let us know no interest but Jesus Christ's. I cannot say that I have already attained this, but my heart is bent on making the endeavour. Too often I take a wrong aim, and miss my mark, but I will tell you the rules I strictly impose upon myself from day to day : Never to lie down, but in the name of God ; not barely for natural refreshment, but that a wearied servant of Christ may be recruited and fitted to serve Him better the next day. Never to rise up but with this resolution, well, I will go forth this day in the name of God, and will make religion my business, and spend the day for eternity. Never to enter upon my calling, but first thinking, I will do these things as unto God, because He requireth these things at my hands in the place and station He hath put me into. Never to sit down to the table, but resolving, I will not eat merely to please my appetite, but to strengthen myself for my Master's work. Never to make a visit, but upon some holy design, resolving to leave something of God where I go ; and in every company to leave some good savour behind. This is that which I have been for some time learning, and am pressing hard after ; and if I strive not to walk by these rules, let this paper be a witness against me.

" I am not now in my former publick capacity, such things being required of me to say and subscribe as I could by no means yield to, without open lying and dissembling with God and men ; yet, that I am unuseful, I cannot say ; but rather think, that possibly I may be of more use than heretofore. I thank the Lord I have not known what it is to want a tongue to speak, but in my sickness ; nor a people to hear ; but so as that we both follow the things that make for peace.

" I perceive you are otherwise perswaded in some things than I am ; but, however, I trust we meet in our end. Since you are in, may it be your whole study to gain souls, and to build them up in holiness, which is with too many the least of their cares. One duty (miserably neglected) I shall be bold to commend to you from my own experience, and that is, the visiting your whole flock from house to house, and enquiring into their spiritual estates particularly, and dealing plainly and truly with them about their conversion to God ; to the usefulness of this great work I can set my *probatum est.*

" I hear you have two parsonages ; O tremble to think how many precious souls you have to look to ! and let it be seen, however others aim at the fleece, you aim at the flock ; and that you have indeed *curam animarum.*"

The following letter appears to have been written about the same period :—

TO A DISSENTING MINISTER IN GAOL.

" WORTHY SIR,—It was but a little after my release from my own confinement, that I heard of yours ; and now write to you, as one that hath taken a higher degree than ever, and more truly honourable, being commenced prisoner of Christ. I was once affected with the picture of a devout man, to whom a voice came down from heaven, saying, *Quid vis fieri pro te.* To which he answered, *Nihil domine nisi pati ac contemni pro te.* Undoubtedly, Sir, it is our real glory to be throughout conformed to Jesus Christ, not only in His sanctity, but in His sufferings. Paul counted all things but dung for this, that he might win Christ, &c.,

and know the fellowship of His sufferings, and be made conformable to His death. I doubt not but your consolations in Christ do much more than superabound in all your tribulations for him. Yet, let me add this one cordial, that now you have a whole shoal of promises come in to you, which you had not before; I mean, all the promises to suffering saints, in which they have not an immediate, but only a remoter right, unless in a suffering state. And doubtless he hath gotten well that hath gotten such a number of exceeding great and precious promises. If the men of the world do so rejoyce when such or such an estate is fallen to them, should not you much more, that have such a treasure of promises fallen to you?

" I can tell you little good of myself; but this I can tell you, that the promises of God were never so sweet in this world to me, as in and since my imprisoned state. Oh, the bottomless riches of the covenant of grace! It shames me that I have let such a treasure lie by so long, and have made so little use of it. Never did my soul know the heaven of a believer's life, till I learnt to live a life of praise, and by more frequent consideration to set home the unspeakable riches of the divine promises, to which, I trust, through grace, I am made an heir. I verily perceive that all our work were done at once, if we could but prevail with ourselves and others to live like believers; to tell all the world, by our course and carriage, that there is such pleasantness in Christ's wars, such beauty in holiness, such reward to obedience, as we profess to believe. May ours and our people's conversations but preach this aloud to the world, that there is a reality in what God hath promised; that heaven is worth the venturing for; that the sufferings of the present time are not worthy to be compared with the glory which shall be revealed in us!

" Verily, Sir, it is but a very little while that prisons shall hold us, or that we shall dwell in dirty flesh. Porphyry tells us of Plotinus, that he was ashamed to see himself in the body ; to see a divine and immortal soul in a prison of flesh (for so they held the body to be) ; but the worst shackles are those of sin. Well, they must shortly off all together ; our Lord doth not long intend us for this lower region. Surely He is gone to prepare a place for us. Doubtless it is so ; yea, and He will come again, and receive us to Himself, that where He is, we may be also. And what have we to do, but to believe, and wait, and love, and long, and look out for His coming, in which is all our hope ? 'Twill be time enough for us to be preferred then. We know beforehand who shall then be uppermost. Our Lord hath shewed us where our place shall be, even at His own right hand ; and what He will say to us, ' Come, ye blessed,' &c. Surely we shall stand in His judgement. He hath promised to stand our Friend. Let us look for the joyful day. As sure as there is a God, this day will come, and then it shall go well with us. What if bonds and banishments abide us for a season ? This is nothing but what our Lord hath told us, ' The world shall rejoice, but ye shall weep and lament ; you shall be sorrowful, but your sorrow shall be turned into joy.' Oh, how reviving are His words ! ' I will see you again, and your heart shall rejoice, and your joy no man taketh away from you.'

" If that miserable wretch leapt chearfully off the ladder, saying, ' I shall be a queen in hell,' with what joy should we do and suffer for God, who have His truth in pawn that we shall be crowned in heaven ? Verily,

x

they are wonderful preparations that are making for us. The Lord prepare us apace, and make us meet to be partakers. It was the highest commendation that ever that worthy R. Baxter received, which fell from the pen of his scoffing adversary, Tilenus, who saith of him, *Totum Puritanismum totus spirat.* Oh, that this may be true of us and ours !

"   .   .   —But what shall I say ? I have more need to receive from you, than ability to give ; only I will tell you my wishes for you : I wish that your body may prosper, as your soul also prospereth. I wish, that you may see the travel of your soul ; that you may find your people thriving under your hands in all manner of holy conversation and godliness, that whosoever converses with them, may see and hear by them, that God is in them of a truth. I wish your enlargement from your bonds, and your enlargement in them : that your prison may be but the lanthorn through which your graces, experiences, communion, and prison attainments may shine most brightly to all beholders. I wish your prison may be a Paradise of peace, and a Patmos of divine discoveries. Lord Jesus, set to this thy Amen.

"I am, Sir,

"Your unworthy brother and companion

In the kingdom and patience of Jesus,

"*Jan.* 10, 1664."   "Jos. ALLEINE."

About April he was able to leave his chamber again, and from that time he persisted in preaching once and sometimes twice every Sunday, as well as in visiting and teaching on other days. It was impossible to go on thus ; and in the summer of

1665, yielding to the advice of his friends, he agreed for health's sake to spend a season of rest in the country.

Reddening its fringe of grass, and the trailing strings of tangled creepers through which it glistens, there is at the village of Seend, near Devizes, a chalybeate spring, now scarcely noticed, but then just beginning to have a brief celebrity. In the year after, some of its waters were taken in phials by Aubrey to a meeting of the Royal Society, and the sages there were " wonderfully surprised" at the experimental effect produced by the oxidation of the iron it contained. An advertisement of its virtues appeared in Mr. Lilly's Almanac. The village became fashionable, and was much frequented by persons who came to be cured of "the spleen." Mr. Alleine went to this Wiltshire Bethesda, and stayed for several weeks. In that summer there was little chance of refreshment for an invalid anywhere, for never had such a sultry season been known. The cattle died, the hedge-leaves were shrivelled, some of the pasture lands were burnt white like the highways, and meadows which usually yielded forty loads of hay, now yielded only four. Though all nature languished around him, the strength of our friend was renewed by his visit, and he went back to Taunton rejoicing in hope.

On his return, he resolved to start on a mis-

sionary tour through Wales. The idea of Wales
as a mission-field was not new to him or to his
flock.   By the establishment of schools, the employment of lay and itinerant agency, and the
appointment of working ministers in the place of
those who were deprived for drunkenness, or
scandalous lives in other respects, the Puritans,
with the questionable aid of the Long Parliament,
had done much to disperse the heathen darkness
that had so long shadowed the principality.   This
may be said with confidence, although, at the same
time, it can scarcely be doubted that hard measure
was sometimes dealt to the Royalist clergy there,
and that a few excellent men suffered ejection with
their numerous less honourable brethren.*   From
the time of Mr. Alleine's ordination, he had joined
in the endeavours to evangelise his Welsh neighbours.   By correspondence with Lord Wharton,
by appeals to his own responsive people, and by
co-operation with Vavasor Powell, through whose
single itinerancy twenty thousand persons were
gathered into Christian congregations†—by these
and other means, he had sent help over to those
whom he called " men of Macedonia." The effects
of such services were now rapidly withering before

---

* Gemitus Ecclesiæ Cambro-Brittannicæ, 4to., 1654.
† Thurloe.   Vavasor Powell was a Baptist.   He was eleven years
in prison for nonconformity, and died in the Fleet Prison, 1670.

the Act of Uniformity. What could be done? He busied his mind with many projects. By his influence, several ministers were sent over, and he was just setting out himself, when the return of his maladies convinced him of his inability to travel, and, entreated by his friends, he mournfully gave up the design.*

In his accustomed rounds, then, this servant of the Lord still determined to toil on—his strength strained to the utmost, and his life beset with perils ; but though many threats were uttered against him by the magistrates, and many warrants out for him, nothing ruffled his placid courage, or shook his firm resolve. He would say, when his enemies were plotting to get him into prison, " They could not do me a greater kindness. I can do but little because of my distempers ; but if I cannot work for God, I can suffer for Him, if He would so far honour me." But the time was not yet come for this, and, till then, he seemed to lead "a charmed life."

All this while the Plague was raging in London. The old Gothic city, with its foul nests of narrow streets, each having in its centre a black rivulet trickling along to the river, seemed marked for such a doom. The avenger had often sent warning of his approach, and now he had come, walking in

---

* Richard Alleine.

darkness, wasting at noonday, and filling the whole scene with horrors which the tongue trembles to utter, and the pen refuses to record.   In the month of September, the terrific number of ten thousand at least, was the weekly average of the bills of mortality.   In one night—a night long to be remembered—it is said that four thousand died.   Shop after shop was closed, door after door was inscribed with a long red cross, having over it the words, "The Lord have mercy upon us," and street after street became still, with the awful peace of death— the doors left open, the casements clapping in the wind, the rooms empty, the inmates gone.   In many parts,

> " The town lay solitary,
> As doth a quite forsaken monastery
> In some lone forest, and we could not pass
> To many places but through weeds and grass." *

The pestilence travelled on until nearly a hundred thousand souls had been swept away before it. Material terrors were often heightened by the workings of an insane imagination.   In the heavens men saw, or thought they saw, blazing stars and flaming swords; and on the earth, spectres were descried scintillating in the twilight.   Fanatics,

---

* G. Wither on the Plague in 1627.   London's Remembrancer, 4to., 1665 ; a Collection of all the Bills of Mortality for this present year, &c.   By the Company of Parish Clerks, 1665.

thinking themselves inspired, went everywhere shouting messages of wrath. One hollow voice made the streets echo with the cry, "Yet forty days, and London shall be destroyed!" Another moaned, night and day, "O the great and dreadful God! O the great and dreadful God!" Survivors thronged to the churches, but with a few honourable exceptions the clergy had fled. Handbills were thrown about the streets, bearing the title, "A Pulpit to Let," on which were printed the following lines :—

> "They that should stay. and teach us to reform,
> Gird up their loins, and run to 'scape the storm;
> They dread the plague. and dare not stand its shock,
> Let wolves or lions feed the fainting flock.
> Think you these men believe with holy Paul,
> For them to be dissolved is best of all;
> Then, their own bodies they would never mind,
> More than the souls of those they left behind.
> Who now, those sons of Aaron being fled,
> Shall stand between the living and the dead?
> We have at home the plague, abroad the sword,
> And will they add the famine of the word?"

An eye-witness declares, that seeing these pamphlets of "A Pulpit to Let" scattered over the thoroughfares, and finding the churches open, many of the Nonconformist ministers ventured to accept the challenge, and fill the pulpits,*—

---

* Vincent's "God's Terrible Voice in the City." The lines quoted above, occur in "A Pulpit to Let," single sheet, 1665.

secure in a toleration decried by law, but allowed by the exigencies of the hour. Among these were William Dyer, author of the book on " Christ's Famous Titles," John Janeway, Dr. John Owen, John Knowles, formerly of Bristol Cathedral, Thomas Vincent, Chester, Turner, Franklin, and Grimes. What these men did, and what they dared so heroically, would furnish materials for many stirring chapters, and made at the time a deep impression on the hearts of the English people.

We naturally ask what their old foes were doing through all this dreary season? Most of them were too absorbed in their own affairs to care for those of others. Some were engaged, as usual, in trifles. We find fussy Mr. Pepys, the type of this class, able, amidst all his fright, to take affectionate and critical notices of periwigs, thus pensively contemplating their fate—" People will henceforth buy no hair, lest it had been cut from the heads of people who had died of the pestilence." *   Some were absorbed in vice—the Plague only rousing them, as it did the men of old Athens, to a wilder fanaticism of license.†   Others, and

---

Guildhall Library.   I think it must be the pamphlet to which Vincent alludes.   Various poems and ballads were printed on the same subject, such as "The Runawaye's Return;" "The Shepherd's Lacker Lacked," &c.

* Diary, 1665.   † Thucydides, ii. 54.

this is our present point, were absorbed in plans of
new persecution ; the self-devoting labour of the
Nonconformists, instead of making them relent,
only seeming to lash up emotions of more pitiless
vengeance. Sheldon, now archbishop of Canterbury, Seth Ward, bishop of Salisbury, and Lord
Clarendon, employed the leisure of their safe retreat
at Oxford in forging the infamous Five-Mile Act,
which received the royal assent on October 31,
1665. This Act set forth a certain oath, which
every Nonconformist minister was to take, declaring
his conviction that it was unlawful, under any pretence whatever, to take up arms against the sovereign, and promising not to attempt any alteration
of the Government, either in Church or State.
It also provided, that those who refused to take
such an oath, should not come within five miles
of any corporate city or town, or within five miles
of any place in which they had heretofore been
settled, or in which they had preached, under enormous penalties.

About thirty, or a few more, consented to take
this oath, Mr. Newton with the rest; but it was
obviously impossible to be taken by the great body
of Nonconformists. The nation does not exist for
the king, but the king for the nation. Among
free men, an oath of allegiance to their ruler means
no more than that they will be faithful to him while
he is faithful to them. When he no longer regards

the object for which he reigns, loyalty is no longer a virtue. The Dissenters were loyal, but the *jus divinum* of kingship, and the political nothingness of citizenship—the doctrine that kings can claim to hold all mankind as property in perpetuity, and that subjects have nothing to do with Government but to be governed—these were not among the articles of their Puritan creed, neither could they help desiring, by all legal means, to obtain some change in the arbitrary laws. The ministers therefore refused the oath, as was anticipated, and were a second time driven from their homes. While they kept in their old haunts, the most persecuted could preach occasionally ; however poor they were, however scorned by the world, they could always be comforted by the presence of a few who held them in unspeakable reverence,—who were ready to give away their last crust to keep them from starvation,—and who, in the most evil day, would have found for them the safest nooks of concealment, or have risked life itself to cover their escape from the troopers. But from this time, their lot was to be cast among strangers, and their final possibility of preaching the Gospel seemed to be taken away.

The only excuse for this act of exquisite wickedness is, that the ends contemplated by the Act of Uniformity could not, at that early stage of its action, have been secured without it. One of its first objects was to make it impossible for any but Conformists to be recognised as ministers in England. But this was defeated by the persistent ministry of those who, being no longer Conformists, were, according to the law, no longer ministers. More than this, they had actually ventured into the empty pulpits of certain churches in London. There were many empty pulpits,—"bells lacking clappers," as Latimer would have said, in the country; and as these resolute men had once defied the law, who could tell where the mischief might end? Preach they would—certainly in their conventicles, and possibly in unoccupied churches; this, indeed, they often actually did.* Preach they would, while they could have congregations, and the only way to prevent their preaching was to drive them from their people. The rulers were right, if they were right in passing the Act of Uniformity. Law must not remain a dead letter on the statute-book. If it be right to make a law, it is right to enforce it. Laws for the soul, like laws for the body, must be enforced by penalty, and the penalty must, if possible, answer its end.

The first Nonconformists have often been represented as a gloomy generation. "But," asks one of their advocates, "is it fair to ruin us, and then reproach us for not being merry? They that

---

* O. Heywood.

wasted us required of us mirth . . . . . but how
shall we sing the Lord's songs in a strange land,
and what other songs can we sing ?   *Shall we set
the Five-Mile Act to music,* and make merry with our
sorrows ?"   " I wonder how any one can laugh,"
exclaimed a poor woman to Alleine, " when God's
church is in such distress."*   Some degree of
gloom was natural, and it hung heavily over the
spirits of many—not, however, as it seems, over the
spirits of Mr. Alleine.   You are eager to know
how the new Act affected his proceedings.   He
resolved to take up his abode at Wellington, a
town more than five miles away ; but, a few nights
before doing so, he obtained the largest room that
could be found, probably one at Fullands,—called
his people together, and held a service of *solemn
thanksgiving !*   The rough notes of his address on
this occasion have been preserved, and we must
spare space for a few sentences here :—

"Most dearly beloved brethren, with no little
joy and thankfulness have I thought of this time,
when I should once more see your faces together ;
and be so truly glad, with so heart-contenting a
mercy, as to ' rejoice with the joy of God's people,
and to glory with His inheritance.'

" It is a time that, to some, may seem unseasonable to set up thanksgivings, when our calamities

---

* Alleine's Remains, p. 32.

are so near approaching. But surely, if I had never hopes to enjoy one day with you more, the last day should be a day of praise. And if I were sure that we were now to take our farewell of Christians and ministers, and of all our former liberties, I should exhort you that we might join once more in lifting up hearts and hands in blessing God for all the mercies that we have met with together. Your condition is never such but your mercies are infinitely greater, and more than your afflictions. Neither may the sense of misery at any time surprise you, so as to drown the thankful acknowledgment of God's mercies. God, that hath been always good to you, hath never been better than since you have had affliction. Elijah was never so happily fed at a full table as when it was a time of great famine; when God sent every bit of bread and flesh by the mouth of a raven. O how sweetly, do you think, that every bit of this bread did relish with the man of God, when he saw that he received it immediately out of God's own hand?

" Brethren, though it hath been a time of great calamity, yet God hath herein heightened His mercy to you ;—you have seen the bush burning, and yet not consumed. The portion of God's children hath been taken away, and yet our cheeks have been fat. We have been cast with Daniel into the lion's den ; but God hath sent His

angel and shut the lion's mouth, and we have not
been destroyed, but are here together to praise the
Lord.

"Methinks there are several periods of time,
since the time of our calamities, wherein God hath
appeared to us, when we thought all had been gone.
One period was when your ministers were shut out
of public by the Act of Uniformity. Another,
when we were cast out of our private meetings by
the Act made against seditious conventicles, so
called by the iniquity of the times. Another, by
this Act that doth now cast ministers out of their
habitations. And, methinks, every period should
end with praise. We read, that when they removed
the ark, that when they had passed such a number
of paces, then they ' slew a sacrifice.' So, methinks,
as we pass these periods of time, at the end of
every period we should offer praise. What ! though
God hath separated your preachers from you, yet,
as He said, if the soldier dies fighting, and the
preacher preaching, and the swan singing, then the
saints should part praising. Oh, Christians, this is
the spirit that should be in you, that whatever God
doth with you for the time to come, you should
resolve to end in His praise for the mercies past.
If it were the last day we should have together,
surely, methinks, we should end in praise.

"The mercies of God are a deep that cannot be
fathomed. Where shall I begin or end ? Let me

this evening show a little of God's mercy to you, and let my message live in your hearts as long as you live."

He first aims to show the mercies enjoyed by his people as *the people of God.* He shows how they may prove the existence of this relation, and then, that this relation involves the following things, on each of which he enlarges:—" You are the election of grace—you are the first-born of God—you are the first-fruits of the creation—you are the burgesses of heaven—you are the members of Christ—you are the living stones of the temple."

He next asks the people to call to mind the particular mercies they have enjoyed *as the inhabitants of Taunton:*—

" Though praise for the higher mercies should ever ring loudest, these should not be forgotten.

" Firstly. He has been a *Saviour* to you. *He hath saved your lives from the sword.* Have you forgotten that you were a people devoted to destruction by the sons of violence? But God disappointed them, and gave your lives for a prey.

" *Your dwellings from the flames.*—The flames have been set in ambush against you, and yet your habitations have not been burnt down to this day.

" *Your lives from the plague.*—It hath devoured others, but it hath not devoured you. How eminently hath God preserved you in this place, in the time of common calamity that hath been among

others! O think not that it was because those
were greater sinners than are in Taunton; no, but
because God hath a peculiar intention of saving
you. Yet I say to you, as Christ to them, ' Think
not that those upon whom the tower in Siloam fell,
were greater sinners than any in Jerusalem. I tell
you, nay; but except ye repent, ye shall all likewise perish.' We have had the same sins, and yet
God hath preserved us.

" *Your persons from the prison.*—How often hath
God preserved you? He hath been like the cloud
upon Israel; ' and upon all the glory there hath
been a defence.' Once, indeed, some of you have
tasted of a prison; but what a mercy was it, that
it was but once.

" Secondly. God hath been a Shepherd to you.
—Therefore, you have not wanted. Who is it
that leads you by the still waters? Whence is it
that you lie down in green pastures? It is because
God is your Shepherd. How hath God provided
for you formerly and of late?

" Thirdly. God hath been a keeper to you.
When you were sent to prison God did keep you.
O do not forget the mercies of a prison! I believe,
that of all the passages of our lives, many of us have
no such experience of God's mercy as in a prison.
O the provision that God did make for us there!

" Brethren, now let us thankfully commemorate
all these mercies. Let me call upon you, as the

Psalmist, ' Rejoice in the Lord, ye righteous ;' and again, ' Rejoice, O ye people, let your voice be heard on high.' ' Let us worship and fall down before the Lord our Maker.' Let it be said, ' Praise waiteth for thee, O God, in Taunton.' Well might praise wait for God in Taunton, for God hath waited to be gracious to us. There was the place where He chose to put His name. ' There brake He the arrows and the spear.' Who is like our God, who rideth on the heaven for our help, and on the sky for our aid ? Blessed is the people that heareth the joyful sound ; they shall rejoice in thee, O Lord. ' The Lord is our deliverance, and the Holy One of Israel is our King.' Shout, therefore, O inhabitants of Taunton, for great is the work of the Lord with you. And now, O Lord, bless them, and accept the work of their hands, and lift them up for ever !''

At Wellington, he preached in a dye-house. Attempts lately made to identify the place by the help of tradition have all failed. It was a very obscure shelter ; but good men, like diamonds, shine in the dark, and light will not remain a secret long. Mr. Alleine was soon discovered by informers, and a warrant placed in the constable's hand for his apprehension. Even had he been silent he would not have been safe, for it was thought that the house in which he lodged was not

quite five miles from Taunton.*   This was a
question about which conscientious magistrates, and
those for whom they acted, desired to be mathe-
matically exact.   According to a statute of Queen
Elizabeth, a mile measured just 1760 yards, and
therefore it was now illegal for an ejected minister
to dwell within a distance of just five times that
measurement of road from the utmost bend in the
boundary of his former parish.   In a doubtful
case, a clergyman has been known to have the
ground measured in the night, so as to compel his
Nonconformist predecessor to move a few yards
further off.†   Philip Henry was charged with living
within the prescribed limit of distance from his old
church.   It was a frivolous and vexatious charge ;
to still the cavillers, however, he took the chain
into his own hand, and measured the distance,
taking care, before doing so, to be justified by

---

* The two towns are nearly seven miles apart ; but the parish of
Hill Bishops joins that of Taunton, and lies between it and Wellington.   Mr. Newton was minister of both parishes, the duties of
the former being chiefly performed by a chaplain, Mr. N. Charlton.
Having been Mr. Newton's assistant, Mr. Alleine's ministry was
regarded as having had the same parochial extent ; and the informer
probably contended that from the limit of Hill Bishops the outer-
most parish, to the house at which he lodged on this side Wellington,
there was not quite five miles space.

† This Nonconformist was the learned Benjamin Woodbury,
who had just refused a canonry of Windsor, offered on condition
of his conformity.

a Scripture text, which he found in Deuteronomy
xxi. 2.*

Mr. Alleine made no attempt to argue the case;
but, as the person in whose house he had found
shelter was threatened with imprisonment in consequence, he immediately went back to Taunton,
saying, " Blessed be the Lord, I shall now give up
two lives for Christ; the one in doing for Him,
the other in suffering for Him. I am worn out in
doing for Him ; and now I can *do* no more, shall
I *suffer* no more for His sake ?"† In the face of
many dangers, both to host and guest, he found in
his own parish many houses open to him ; and he
went from one to the other, adopting the language
of holy Mr. Dodd, " I have a hundred houses for
one I part with."

Though a sick man, and greatly needing rest,
we are told that he gladly lived this life of changes,
because " he knew not how soon he might be carried
again from his people to prison; and, by living
with them successively, he had opportunity of
being intimately acquainted with them, and the
state of their souls; how it fared with their children
and servants ; and how they performed their duties
to each other in their families." These were only
visits ; and his real home all the time was Fullands,

---

* Philip Henry's Life, p. 108.
† Notes by Mr. F., in whose house he lodged.

the house of Mr. John Mallack, a merchant who lived about a mile from the town.* "Here," Mrs. Alleine says, " he was exceedingly taken with God's mercy to him, in Mr. Mallack's entertaining him and me so bountifully, the house and gardens and walks being a great delight to him, being so pleasant and curious, and all accommodation within so suitable, that he would often say that he did as Dives, fare deliciously every day."

About this time, three probationers were ordained in Somersetshire to the Christian ministry, and there is reason to believe that Mr. Mallack's house was the scene of the event. Theses were read, examination was gone through on difficult points of divinity, Mr. Alleine offered the ordination prayer, and then Mr. Ames Short, Mr. Thomas Lye, Mr. William Ball, Mr. Robert Atkins, and Mr. John Kerridge, together set the young men apart to the work of Christ " by the laying on of hands."† " We never heard of these preachers before,—well-meaning men, perhaps, though of course sad annoyances to the authorised and learned clergy,—pity that they left their original vocation of the plough, the loom, or the last." So says the believer in Clarendon or Walker. But the simple

---

* It appears from a tablet in the church that " John Mallack, of Fullands, gentleman, departed this life November 23, 1678." Fullands-house is now occupied as a school.

† Life of Trosse, by J. H.

man has been imposed upon. All were gentlemen ; all were scholars of distinction at one or other of the universities ; although all were now wandering, poor, and homeless. Great indeed had been their reverses ; but all might have kept caste, and most might have enjoyed preferment, if conscience had allowed them to conform. Golden persuasives to conformity had been offered and refused. One of them, praised by the bishop of Chester as one of the best preachers in the country, had refused great offers, made particularly by the lord-lieutenant of Ireland ; " but the offer of a mitre could not move him to act contrary to his sentiments."* Another, who had been urged in vain to accept a deanery, had, within a few days of this ordination service, been pursued by dragoons, been searched for in chimneys, chests, and boxes, and had at last escaped safely to Taunton through the bravery of his son, a little child, who refused to betray his father's hiding-place, even when a pistol was held to his breast by a constable, who furiously demanded to know the secret. George Trosse, the only one of the three candidates whose name is known, was himself " a good clerke of Oxenford," and no mean scholar. " He afterwards confessed to a friend that he had read over all the books in his study, besides about sixty folios which stood in his bed-

---

* Calamy on Atkins.

chamber, and that he had read over the Bible, in English, Latin, Greek, Hebrew, and French, a hundred and a hundred times."*   " Though fired with holy zeal," writes his biographer, " he had some hesitation about entering upon the sacred office before ; but when the Oxford Act drove Dissenting ministers from cities, corporations, and their own benefices, he consented, and was solemnly set apart to the work."† Solemnly indeed! solemnly set apart to a ministry which could only be exercised in partial safety at midnight meetings in the woods ; solemnly set apart to scorn, penury, and bonds, for the sake of Christ's holy Gospel ; solemnly set apart to such a life by reverend men who were themselves passing through its great tribulation.   We must search the legends of primitive martyrs and fathers to find an ordination scene of equal solemnity.   It ill becomes the church of the conventicle to treat with disrespect the solemnities peculiar to a church installed in cathedrals, enriched with the spoils of ancient Romanism, and adorned with the spells of royalty, of chivalry, and of historical prescription ; but it acts a still less-becoming part when, with bustle and flaunting show, it seeks to rival such attractions.   From its very nature it never can succeed, however it may

---

* Gilling's Life of Trosse, 1715, p. 33.
† Gilling.

stoop to try. The effort is as needless as it is useless, for it has its own poetry, its own grand and moving stories, and its own powers of impression, although they are not of this world,— they are only of the kind shown in the lives of our ancestors, and in the truths for which they lived and died.

Still weak and sickly, it was deemed needful for Mr. Alleine to take a second pilgrimage to Devizes to drink the mineral waters. Before setting out, he resolved to convene his friends, and set apart a day of thanksgiving for all mercies to him and them. Accordingly, on the 10th of July, 1666, there was a large assembly gathered at Fullands to keep this festival of praise. He then preached from the words of David, " He hath not dealt so with any nation. Praise ye the Lord."—Psalm clxvii. 20. The following is a sketch of the discourse:—As God deals with singular mercy to His people, they owe Him singular praise. Review the historic mercies of the nation. The Gospel is its brightest mercy ; for as the earth without the sun, would be the land without the sun of souls. Gospel light was kindled in primitive times. After it had been clouded over for a season by the Saxon invasion, Austin came from Rome, and suddenly a light shone through the ministry of other famous preachers. When, after that, it was clouded again by the power of Antichrist, others were raised,

some to testify by living, some by dying for the
Word.   Even the deaths of martyrs, our own kindred, have proved to be amongst the mercies of the
church, for, according to the holy prophecy of
Latimer, " God hath lighted such a candle in England that it never shall be put out."   The scat-
tering of the Spanish Armada—the detection of the
gunpowder plot—and other deliverances from the
power of darkness, were all our mercies, though not
in our days, for God hath thus kept alive that light
which He once commanded into the nation.   But
come nearer and look upon Taunton, the place of
our solemnities and desires, and you shall find that
He hath not dealt so with any other place.   No
need, like David, to bemoan yourselves that you
dwell in the tents of Kedar.   Threescore years
hath God waited on Taunton, and you have all
been born under the powerful preaching of the
Word.   Even until now, your eyes behold your
teachers—He hath not dealt so with other places ;
there, excellent lights have been put out, and you
scarce find even the footsteps of religion.   You
behold many maintaining the profession of the
Gospel, but many parishes there are whose professors are so few that they are for signs and
wonders to be pointed at.   You behold " how
good and pleasant a thing it is for brethren to dwell
together in unity."   Bless the Lord that the hearts
of believers have all been made one in this place.

Bless the Lord, you His people, because the Lord hath blessed you with peace!

By far the larger part of the sermon relates to the peculiar mercies belonging to God's peculiar people. In the course of these appeals he says, " He doth single you out before the world, to tell the world what a God can do for a poor creature; to make you the monuments of His magnificence and bounty; to show how He could exalt the dust of the earth. This is the use you serve for in the world. Do not live as if you were made for little things, and for little use; you are made for this use—that you should be vessels prepared to have the infinite fulness of God pouring into you, as vessels standing by for the same purpose, and running over to all eternity, when you shall be ever full and running over with the glory of God—when the all-sufficiency of God shall be for ever emptying itself into you. How is it that God hears no more of you? Hath He done so for any other?"

In the close he says, " What if in this world you suffer more than others ?

" You are better fed than others; for God Almighty hath fed you by extraordinary providence.

" You are better taught than others.—Who is like to you, O people, about whose tents the manna always raineth ?

" You have more promises than others.—Now

there are come in to us a whole shoal of promises, that we would not so properly claim before.

"God hath honoured you more than others.— To others with you it is given to believe; but to you it is given to suffer for His sake; which the apostle reckons as a step higher than others can attain.—(Phil. i. 29.)

"God hath intrusted you with His honour more than others. He hath put more into your hands, than into the hands of any other. God's glory is trusted more with the sufferers of Christ than with any others. O be infinitely tender of His honour! See that you love Him more than others; praise Him more than others."

While all were lost in thoughts like these, the door was suddenly shattered open, and in burst helter-skelter, with a crash of harsh laughter, a party of men flourishing drawn swords. Two magistrates hounded them on, and in a moment the scene was one of clamour and fury. The door had not been fastened, but the heroes adopted this method of opening it, in preference to the usual one of lifting the latch, in order to render the ceremony of their entrance more impressive. With much abusive language the names of all present were taken down, and the constables charged to bring them next day before the justices assembled at the Castle Tavern, "there to be dealt with akordin to law." They appeared at the time appointed, and after two days' tedious attendance, were all "convicted of a conventicle," and sentenced to a fine of three pounds each, or to be committed to prison threescore days. Of the persons thus sentenced, few paid the fine, or allowed others to do it for them. Mr. Alleine, therefore, with his wife, his aged father, seven ministers, and forty private persons, were committed to the prison at Ilchester.

A sufferer in the same cause was at that time singing in a distant prison :—

> " 'Tis not the baseness of this state
>   Doth hide us from God's face ;
> He frequently, both soon and late,
>   Doth visit us with grace.
>
> " Here come the angels, here come saints,
>   Here comes the Spirit of God,
> To comfort us in our restraints
>   Under the wicked's rod."

This might have been the song of our imprisoned congregation. Indeed it was in spirit the song of their minister, for he is reported to have said to his wife, " Well, though we have not our attendants and servants as the great ones and the rich of the world have, we have the blessed angels of God still to wait on us, to minister to us, to watch over us while we are sleeping ; ready to be with us when journeying again, and still to preserve us from the rage of men and devils." The prison had but little gloom in it for him, and was allowed to place no check upon his labours. He ministered sedulously to those members of his flock who were there, and the rest he visited by letters, eight of which have been printed. Two sermons were preached nearly every day ; and he invariably took his turn in preaching, as well as in other devotional exercises. His last exhortation, delivered on the morning of the day when he and those who were committed with him were set free, has been thus preserved in the short-hand notes of a listener:—

" Dearly beloved Brethren,—My time is little, and my strength but small, yet I could not consent that you should pass without receiving some parting counsel ; and what I have to say at parting shall be chiefly to you that are prisoners, and partly also to you our friends, that are here met together. To you that are prisoners, I shall speak something by way of exhortation, and something by way of dehortation.

" *By way of Exhortation.*

" First.—Rejoyce with trembling in your prison comforts, and see that you keep them in a thankful remembrance. Who can tell the mercies that you have received here ? My time nor strength will not suffice me to recapitulate them. See that you rejoyce in God, but rejoyce with trembling. Do not think the account will be little for mercies so many and so great. Receive these choice mercies with a trembling hand, for fear lest you should be found guilty of misimproving such precious benefits, and so wrath should be upon you from the Lord. Remember Hezekiah's case: great mercies did he receive ; some praises did he return, but not according to the benefit done unto him ; therefore was wrath upon him from the Lord, and upon all Judah for his sake, (2 Chron. xxxii. 25.) Therefore go away with a holy fear upon your hearts, lest you should forget the loving-kindness of the Lord, and should not render to Him according to what you have received.

" Oh, my brethren, stir up yourselves to render praise to the Lord. You are the people that God hath formed for His praise, and sent hither for His praise ; and you should now go home as so many trumpets to sound forth the praises of God, when you come among your friends. There is an expression (Psalm lxviii. 11) ' The Lord gave the word, great was the company of them that published it.' So let it be said of the praises of God now, great was the company of them that published them. God hath sent a whole troop of you here together, let all these go home and sound the praises of God wherever you come ; and this is the way to make His praise glorious indeed. Shall I tell you a story that I have read ?—There was a certain king that had a pleasant grove, and that he might make it every way delightful to him, he caused some birds to be caught, and to be kept up in cages, till they had learned sundry sweet and artificial tunes ; and when they were perfect in their lessons, he let them abroad out of their cages into his grove, that while he was walking in this grove he might hear them singing those pleasant tunes, and teaching them to other birds that were of a wilder note. Brethren, this King is God, this grove is His church, these birds are yourselves, this cage is the prison ; God hath sent you hither, that you should learn the sweet and pleasant notes of His praise. And I trust that you have learned something all this while, God forbid else. Now God opens the cage, and lets you forth into the grove of His church, that you may sing forth His praises, and that others may learn of you too.   Forget not, therefore, the songs of the house of your pilgrimage, do not return to your wild notes again ; keep the mercies of God for ever in a thankful remembrance, and make mention of them humbly as long as you live ; then shall you answer the end for which He sent you hither.   I trust you will not forget this place. When Queen Mary died, she said, 'That after her death they should find Calais on her heart.   I hope that men shall find by you hereafter, that the prison is upon your heart, Ilchester is upon your heart.

   " Secondly. Feed and feast your faith upon prison-experience.   Do not think that God hath done this only for your present supply.   Brethren, God hath provided for you, not only for your present supply in prison, but to lay up for all your lives that experience that your faith must live upon, till faith be turned into vision.   Learn dependence upon God, and confidence in God, by all the experiences that you have had here.   ' Because thou hast been my help (saith the Psalmist), therefore under the shadow of thy wing will I rejoice.'   Are you at a loss at any time ? then remember your bonds.   We read in Scripture of a time when there was no smith in all Israel, and the Israelites were fain to carry their goads and other instruments, to be sharpened, down to the Philistines. So when your spirits are low, and when your faith is dull, carry them to the prison to be sharpened and quickened. Oh, how hath the Lord confuted all our fears! cared for all our necessities !   The faith of some of you was sorely put to it for corporal necessities.   You came hither, not having any thing considerable to pay for your charges here, but God took care for that.   And you left poor

miserable families at home, and no doubt but many troublesome thoughts were in your minds, what your families
should do for bread, but God hath provided for them.

" We that are ministers, left poor starveling flocks, and
we thought that the countrey had been now stript, and yet
God hath provided for them. Thus hath the Lord been
pleased to furnish us with arguments for our faith, against
we come to the next distress. Though you should be
called forth to leave your flocks destitute, you that are my
brethren in the ministry, and others their families destitute,
yet doubt not but God will provide. Remember your
bonds upon all occasions. Whensoever you are in
distress, remember your old Friend, remember your tryed
Friend.

" Thirdly. Let divine mercy be as oyl to the flame of
your love : ' O love the Lord, all ye His saints.' Brethren,
this is the language of all God's dealings with you; they
all call upon you to love the Lord your God with all your
hearts, with all your souls, with all your strength. What
hath God been doing ever since you came to this prison ?
All that He hath been doing since you came hither, hath
been to pour oyl into the flames of your love, thereby to
encrease and heighten them. God hath lost all these
mercies upon you, if you do not love Him better than
you did before. You have had supplies ; to what purpose
is it, unless you love God the more ? If they that be in
want, love Him better than you, it were better you had
been in their case. You have had health here, but if
they that be in sickness love God better than you, it were
better you had been in sickness too. See that you love
your Father, that hath been so tender of you. What
hath God been doing, but pouring out His love upon you ?
How were we mistaken ? For my part, I thought that

God took us upon His knee to whip us, but He took us upon His knee to dandle us. We thought to have felt the strokes of His anger, but He hath stroked us as a father his children, with most dear affection. Who can utter His loving kindness! What! (my brethren) shall we be worse than publicans? The publicans will love those that love them. Will not you return love for so much love? Far be this from you, brethren; you must not only exceed the publicans, but the Pharisees too; therefore, surely you must love Him that loveth you. This is my business now to bespeak your love to God, to unite your hearts to Him; blessed be God for this occasion; for my part I am unworthy of it. Now, if I can get your hearts nearer to God than they were, then happy am I, and blessed are you. Fain I would, that all these experiences should knit our hearts to God more, and endear us for ever to Him. What! so much bounty and kindness and no returns of love? At least no further returns? I may plead in behalf of the Lord with you, as they did for the centurion : ' He loveth our nation (say they) and hath built us a synagogue.' So I may say here, He hath loved you, and poured out His bounty upon you. How many friendly visits from those that you could expect but little of? Whence do you think this came? It is God that hath the key of all these hearts. He secretly turned the cock, and caused them to pour forth kindness upon you. There is not a motion of love in the heart of a friend towards you, but it was God that put it in.

"Fourthly.—Keep your manna in a golden pot, and forget not Him that hath said so often, ' Remember me.' You have had manna rained plentifully about you; be sure that something of it be kept. Do not forget all the sermons that you have heard here ; O that you would labour to repeat them over, to live them over ; you have had such a stock that you may live upon, and your friends too (if you be communicative), a great while together. If anything have been wanting, time for the digesting hath been wanting. See that you well chew the cud, and see that you especially remember the feasts of love. Do not you know who hath said to you so often, ' Remember me ?' How often have you heard that sweet word since you came hither ? What ! Do you think it is enough to remember Him for an hour ? No, but let it be a living and lasting remembrance. Do not you write that name of His in the dust, that hath written your names upon His heart. Your High Priest hath your names upon His heart, and therewith is entered into the holy place, and keeps them there for a memorial before the Lord continually. O that His remembrance might be ever written upon your hearts, written as with a pen of a diamond, upon tables of marble, that might never be worn out! That as Aristotle saith of the curious fabrick of Minerva, that he had so ordered the fabrick that his name was written in the midst, that if any went to take that out, the whole fabrick was dissolved. So the name of Jesus should be written upon the substance of your souls, that they should pull all asunder before they should be able to pull it out.

" Fifthly.—Let the bonds of your affliction strengthen the bonds of your affection. Brethren, God hath sent us hither to teach us, among other things, the better to love one another. Love is lovely, both in the sight of God and men ; and if by your imprisonment you have profited in love, then you have made an acceptable proficiency. O brethren, look within ; are you not more endeared one to another ? I bless the Lord for that union and peace

z

that hath been ever among you. But you must be sensible that we come very far short of that love that we owe one to another; we have not that love, that indearedness and tenderness, and complacency, that compassion towards each other, that we ought to have. Ministers should be more endeared one to another, and Christians should be more dear to each other than they were before. We have eaten and drunk together, and lived on our Father's love in one family together; we have been joined together in one common cause, and all put into one condition. O let the remembrance of a prison, and of what hath passed here, especially those uniting feasts, ingage you to love one another!

"Sixthly.—Let present indulgence fit you for future hardships, and do not look that your Father should be always dandling you on His knee. Beloved, God hath used you like fondlings now, rather than like sufferers. What shall I say? I am at a loss when I think of the tender indulgence, and the yearnings of our heavenly Father towards us. But, my brethren, do not look for such prisons again.

"Affliction doth but now play and sport with you, rather than bite you; but do you look that affliction should hereafter fasten its teeth on you to purpose; and do you look that the hand that hath now gently stroked you, may possibly buffet you, and put your faith hard to it, when you come to the next tryal. This fondness of your heavenly Father is to be expected only while you are young and tender; but afterward you must look to follow your business, and to keep your distance, and to have rebukes and frowns too when you need them. Bless God for what you have found here, but prepare you, this is but the beginning (shall I say the beginning of sorrow?

I cannot say so, for the Lord hath made it a place of rejoycing); this is but the entrance of our affliction; but you must look, that when you are trained up to a better perfection, God will put your faith to harder exercise.

" Seventhly.—Cast up your accounts at your return, and see whether you have gone as much forward in your souls, as you have gone backward in your estates. I cannot be insensible but some of you are here to very great disadvantage as to your affairs in the world, having left your business so rawly at home in your shops, trades, and callings, that it is like to be no little detriment to you upon this account. But happy are ye if you find at your return, that, as much as your affairs are gone backward and behind-hand, so much your souls have gone forward. If your souls go forward by grace in your sufferings, blessed be God that hath brought you to such a place as a prison is.

" Eighthly.—Let the snuffers of this prison make your light burn the brighter, and see that your course and discourse be the more savoury, serious, and spiritual for this present tryal. O brethren! Now the voice of the Lord is to you, as it is in the prophet Isaiah lx. 1 :—' Arise, and shine!' now ' let your light so shine before men, that others may see your good works, and glorifie your Father which is in heaven.' It is said of those preachers beyond sea, that have been sent into England, and here reaped the benefit of our English practical divinity, at their return they have preached so much better than they had wont to do, that it hath been said of them, ' *Apparuit hunc fuisse in Angliâ.*' So do you, my brethren, live so much better than you had wont, that when men shall see the change in your lives, they may say of you, ' *Apparuit hunc fuisse in Custodia.*' See that your whole course and discourse be more spiritual and heavenly than ever ; see that you shine in your families when you come home ; be you better husbands, better masters, better fathers ; study to do more than you have done this way, and to approve yourselves better in your family relations than you did before ; that the savour of a prison may be upon you in all companies : then will you praise and please the Lord.

" Ninthly, and lastly.—See that you walk accurately, as those that have the eyes of God, angels, and men upon you. My brethren, you will be looked upon now with very curious eyes. God doth expect more of you than ever ; for He hath done more for you, and He looketh what fruit there will be of all this. Oh ! may there be a sensible change upon your souls by the showers that have fallen in prison, as there is in the greenness of the earth by the showers that have fallen lately abroad.

"By way of Dehortation also, I have these four things to leave with you.

" First.—Revile not your persecutors, but bless them, and pray for them, as the instruments of conveying great mercies to you. Do not you so far forget the rule of Christ, as when you come home, to be setting your mouths to talk against those that have injured you. Remember the command of your Lord—'Bless them that curse you, pray for them that despitefully use you, and persecute you.' Whatever they intended, yet they have been instruments of a great deal of mercy to us ; and so we should pray for them, and bless God for the good we have received by them.

" Secondly.—Let not the humble acknowledgment of God's mercy degenerate into proud, vain-glorious boast-

ing, or carnal triumph. I beseech you, see that you go
home with a great deal of fear upon your spirits in this
respect, lest pride should get advantage of you, lest instead
of humbly acknowledging God's mercy, there should be
carnal boasting. Beware of this, I earnestly beg of you,
for this will very much spoil your sufferings, and be very
displeasing in the sight of God. But let your acknowledging of His mercy be ever with humble, self-abasing
thankfulness, and be careful that you do not make His
mercies to be the fuel of your pride, which were to lose
all at once.

" Thirdly.—Be not prodigal of your liberty upon a conceit that the prisons will be easie, not fearful of adven-
turing yourselves in the way of your duty. Alas! I am
afraid of both these extreams; on the one hand, lest some
among us, having found a great deal of mercy here, will
now think there is no need of any Christian prudence,
which is always necessary, and is a great duty. It is not
cowardice to make use of the best means to preserve our
liberty, not declining our duty. On the other side, there
is fear lest some may be fearful, and ready to decline their
duty, because they have newly tasted of a prison for it.
Far be it from you to distrust God, of whom you have
had so great experience, but be sure you hold on in your
duty, whatsoever it cost you.

" Fourthly.—Do not load others with censures, whose
judgment, or practice, differs from yours, but humbly bless
God that hath so happily directed you. You know all
are not of the same mind as to the circumstances of suffering, and all have not gone the same way. Far be it
from any of you (my brethren) that you should so far forget yourselves, as to be unmerciful to your brethren, but
bless God that hath directed you into a better way.

Your charity must grow higher than ever; God forbid that you should increase in censures, instead of increasing in charity.

"Having spoken to my fellow-prisoners, I have two words to speak to you, our friends and brethren with us.

"First.—Let our experience be your incouragement. O love the Lord, ye our friends, love the Lord; fear Him for ever; believe in Him, trust in Him for ever, for our sakes; we have tasted of the kindness of God.

"You know how good God hath been to us in spirituals and in temporals. Encourage your hearts in the Lord your God, serve Him the more freely and gladly for our sakes. You see we have tryed, we have tasted how good the Lord is; do you trust Him the more, because we have tryed Him so much, and found him a Friend so faithful, so gracious, that we are utterly unable to speak His praise. Go on and fear not in the way of your duty; verily there is a reward for the righteous. God hath given us a great reward already, but this is but the least; we look for a kingdom.

"Secondly, and lastly,—My desire is to our friends, that they will all help us in our praises. Our tongues are too little to speak forth the goodness and the grace of God, do you help us in our praises. Love the Lord the better, praise Him the more, and what is wanting in us, let it be made good by you. O that the praises of God may sound abroad in the country by our means, and for our sakes."

Chapter XIV.

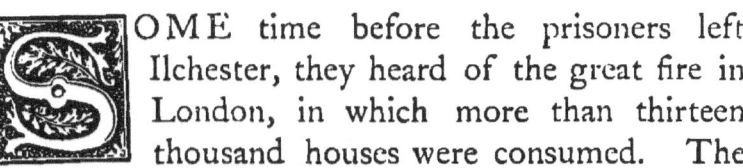

𝕱aint, 𝕡et 𝕻ursuing.

" Oh what a livelie life, what heavenlie power,
What spreading virtue, what a sparkling fire ;
How great, how plentiful, how rich a dower,
Dost thou within this dying flesh inspire."

SIR JOHN DAVIES.

SOME time before the prisoners left Ilchester, they heard of the great fire in London, in which more than thirteen thousand houses were consumed. The spirit of the times was curiously shown, day by day, in the various popular accounts and speculations that came drifting in to them along with the news. Some persons thought that the disaster was the work of the Romanists ; others thought that surely the Baptists had set the houses on fire ; indeed, this charge had actually been reported in a letter from the

Court ; how, then, could it be doubted !* Opinions
in the outside world were equally conflicting as to the
particular lesson which this judgment was intended
to teach the nation. Some said that it marked the
displeasure of Heaven at the leniency shown by
the church to Nonconformists ;† others declared it
to be the terrible voice of God to the chiefs in
Church and State, crying, " Let my people go,
that they may serve me ; and if ye will not, behold,
thus and thus I will do unto you."‡ Our friends
probably inclined to the latter belief, but to their
honour, their deep concern took a practical rather
than a speculative form. Affliction had made
them know " the heart of a stranger," and taught
them to sympathise with the citizens who, shelter-
less and in despair, were wandering over the fields
in sight of the waste where their homes had been.
They longed to help them, but what could they

---

* Attempts were made to bring fresh odium on the 'sect every-
where spoken against ' by charging on its members this evil deed.
Among other instances see a letter from the Duke of Buckingham,
September 6, 1666, who says, " A great many Anabaptists have
been taken setting houses on fire."—MS. in the Guildhall Library.
Of course these charges were brought by informers in pay of the
Government.

† Seth Ward, bishop of Exeter, preached a sermon before the
House of Lords, October 10, 1666, in which he laboured to prove
that the fire was intended to establish the church, by rousing Government " to uphold religion in the sincerity and *uniformity* thereof, to
prevent it from undermining *toleration.*"

‡ Philip Henry.

do ? Though they would be soon out of prison,
it would be with the prospect of soon entering it
again. Their trade was gone ; all the world was
against them ; and poor as they had been made by
a life of penalties, on them alone rested the responsibility of keeping alive their many ministers and
co-religionists who had been made poorer still.
However, the first thing they did when set free,
was to join in making a collection for the sufferers
in London. To this collection Mr. Alleine gave
a sum, which from its liberal proportion was intended to be a stimulus to others, and, at the same
time, as it was afterwards discovered, he gave
more than as much in secret. In this way he and
his people offered God praise for their deliverance.
To be grateful, is something more than to feel
beautiful and bounding sensations of delight, to offer
complimentary acknowledgments in language, or to
thunder back thanksgiving songs ; it is essentially
a practical thing, and its first question is, " What
shall I render to the Lord for all His benefits ? "
So they thought.

His last imprisonment, both by its direct influence, and by depriving him of his intended visit
to Devizes, had greatly increased his disorder.
All through the winter and spring it continued to
gain ground ; but, weak as he was, he preached, kept
many days of fasting and thanksgiving, and frequently administered the Lord's Supper to his people.

In June, 1667, he went to Devizes again. Informers, constables, distraining officers, turnkeys,
and such-like disreputable ministers of religion, were
not so active here as in some other places. On this
account, therefore, as well as on account of the
medicinal advantages which the sick man primarily
sought, Devizes was always an attractive retreat.
In a letter to Taunton he thus alludes to it :—

"You may not think that I have forgotten you,
and consulted my own ease and pleasure : but if
God prosper my intentions, I shall be found to have
been daily serving you in this retirement. I will
assure you, I am very tender of preserving all that
little strength that God doth add to me entirely for
your sakes. I bless the Lord I am in great tranquillity here in this town, and walk up and down
the corporation without any questioning me. I
seem to myself to be retired to this place, as a
vessel rent and shatter'd and torn in the service,
that is come to recruit in the harbour. And here I
am, as it were, rigging, and repairing, and victual-
ling, to put forth again in the service ; which I
shall do with the first wind, as soon as I am
ready."

A week after this he writes :—" I longed to hear
of your welfare, but by reason of the carryer's in-
termitting his journeys, could not till now obtain
my desires, neither had I opportunity till the last
week of writing to you. I rejoyce to hear, by

Mr. Ford, of God's continual goodness towards you ; He is your Shepherd, and therefore it is that you do not want. 'Me you have not always, but He is ever with you, His rod and His staff shall comfort you.'

"O beloved flock, I may give you the salutation of the angels, 'Hail, you are highly favoured of the Lord, blessed are you among men ;' though you are but poor and despised, like little Benjamin among the thousands of Judah, you carry away the blessing and the privilege from all the rest. God hath done more for the least of you than for the whole world of mankind besides, put all their mercies together. Fear not, little flock, it is your Father's good pleasure to give you the kingdom. 'Blessed are you of the Lord, for yours is the kingdom of heaven.' All that the Scripture speaks of that kingdom of glory, that kingdom of peace, of righteousness, that everlasting kingdom, it speaks to you. Behold your inheritance, see that you believe.

"I charge you to beware of the world. When Saul had gotten his kingdom, he left off taking care for the asses. O remember, yours is the kingdom! What are you the better that you have all this in your Bibles, if you do not weigh it by frequent and serious consideration, and ponder these sayings in your hearts ? Beloved, I have written these things to you, that your joy may be full."

While staying at Devizes, several old clerical friends of his, living there or in the county, would, when they heard of his visit, seize the rare chance of spending an hour in his company.

One of these was Mr. Timothy Sacheverell, of Trinity College, Oxford, and late minister of Tarrant Hinton. At this time he was living at Winterbourne in Wilts, but would be occasionally at Devizes, and soon made it his home. He was held in extraordinary respect even by his opponents. Bishop Kennett speaks of his "great worth, temper, and learning."* He was fervent in spirit, serving the Lord; and although no Syrian hermit was ever a greater lover of peace, no knight of Gothic romance was ever inspired with a grander bravery. Not long before this visit, while he was kneeling in prayer with his family one morning, several troopers rushed into the room, and one of them, holding a pistol at his back, commanded him in the King's name immediately to stand up, but he still continued praying. When he had concluded, he rose and calmly asked the trooper how he durst thus pretend in the King's name to interrupt him, while he and his family were presenting their petitions to the King of kings!

Another person of note amongst the Nonconformists here was Mr. Benjamin Fflower, the

---

* Register, p. 915.

ejected vicar of Cardiff. His family, like that of
Mr. Alleine, had been known about the neighbourhood of Devizes for some centuries past, and these
had lately been drawn yet more closely together by
intermarriages. Though not yet living in the town,
his house was not far away, and he would not
neglect this opportunity of seeing his eminent
kinsman. Mr. Fflower was a man of glowing
piety, and his great labours have led to his being
called " the Apostle of Wiltshire Dissenters."
Shortly after this interview, a Presbyterian church
was organized in the town, and he became its first
pastor ; and perhaps we may have leave for a
moment to glance beyond the strict limit of this
history just to notice the fact, that this gentleman,
in his own belief at least, lived to be the last
survivor of the two thousand confessors. Preserved in the archives of this church, there is
a paper extracted from the diary of Defoe's
friend, Thomas Webb, once a member, in which
the story of the pastor's resignation is thus
related : —

" 1709. *April* 10.—The reverend Father in
God,* Mr. Benjamin Fflower, administered the
Lord's Supper to us, this day being by him desired

---

* ' Those ministers who beget converts to Christ may most
properly be called *Fathers in God.*'— Sermon on 1 Cor. iv. 15,
preached by Mr. Atkins before Bishop Gauden, in 1662.

to be his last day of doing so; his great age, being eighty-two years old, not admitting him to take the journey, or so hard work upon him ; therefore he desired the whole work might be left to Mr. Chauncey,* and he excused, which was agreed unto. And so accordingly, after the Sacrament, he took his leave of us, which made tears run from the eyes of almost all the congregation, telling us he was superannuated for the work, and he knew not one alive but himself that was thrust out by the Bartholomew Act ; all his brethren having got the start of him, and got home before him ; and what he was left behind so long for, God only knew ! But we have received much good from his lips ; they have dropped honey and the honey-comb !"†

Another, whose friendly face might be sometimes seen, was Mr. William Gough, of Queen's College, Cambridge, who, since the passing of the Five-Mile Act, had been minister of a Baptist congregation at Earl Stoke, a little over five miles from Devizes, but he was frequently in the town, and was afterwards a pastor here.

It is certain that he often saw the excluded vicar

---

* Mr. Chauncey died at Devizes, May 26, 1750.—Wilson MS.

† This MS. furnishes a clear refutation of the report printed by Bishop Kennett, to the effect "that Mr. Fflower, after the Restoration, returned to his native country in *Gloucestershire*, conformed, and had a benefice there."—Kennett's Register.

of Compton, worthy Mr. Frayling, a meek-looking old' scholar, in shabby skull-cap and threadbare cloak, who at this time, and ever since his trouble, had preached at Devizes secretly, on alternate Sundays, with Mr. Obadiah Wills.* There, and in surrounding places, he kept on his patient services even after he was blind with years, and had to be led by a friend across the downs from village to village. When he died, his neighbour Mr. Gough eulogized him as "a Moses for meekness, a Nathaniel for uprightness, and one of Eliphaz's happy men, who came to his grave in full age."

Another of Mr. Allcine's companions during this month was Mr. Ford, once one of the most famous tutors at Magdalen College, Oxford, and after that, a member of the Westminster Assembly. It is pleasant to picture these *doctores umbratici* together, enjoying a short holiday for once in their lives, now walking through the fields in company, now standing by the "bowery clefts and leafy shelves" of the lane-side, where the spring is flowing, and now meeting in some cottage or garden-croft to a feast of yet holier happiness. In some of their meeting-places, however, great secrecy was needed, and watchers had to be on the look-out, for their happiness was likely to suffer interruption

---

* Obadiah Wills, M.A , formerly rector of Alton Priors.

from visitors, profane as the harpies that descended
on the feast of Æneas.

But their intercourse was made peculiarly solemn
by the sudden though joyful death of Mr. Tobie
Alleine.

Joseph writes :—"It hath pleased the Lord to add
to my affliction since my coming by taking
away my dear father,—the day of whose glorious
translation was the day after my arriving here.
But I bless the Lord, I do believe and expect the
return of the Redeemer with all His saints, and the
most glorious resurrection of my own dead body
with all believers ; and this makes me to rest in
hope, and fills me with unspeakably more joy than
the death of myself or any other saint can with
grief."

This trouble came not alone.   The waters failed
to produce the usual effect on the invalid, and in
July he was stricken down with a fever.   When to
all appearance he was lying at the point of death,
he dictated a long letter to his people, closing with
this prayer :—

"O Father of spirits, that hath set me over thy
flock to watch for their souls, as one that must
give an account; I have long studied thy will,
and taught in thy name, and do unfeignedly bless
thee that any have believed my report.   I have
given unto them the words which thou gavest me,
and they have received them.   I have manifested

thy name unto them, and they have kept thy
Word. And now I am no more with them, but I
come unto thee. Holy Father, keep them through
thine own name; for they are thine. As they
have kept the word of thy patience, so keep thou
them in the hour of temptation. They are but a
flock—a little and a helpless flock—but thou art
their Shepherd; suffer them not to want; do thou
feed them and fold them; let thy rod and thy
staff comfort them, and let not the beasts of prey
fall upon them to the spoiling of their souls.

" But what shall I do for them that will not be
gathered ? I have called after them, but they would
not answer ; I have charged them in thy name, but
they would not hear ; I have studied to speak
persuasively to them, but I cannot prevail. Then
I said, I have laboured in vain ; I have spent my
strength for nought, and in vain ; yet I cannot give
them over, much less may I give Thee over. Lord,
persuade Japhet to dwell in the tents of Shem.
Lord, compel them to come in, and lay the hands of
mercy upon them, as thou didst on lingering Lot,
and bring them forth, that they may escape for
their lives and not be consumed. Lord, I pray
thee, open their eyes that they may see, and lay
hold upon their hearts by thy omnipotent grace.
Do thou turn them, and they shall be turned. O
bring back the miserable captives, and suffer not
the enemy of mankind to drive away the most of

the flock before mine eyes, and to deride the fruit-
less endeavours of thy labourers, and boast over
them, that he can do more with them, though he
seek to ruine them, than all the beseechings, counsels
and charges of thy servants that seek to save them.
Lord, if I could find out anything that would pierce
them, that would make its way into their hearts,
thou knowest I would use it. But I have been
many years pleading thy cause in vain ; O let not
these endeavours also be lost ! O God, find out
every ignorant, every prophane sinner, every
prayerless soul, and every prayerless family, and
convince them of their miserable condition while
without thee in the world. Set thy image upon
their souls—set up thy worship in their families.
Let not pride, ignorance, or slothfulness, keep them
in neglect of the means of knowledge. Let thine
eyes be over the place of my desires for good, from
one end of the year to the other end thereof. Let
every house therein be a seminary of religion ; and
let those that cast their eyes upon these lines find
thee sliding in by the secret influence of thy grace
into their hearts, and irresistably engaging them to
do thy pleasure. Amen, amen."

In six weeks' time the sentence of death seemed
to be revoked, and he was able to travel back to
Taunton. He only remained there for a short
period, and in September we find him at Dorchester.

There lived at Dorchester, in those days, "a very worthy and reverend physician," one Dr. Loss, a great helper to the persecuted ministers, whose Latin memoranda respecting them afforded assistance to Antony Wood.* Unhappily, that note-book, though much searched for lately, cannot be found. Most likely it contains some account of Mr. Alleine's last days, for the doctor became his kind friend. Till now they had never met, but prescriptions and medicines had come by carrier. Now, a personal interview was needful, and this was the reason for the journey.

Dr. Loss advised Mr. and Mrs. Alleine to stay in the town for a fortnight; but the small-pox then raging everywhere, they could not hire a chamber, and were in great perplexity until a certain Widow Bartlett† found out their inn, and courteously invited them home. Two or three days after this, the sick man suddenly lost the use of all his limbs. Looking at his dead hands, he said, "the Lord gave, and the Lord hath taken away, and blessed be the name of the Lord." He could not lift a finger. Two attendants were needed even to turn him in bed, and this they sometimes did forty times in a night. In this living death he lay from September

---

* Athenæ, iii. 404. Lansdown MSS. 1236, folio 104.

† Mr. Bartlett had been minister at Tiverton, and, it is said, great labours hastened his end.—Nonconformist's Memorial, vol. i., p. 464.

the 28th to November the 16th, and all through the winter there was but little change. But even this forlorn estate had its alleviations; for when the Nonconformists of the place knew of his presence and affliction, all were constantly eager to cheer him with new surprises of kindness.

The doctor came twice every day for fourteen weeks, ever refusing fees; and the gentry living near supplied everything that could be invented to give him comfort. All this made him say, " I was a stranger, and Mercy took me in ; in prison, and Mercy came to me; I was sick, and Mercy visited me."

Some old friends from Taunton having come to see him once more, he was much revived. Propped up with pillows, and the curtains drawn back, " He desired them," says Mrs. Alleine, " all to stand round the bed, and would have me take out his hand and hold it forth, that they might shake his hand though he could not shake theirs." Then, as he was able, he thus spake to them :—

" O how it rejoices my heart to see your faces and to hear your voices, though I cannot speak as heretofore to you. Methinks I am now like old Jacob, with all his sons about him. Now you see my weak estate ; thus have I been for many weeks since I parted with Taunton, but God hath been with me, and I hope with you ; your prayers have been heard and answered for me, many ways ; the

Lord return them into your own bosoms. My
friends, life is mine, death is mine ; in that covenant
I was preaching of to you, is all my salvation and
all my desire ; although my body do not prosper,
I hope, through grace, my soul doth.

" I have lived a sweet life by the promises, and
I hope, through grace, can die by a promise. It
is the promises of God, which are everlasting, that
will stand by us. Nothing but God in them will
stead us in a day of affliction.

" My dear friends, I now feel the power of
those doctrines I preached to you, on my heart—
the doctrines of faith, of repentance, of self-denial,
of the covenant of grace, of contentment, and the
rest ; O that you would live them over, now I
cannot preach to you !

" It is a shame for a believer to be cast down
under afflictions, that hath so many glorious privileges, justification, adoption, sanctification, and
eternal glory. We shall be as the angels of God in
a little while. Nay, to say the truth, believers
are, as it were, little angels already, that live in the
power of faith. O, my friends ! live like believers, trample this dirty world under your feet ;
be not taken with its comforts, nor disquieted with
its crosses ; you will be gone out of it shortly."

When they again came to take leave of him, he
prayed with them as far as his weak state would
suffer him, and, in the words of Moses and the

apostles, the same he always used after a sacrament, he blessed them, saying—

" The Lord bless you and keep you, the Lord cause His face to shine upon you, and give you peace.   And the God of peace, that brought again from the dead our Lord Jesus, through the blood of the everlasting covenant, make you perfect in every good work to do His will, working in you that which is well-pleasing in His sight, through Jesus Christ, to whom be glory, for ever and ever. Amen."

Then he spake thus :—

" Farewell, farewell, my dear friends. Remember me to all Taunton.   I beseech you and them, if I never see your faces more, go home and live over what I have preached to you, and the Lord provide for you when I am gone.   O ! let not all my labours and sufferings, let not my wasted strength, my useless limbs, rise up in judgment against you at the great day of the Lord."

In the last week of January, 1668, modern style, while he was lying helpless on the bed, a messenger came with the heavy tidings of his brother Norman's death.   Mr. Norman had evidently sunk a victim to the agencies which were now wasting away the life of his friend.   Long imprisonment had made the strong man weak.   Determination to fulfil his ministry amidst persecutions, and to do by incessant and multiplied services, in small and secret companies, what the law forbad his doing in a public and comprehensive way, had made him weaker still. Sorrow for the sorrows of the church, and shame for the shame of his country, now left without a hand or a voice to vindicate her stricken strength or lift her degraded name, weakened him still more. The hardships endured by his relatives for nonconformity—the fines, expensive processes, and impediments to trade which had at last compelled Humphrey Blake, his wife's father, to sell the estate which the admiral had left him, and emigrate with his family to Carolina,* were troubles which, joined to all the rest, broke his noble heart, and brought him to an early grave. He was not forty when he died. In the register of St. Mary's, Bridgewater, where he was buried, the officiating clergyman has written :—" Feb. 9, 1668. Johannes Norman, *Presbiter Doctus.*"

Norman and Alleine were as truly martyrs as were Ridley and Latimer. The only difference visible is, that the two former were put to death by Romanists—the two latter, by Protestants ; the former died in a fire lighted by a torch—fire that

---

* Mr. Blake left two daughters in England, one married to George Crane, ex-M.P. for Bridgewater, the other married to Mr. John Norman. Sarah, his eldest daughter, afterwards married Joseph Moreton, Esq., governor of Carolina ; and Joseph, his eldest son, succeeded Mr. Moreton to the governorship, continuing, like his father, a firm Dissenter.

wrapped the body in its waves, and did its work in an hour ; the latter, in fire lighted by a legislative enactment, the fire of sickness and sorrow, that stung both body and soul—a slow, silent fire that lasted for years. Mr. Alleine's hour was not yet come, but, as Dr. Annesly said of him, " it was impossible that anguish like his could continue long, and at last his sufferings for Christ hurried him to heaven in a fiery chariot."*

A few days after this bereavement he was much better, and such was his strong wish to see Taunton again, that Dr. Loss gave his consent, though with many fears for the issue of the experiment. He was borne thither in a horse-litter, and the sight of friends flocking round him seemed to give new strength ; but it was only a deceptive excitement, to be followed by long pauses of exhaustion. He could not bear the joy, and was therefore carried out of the way to the quiet mansion at Fullands. The story of the few following months is only one of convulsions and terrific pains interchanging with paralysis, a story too afflicting to write or read. Yet " he was full of the praises of God for mercy," praises sung from off the rack of physical anguish, his spirit making " songs in the night."

The poor wife had one more hope left. They

---

* Dr. Samuel Annesly, in 1692.

would try Bath. Huddled within an old wall, a mere maze of five hundred houses, " streets, narrow, uneven, and unpleasant," meanly built, yet full of loud life, the town itself would not be so reviving to him as his former lodging had been, in the peaceful village grange; but the " King's Bathe was the fairest in Europe," and many of those wonderful books on the virtues of its waters had already been written, which, with a few modern ones, would " fill a decently-sized library."* About the beginning of July, when he was somewhat stronger than usual, a horse-litter being again procured for him, he ventured on the journey of forty miles, and in two days accomplished it. " The doctors were amazed to behold such a wasted object, professing they never saw the like, much wondering how he was come alive, and on his appearance at the bathe some of the ladies were affrighted, as though death had come amongst them." In three weeks' time he was so marvellously restored, that, although he could never afterwards walk without assistance, physicians thought that there was no doubt of his ultimate recovery.†

---

* Knight's Land we Live in.

† Mr. Pepys was here a fortnight before. An interesting account of Bath and its visitors may be seen in his Diary, 13th, 14th, and 15th of June, 1668.

It was but the last bright flicker of a dying
flame, but it was truly bright, and he made it so
shine before men, that they, seeing his good works,
might glorify his Father in heaven.   Every day,
from five till seven o'clock in the morning, he was
alone for prayer, and three other short intervals
before night were set apart for the same special
retirement; at seven he was carried to the bath.
Much grieved by " the oaths, drinking, and ungodly carriage of the persons of quality there, he
did always give his faithful reproofs.   His way
was," adds his memorialist, " first to converse *of
things that might be taking with them,* for, being
furnished by his studies for any company, he did
use his learning for such ends, and by such means
hath caught many souls.   There were none but did
most thankfully accept his reproofs, though close
and plain, and showed him more respect after; the
vilest one among them, as I was by several informed,
saying of him ' that he never spake with such a
man in his life.'"

About three o'clock he used to be carried in a
chair to visit all the schools and almshouses. When
on these rounds, one of his efforts was to persuade
the teachers to make the Assembly's Catechism one
of their class-books.   Many copies of it, and also
of other small books, he would give for distribution
amongst the scholars, and engage to come a week
or fortnight after, to see what progress they had

made. He always had a school of sixty or seventy
poor children at his lodgings on Sunday, to receive
Christian instruction—perhaps the first Sunday
school known in all history. No wonder that such
a novelty excited alarm, and that the threatened
citation of several persons to Wells, before the
bishop, to give an account of their implication in
it, led to its dissolution. In his daily visits to the
poor he would open searching conversations with
them respecting their spiritual state, would pray
with them, and where it was needed, bestow money.
On one occasion he sent for all the "godly poor"
that could be found in the place, and gave to every
one "a thank-offering" for God's mercy to him.
Also inviting all to come, with his more intimate
friends, to join in keeping a day of thanksgiving.
On the day appointed, Mr. John Howe, Mr.
Fairclough and himself conducted the services.

"That greatest of the Puritan divines," John
Howe, was here during these months as a homeless
fugitive. Since black Bartholomew day he had
procured a doubtful and slender living, by performing any service, however humble, of which he was
capable. "Impelled in all probability by necessity,"
remarks Mr. Henry Rogers, "he published his
celebrated treatise entitled, 'The Blessedness of
the Righteous.'" This was the very time of his
doing so. There is no need now to tell of his
lofty life, or his well-known writings ; but, for Mr.

Alleine's sake, it is good to know that he was a charming companion as well as teacher. The note-book of his friend Dr. Sampson gives proof of this, which ought to be published. Courtly and learned, at home as much with princes as with scholars, delighting to " tilt with lance of light in lists of argument," pouring out in conversation a stream of pleasantry, sparkling anecdote, and varied knowledge of the world—yet most happy in those holiest of exercises which gave most joy to his suffering friend—his presence must have been welcome as the day.

Mr. Richard Fairclough, the ejected rector of Mellis, was on terms of most endeared intimacy both with Howe and Alleine. Our knowledge of the latter has been assisted by a paper containing some of Mr. Fairclough's reminiscences. He and his family had parted with a thousand a year for nonconformity; and now he would say to his friends, "I have no treasure but in heaven." When in possession of his rectory he gave away all he had, and in his advanced life the grateful offerings of a few London citizens kept him from dying of want. In addition to these facts, the only in-formation we have of this extraordinary man is contained in the sermon preached by Mr. Howe on the occasion of his death in 1682. He says " that about twelve years he continued student (whereof divers, a fellow) and great ornament

of Emanuel College, Cambridge. He was a man
of clear, distinct understanding, of a very quick,
discerning and penetrating judgment, that would on
a sudden strike through knotty difficulties into the
inward centre of truth, with such a felicity that
things seemed to offer themselves to him which are
wont to cost others a troublesome search." "When
rector of Mellis, the fame of his preaching made
an obscure country village soon become a most
noted place ; from sundry miles about, thither was
the great resort, so that I have wondered to see so
thronged an auditory. . . . His labours here
were almost incredible. Besides labours on the
Lord's day, he five times in the week prayed
and preached an expository lecture to a considerable congregation ; nor did he ever produce in
public anything which did not smell of the lamp.
. . . . He also found time not only to visit
the sick, but also, in a continual course, all the
families within his charge, personally and severally
to converse with every one that was capable,
labouring to benefit their souls, for his whole heart
was in his work. Every day, for many years
together, he used to be up by three in the morning,
or sooner, and be with God, which was his dear
delight, while others slept. The bent of his soul
was towards God. He was a mighty lover of
God and men. He was ever made up of light and
love. . . . All this made that rare and happy

temperament with him which I cannot better express than by a pleasant seriousness. What friend of his did ever at first congress see his face but with a grave smile? When unexpectedly and by surprise he came in among his familiar friends, it seemed as if he had blest the room, as if a new soul or some good genius had come among them."*

These were Mr. Alleine's chief companions while staying at Bath. We are glad, though not surprised, to hear his wife say, " He was now more cheerful than formerly, and seemed to be more quick in his converses, whatever he was put upon, either by scholars or those that were inferior ; and he was likewise more exceedingly affectionate in his carriage to me and all his friends, especially to such as were more heavenly, as Mr. Fairclough and his wife, Mr. How of Torrington, Mr. Joseph Barnard and his wife, several of our Taunton friends, Bristol ministers and others, which were a great comfort to us."   •

Dr. Sampson's note-book contains an anecdote of a fact connected with this visit, which we may here give, not so much because of its intrinsic importance, as because it has never yet been printed ; and because, also, it brings into the circle of our acquaintance the Rev. Joseph Glanvil, rector of Bath Abbey, prebend of Worcester, chaplain in

---

* Howe's Works, vol. iii., p. 413.—Hunt's edition.

ordinary to his Majesty, and likewise a most distinguished authority on the subject of ghosts and
witches.

"*Of Mr. Glanvil.*

" When he was minister of the Bathe, he was
very desirous to heare the converse of Mr. Howe,
which Mr. Howe was shy to afford, though then at
the Bathe, and therefore leisure enough. At last, he
visits Mr. Howe, and after kind expressions pressed
him to preach, which Mr. Howe not yielding to, he
promised al safety imaginable : he would needs know
the reason of this refusal. After much urging,
Mr. Howe said, ' Shal I preach for ye man who
said he would as soon worship a Lleek or an Onion
as the God of the Calvinists?' Mr. Glanvil
pressed him hard to know who was his informer ;
and he would not tel him. ' I know,' said Mr.
Glanvil, ' how it was : when I saw that venerable
person, Mr. Joseph Alleine there, it put such an aw
upon me, that I knew not what I said ; I know I
was preaching about and against the supra-lapsa-
rians, but what, I have clene forgot.'

" From Mr. Howe."

" What a strange passion is indignation against
a man, that we fear can over-argue and confound
us,—either passion or pride made him mad for

the time, or he was afterwards guilty of great
flattery and hypocrisy."*

Some of Mr. Glanvil's friends thought of him
as an ingenious, amiable, not very earnest man,
who walked circumspectly, kept his eye open
to most chances, and had an instinctive tendency to
the safe and sunny side of life.   It was a curious
thing in those days, it would be even in our own,
for a church dignitary to ask a Dissenting minister
to preach in his pulpit; and it is much to be feared
that Mr. Howe regarded his courtesy only as the
vibration of a church weathercock, showing a change
in the wind.   The bitter persecution of the Dissenters, combined with the utter unworthiness of
the men who now held political and sacerdotal
power, had led to a strong though brief re-action of
popular feeling.   Mr. Evelyn had lately predicted
the speedy return of the nation to a commonwealth.
Our friend, Mr. Pepys, had just written, " The
Nonconformists are mighty high, and their meetings frequented and connived at, and they do expect
to have their day soon."†   "Mr. Hollier dined
with my wife and me, and had much discourse
about the bad state of the church, and how the
clergy are become to be men of no worth in the
world ; and as the world do now generally discourse,

---

* Add. MSS. 4460.
† 21 December, 1667.

they must be reformed, and I believe the hierarchy will be shaken, whether they will or no."* At the very time when the little incident under review occurred at Bath, the worthy diarist wrote :— "July 18.—My old acquaintance Will Swan to see me, who continues a factious fanatic still, and I do use him civilly, in expectation that these fellows may grow great again." By a stroke of skilful policy, was Mr. Glanvil seeking to use John Howe as our other friend was using Will Swan? The thought will obtrude itself, but let us dismiss it. The writings of the Bath rector contain some truly liberal sentiments. A few leaders of all parties thought well of him; and if we had no other evidence in his favour, we should be inclined to think that he must, upon the whole, have been a good minister, or he would not have been stigmatised as a bad one by Antony Wood.

---

* February 16, 1667–8.

Chapter XV.

𝕮oll for the 𝕭rave.

" Bene inquit, veritatem dixisti : consummatum est ; . . . . .
Et sic pavimento suæ casulæ decantans : ' Gloria Patri. et filio et
Spiritui Sanɓo.' Cum Spiritum Sanɓum nominasset, spiritum e corpore
exhalavit ultimum, ac sic regna migravit ad celestia."

CUTHBERTI EPISTOLA DE OBITU VENERABILIS BEDÆ.

Y work is done. One day, when, for four hours, attendants had been waiting in the hush of strained expectancy for the last moment of Joseph Alleine's life on earth,—when they almost thought that all was over,—when the physician, watch in hand, had whispered, " Only a few minutes now,"—these words broke from his lips like a distant sound, " Weep not for me ; my work is done."

He was mistaken. He had yet more work to do. When just passing through the shadows that border the spirit-land, he was summoned to turn back into the daylight of this world again for work. The pleasant sojourn at Bath, and all the works done there, came after this—but we have now nearly reached the end of the story.

Faithful unto death, his last work on earth contemplated the religious instruction of children. With great difficulty, he accomplished a journey of five miles to see his friend, Mr. Joseph Barnard, who had, like himself, just "had a great deliverance ;" but whether from sickness, or prison, or both, has not been told us. He proposed that they should unite in presenting " a thank-offering to God," by printing, at their own expense, six thousand copies of the Assembly's Catechism ; and that they should then engage the assistance of their friends to send a hundred copies to each minister in Wiltshire and Somersetshire who would promise to undertake their distribution among the children around them. Mr. Barnard consented, the plan was completed, a letter was drawn up to be sent to each minister in their names conjointly, arrangements were made for receiving the report of results, and now the work of life was done.

While at Mr. Barnard's house his strength dropped rapidly, and the horse-litter was again sent for to take him back to Bath. On the 3rd of November, he felt that the hand of death was on him, and asked his friends to pray for him, " because his time was very short." Let the close of

the story be told by his wife :—" At night he said
to me, ' Well, now, my dear heart, my companion
in all my tribulations and afflictions, I thank thee
for all thy pains and labours for me, at home and
abroad, in prison and liberty, in health and sickness.'   Reckoning up many of the places we had
been in, in the days of our affliction, and utter-
ing many most endearing and affectionate expressions, he concluded with many holy breathings to
God for me, that He would requite me, and never
forget me, and fill me with all manner of grace
and consolations ; and that His face might still
shine upon me, and that I might be supported and
carried through all difficulties.

   " After this he desired me to see for a ' Practice
of Piety ;' and I procuring one for him, he turned
his chair from me, that I might not see, and read
the ' Meditations about Death' in the latter end
of that book ; which I discerning, asked of him
whether he did apprehend his end was near ?   To
which he replied, he knew not, in a few days I
would see ; and so fell into discourse, to divert me,
desiring me to read two chapters to him, as I used
to do every night ; and so he hasted to bed, not
being able to go to prayer ; and with his own hands
did very hastily undoe his coat and doublet, which
he had not done in many months before.   In a
quarter of an hour after, he fell into very strong
convulsions ; which I being much affrighted at,

called for help, and sent for the doctors, who used all
former and other means, but no success the Lord
was pleased to give then to any. But they continued for two days and nights, not ceasing one hour.

" This was most grievous to me, that I saw him
so like to depart, and that I should hear him speak
no more to me; fearing it would harden the wicked
to see him removed by such a stroke; for his fits
were most terrible to behold. And I earnestly
besought the Lord, that if it were His pleasure, He
would so far mitigate the heavy stroke I saw was
coming upon me, by causing him to utter something of his heart before He took him from me,
which He graciously answered me in; for he that
had not spoke from Tuesday night, did on Friday
morning, about three o'clock, call for me to come to
him, speaking very understandingly, between times,
all that day. But that night, about nine o'clock,
he brake out with an audible voice, speaking for
sixteen hours together, those and such-like words as
you formerly had account of; and did cease but a
very little space, now and then, all the afternoon.

" About three in the afternoon he had, as we
perceived, some conflict with Satan, for he uttered
these words :—' Away, thou foul fiend, thou enemy
of all mankind, thou subtile sophister, art thou
come now to molest me—now I am just going—
now I am so weak, and death upon me? Trouble
me not, for I am none of thine! I am the Lord's;

Christ is mine, and I am His; His by covenant.
I have sworn myself to be the Lord's, and His
I will be.   Therefore, be gone!' These last words
he repeated often, which I took much notice of.
Thus his covenanting with God was the means he
used to expel the Devil and all his temptations."

At six o'clock on Saturday evening the great
victorious spirit passed away.

The mourners could not forget the charge given
by their beloved minister while yet with them,—
" If I should die fifty miles away, let me be buried
at Taunton;" and a grave was, therefore, found
for him in St. Mary's chancel.

To-day, as you stand alone in the stone-chamber
near it, with the ancient register before you, having
suddenly lighted upon the entry, fresh as if written yesterday—" Mr. Joseph Alleine, minister,
November 17, 1668,"—it is startling to think that
perhaps the last time these words were looked at,
poor widowed Theodosia was standing by.   The
thought is magical. All at once you are living back
in that old November day,—" a certain trembling
consciousness seems to breathe through the air,"—
faces and forms seem to hover and glow out of the
blank twilight ; and though alone, you are in
solemn company ;—a vast congregation is in the
church, and all around it.   There ! you see John
Howe and Richard Fairclough, just come from

Bath with the sorrowing train. Old George Newton is close at your side, " leaning upon the top of his staff;" and you catch the very tones of the moment while he is saying, " Beloved, it is not rebellion for me to mourn. In holy writ, you find an old prophet burying a prophet, and as he stood over his grave he melted and said, Alas, my brother !" Thus you may live in the past, until its long-vanished voices and scenes strike you at times with the force of present reality. All that your mind has now pictured was once real. The words quoted were actually spoken; and it was truly amidst such demonstrations of public sorrow that the remains of the devoted minister were committed to their last resting-place. The spot was afterwards marked by a brass plate in the pavement thus inscribed :—

HIC JACET DOMINVS JOSEPHVS ALLEINE
HOLOCAVSTVM TAVNTONENSIS
ET DEO ET VOBIS.

An old poet has said :—

" It is not growing like a tree
In bulk, doth make man better be.
A lily of the day
Is fairer far in May,
Although it fall and die that night,
It was the plant and flower of light ;
In small proportions we just beauties see,
And in small measures life may perfect be."*

* Ben Jonson.

This is true ; but we have more to say of the short life that has now been recorded.

The short life of a flower may be as perfect as the long life of a tree, and it may equally answer its own peculiar ends, but those ends are not equally important.   The short life of a Christian may be filled with a power of usefulness, that shall reach to heaven and live for ever.   We have here an example, at once for our rebuke and for our encouragement, to show what divine attainments may be made, and what noble service done, in a short life.   He was not thirty-five years old when he died; but his life was so rich, and so full of efficacy, that he never seemed to be so much alive, even on this earth, as after he was taken from it. His work still went on ; he still preached the glad tidings, and hundreds of thousands have heard him. On many a cottage-wall was seen, soon after his funeral, a broad sheet, on which were printed his last words.   The title was, " The Golden Sayings, Sentences, and Expressions of Mr. Vavasor Powell ; with some Choice Sayings of that godly divine, Mr. Joseph Alleine, of Taunton, in Somersetshire."*
His letters were then collected, and along with a simple and affectionate biography, written by his widow, were almost immediately translated into Welch, German, and other languages, and have

---

* British Museum.

since passed through almost countless editions.*
In 1671, his "Alarm to the Unconverted" first
saw the light. It appears to be the substance of
sermons preached on conversion. Of this book
Dr. Calamy, writing in 1702, remarks, "Multitudes will have cause for ever to be thankful for it.
No book in the English tongue (the Bible only
excepted) can equal it for the number that hath
been dispersed; there have been twenty thousand
sold under the title of the 'Call,' or 'Alarm,' and
fifty thousand of the same under the title of the
'Sure Guide to Heaven,' thirty thousand of which
were at one impression."† "It is a wonderful
amount of good" says another writer, "which has
been accomplished by the solemn and pathetic
appeals contained in the 'Alarm to the Unconverted.' As one example it may be mentioned,
that towards the close of the last century a minister, more eminent for scholarship than fervour,
repeated the substance of its successive chapters to
his Highland congregation, as he was engaged in
translating the work for some Society; and the
result was a wide-spread awakening, which long
prevailed in the district of Nether Lorn."‡ In
1674, his "Remains" were published, under the

---

* Moreri. Le Grand Dictionnaire Historique. 1740.

† Calamy's Account of the Ejected Ministers, vol. ii., p. 577.

‡ Hamilton's Sacred Classics, vol. ii., p. 219.

editorial care of his father-in-law; and, later still, appeared " The Saint's Pocket Book." A complete list of his works will be found in the Appendix.

The late William Rhodes, whose kindred spirit so fitted him to understand this holy confessor, has left some remarks on his life and works, which, though not intended by him for the public eye, may be given here with propriety. A friend having alluded to Joseph Alleine in the course of a letter to him, he thus replied, " I borrow the hand of another, as I have been obliged to do for so many years past, to write the few lines I may be able to dictate. . . . . You have awakened into fresh love and delight my recollections of one whom I have admired, and aspired to imitate from my earliest days. . . . . . I cannot tell you how much I love the memory and character of that most excellent man, nor the value I put upon his life and Christian letters, which no person of devout sensibility can read for the first time without finding himself transported for a while to the finest climate of the spiritual world, and moved with higher aspirations towards the life and beauty of holiness. The lights and powers of the world to come are upon him there, as they ruled and delighted the heart of the writer. He possessed all the intensity and refinement of the Puritan piety,—a piety hitherto unequalled in the history of our race,—without any tincture of its undue austerity and seclusion from the innocent graces of life. In religious fidelity and tenderness—in holy severity of self-government—in constant solicitudes and toils for the salvation of men—in ardour and elevation of soul under prolonged sufferings—in frequent and lofty converse with eternal things, he was scarcely inferior to Paul himself, the first of human teachers, the inspired prince of mankind. I do not, of course, for a moment, place Mr. Alleine on a level, in intellectual endowments, with the great religious minds of that great period : not with Bunyan, who stands alone in profound wisdom and genius, so rich in the illuminations that come from above: nor with Baxter, in his wonderful amplitude of capacity and labour : nor with Howe, in his serene majesty of spirit and magnificence of thought. These were not his distinctions ; but in heavenliness of temper and action he was equal to the best, if he did not surpass them all. He united in perfection what is so seldom attained—the delight and grandeur of contemplative devotion, with untired activity in performing the common duties of time."

Some information will be welcome respecting the final history of Alleine's companions. And, first, it will be asked, "What became of his widow, the companion of all his tribulations?" She was left with no children. No authentic account can be found of her last years, beyond the simple fact that

she died before the horrors of the Monmouth rising
began. We should like to know more of her, but
from the little that we already know, we are bound
to give her a place in the praise of all the churches
along with such women as Lucy Hutchinson, Lady
Falkland, and Mrs. Margaret Baxter. Next it will
be asked, " What became of his companions in the
ministry, and the people of their united charge ?"
Mr. Newton's last days were full of trouble. As
we have seen, he was not a man of courage, but
courage came as faith grew stronger, and he returned
from his weary concealments about London to serve
his former flock, just when the decline of Alleine's
power made that return doubly welcome. In 1672,
Paul's Independent Meeting was built for him, and
a license was obtained for it, in accordance with a
declaration in favour of the Nonconformists, by
Lord Clifford. His peaceful ministry was not
permitted to last long. Antony Wood asserts that
" he was seized and imprisoned for several years,
and justly suffered as a mover of sedition." Such
was the ecclesiastical estimate of his loving labours,
and such was its reward. The date of his imprisonment is now uncertain ; we only know that
after his release, though bowed with infirmities, he
set forth to face the storm once more, and continued preaching just as ever ; the interruption he
suffered from the legalized fury of bad men, and
from the mistakes of the good, only moving him

to say, "Let us earnestly beseech the good Lord
to leave His children now no longer out at school,
but speedily to fetch them home, and teach them
all Himself, and then we shall have great peace."
In 1681, when bordering on his eightieth year, persecution still raging round him, the good father fell
asleep. Again, even scorners were silenced into
reverence, and again they allowed the ground within
the chancel rails to be opened for a Nonconformist's
grave.

> "See now his peaceful breast,
> Rocked by the hand of death, takes quiet rest;
> Disturb him not, but let him sweetly take
> A full repose, he hath been long awake." *

He was taken from the evil to come. Only two
years after his death a heavy trial befel his people.
Their chapel, and that occupied by the Baptists,
were both sacked by order of the mayor, who,
writing to Sir Leoline Jenkins, says: "We burnt
ten cart-loads of pulpit, doors, gates, and seats, in
the market-place. We staid till three in the morning before all were burnt. We were very merry.
The bells rang all night! The church is now full;
thank God for it! The fanatics dare not open their
mouths." † In about a month, the magnate's note
of thanksgiving was changed for one more pensive,

---

* Quarles.

† August 11, 1683. State Paper Office, Sir L. Jenkins, xiii.

for by that time it was reported that the people met under the roof of private houses, in seven or eight places simultaneously.*   Long may their successors meet, and continue to enjoy their rich inheritance of blessing!

" What became of Mr. Norman's congregation ?"   Their meeting-house suffered at the same time a similar fate.   Lord Stowel gives the account in the following words :—" We found the House of Worship which was sooner pluckt down than built and so ought to have bin all the phanatick houses in Bridgewater if they had the least incouragement for they were all able workmen the materialls of the conventicles were carried upon the cornhill which made a bonfire fourteen feet high atopp of which was placed the pulpit and the cushing. Wee only wanted the levit to have given us a farewell sermon there were severall gentlemen of the country that came into us. . . . . We stood round the bonfire, and healths were not wanting. The mittig hows was made rown like a cockpit and ould hould sum 400 parsons."†

" What became of the Dissenters generally ?" The cases just related may be supposed to be rare and exceptional, but in reality they are only average specimens of what took place throughout

---

* September 2nd and 22nd.

† State Papers.   The " Levit " alluded to was Mr. John Moore, A.M., of Brazenose College.

the nation. It was a common thing to deal thus with the chapels of the Nonconformists. The worshippers often anticipated the visits of such destroyers, and to escape some of the terrors of their mirth, that "grew so fast and furious," they quietly destroyed their chapel furniture with their own hands.

The mobs who once smashed cathedral windows were just as ready to burn conventicle benches. They were not composed of Puritans in the one case, nor of decent ceremonialists in the other ; but of the volatile rascality that will always rejoice in the excitement of a political party, and shout with the winning side. Only be it remembered, that in the one case the outrage was against the order of Government ; in the other, it was in obedience to it. In the one case, most of the accounts of sacrilegious violence are detected exaggerations ; in the other, they are reports sent to the Secretary of State, and placed among the archives of the nation.

Zeal for the Act of Uniformity did not idly waste itself in attacks on mere timber and stone. Persons, not things, were its objects. Within the compass of three years, the Dissenters of England suffered, in penalties inflicted for the worship of God, to the amount of two millions sterling.* From the Restoration to the Revolution, these losses

* Defoe's Preface to Delaune's Plea.

from the same causes rose to twelve or fourteen millions.* In the same space of time, sixty thousand persons are said to have suffered on a religious account. The lists of these sufferers were collected with great care and cost by Mr. Jeremy White, who told Lord Dorset that when King James offered him a thousand guineas for the manuscript, he refused to surrender it, knowing that it was only wanted in order to strengthen the interests of Popery.†

These sufferings included fines, bonds, transportation, voluntary exile to Holland or America, and death in prison. White gives the number of such deaths as 5,000; William Penn states the same number. Picart reports 8,000;‡ Daniel Defoe says, near 8,000.§ It is impossible for us to know with certainty the statistics of that black record, until the books are opened at the judgment day. One who lived through those times remarks, "I have read concerning Zoroaster's book, entitled, 'The Similitude,' that it required no less than 1,260 ox-hides for the covering of it. I know not how far the sufferings of the Nonconformists under

---

the Caroline persecution would go to fill a book of such enormous dimensions,—this I know, it was a persecution too terrible to admit of a similitude, and there is a worthy writer who does not scruple to say, that if the sufferings of good men in this persecution were distinctly written, our largest books of martyrs would be but an Enchiridion in comparison with such a history."*

It has often been argued that the shameless immorality that suddenly flooded the nation at the return of the exiled King, gave proof that the religion of Puritanism, which appeared to prevail just before, was only a hollow and pretensive show; the maxim being true of nations as of individuals, that none can be supremely wicked on a sudden. This is unfair to the Puritans. The facts of the case only prove—what needs no proof—that the large majority of men, even then, were worldly; that many, of course, were willing to profess from worldly motives State religion—the religion that stood connected with highest rank and honour, whatever that religion might be; and that many more were desperate haters of godliness, eager to throw off the restraints which it had imposed upon them. It must still be contended that Christians have seldom been so numerous in proportion to other men as in those days, and that piety has seldom had a higher tone.

---

* Eleutheria. London, 1698, p. 83.

C C

Evidence for this is seen in the vast number of
sufferers for Nonconformity, and in the great fight
of afflictions which they so long endured. Would
the Son of man find so much " faith on the earth "
now? It may well be doubted.

Let all honour be given to this noble army of
martyrs. Let their living representatives strive
without ceasing to act a part worthy of such an
ancestry. Let them be upon their guard lest prosperity foster effeminacy, and make them " feebler
sons of feebler days." Two things in the conduct
of our fathers, and especially of their ministers,
should be admired and imitated ; first, their determination to maintain, at all costs, that in all matters
of religion the sole standard of authority is the
word of God, as interpreted by the Spirit of God
—the Spirit promised " to every one that asketh ;"
next, their determination to maintain a clear, free,
and living conscience. In their view, there were
many things in the English Episcopacy, considered
as a church, but not as an establishment, which
were not in accordance with their one standard ;
they therefore refused to take orders. They might
have accepted the articles as " articles of peace."
They might, while thinking some particulars in
them *contrary* to the word of God, have pledged
themselves to an acknowledgment of them all as
" *agreeable* to the word of God," secretly meaning,
by that phrase, " agreeable in so far as they are

agreeable." When the plain words of creeds, forms,
and offices conveyed teachings which seemed to
them at variance with the teachings of inspiration,
they might, with a little ingenuity, very easy to such
practised casuists, have put upon them a private
and reserved construction. They might have persuaded themselves that many things which they
thought unscriptural in the Prayer-book were only
little things ; that therefore they could safely avow
their unfeigned assent and consent to them, regarding untruthfulness or dishonesty in little things to
be only a little sin, especially when demanded as
part of a formal introduction to a ministry of holiness and truth. They might have thought the act
of subscription an insignificant price to pay for all
the splendid advantages of clerical conformity.
They might have refused to think at all. But
such was not their course. They thought that with
their faith differing in many important respects from
the Anglican formulas, the act of subscribing to
those formulas would either imply that the moral
sense within them was dead, or would inflict a
wound upon it of which it soon would die. They
thought that any attempt to satisfy conscience, by
giving their own " private interpretation " to that
which they subscribed, any attempt to pervert,
resist, or explain away the meaning of plain words
in this particular instance, might injuriously affect
their power of using or understanding plain words

in other instances. They thought that expediency
so subtle and evasive might not only destroy their
own self-respect, but bring suspicion on their teaching and discredit on their cause. They therefore
declared themselves to be Nonconformists, their
people joined them, and all spent the rest of their
days in a driving tempest of persecution.

We hold these men in reverence for acting out
their principles so far as they had opportunity of
tracing them, but there was one legitimate conclusion which they had not reached. It had thus been
expressed by Sir Harry Vane,—" The province of
the magistrate is the world and man's body ; not
conscience and the things of eternity." Only a few
thought with him. It would be impiety for us to
reproach them because they only saw this truth as
" in a glass darkly." It is our vocation to utter it ;
but it was not theirs, for the time had not come.
They were heroes, true, masculine, and grand ;
they had their own work to do, and they did it
well ; their own battle to fight, and they fought it
nobly ; their own special truth to utter, and they
told it with power from heaven ; but the doctrine
of religious liberty they had yet to learn through
trials, and we are inheriting the knowledge that
came out of their experience. Gradually they
learned to look beyond the hand that smote them,
to the hidden life that set it in motion and nerved it
with strength. This they found to be the spirit

which claims infallibility, and the right to rule over
conscience—a spirit which is not peculiar to any
single sect, but has been the common sin of all
when in circumstances to exercise it. Since alliance
with the State is certain to create those circumstances, modern Dissenters have added to the
theoretic basis of dissent adopted by their ancestors, the principle that every church should, in
matters of religion, renounce State patronage and
be free from State control. This they regard as
only a further development of Puritan scripturism.
Holding this tenet, their opinion differs from that
of the majority of men, but, in deciding any religious question, they attach little value to majorities.
It was a majority that crucified Christ. Christian
truth is not with the multitude. The votes for
such truth are not to be numbered but weighed,
and weighed only in the balances of Scripture.
Holding this tenet does not imply the assumption
to themselves of any superior intelligence or conscientiousness over those from whom they differ.
It does not imply hostility to the church of
England, or injustice to the reputation of the great
and holy men who have adorned and still adorn it ;
it does not imply that they love their fellow-
Christians the less because they may belong to that
communion. It rather implies that, to them,
differences of practice as to church order can inter-
pose no bar to Christian love, or perfect equality.

They would give to others what they claim for themselves — equal social rights, and warmest Christian affection, without first asking for uniformity. In their belief, all healthy life protests against the demand for uniformity. "Attempt to construct some outward framework of uniformity for nature, and the oaks and elms, the informal lilies of the field and the fowls of the air, will breathe forth their protest in beauty, and sound it in song." The life of grace, like the life of nature, though million-formed, is one,—and that power from without which most succeeds in binding it into sameness of aspect, will, in the end, only make it dwindle and pine. We would rather seek for ourselves and for all Christians greater vitality of faith in Christ, the mediating principle by which alone man can be led into the light of God, the combining fact, in virtue of which alone all believers have a unity which underlies all visible variety, and makes variety beautiful.

APPENDIX.

No. I.—p. 79.

Letter from the Church at Taunton, in America, under the pastoral care of the REV. MR. EMERY, *to the* REV. HENRY ADDISCOTT, *and the First Independent Church at Taunton, in England.*

Taunton, Mass., U.S., Feb., 1854.

REV. AND BELOVED,—We are moved to address you, by reason of our common origin, and our common Christian faith. *Your* fathers were *our* fathers ; and the Deans, the Reeds, the Blakes, the Attwoods, and the Halls, from whom some of *you* sprung, have descendants in *our* church and town, who would gladly become better acquainted than they now are with those who claim a common descent in the mother-country. Our ancestors were led to remove hither, as you are well aware, for the sake of planting a church in this western world.

The church which the first settlers of Taunton formed in 1637 still lives, and adheres to the faith of the fathers of New England—the faith which has so long distinguished all true saints. There are *three* colonies from the original church, which are Calvinistic Congregational churches; and of these the church which we represent is one—adopting the same confession of faith and covenant in substance, desiring to perpetuate the great truths gathered out of the Word of God, and embodied in the Westminster Shorter Catechism. There are *other* churches in town, which are generally regarded as evangelical, a Calvinist Baptist, a Protestant Episcopal, two Protestant Methodist, and a Presbyterian. There are also several which are *not* so regarded, but which we will not particularly name. The prevailing sentiment of the town, which contains a population of some 12,000, is what would be termed, with us, *orthodox.* We have a desire to know how it is with *you.* Rev. Mr. Bingham, the pastor of the Unitarian Society in Taunton, spent a Sabbath with you some months since, and preached, as we are informed, in one or more of your churches. From his published letter, we learn that about half of your people are Dissenters. We should like to know what are the *doctrinal views* of these Dissenting churches, and so much of your ecclesiastical history as you may be disposed to give us. Our own history is put in a permanent form, and is herewith transmitted to you. If you have documents of any kind, printed or otherwise, which would make us better acquainted with you, we should prize them highly. There is a history of your town by Toulmin, of which we have heard, but not seen. *Our* church has recently erected a new place of worship, in a more central part of the town, and dropping the original name, which indicated the *Street* in which they worshipped (Spring Street), have adopted the name of *Winslow,* in memory of Edward Winslow, one of the pilgrims, the third governor of Plymouth colony, and the *first* Englishman who ever touched Taunton soil. History warrants us in believing he was an eminently good man, and that *his* was a name *worthy* to be thus perpetuated in the place.

Wishing you grace, mercy, and peace, we remain, *yours*, in the fellowship of the Gospel, and on behalf of the Winslow church,

S. HOPKINS EMERY, *Pastor.*

EDGAR H. REED,
C. WOOD,
WILLIAM T. BLAKE, } *Committee.*
P. W. DEAN,

No. II.—p. 378.

A List of MR. ALLEINE'S *Works.*

Title.	Date of original publication.
1. Prayers for the Use of the People............	
2. Useful Questions, whereby a Christian may examine himself. Folio sheet	Some-time be-tween 1655 and 1661.
3. Directions for Covenanting with God. Folio sheet	
4. Rules for the more Profitable Management of Family Worship. Folio sheet.........	

Title.	Date of original publication.
5. Theologia Philosophica : licensed in	1661
6. Call to Archippus. 4to........................	1664
7. Explanation of the Assembly's Shorter Catechism, with a Letter to his Flock, and Rules for daily Self-examination. 12mo...	1664
8. Synopsis of the Covenant of Grace. Folio sheet.	1664
9. A Soliloquy : representing the Believer's Triumph in God's Covenant, and the various Conflicts and glorious Conquests of Faith over Unbelief. First published in Part III. of the Vindiciæ Pietatis	1665
10. Directions to the Ministers of Somersetshire and Wiltshire for the Instructing of Families, &c...............................	1668
11. Letters full of Spiritual Instructions, tending to the promoting of the power of Godliness. Forty Letters; afterwards increased to Forty-five	1671
12. An Alarm to Unconverted Sinners: 8vo.	1671
One edition of this appeared under the title, "The true way to Happiness," 1675: another under the title, "A Sure Guide to Heaven," 1691.	
Included in the first edition of the "Alarm," were the three following tracts, which had before been published separately, without date :—	
13. Counsel for Personal and Family Godliness.	1671
14. Divers Practical Cases of Conscience, judiciously solved................................	1671
15. Counsels and Cordials for the Converted ...	1671

Title.	Date of original publication.
16. The Remains of that excellent Minister of Jesus Christ, Mr. Joseph Alleine, being a Collection of Sundry Directions, Sermons, Sacrament Speeches, and Letters, not heretofore published......................	1672
17. A Treatise called The Voice of the Herald before the Great King. The Voice of God speaking from Mount Gerizim. The Voice of the Redeemed after the Proclamation	1684
18. A Treasure of Gospel Promises, left in Legacy by Jesus Christ...............	Unknown date.
19. Promises for the Saints' Support in Times of Trouble and Persecution	Unknown date.

  Treatise 17, 18, and 19, along with the "Soliloquy" before named, were afterwards published under the title of the "Saint's Pocket Book."

INDEX.

ERRATA.

P. 32, *note, for* Gangrœna, *read* Gangræna.

P. 60, line 17, *insert* Musarum *before* Oxoniensium.

WORKS BY THE SAME AUTHOR.

A SECOND AND CHEAPER EDITION,

In foolscap 8vo., price 2s., cloth lettered,

POWER IN WEAKNESS: MEMORIALS OF THE REV. WILLIAM RHODES.

" It is refreshing to meet with a book like this—the brief, modest, and withal lively and graceful record of a man who, to the great mass of the religious public, lived and died unknown. In marked contrast with the gold-leaf style of life-making, in which whatever is really good is beaten out into invisible thinness and tenuity, this memoir is a solid ingot, small in bulk, but with valid mint-mark, and precious in every grain of it."— *Family Treasury.*

" The record of a beautiful mind, and of a career which, but for such a record, would have been almost frustrated."—*Rev. Dr. J. Hamilton* (in the *Witness*).

" . . . This unpretending and interesting narrative."—*British Quarterly Review.*

" Greatest minds are often those of whom the noisy world hears least. The once obscure spirit of wisdom flashes through the whole firmament after it leaves the mortal frame. Mr. Rhodes lives in his best thoughts. This full-length picture is painted by a most able hand; and here men shall learn that which he most desired to teach when alive." —*Christian Spectator.*

" He was a hero in humble life; a thinker of whom the world knew nothing; a worker whose deeds found almost their sole observers in God and the angels; and yet a hero, and a thinker, and a worker who may well be an encouragement and a lesson, and an example to those who come after him. We cannot but thank Mr. Stanford for having furnished us with so interesting and useful a volume."—*The Freeman.*

" This is a small book, but it contains more solid, sterling material than many volumes of the weary biographical common-places so often to be met with. It is a brief sketch of the life of a remarkable man, for many years weak and afflicted in body, but, to the last, strong in mind and in faith. The materials for this memoir could not have been placed in better hands than the Rev. Charles Stanford's—what he has written is a model for Christian biographers." — *English Presbyterian Messenger.*

" We think it a piece of superior biography in its style, contents, and adaptation for usefulness."—*Patriot.*

" Mr. Stanford has done his part as biographer wisely and well, and we feel under deep obligations to him for having set before us the example of one who believed, and wrought, and hoped against hope."— *Eclectic Review.*

" We have perused this volume with intense gratification."—*Scottish Congregational Magazine.*

LONDON: JACKSON, WALFORD, & HODDER, 18, ST. PAUL'S CHURCHYARD, E.C.

In one handsome volume, square crown 8vo., red edges, cloth antique,
Price Six Shillings and Sixpence, post free,

CENTRAL TRUTHS.

"There are to be found in these pages a singular refinement of illustration and a peculiar felicity of language, which the cultivated and tasteful will prize and admire, however much it may be lost on common, hasty readers. Mr. Stanford has an order of mind, and has acquired habits of study, eminently adapting him to be a teacher of wise and thoughtful men."—*Evangelical Magazine.*

"This book supplies what we have long felt wanting, a brief and sound view of Evangelical truth in attractive language.—The style possesses the uncommon charm of being at once rich and clear. We should rejoice in seeing this beautiful volume on every drawing-room table."—*The Record.*

"Its pages are replenished with wisely simple and unassumingly graceful utterances."—*Christian Spectator.*

"We have rarely read a volume of sermons with such unmixed pleasure. It is impossible to read a page of this volume without being struck by the intimate--we were about to say microscopic—acquaintance with Scripture which it displays. Passages of inspired teaching and revealed truth are constantly quoted in senses which, though perfectly obvious when pointed out, have been unnoticed before, and a feeling of pleased surprise is thus constantly produced in the reader's mind."—*Baptist Magazine.*

"Beautiful conceptions, clothed in fascinating language, with scintillations of genius and fancy, grow in every page, combined with solid thought and the fruits of diligent and well-directed study. But the work merits far higher than mere literary commendation. It is so thoroughly evangelical, its views of Christian truth are so clear and so scriptural, it is so entirely in sympathy with the great and solemn verities of man's apostacy and of his redemption by the vicarious sufferings and death of the Redeemer, that we heartily wish for it a wide circulation in Christian families."—*Evangelical Christendom.*

Fourth Thousand, in 18mo., price 3d. sewed, or 2s. 6d. per dozen,

SECRET PRAYER.

"An exceedingly beautiful discourse; displaying at once a cultivated mind, a devout heart, and an original genius."—*Congregational Pulpit.*

"Of this beautiful discourse we need say no more than that it is worthy of a place in the volume of 'Central Truths.'"—*Baptist Magazine.*

"Eloquent, earnest, and useful; full of devout feeling and stimulus."—*Patriot.*

Fifth Edition, 18mo, price 3d., sewed, or 2s. 6d. per dozen,

FRIENDSHIP WITH GOD.

". . . Rich with consoling and ennobling sentiments."—*English Presbyterian Messenger.*

"This exquisitely beautiful discourse."—*The Freeman.*

LONDON: JACKSON, WALFORD, & HODDER, 18, ST. PAUL'S CHURCHYARD, E.C.

www.ingramcontent.com/pod-product-compliance
Lightning Source LLC
Chambersburg PA
CBHW050902130726
47900CB00015B/1704